Strangers

BARBARA ELSBORG

ELLORA'S CAVE
ROMANTICA PUBLISHING

An Ellora's Cave Romantica Publication

www.ellorascave.com

Strangers

ISBN 9781419962837
ALL RIGHTS RESERVED.
Strangers Copyright © 2009 Barbara Elsborg
Cover art by Syneca.

Electronic book publication December 2009
Trade paperback publication 2011

STRANGERS

Trademarks Acknowledgement

Mars: Mars Incorporated

Marsala: S.A.V.I. Floria-Ingham Whitaker-Woodhouse & C Corporation

Nobu: Matsuhisa, Nobuyuki Individual

Post-It: 3M Company

Red Bull: Red Bull GmbH Limited Liability Company

Selfridges: Selfridges Retail Limited

Sky TV: BSkyB Ltd.

Twiglets: United Biscuits UK Limited

Twister: Hasbro, Inc.

Woolworths: F. W. Woolworth Co.

Chapter One

ஒ

GOODBYE

Kate stared at the letters written in the sand and laughed. If that wasn't a sign, she didn't know what was. Three more steps and a cold wave swept over her feet. Kate gritted her teeth and waded forward until the water reached her waist. One shuddering plunge and she began to swim. Moments later her sandals slipped from her feet. Damn, they were her favorites. Kate snorted with laughter, inhaled a lungful of saltwater and tried to stand. When her feet failed to touch bottom, she flailed around until she got her breath back and could swim again.

It didn't take long before she was shivering. Kate pictured herself sliding into a deep sleep and drowning. Then pictured herself struggling to breathe as water rushed into her throat. She batted away a hard ball of fear. No going back.

Flipping over, she looked up into the pale gray early morning sky. It would have been good to see the sun for the last time. Kate let herself sink and moments later her legs kicked her to the surface. She gave an annoyed grunt. She'd even held her breath. This wasn't going to be as easy as she thought. How weird if she swam as far as France. More likely a tanker would mow her down.

The blow caught her on the end of her nose. Kate gasped as she went under, swallowed water and panicked. Drowning was one thing, being attacked by a shark something else entirely. She kicked her way to the surface, the horror of being eaten turning her into a writhing mass of fear. When her feet connected with something solid, fear turned to terror.

"Oww!" yelped the shark.

Kate thrashed harder.

"What the fuck are you doing?" the shark demanded.

Having an entertaining hallucination. Kate swiveled round. She'd not slept last night and her tired mind had imagined someone with her. Fortunately not a shark. She'd conjured up a real humdinger—an angry, dark-haired man who needed a shave. Despite the sooty shadows under his eyes, he was gorgeous. A shiver of lust joined Kate's other shivers. Of course he could have the body of a hippo, since she could only see his head and bare shoulders.

"Oh God, your nose is bleeding. Sorry," he said.

Kate touched her face and saw the blood on her fingers before a splash of water washed them clean.

"I wasn't looking where I was going. I didn't expect anyone to be out this far," he said.

She continued to tread water, wondering if she could keep him with her.

"Aren't you going to say anything?" he asked.

Kate opened her mouth, considered the sense in talking to someone who wasn't there, and closed it.

"Are you a mermaid?" He dropped under the waves.

Was he a merman? But then he'd know she wasn't a mermaid. He surfaced beside her, closer than before, a haunted look in his huge, soft brown eyes.

"Toes," he spluttered, spitting on her face. "With red nail polish. I'm so disappointed."

Kate's heart sank. A figment of her imagination would neither complain nor spit at her. He was real.

"I thought you were a shark," she said. "Then I thought I'd imagined you."

"A shark?" He turned in a jerky circle. "Oh Christ, and you're bleeding. They can scent tiny amounts of blood in the water from oceans away. A squad of them are probably zooming over to tear us apart, limb by limb. If you feel a sudden tug, that'll be your leg gone."

Kate wiped her nose again. Still bleeding.

"Sorry. I hope I didn't break it," he said.

"Don't worry about it."

"So…do you do this often?" He bobbed up on a wave as she dropped into a trough.

Kate was torn between laughter and tears. "What?"

"Swim out to sea in your clothes?"

"Yes, it's fabulous exercise. I'd better get going." She didn't move.

"What's your name?" he asked.

"Kate."

"I'm Charlie."

"Well, hello and goodbye, Charlie."

She swam out to sea using strong and decisive strokes.

"You're going the wrong way," he yelled.

"Not finished yet. Got to burn off the seventeen Mars Bars I ate last night. Squillions of calories to go."

He came up next to her, doing the breaststroke like her. They swam side-by-side in silence.

"Did you ever see that film *Open Water*?" Charlie asked suddenly.

Kate had been trying not to think about it. "Unlike that poor couple, we're not lost. The beach is behind us."

"I don't want to go back to the beach," he said.

Kate glanced across. Bloody hell, what were the chances of them picking the same spot to disappear? All that water and they ended up in the same place?

"I was here first," she said.

"How do you know?"

He was right. She didn't.

Light dawned. "Was the message in the sand yours?" Kate asked.

"See, I *was* here first. Anyway, there's enough water for both of us."

True. Kate wondered about diving, then opening her mouth to let the sea flood her lungs. Would it work? Would it be quick?

"Your nose is still bleeding," he said.

"Shit."

"I'd have thought you'd welcome a shark."

Kate caught the hint of a smile on his face and glared. "I'm choosing the way I die, and I'm not choosing Jaws."

"Me neither," Charlie said. "Why don't we stop swimming?"

"I already tried. My legs won't cooperate. Watch."

Kate stopped moving and almost instantly started to tread water. Charlie held himself still, went under, then popped up next to her, water streaming down his face.

"This is crazy." His teeth were chattering.

"Feel free to change your mind. No one's forcing you."

Then Kate screamed and Charlie shot straight out of the water. She noticed he had great pecs, then panic overwhelmed every thought.

"Jesus, what's the matter?" he gasped.

"There's something behind me. Brushing against my back. Oh God. Jellyfish."

Charlie swam around, and then a swag of seaweed plopped onto her head. Kate screamed again and shot into hyper-speed, arms and legs powering her away.

"It's not a jellyfish," he called. "It's seaweed."

"I don't like seaweed either."

Charlie caught up. "Why the hell choose to do things this way, if you're frightened of jellyfish, sharks and seaweed? Anything else to add?"

"Crabs, eels and oil tankers."

He sniggered. "How about giant squid?"

She gulped. "I thought if I kept my clothes on, I wouldn't mind slimy things, but I was wrong. I hadn't thought about sharks until you mentioned them. Nor squid. Anyway, I'm not the only one who doesn't like sharks."

one of Turner's paintings with no detail, only color to express mood. Every time she tried to gulp air, she swallowed water. Kate coughed, choked and screamed for Charlie. She'd turned in circles looking for him and now the beach was lost.

"Charlie!"

When she caught sight of his white face at the crest of a curling wave, Kate swam frantically in his direction, fighting the water to get to his side. Through her stinging eyes, Kate saw him swimming toward her.

"I thought I'd lost you." She reached out to touch him.

He coughed and spat out water. "I'm hard to get rid of. I'm so fucking cold and tired. This was supposed to be what I wanted, only now I don't."

Beneath the shadow of his unshaven face, his skin appeared almost translucent. The hollows below his cheekbones looked deeper, as though he was turning into a corpse in front of her.

"Keep swimming," Kate said.

"Which way? Where's the fucking beach?"

"I don't know."

They looked at each other and Charlie gave a wry smile. "Maybe we weren't meant to change our minds."

He held his hand above the water and Kate reached for his white fingers.

"Don't let me go," she gasped.

"Don't let *me* go," Charlie said.

And they let the sea choose whether or not it wanted to keep them.

Chapter Two
Kate's Story

ଛ

"Guess what?" said Lucy, occupier of apartment four, Elm Gardens, Greenwich, below Kate in number five.

"What?" asked Kate.

Pinball Lucy barged into Kate's apartment and bulldozed through to the lounge.

"I've got us press tickets to a new venue in Knightsbridge."

"No thanks," Kate said.

"It's called 'The Wedding Party'."

"Not interested."

The two words bounced off Lucy.

"It's going to be great," Lucy said. "Of course you want to go."

Kate finished washing the dishes. "No, I don't."

"Obviously I haven't made this sound enticing enough. Listen to the publicity handout. *'The evening is a cross between a mock wedding reception and a dating event. Whilst enjoying a wedding-themed comedy dinner'*, which is going to be a load of laughs, *'you also get the chance to meet new people.'* Isn't that a great idea?"

"No." Kate began to clean the handles on the kitchen cupboards.

Lucy's shoulders dropped. "Why not?"

"Don't you think it's a bit odd, trying to pair up singles at a dysfunctional wedding?"

Lucy thought about it and then shrugged. "The tickets are free."

"No." Kate moved on to the skirting boards.

"There's a seven-course banquet and unlimited booze."

That was tempting but—"No."

"It's going to be a fun, drunken night out," Lucy said in exasperation.

"Not a desperate search by desperate single men and desperate single women?"

"Well, I'm not single," Lucy said.

"And I'm desperate *and* single?" Kate pulled the vacuum cleaner out of the cupboard.

"Course not. Rachel and Dan are going. Please?"

Kate gave in.

And found out on the way there, that Dan who lived next to Kate in number six, and Rachel who lived below in number three, only agreed to go because Lucy told them Kate would only go if they did.

"You conniving little minx," Dan said.

Lucy grinned. "Hey, I can't help being persistent and persuasive. If I listened when people said no, I'd never have got the job with Metro Radio."

Since Lucy was now going out with married boss Nick, Kate wondered how persistent and persuasive she'd really had to be.

When the four of them walked into the wedding marquee, erected inside a building, their jaws dropped. Acres of glittering white material covered the walls, while above their heads thousands of lights twinkled in a black canopy. Each circular table had eight silver chairs, and above the center of each table three red heart-shaped balloons were anchored by melting ice sculptures. The entwined bride and groom had already morphed into a risqué pose.

A microphone squawked and a disembodied voice instructed the women to find their seats and the men to stand together at the far side of the room.

"I hope they don't pick Nick," Lucy whispered.

"But he'd choose you," Kate said.

Lucy's eyes widened. "I hadn't thought of that."

Kate watched the circle of light dance from one man's face to another. Each time the light paused, the reaction was different— pleased, horrified, smug, cross, oblivious. When the light landed on Dan, he looked so terrified, Kate sniggered. Then the spotlight did a wild dance, anticipation heightened by a long taped fanfare before the light settled. As the guy walked forward, Kate applauded with everyone else. He was good-looking, tall, with neat brown hair, very white teeth and a square jaw. He also had a nervous smile on his face.

"Pick me, pick me," Rachel said.

Kate glanced at her friend. She had straight brown hair that fell to her shoulders and curled out at the edges. Her nose turned up and her lips were red and full. She stared at the guy and hovered above her seat in an attempt to look taller. On the opposite side of the table, Lucy gazed in a different direction. She didn't want to be picked because it wasn't Nick doing the choosing, but who could resist her long, white-blonde hair, bright blue eyes and cheekbones sharp enough to slice Parma ham.

Grabbing her champagne flute, Kate sank as far down under the tablecloth as she could, which was not very far with a table leg wedged between her thighs. She took a gulp of the tepid liquid and winced. Not that she was an expert, but if this was champagne, she was a supermodel. It was too sweet, too fizzy and had about as much alcohol as a sports drink.

"Oh my God, he's coming this way," Rachel squeaked.

Lucy, like Rachel, was now focused on the guy strolling past the seated women. Kate took in their sultry smiles, promising pouts and fuck-me eyes and saw faces fade when he passed by. He made straight for Kate's table. Lucy was pretty irresistible, only lover-boy Nick wouldn't be too happy if she had to spend the evening being nice to another man.

It took Kate a moment to realize that someone was trying to pull her hand away from the edge of her chair. Another moment before she registered that the guy with the square jaw and embarrassed smile had dropped down on one knee next to her and not next to Lucy, not even next to Rachel.

"Will you marry me?" he asked.

Everyone in the room went wild, whooping and whistling for several seconds.

Kate's champagne flute fell from her fingers. She watched it tip over on the table. The liquid sank into the pristine white cloth and spread like an orange fungus. She couldn't tear her eyes away from the stain. Rachel poked her with a fork, hissing something in her ear. Kate turned to look at the man who waited at her feet. The uncomfortable look on his face became more evident as the seconds ticked by. The room slipped into silence. Everyone waited for her to speak. The fork hit her again and she flinched.

"All right," she forced out.

Her groom laughed. He got to his feet, pulled her up and whirled her away from the table.

Kate had a few moments of pure panic when she couldn't breathe. He'd whisked her through a door, away from the noise and faces before she managed to fill her lungs.

"Christ, I thought for a minute you were going to say no." He grinned at her, his smile a little off-center.

Kate swallowed hard. She'd wanted to say no, been desperate to say no, had "no" on her lips, together with "pick Lucy, you idiot" or even "Rachel is desperate", for which Rachel would never have forgiven her, but somehow "all right" had come out.

A man in black leather trousers and a frilly white dress shirt rushed down the corridor toward them. He wore a headset with a microphone that curved across his cheek like a fat-headed black snake.

"Our very first happy couple. Fabulous. Follow me."

He walked backward and Kate was tempted to do the same.

"I'm Chris. Your names?"

"Richard Winter."

"Kate Snow."

Richard turned to Kate and gave her a cheesy grin. "Hey, Winter and Snow on the hottest day of the year. Definitely destiny."

His eyes crinkled and she smiled back.

"I'm so glad you said yes," Richard said, "because you know what? I really want to marry you."

Kate laughed. This might turn out to be fun, she thought, though if she'd had a choice, she'd have turned him down. When she'd agreed to come with Lucy and the others, it never crossed her mind she might be chosen as the bride. Now she felt obliged to go through with it. Kate didn't like to let people down.

She and her groom were ushered into separate rooms. "Strip," was the first word Kate heard.

The organizers talked to her and the bridesmaids as they got ready, told them what they had to do and gave them some idea of what to expect, though not all of it, because they wanted spontaneous reactions. Kate wished she could spontaneously combust before she threw up and they freaked out. The first-night nerves of those running the event rubbed off on Kate and the others. When Chris reminded them how many of their friends and colleagues were out there, they'd all turned pale.

"The press don't care who they murder," Chris said.

Kate was levered into her dress, the largest thing she'd ever seen, layer upon layer of white fluff. She looked like an upside down stick of cotton candy at best and at worst like Barbie's grumpy, ugly sister. The woman messing with Kate's hair swore when it failed to flatten, and eventually gave up. Kate smiled to think at least her hair had a mind of its own. A sparkling princess tiara was pinned on her head and a short stiff veil fastened in place.

By Kate's side, the three bridesmaids had been zipped into puff-sleeved, scoop-necked, flowered monstrosities in lime green, fuchsia pink and muddy brown. You don't need adjectives with brown, Kate thought. She watched in sympathy as Brown burst into tears, consoled by a relieved Pink and Green.

Back in the main room, everyone applauded their entrance. Kate knew her cheeks approached the shade of the carpet, but she kept her head up and strolled toward the spot where her groom and the make-believe vicar stood waiting. The Wedding March blared out, interrupted every couple of seconds by a static-strewn police radio transmission concerning a raid on a massage parlor.

When her husband-for-the-evening turned to look at her, Kate's breath caught in her throat. Richard wore a tuxedo with a neon pink bowtie. He looked gorgeous and genuinely thrilled at the sight of her. So Kate didn't understand why there was a voice in her head telling her to do a Julia Roberts and get the hell out of there.

The vicar hiccupped and stuttered through the service. He got their names wrong and the words, switching between a christening and a wedding. When the humiliation was over, the bride and groom were seated at a long top table.

"Bet you didn't think you'd get married today," Richard said.

Kate didn't think she'd ever get married. "What made you choose me?"

"That wince you gave when you took a mouthful of this crap." He lifted his champagne glass.

That serves me right. She was usually much better at hiding her feelings.

"So what does my wife do for a living? Anchor for the six o'clock news? Political correspondent for *The Times*? Gossip columnist for the *Sun?*"

"Waitress."

There was a pause. Kate knew he either wished he'd picked someone more interesting or was waiting for her to ask what he did. She kept silent, wondering if he'd pass the test.

"I'm an investment banker."

Failed it.

"But I have a feeling that when we hear the best man's speech, he'll have invented a more interesting career for me. Your father for you too, probably, but I am in banking, honestly. I'm afraid I'm a boring shit."

Maybe she'd judged him too quickly.

"I'm glad I picked you. You don't seem boring at all," he said.

He gave her a little smile and Kate's defenses began to shake.

As the first course was being removed, a gong sounded and the men got up and changed tables.

"Hope you aren't feeling short changed," Richard said. "I'm afraid we're stuck with each other for the evening."

"That's okay." Kate meant it. She hadn't come looking for a guy but Richard seemed nice. Kate didn't talk much, but he was attentive and listened when she *did* speak and she began to enjoy herself.

That didn't last long.

"I think your father's about to embarrass you." Richard put his hand on her arm.

Far from being embarrassed, Kate felt adrift from what was happening. The jovial bald man standing next to her looked nothing like the father Kate remembered.

"Welcome," the hairless Santa boomed. "Welcome, all you lying reporters, amateur photographers, TV and radio would-be stars, those freelancers from Aunt Lizzie's care home for the hopelessly insane, paparazzi bottom-feeding scum, friends, relations and complete strangers."

That set the tone. Apparently, Richard was a gynecologist and Kate was a proctologist. A perfect match. Stories of Kate showing the world her bottom in Marks and Spencer and Richard getting his hand stuck in a turkey were two of many anecdotes. It was only when her mother, a tall, thin woman wearing the largest hat Kate had ever seen, got up to speak and began arguing with her husband, that Kate's composure was shaken. When Richard lifted her hand from the table leg and squeezed her fingers, as if he guessed something was wrong, she knew she wouldn't mind seeing him again.

After the collapsing wedding cake, the hysterical mistress, the screaming baby, the police raid, the embarrassing wedding presents and the fight over the bouquet by the ushers—at which point Kate wondered how much more they could cram in—the torture was almost over.

Kate and Richard had the dance floor to themselves for one slow number. The twangy voice of Tammy Wynette singing *D.I.V.O.R.C.E.* filled the room. Then the night was theirs to do what they wanted, but the moment Richard pulled Kate into his arms, she doubted she'd dance with anyone else. She felt his heart beating against hers. His fingers trailed over her back and he pressed his face into her hair, talking to her as though he was declining a verb.

"Can I kiss you? Let me kiss you. I have to kiss you. I've got to kiss you."

He moved his hands to her throat and angled her face as he pressed his lips to hers. Once she'd opened her mouth, he slid one hand down her back and pulled her to him, his hips shoved tight against hers. Even through the thick layers of her horrible dress, Kate felt his erection pressing into her stomach. No mistaking his interest. The kiss started slow and warm, but segued in an instant to fast, hot and greedy. She became aware of hooting and cheering and pulled away to find others moving onto the dance floor around them.

Richard whispered in her ear, "You look delicious and now I know you taste delicious."

"You like meringue?"

"I like whipped cream better."

Kate laughed. His hands slid around her waist, and he lifted his thumbs so they grazed under her breasts. Kate wobbled. She had a sudden vision of a bed waiting for them in another room, together with a pile of sex toys. The bed would be surrounded by tiered seating and their first night would be observed by every guest, all judges at the Wedding Night Olympics, scoring out of ten. She shuddered.

"What are you thinking?" Richard asked.

Kate wasn't sharing. "If my friends were okay."

"You want to know what I'm thinking?"

She thought she already knew.

"I don't want you to wear a dress like that when we get married. I picture you in something sleek and elegant."

Not what she expected.

"Can I come back to your place?"

That was.

He looked at her with his lopsided smile, and Kate was torn between finding it cute and disconcerting.

She pulled away. "No."

"Do you want to come back to mine?"

"No."

She liked the fact that he laughed, but Kate didn't trust herself with this guy.

Richard ran after Kate's taxi, blowing kisses as she watched through the back window. Once she'd gone, he returned to his friends standing in line for a cab and didn't try to hide his smug look.

"Fifty quid for each of us," Simon said to Richard, holding out his hand.

Richard held up his mobile, displaying Kate's number.

"It's only a phone number and it could be the one for Battersea Dog's Home," Simon pointed out.

"It's only you girls give that to." Richard smirked. "Fancy raising the bet? I've had another idea."

His two friends exchanged glances. Richard knew Simon would be up for it. He was a reporter for the daily rag, 24/7, ergo he was up for anything. He wasn't so sure about Alexander Philo, known as Fax, who was a freelance photographer. Richard hadn't known him for long.

"You're making excuses. Pay up," Simon said.

"Okay, so she didn't sleep with me tonight, but I bet I can get her to marry me inside two months."

Fax and Simon burst out laughing.

"I'm serious," Richard said, pissed off they were laughing so hard. "In fact I'm so serious, I'll give you a thousand quid each if I fail to get her into a registry office inside eight weeks. But I won't fail, so you'll be paying me."

There was a sudden silence.

"I don't like it." Fax shook his head.

"What's not to like about that sort of easy money?" Simon asked. "Not that I should encourage Richard in his despicable gambling addiction, but I'm in. Rich, you'll never do it. In fact, if Fax isn't interested, I'm up for the two thousand."

Richard lit a cigarette. "You sure?"

Simon nodded.

"Hey guys, drop it," Fax said. "You shouldn't fool around with someone like that."

Richard snorted. "It's a bit of fun. Lighten up." He caught the look in Simon's eye. "You're not going to write about this, Baxter."

"Okay, no article, but I'm definitely in on the bet. You aren't that persuasive. You can take the pictures, Fax." Simon nudged him in the ribs. "I'll want proof."

"No interfering, either," Richard said. "I don't want you telling her I've got herpes or something."

"Cleared up then, has it?" Simon asked.

"Wanker." Richard laughed.

"You're both wankers," Fax said.

On a Friday night, five weeks to the day after "The Wedding Party", Kate and Richard were walking hand-in-hand through Greenwich Park, Fax and Simon tagging along behind. The four of them had been for a meal in Crispies, the café where Kate worked. She'd rather have eaten elsewhere but Richard had insisted.

"Stop right here," Richard said, looking up at the green laser light overhead, shining from the Observatory on the hill. "You're in the eastern hemisphere and I'm in the west."

He waited for Fax and Simon to catch up. "You can witness this," he said and dropped on one knee on the gravel path. "Kate, my love, will you marry me?"

Because he said he loved her and because he wanted her and made her feel safe, Kate thought that was enough. She started to say yes, then remembered what she'd said the first time. "All right."

Richard laughed, more excited than she'd ever seen him before. He whirled her in a circle on the path, then high-fived his friends.

"Right. I'll arrange everything," he said. "Registry office, flowers, photos, honeymoon. All you have to do is turn up at the registry office in a beautiful dress, looking sexy, ready to say yes and not—all right."

"Slow down." Kate smiled at his exuberance.

"We're getting married," he shouted. "She said yes."

"Actually, I said all right." Kate jumped into his arms to give him a kiss.

"Blimey, you've only known one another a few weeks. Sure you're not rushing it?" Simon asked.

"That's exactly what we're doing—rushing it." Richard grinned.

"Are you all right with a registry office wedding?" Simon asked Kate. "Or did you want to walk down the aisle?"

"We can do it in church if you want," Richard said. "Though I'd prefer not."

"A registry office is fine." Kate didn't want the trimmings.

"When are you going to tie the knot?" Fax asked.

"As quickly as possible. Today if we could. Now fuck off you two. My fiancée and I have things to discuss."

Richard took her hand in his and pulled her faster toward her apartment.

"They didn't say congratulations," Kate muttered.

"Fax is jealous. He fancies you himself."

She couldn't believe that. Fax was always asking about Lucy.

"Let's keep this a secret," Richard said. "Not tell anyone until it's done. I know we haven't known each other long, but we don't want people telling us it's too soon. That's probably the reason for Fax's horse face. He's so bloody cautious, it's a wonder he ever takes a photo."

Richard tugged her into his arms. "We'll get married and afterwards we'll have a party and invite your friends and relations and mine."

Kate knew there wouldn't be many of her friends, and no relations. She'd told him her parents were dead.

"I don't want thousands of my relatives there and none of yours." Richard stroked her cheek. "This way, it's our special day. Nor do I want my mother interfering. God, I'd love to turn up on my parents' doorstep, holding your hand, telling them you're my wife. Where do you want to go on honeymoon?"

Kate felt as though she'd been shot up in a rocket and was exploding in every direction.

Richard squeezed her hand. "Where do you want to go, Kate? Let me make your dreams come true."

Could he? At that moment he seemed capable of anything.

"Hawaii," she said.

"It's yours." Richard grinned.

Kate gasped with shock, but she believed him.

✳ ✳ ✳ ✳ ✳

Fax downloaded the pictures into his computer and stared at the screen, wishing by willpower alone he could make it not have happened. The first image showed Kate arriving at Woolwich registry office looking so happy, her face glowed like a newly opened flower. He'd taken several shots of her between the limo and the door. She'd even turned at the entrance, looked back and laughed, as though she'd been posing for his camera, although Fax felt certain she hadn't seen him.

That particular image was wonderful and terrible. It captured her joy, the last moment of her happiness. He could have stopped her going inside, but he'd been a coward. Fax had convinced himself there was no point, because it was too late. Kate thought Richard was going to marry her and she'd turned up in a stunning ivory wedding dress. The damage had been done and the bet lost or won depending on how you looked at it. Richard was the loser, but the prick wouldn't see it.

As Fax waited outside, his mood was briefly lightened by the hope that Richard *was* inside, or would turn up late, because whilst he might not have started out loving Kate, he'd fallen in love on the way. On the other hand, Fax knew Kate deserved far better than to be married to a dickhead like Richard Winter. This way, she'd be hurt, but would survive.

Fax clicked to the next photograph. There had been no need for him to wait after Kate walked into the building, but he had. The longer he stood there the more certain he was that Richard wasn't inside. Fax knew no matter how bad he felt, it was nothing compared to what Kate had to be feeling. Other couples had come and gone, and still Fax waited because Kate still waited. He rang Richard but the bastard had his mobile off.

When she emerged, Fax had raised his camera almost as a protective barrier. She looked smaller, as though she'd lost something. That's what Richard had done, Fax thought. He'd sunk his teeth in her neck and sucked the life out of her. It was almost enough to make Fax believe in vampires.

Kate's face was as pale as her dress. He could have approached her, but to say what? Instead, Fax followed her to Greenwich, taking more bloody pictures hoping now she'd turn round, see him and hit him so he felt less guilty. She'd sunk so deep inside herself, Fax thought he could have sat next to her on the bus without her seeing. He trailed her to her apartment. Kate took a key from her shoe and went in. While Fax was too much of a coward to talk to her, he was not too much of a coward to talk to Richard.

Armed with copies of the photographs, he went to Richard's apartment.

"Brought your money?" Richard asked.

"Fuck off, you bastard."

Richard grabbed the brown envelope from Fax's hand and ripped it open. Fax watched as he went through the pictures, expecting a flicker of remorse, hoping the photographs would achieve at least something worthwhile.

"God, she looks a bit pissed off." Richard grinned.

Fax gasped. "She was more than a bit pissed off, you fuckwit."

"She'll get over it."

"I thought you loved her. *She* thought you loved her."

"She wasn't a bad fuck, but she's only a waitress."

A flash of rage swept through Fax. "She's better than you, Richard."

"You knew about the deal. If you're so bloody pious, why didn't you tell her?"

"I wish I had."

Richard narrowed his eyes. "When are you going to pay me?"

Fax's hands clenched into fists. "I never agreed to this, but I made the mistake of giving you the benefit of the doubt. I watched you with her and thought you cared. If you had an ounce of decency you'd tell her you got cold feet or something."

"Tell Simon he owes me." Richard slammed the door.

Fax couldn't ride off straightaway. He was shaking too much. By the time he'd put on his helmet, he knew what he had to do. Telling Lucy meant he'd never have a chance with her because she'd think he was a complete bastard, but that was his punishment for ever wanting Richard Winter to be his friend.

"You complete bastard," Lucy gasped.

"I thought he loved her. I would have said something sooner, but I really thought he loved her." Fax couldn't even convince himself.

He sat in Lucy's place, fidgeting on the edge of the couch. He'd longed to be sitting on the bloody thing, only with Lucy in his arms, and instead she glared at him as if he'd sprouted horns and grown a forked tail. Fax lifted his hand and smoothed down his spiky hair, checking for emerging lumps. Even furious she was lovely.

"I need to speak to her," Lucy said, but stayed where she was.

"I could come, if you think it might help."

Another death ray shot in his direction.

"I'll do anything." Fax tried not to look at her chest.

Lucy sighed. "Rachel and Dan are out. I suppose you're better than nothing."

Fax was pathetically grateful even for that.

Kate lay in her wedding dress, curled up on the floor inside her apartment, barely able to breathe. She'd risked expanding her world for Richard and now had no safe place left. Her heart had been shredded, minced and liquidized because she'd allowed herself to believe he loved her. And all Kate could think was that it served her right.

She flinched as Lucy banged on the door.

"Kate, are you there?"

Kate reran the last few weeks, searching for what she'd missed.

"Kate! I know what happened. Fax told me. I can't believe Richard would do that. Please open the door."

Denied the chance to pretend it had never happened, Kate's heart faltered.

"Kate, please."

How stupid to think anything had changed, when *she* hadn't changed. Had Richard uncovered something so bad he no longer wanted to marry her? Her breath jammed in her throat, stopped it up. Maybe that was it. No one ever would want her. Kate wished she were dead, wished her heart would stop pumping blood.

"Kate, open this door right now," Lucy said.

Kate's heart twisted as if Richard squeezed it with his hands. She willed her veins to shrink, arteries to clog, brain to freeze.

"Kate, let's open a bottle and talk about what a shit he is," Fax called.

"He's a fucking monster. I'd have fallen for it, too," Lucy said.

And for a moment, Kate's blood *did* falter. Fallen for what?

"Fax never thought Richard would go through with it, otherwise he'd have told you at the beginning. Kate, Richard's planned this since 'The Wedding Party'."

Kate trembled. So Richard hadn't changed his mind, had an attack of nerves or discovered her secret. He'd deliberately seduced and then dumped her.

"He shouldn't get away with playing with people like this," Lucy said.

A game? No, a bet. Richard liked to gamble. Horses, dogs, cards. One of the few things about him that made Kate uncomfortable.

"I don't think she's there," Fax said. "Maybe she's gone away."

"Her car's outside."

"She might want to be on her own."

Please.

She listened to the retreating footsteps and curled up tighter. Overwhelmed by a wave of deep inadequacy, Kate found it easy to believe it was her fault Richard had done this. She wasn't good enough, pretty enough or clever enough to see through him. Her failure, not his.

At the end of a sleepless night, Kate realized there was nothing she could do to make things right and only one way to make it all go away.

Chapter Three
Charlie's Story

ဢ

"I think you're loads better than Robbie Williams," the girl whispered in Charlie's ear.

He gritted his teeth. He was a lot fucking better than Robbie Williams.

"Do you?" Charlie stared at her. God, he couldn't remember her name. "Have you fucked Robbie, then?"

She giggled. "No, I meant at singing."

Charlie threw off the sheet and stood up, stark naked. "I don't sing anymore."

He looked for his boxers.

"You could sing for me. Come back to bed."

He glanced at her. Why did he always think he'd meet a different sort of woman, when he kept going to the same sort of places? She'd thrown herself at him and he'd said yes. He was obliged to be charming and sexy, the guy every woman wanted in her bed and a lot of men, too. But Charlie was tired of waking up and wondering who lay next to him.

This one was like all the others. Hot body, single brain cell. Charlie hadn't even been to sleep and he still couldn't remember her name. He focused on her chest as she ran her hands around her perfectly round breasts, pointing little brown nipples in his direction, her weapons of destruction. His cock twitched and he licked his lips.

"Don't you want me, Charlie?"

Yes and no. He looked under the bed. No underwear but plenty of empty condom wrappers. He grimaced. Charlie gave up, grabbed his jeans and went commando, zipping himself up carefully. The bitch had probably hidden his boxers so she could sell them on eBay. It wouldn't be the first time.

"Charlie?"

"Sorry, I've got a job first thing tomorrow," he lied.

"Got any coke, then?" She lay back, tweaking her diamond-hard nipples with fidgeting fingers.

He'd wondered if her tits were fake because they were so perfect. He hadn't seen a scar, though he'd heard surgeons could go in under your armpit. Charlie had a vague interest in checking, but didn't want her to get the wrong idea, plus she looked too young to have had that sort of surgery. She looked very young. *Shit.*

"How old are you again?"

"Sixteen. Do you think I'm big enough?" She squeezed her breasts.

"Yeah, you're great," Charlie said. *Jesus, sixteen!*

He slipped on his shirt and pulled a foil wrap from his pocket. He tossed it onto her flat stomach, looked for his shoes, and remembered he'd left them downstairs.

"Great fuck, thanks a lot," he said and left without a backward glance.

Downstairs the party was still in full swing, swing being the operative word by the look of the two half-naked men and one naked woman entwined on the couch, but he'd had enough. Charlie located his shoes and left.

It wasn't until the next day, when Charlie heard a TV newsreader say it, that he remembered her name. India Westerby. Age sixteen. In a coma after a party at the home of Justin Denton, lead singer of "Blast". Charlie's first thought was, thank God she really was sixteen, then, thank God it happened after he left, and then, fucking hell, had he done that? He looked at the wrap of coke in his fingers, thought about using it and tossed it in the toilet. The poor kid, he thought and threw up.

Justin didn't answer his calls until late afternoon.

"What happened last night?" Charlie's heart hammered so hard and fast, he imagined it was the start of a heart attack. It would serve him right.

"Christ, it's been a fucking nightmare. I went upstairs about three this morning and found her on the bed, coke and blood all over her face. Brian Jackson was in the corner, gibbering like a baby. I had to call the police. Brian admitted he'd given her coke and they arrested him. God, I am so fucked over this. My house," Justin wailed.

Charlie tried to swallow the lump in his throat and failed. "Did the police want to know who was there?"

The pause said everything.

"I had to, mate. Everyone saw you. You were with her for a while."

"Umm."

"Don't get in a twist about it. She was down here dancing topless after you left, dipping her tits in Grand Marnier and letting everyone have a suck. The stupid bitch. My manager's back again. I got to go."

Charlie's hands shook as he put down the phone. Brian Jackson, drummer of "The Flakes" might have given India coke, but so had he. The packet had his prints on it. His fucking boxers were still in the room. Probably. Had he flushed the condom? Charlie couldn't remember. He retched. He was pathetic. He could have killed her and all he could think about was saving his own ass. The contents of his stomach rose into his mouth yet again and he rushed to the bathroom.

When he looked in the mirror, Charlie didn't recognize the person staring back. Everyone kept on about his fabulous face, but he looked like shit. Dark circles rimmed his bloodshot eyes and his skin was sallow, despite weeks spent filming in the Arizona desert. He needed a shave. His breath would have made a flower wilt. Jesus Christ, sixteen years old? He was a walking fucking disaster. How many more lives was he going to destroy?

Charlie attempted to smile at his agent's secretary, but when Alicia wouldn't look at him, he knew he was in trouble. She'd called to tell him Ethan wanted to see him—now—and Charlie wondered how he'd found out he was at the party. But then Ethan was God. He knew everything. He'd been his agent since the outset and the closest thing to a friend Charlie had.

"Go straight in," Alicia said.

Ethan Silver stood staring out of the window when Charlie pushed open the door. His agent was in his forties, taller than him, with short gray hair beginning to recede.

"Sorry," Charlie said, the best way to open any conversation he had with anyone.

Ethan turned and Charlie swallowed hard. Ethan's jaw was tense, his narrowed eyes black with fury.

"I want to kill you, you stupid fucking wanker." Ethan's voice started soft but by the end of the sentence he was yelling.

He strode across the room with his tie askew, his face flushed. He stopped in front of Charlie and Charlie cringed.

"What the fuck's the matter with you? Do you have a brain? Don't answer that. Did you know you lose brain cells every time you fuck? You are literally fucking your life away," Ethan shouted.

"Count to ten slowly. I find it helps," Charlie said.

Ethan gave a snort of disgust and returned to his desk to slump on his chair. He pointed to the low black leather seat opposite. Charlie sat.

"Right—eight, nine, ten. You are still a stupid fucking wanker. As if my job isn't stressful enough without dealing with morons."

Ethan snapped his pencil in half and Charlie pressed himself back in the chair. He knew Ethan had chosen it so he towered over anyone who sat there. As if the guy wasn't intimidating enough. Ethan picked up another pencil and snapped that one too.

"Do you know why I'm breaking my pencils, Charlie?"

Charlie shook his head.

"Because although snapping your neck would give me a greater sense of satisfaction, I'd get sent to prison for that."

Charlie stayed quiet.

"I don't know what's wrong with you. That was your fucking part."

The fog cleared in an instant and Charlie perked up. Ethan didn't know about him and India. "I didn't get it?"

"Of course you fucking didn't get it," Ethan yelled.

"Okay."

"Is that all you have to say?"

"What do you want me to say?"

"You were a shoo-in, Charlie. All you had to do was fucking walk into the room and turn on your smile. How difficult could that be?"

Charlie opened his mouth and closed it again.

"Apparently you were drunk, stoned and rude. Did I miss anything?" Ethan rose from his chair and paced again.

Charlie felt like a mouse being played with by a cat. Any moment Ethan would crunch and swallow him. Charlie's memory of the audition was a bit hazy. Drunk, stoned and rude about covered it. "No," he said. "You didn't miss anything."

Ethan ground his teeth.

"You're going to wreck your dental work."

"You're lucky I'm not wrecking yours." Ethan kicked his waste paper basket straight at the door.

Charlie jumped at the noise and his headache flared up again.

Alicia rushed in. "Are you all right, Mr. Silver?"

"You're fired," Ethan said.

Her chin wobbled, she dissolved into tears and fled.

"What was that for?" Charlie asked.

"The woman's useless. I've had enough of useless people. I need a different job. A complete change of career. Instead of trying to find work for wankers like you, maybe I should take up something less stressful, like working as Naomi Campbell's personal assistant."

Charlie didn't dare laugh. "Sorry," he muttered.

"Get yourself straight, Charlie, or you're out. I don't represent losers."

"I'm not a loser." He figured this wasn't the time to tell Ethan about India.

Ethan sat down again, moderating his voice. "Look, Charlie. I don't want to lose you as a client. I knew you were a gold mine the first time I met you, but the gold is sinking deeper and deeper and pretty soon it's going to be inaccessible."

Charlie nodded, trying to look contrite.

"I want you back on the right track, Charlie. And if I can't do it with the promise of the role of a lifetime, how the fuck can I do it?"

Charlie drove away in a temper. Ethan was furious with him and Charlie was furious with himself. It wasn't as if he wanted to wreck his life. After giving up a very successful career as a singer/songwriter, Charlie had landed several bit parts in films that barely made it to general release, until he got his break. He'd just completed his first major role in a Steven Spielberg production and he'd been good. Steven had said so. The film was due out in a few months, but word was already circulating that it could win Oscars. Probably not for Charlie, but association with an award-winning film would boost his career.

On the back of Charlie's work for Spielberg, Ethan arranged an audition for a film where he'd be the lead. It was a project of one of the big American studios and Charlie hadn't quite been able to believe it. Provisionally entitled *The Green*, it was about a guy whose wife had been whisked off into a parallel world. Once Charlie read the script he'd wanted it, thought it was his and he'd fucked it up. No surprise there.

Charlie decided he needed cheering up, something to take his mind off his problems. Jen's mobile was switched off so he rang her house, hoping he didn't get her mother.

Arabella, Jen's sister, answered. "Jen's out shopping. She won't be long. Want to come over and wait?"

"Yeah, all right," came out of his mouth, when he should have said no. The story of his life.

Charlie looked at the woman lying naked next to him on the bed. Arabella had a self-satisfied smirk on her face. Then he looked at the two women standing in the doorway. One was Arabella's mother, Veronica and the other was Arabella's sister, Jennifer. Now he'd slept with all three.

"I think it's time for me to leave." Charlie stood up, not caring that he was naked and had the remains of a hard-on. He grabbed his boxers.

Veronica glared at him and Jen cried without making a sound, fat tears rolling down her cheeks.

"Sorry, Jen," he muttered, dressing as quickly as he could.

"You will be, you little shit," Veronica hissed. "My husband will make sure you never —"

"Work in this town again?" Charlie couldn't help grinning. He strode over and put his face close to hers. "Maybe he'd reconsider, if I offer to tell the Sunday papers about the kinky sex his wife enjoys and how thirty minutes ago, his youngest daughter stuck her hand in my pants while I stood at the front door. Probably captured on your CCTV camera. If you get it on *The UK's Funniest Videos*, use my share to buy yourself some wrinkle cream."

He smiled his apology to Jen, but her mouth dropped open and she fled.

"Get out," Veronica gasped.

Charlie escaped while he still could.

He'd been stupid again. He liked Jen. Well, he half had, until she got clingy, but her father was not someone he needed to piss off. Malcolm Ward headed the music company Charlie used to be signed to. He wasn't going to be very happy if he got wind of how well Charlie knew all the women in his household. And if Ethan found out, he'd kill him. *When* he found out, Charlie corrected. So he was as good as dead. *Shit.*

Charlie hadn't even reached his apartment before Ethan was on the phone.

"Are you incapable of keeping your dick in your pants? You've just finished a movie that's going to make you a mega star and you're pissing it away. What the hell is the matter with you? Has someone pressed your self-destruct button?"

Charlie switched Ethan off in mid-rant and called Justin.

"Fancy a pint?"

Charlie was already drunk by the time Justin got there. A group of girls stood by the bar, egging each other on as Charlie stared at them. Justin collected a couple of pints and joined him at his table.

"Don't waste your time with them. They're all dogs," Justin said.

"Because they didn't take any notice of you?" Charlie continued to eye flirt with the ugly one to wind up the others.

Justin shook his head. "If you winked at a statue, the fucking thing would go wet between the thighs."

Charlie grinned, then turned his back and helped himself to one of Justin's cigarettes.

"Thought you were giving up?" Justin asked.

"Buying them, not smoking them."

"You'll get us thrown out if you smoke in here."

"Not until I've had a couple of drags."

Charlie saw Justin's eyes focus somewhere over his shoulder and turned to see the ugly one staring at him, her eyes wide open in excitement. She looked like a pug, her nose all squashed up on her face, with tiny piggy eyes and wrinkles.

"Can I have your autograph?" She offered him a beer mat.

"Piss off," Charlie said.

He heard her sob as she fled back to her friends.

"What did you do that for?" Justin stared at him.

"She didn't say please."

"You're a mean bastard."

He *was* mean. He didn't care. He didn't care about anything. That was his problem.

"Word is, India died of an overdose," Justin said under his breath. "Enough coke in her system to keep you and me going for a week."

"Fuck."

"How about giving *me* your autograph?"

Charlie turned to see one of ugly girl's friends. Pretty face, dimples, vacant eyes.

"Sure." He smiled. "Lift your skirt."

As he wrote on her thigh, she squealed with delight. He handed back the pen and patted her on the bottom.

A moment later, there was a wail of fury.

"What did you write?" Justin asked.

"Robbie Williams."

"You shit. Want to go to a club?"

"Why not?"

Yet Charlie could think of hundreds of reasons why not. The biggest one being he was tired of not being able to be himself. He'd no sooner gone into the club than he'd been pestered. Everyone wanted a part of him. They had pictures of Charlie Storm on their phones, on their walls, in their hearts. They knew the details about his body almost better than he did — his height, weight, collar and shoe size, blood group, the exact location of every scar. He belonged to them. He sometimes felt he only existed because of them and Charlie hated his life and hated himself.

He got a taxi home. Being a sex god was exhausting. He knew that sounded pathetic, but while he loved women, loved going out with them, loved fucking them, part of him was bored with it all. Predatory females swarmed around him like flies on a corpse and that was what he felt like sometimes, a fucking corpse.

He'd had so many letters from women begging to sleep with him that he could have papered his entire house and shagged a different bird every day for years, probably for the rest of his life.

Plenty of them wanted to have his babies. Charlie always carried condoms and let Ethan's staff deal with his letters now.

The funny thing was he hadn't slept with nearly as many women as people thought. For a start, he hadn't fucked Jody Morton, the leading lady on the Spielberg film, despite rumors to the contrary and her obvious interest in having him in, outside or under her trailer. The idea of being bitten by a snake had been enough to squash the last. Jody had a fabulous body, but she was too intense. Charlie had been trying to prove something to himself by not sleeping with her, but he *had* helped himself to his makeup girl and one of the production assistants.

Although he knew he was fucked up, Charlie bridled at Ethan's insistence that he see a shrink. He didn't need to talk about it because Charlie knew what his problem was. He was unlovable. Sure, women said they loved him, but they loved the idea of him, his face, the Charlie with his guitar singing *Angel Eyes*, *Just One Look* or *Fade Away*. That was who they loved and the Charlie on the screen, even when he was a bastard, not the real Charlie because they didn't fucking know him. Otherwise, they'd have run screaming in the other direction. He didn't deserve to be loved. He didn't deserve to be alive.

Charlie only felt better when he was drunk or stoned or preferably both because it stopped him from thinking. He hated his life so much it frightened him.

The moment he walked into his house, his phone rang. Charlie's heart jumped. It was only ever bad news.

"We're done," Ethan said.

"What?"

"You heard me. It's over."

"You're fucking dumping me?" Charlie raged at his agent.

"I don't know who I'm representing anymore, Charlie. You're not the same guy I took on."

"Please, Ethan. I'll try harder."

"It's not working. Every time I try to help you, you fuck up. Even the shrink couldn't sort *your* head out."

"I'm not fucking psycho."

"That's a matter of opinion," Ethan said. "If you'd like to try another psychiatrist, I'll recommend one, but you have to talk to them, Charlie, not sit there staring at the carpet."

"It was supposed to be confidential."

"Telling me you won't talk is hardly breaking a confidence."

"If I see someone else, will you keep me on?" Charlie said. "Please." He knew he sounded desperate and he hated himself for it, but he *was* desperate. Without Ethan, he was fucked.

"No," Ethan said.

"Say you'll think about it," Charlie asked.

"No."

The rage rose in him like a tidal surge, boiling up, overflowing, spewing from his mouth. "Ethan, you are a fucking, selfish wanker."

"Fuck off, Charlie. I've done my very best for you. But Veronica Ward *and* her daughters? For Christ's sake, what were you thinking? Sort yourself out."

"You need me," Charlie said in desperation. "I pay the fucking mortgage on your place in Mayfair. I paid for your fucking car. I've bought you."

"I've created a monster." Ethan laughed.

"When I fucking kill myself, I'll mention you in the note," Charlie yelled.

"You're not going to kill yourself, Charlie."

"We'll see about that."

Charlie switched off his phone, threw it across the room and slumped on the couch. Was Ethan right? Didn't he even have the guts to do that? Charlie didn't understand how everything had been so right and then gone so wrong.

After he and his band were spotted at a union gig by a guy from EMI, their rise had been meteoric. When Charlie fell out with the others, particularly Jed, the arrogant drummer, and decided to go solo, Charlie shot into another galaxy, while the rest of the guys stayed on the same planet. Then, once he got up there, he lost interest. Charlie still liked writing songs, but he no longer

42

wanted to sing in front of an audience. He'd done the big festivals like Glastonbury and Reading. He'd filled the National Exhibition Center. He'd had more success in the States than Robbie had managed and without taking his kit off, but it hadn't been enough.

Charlie had always liked acting. He'd been in all the school productions. He loved pretending to be someone else. Given words to speak, he could taste them, roll them around in his mouth, spit them, dance them, blow them out. He could enchant, disgust or seduce. The three minutes as a twisted killer in his first film had been a bit different to his schoolboy Romeo, but Charlie had been hooked and discovered he was good at being bad. No surprise there. Furthermore, he found being paid to rape, murder and mutilate a huge turn-on—not that he could ever tell anyone, particularly not Ethan's shrink. They'd really think he was nuts.

The house phone rang and he glanced at caller display. He hoped for Ethan, but it wasn't a number he knew.

"Simon Baxter from 24/7 looking for your reaction to the claim that you supplied the coke for Justin Denton's party."

"What?"

"You deny it then?"

Charlie slammed the phone down. It rang again almost at once. This time it was a reporter from the *Sun*.

"Any comment about fourteen-year-old India Westerby? Sources tell—"

Charlie dragged the cord out of the wall. Fourteen? They'd said sixteen. That was bad enough, but fourteen? How could she have only been fourteen? He raced into the bathroom and threw up before he reached the toilet. He was retching and crying at the same time, lying on his beautiful limestone-tiled floor, covered in tears and vomit and wanting his mum, only he couldn't have her because he'd blown that too.

He found himself looking for his "absolute emergency" stash and then threw it into the pan and flushed before he could change his mind. The police might come round any minute. He had to use his head, not trip out of it.

Everything had been his. According to Ethan, Charlie was on the point of becoming the most lusted after heartthrob in the western hemisphere and he'd thrown it all away. His mind ached with the stress of trying to figure out what to do, a way to put things straight.

At the end of a sleepless night, Charlie realized there was nothing he could do to make things right and only one way to make it all go away.

Chapter Four

80

Charlie yelped when his toes scraped against something and his fear made Kate panic. She squealed and kicked out.

"Oh God, is it the shark?" she yelled.

Sand shifted under his feet and he sighed. "Put your feet down."

Kate gasped in relief. "Oh God."

Charlie watched her struggle through the waves and fall forward onto the beach.

"We made it," she shouted and turned to look for him. "What the hell are you doing?"

"Swimming back to my clothes. It's warmer in here than out there."

Possibly true, though not the reason he'd stayed in the sea. Charlie had left his clothes on the beach, including his boxers, though he wished he'd kept them on. A couple of times something had brushed against his cock and whilst he didn't mind being eaten when he was dead, he took objection to anything dining on him while he was alive, particularly if it started on the pieces of him that stuck out. Not that much had stuck out since he'd entered the water. The mere thought of a shark had terrified his tackle into retreating in a way he'd thought physically impossible.

Kate stood with her arms wrapped around her body. He could see her legs shaking. The wind blasted across the sand, whipping at her ankles. All she wore was a white shirt, currently plastered to her skin.

"That way," Charlie yelled above the sound of the crashing surf and pointed left.

As he swam parallel to the shore, he knew Kate watched him. If he turned and headed out to sea, she'd follow.

Charlie recognized the place where he'd left his clothes, a large gorse bush at the back of the beach. The sea had dumped the pair of them back not far from where he'd started.

"My stuff's up there," he shouted. "Keep walking."

"Why? Aren't you wearing anything?"

"An embarrassed smirk. Everything shrinks in cold water. I don't want you getting the wrong impression of my magnificent manhood."

He'd also had a sudden irrational fear that photographers with powerful telephoto lenses might be lurking in the dunes, ready to zero in on what was currently his not very impressive cock. They'd all learned lessons from Jude's alfresco strip and, to be honest, Charlie didn't think Jude's shaft was undersized, but that was the press for you.

Kate found his clothes and walked back into the water with his black silk boxers.

"They're wet," he said in disgust.

"It's raining."

She waded back through the surf and slumped on the sand. A few moments later, Charlie dropped at her side.

"God, we nearly drowned," he said, in a serious voice.

Kate started to laugh. So did Charlie and found he couldn't stop. They lay back, shivering, spattered with sand, lashed by rain and still laughed. Charlie reached for Kate's hand. Her fingers interlaced with his and held on tight and they lay together, cold, wet and alive.

Charlie turned his head toward her and waited for her to turn to him. When she did, he spoke. "So."

"So what?"

"Aren't you going to ask me what I was doing out there?"

"None of my business."

Charlie gave a short laugh. Everything he did was somebody else's business.

"You know who I am." It wasn't a question. Of course she knew.

Kate's brow furrowed. "No, though you look familiar."

Charlie smiled. He didn't believe her. "Do you live near here?"

"London."

"Whereabouts?"

"Greenwich."

"That's nearer than Islington. Going to invite me back?"

When she didn't answer, he continued, "All that swimming has made me hungry."

"I shouldn't talk to strangers. You could be a murderer."

They laughed again.

Fuck it, I'm still alive. I'm glad.

Charlie sat up with a groan and got to his feet. He pulled Kate to hers. They were both shaking, their teeth chattering. He stared at her. He guessed she was in her mid-twenties, a few years younger than him anyway. She was tall and skinny, her dark, red-tinged hair shorter than his. Her ears stuck out a little and were pointed at the top like a pixie's. As she turned her pale face and dark eyes on him, he felt a familiar tug in his groin. His cock coming back to life. He dropped his gaze and got stuck on her legs. They went on forever.

"So you're not a hippo," she said.

"What?" Charlie looked back at her face.

"I've spent the last couple of hours with your head and shoulders. I know you have messy dark hair and big, sad eyes, but I wondered what the rest of you was like. Fat, thin, tail, flippers?"

"I thought you were a sexy mermaid and you thought I was a fat hippo? I'm offended."

"Maybe I have a thing for hippos."

"So, do you see a hippo?" Charlie asked, opening his arms.

Kate looked him over. "An anorexic hippo."

He smiled. "What about a drink, then?" He picked up his wet clothes and boots.

Kate started walking.

"I could do with a lift," he said, when she didn't answer.

She sighed. "Me too, probably. I left the keys in the car. Somebody's bound to have nicked it."

When they got to the car park, there was only one car. A red wreck held together by a complex mixture of rust. Charlie almost hoped someone had nicked Kate's car but she headed straight for it. The sun came out and the vehicle looked even worse.

"I'm not surprised it's still here," Charlie said.

"If you're going to be rude about my car, you can forget the lift."

Kate got in and slammed the door. Charlie winced, waiting for it to fall off. He got in the passenger side and dumped his boots and wet clothes at his feet.

"A palace on wheels, to be sure. It's a sign." Charlie used a line from his last film.

"What's with the strange accent?" Kate asked.

He frowned. "Hey, I was pretending to be Irish."

"What for?"

Did she really not know who he was?

"So if you didn't come by car, how did you get here?" Kate asked.

"Train to St. Somewhere-or-other, then walked."

As Kate started the engine, her foot slipped off the accelerator. The car juddered and stalled. Charlie braced himself against the dashboard.

"Sorry, combination of frozen toes and no shoes," Kate said with a smile.

"Just try not to kill us," he said.

They looked at each other and both sniggered.

In the warmth of the car, Charlie fell asleep. Kate kept glancing at him. Now his face was relaxed, he looked familiar, but she didn't think she knew him. Was he famous? Kate tended not to look people in the face, particularly not men. Better to keep her head down, mind her own business. Maybe he'd been into Crispies, the café where she worked. Maybe he knew Richard. Kate suffered a moment's cramping panic wondering if he was one of Richard's friends and then the moment passed. Pure craziness. Richard had already shown he didn't care about her. Why would he send anyone to follow her?

Charlie's head rested against the window. His mouth hung open and Kate could see the tips of his very white teeth. He was older than her but looked younger now. Not worried anymore. A little lost boy. Except he wasn't a boy, but a man. A good-looking man. Kate knew nothing about him, yet they'd shared a more intense experience than most couples ever did. They wouldn't have survived without each other and maybe a touch of luck. It was a strange sort of bond. Maybe the sooner they went their separate ways, the better.

By late afternoon, they were snarled up in city traffic. For the last ten miles, the engine had survived on sniffing the gas tank. Kate had no money for fuel. Her purse was back at the apartment. She'd thought long and hard before she'd purchased the car. It was an expensive safety net. When she'd driven away that morning, she'd planned to use her escape pod to crash into a wall. A non-starter once she realized she might end up injured, maybe paralyzed and others might be hurt. She needed something certain. So she'd ignored all walls and carried on driving until she reached the coast. Only then did she appreciate the particular suitability of the sea. She could hide forever. The idea of bumping into another suicidal maniac never entered her head.

The closer she drew to Greenwich, the more anxious Kate became, her mood sinking faster than the Titanic. Now she'd returned — Lucy, Dan and Rachel would want to talk to her about the wedding that wasn't. Maybe she'd go back to the beach tomorrow and try again. After all, nothing had changed. Her life was still shit. If Charlie hadn't come along, today would have been her last. Now tomorrow could be. More clothes would help. A couple of sweaters to weigh her down. As if she didn't feel down enough. In the mirror, she saw the ghost of a smile flit across her face.

She activated the remote to open the gates, reversed into her parking place at the back of the block and turned off the engine. Kate glanced up at the windows of her apartment. She thought she'd taken her last look that morning but she wouldn't be dying today.

Charlie stirred and groaned. He opened his eyes and sat up, wincing as he peeled his bare shoulders away from the vinyl.

"Are we back?" he muttered.

"From where?" Kate pushed open the door and stepped from the car.

Her linen shirt had dried to an uncomfortable sandpaper sack, her legs marbled by salt, sand and mud. Charlie picked up his soggy clothing and joined her on the path.

"We're going to make a mess," he said as they walked toward the building. "We've brought half the beach with us."

On the concrete, next to a small flower bed, a green hosepipe lay coiled like a sleeping snake.

"We could clean ourselves off with the hose. I'll let you do me first," he said.

He put his clothes down by the door and then stood in the middle of the parking area with his arms outstretched, his perfect body as irresistible as a dark god's. Kate turned on the tap, picked up the gun and used the initial flurry of warm water on her feet. The moment the temperature changed, she aimed the jet at the middle of Charlie's chest and blasted him with cold water.

"Fucking hell," he yelped. "I've changed my mind."

He hopped sideways, trying to hold back the torrent with his hands. Kate directed the jet down his legs and he spun around so he faced away from her. As he moaned and whined, she realized she was enjoying herself.

"Aren't you done yet?" he shouted.

"Nearly."

She pushed him too far. Kate found the gun wrenched from her hand. She screamed and ran, but there was no escape. When she tried to dodge by the side of a larger vehicle, Charlie adjusted the jet to reach further and blasted her over the top of the car. Kate squealed. The sea had been warmer.

"You can run, but there's nowhere to hide," Charlie drawled in a bad Clint Eastwood impersonation.

She wriggled around the front of one car and tried to duck by the side of another.

"Take your shirt off," he said. "There's some seaweed or something hanging out the back."

Kate heard the word seaweed and freaked out. She leaped from her hiding place and whipped the shirt off so quickly, one of the buttons pinged Charlie on the cheek. His finger released the trigger and the water spluttered to a halt.

"Jesus Christ, Kate. What the fuck are you wearing?"

"Underwear."

"It doesn't look like underwear."

"Pretend it's a bikini."

"That doesn't help," he said, a pained expression on his face.

"Get rid of the seaweed and rinse me off before we freeze to death."

Charlie obliged. This was like no underwear he'd seen before and he'd seen more than his fair share. Fire-engine red, frilly, lacy and disturbingly exotic. The material was dotted with little black flowers and at their heart nestled a tiny red bead. Except there were no flowers over her nipples. He could see those just fine — sharp little pencil erasers jutting out in front of her. The matching strip of material around her hips was a straight band, but at the back, almost nonexistent. She had the sweetest, most bitable backside Charlie had seen in ages. Blood surged to his groin as Kate dashed into the lobby. Good to know the cold water hadn't had a lasting effect.

He switched off the hose at the tap and then followed her up the stairs, his wet clothes bunched in a ball to hide his erection. One flick of his fingers and her bra would be off, only he usually knew how a woman would react to that and with Kate he wasn't sure. As he moved his gaze up her smooth, tanned back, his eyes lingered on a straight white scar about three inches long, lying below her shoulder blade. Operation? Assault? Inside her apartment, she opened a cupboard, grabbed a couple of towels from a shelf above a boiler and tossed him one. The other went round her chest.

"Clothes," she demanded.

Charlie grinned and handed them over.

"Anything in the pockets?" Kate opened another door and pushed everything into a washing machine, along with her shirt.

"No."

He'd locked his phone, wallet and keys in his apartment. Bad move.

"Here, you may as well have these, too."

He reached under the towel, shuffled off his boxers and held them out with a grin. No reaction. He frowned as Kate snagged them from his hand, pushed them into the drum and turned on the machine.

Charlie followed her into the main room and recoiled. "Christ, you've been burgled."

The room was almost bare. A kitchen occupied a small part of it, but in the other section the only item was a tatty couch, piled with cushions, lying at an angle across the room. No TV, no music system, no plants, no ornaments, no pictures, no curtains.

"Nope, this is what it's normally like."

Out of the corner of his eye, Charlie saw Kate pull down a note she'd taped to a cupboard door. She screwed it into a ball and kept it in her hand. He came up behind her.

"I thought you were kidding about the Mars Bars." He nodded at the wrappers on the counter.

"I only ate nine. Then I was sick."

"Why did you eat so many?"

"I didn't want to waste them." Kate grinned and he laughed.

"What do you have to drink?" he asked.

"Tea, coffee, hot chocolate."

"No beer, Jack Daniel's or similar?"

"No."

"Then hot chocolate would be great. Thank you." He smiled at her, but Charlie could see she'd gone somewhere in her head. He took the box of drinking chocolate from her fingers and spooned it into two mugs.

"I don't suppose you have any marshmallows?" he asked.

"No."

"Whipped cream?"

"No."

"Twiglets?"

Kate shot him a glance.

"I like Twiglets," he said. "Mmm, crunchy sticks coated with Marmite. My favorite."

"I like them too, but not in hot chocolate."

"Try it. It's a real treat."

He watched her mind slide away again and chewed his lip.

"Go and sit down. I'll make the drink," he said.

He poured in the water and whisked with a spoon in each hand. Kate hadn't moved, and took the mug he offered.

"Do you want to use the bathroom first? There's a bath and a separate shower," she said in a flat voice.

"After you." Charlie bit back the automatic "with you".

Much to his disappointment, Kate took the scrunched up note with her, but while she was occupied elsewhere, he explored. The first door he opened took him into a room almost as empty as the main one. Bare boards, no rugs, no curtains. The single piece of furniture was a trestle table pushed against a wall, a plastic chair tucked underneath. On top of the table sat an old computer and a sewing machine and, underneath, three cardboard boxes. He opened the flap of one. It was full of slinky black material.

When Charlie opened the door to her bedroom, the breath caught in his throat.

He felt as though he'd stepped into another world, certainly into a different apartment. The room was dominated by a four-poster bed with an elaborate twisted-metal headboard decorated with bronze butterflies. Cream linen drapes smothered with multicolored appliqué butterflies had been tied up with silver cords at each metal corner post. Charlie had a sudden vision of the pair of them on that bed, naked in each other's arms, the drapes pulled across to cut them off from the world. He groaned as his cock tented the towel. He thought too much.

His fingers moved toward the chest of drawers. He shouldn't, but he did. He gulped when he saw underwear in every imaginable color and material — lace, velvet, cotton, leather, silk, denim. He closed the drawer, not daring to look any further. He stood for a moment and then went back to the bathroom.

"Kate, I need to use the toilet," he called through the door.

"You've just had hours in the sea. Couldn't you have gone then?"

"Mum told me to get out of the water first."

"What, even the ocean?"

"It's wrong to pollute." He tried to sound serious.

He could have nipped into the car park or even used the kitchen sink — it wouldn't have been the first time — but he had an ulterior motive and thought she just needed a bit of encouragement. Anyone with a drawer full of sexy underwear had to be up for it. She'd bounced up the stairs in front of him, knowing she looked practically naked from behind, so he only needed to turn his charm up a notch. He really wanted to climb into the bath with her, but it was the sort of move that had got him into this mess in the first place. *Go slow*.

"Please," he pleaded, in his very best seductive voice. "I'm getting desperate."

Kate looked around. The bubbles covered everything, but she didn't care anyway. She'd had modesty knocked out of her years ago. She'd spent all her life sharing bathrooms and bedrooms. Any sign of shyness and you were finished.

"There's no lock on the door," she said.

Charlie didn't even try not to look at her.

"Warm again?" he asked.

"I didn't ask you in to start up a conversation."

"Sorry."

Kate listened to the tinkling sound and thought of Richard. He'd never felt comfortable enough to take a leak while she was in the bathroom. She sank back into the water, pushing up her knees so her head slid below the surface. What a mess, she thought. What a shitty, fucking, awful mess. She wasn't dead, but she felt dead.

When she resurfaced, Charlie was kneeling by the side of the bath. Who did he remind her of? He wiped a smear of bubbles from her lips.

"Can I get in?"

"No."

He sighed. "Couldn't you have pretended to think about it?"

"No."

"Not even a bit of a pause?"

"No."

"So why were you trying to kill yourself?" he asked.

"You may as well have a shower while you're in here. There are more towels in the cupboard."

By the time he got out of the shower, Kate had gone and taken the scrunched-up note, which made him even keener to read it. Under the wash basin, Charlie found a packet of razors, a can of men's shaving gel and three boxes of condoms. All opened. He wasn't sure if he was pleased or not about that. He hadn't checked in the wardrobe for men's clothes, but Charlie didn't get the feeling Kate lived with or had lived with a guy. No guy could survive without a TV. Maybe the boyfriend only came around for a shave and sex. Bit like him. Except not the shave, because Charlie waited until he got home. Now, he took a perverse pleasure in shaving with another man's gear. He wasn't sure why, but he didn't like the idea of Kate having a boyfriend, although he guessed she wouldn't have been in the sea if she had.

Could she be pregnant? Maybe the guy didn't want it. Charlie bristled with anger. Whoever this guy was, he was a wanker. Even as the thought curled around in his mind, filtering like smoke into every crevice, Charlie realized he was being stupid. He knew nothing about her. It was because Kate had shown no interest that he wanted her even more. He still couldn't figure out how she felt about him. Charlie scraped the razor down his cheek but when he heard banging at the front door, his hand jumped and a bead of blood oozed through the foam. He swore and looked down at his naked body. He hoped this wasn't Kate's guy.

"Kate, I bloody well know you're in there."

Charlie relaxed when he heard a woman's voice.

"Your car was there, then it disappeared and now it's back. Let me in. I want to talk to you."

"Hi, Lucy," Kate said.

"Are you all right?" Lucy asked.

"Fine."

"Fine?" The voice rose to a shriek.

Charlie was glad Lucy could see Kate wasn't fine.

"We know what happened yesterday. You must be devastated."

And what did happen yesterday, he wondered.

"Can I come in?" Lucy asked.

No, Charlie thought and called, "Kate, I need some clothes, unless you'd prefer me to walk around naked."

"Oh, maybe not that devastated," Lucy said.

Charlie sniggered.

"I've got a friend staying," Kate said. "I'll talk some other time."

He heard the door close. Then the door of the bathroom opened. A white T-shirt and a pair of sleep pants hit him in the chest.

56

Charlie dressed and found Kate in the kitchen.

"Going to admit you recognize me now?" he asked.

Kate turned to face him and a flash of heat rushed to his groin. She wore the same as him and looked so sexy, with her hair damp and messed up, he had to force himself not to pull her into his arms and fuck her nonexistent socks off.

"Charlie, my pet sea hippo," she whispered.

Did she really not know who he was? "Try again."

Kate screwed up her eyes.

"Why are you looking at me like that?"

"You're rather blotchy," she said.

Charlie burst out laughing. That was a word never applied to him before—gorgeous, seductive, beautiful, never blotchy. "It's the razor."

"Oh. Hungry?"

"Starving."

"Do you eat meat?"

"I eat anything. Almost," he corrected, in case she was into braised brain or grilled gizzards. "Got any wine?" He looked at the empty bottle next to the sink.

"Only champagne."

Kate took two containers from the freezer, removed their lids and put them in the microwave to defrost.

"Is the champagne in the fridge?" he asked and opened the door.

Kate lurched toward him and slammed it shut.

"Whoa." He backed off, hands in the air.

"Sorry. I'll get it."

"What do you have in there? Body parts?"

"Oh God, you guessed. I like to feed bits of the last guy to the next guy and so on. A little quirk of mine. I suppose you don't want to stay for something to eat now."

Kate balled up the note taped to the champagne and handed him the bottle.

Charlie gawped at the label. No furniture and she bought Cristal?

"Bloody hell. This for a special occasion?" he asked, brandishing the bottle.

"I don't think there could be a more special occasion than this."

"Having me in your house, yeah, you're right."

Kate chuckled and Charlie smiled. She looked so different when she laughed, as though every worry had gone. He'd get the next one in, while she was still up.

"Can I stay the night?"

A few worries came back.

"I don't have a spare bed."

"I can sleep on the couch." When she didn't say anything, he added, "Or I could go. I'd need a lift."

"I think," Kate said, "I'd like it if you stayed."

Charlie felt as though she'd put a soothing hand on his brow. He eased the cork out of the bottle with a gentle pop and poured. "What shall we drink to?"

"Me and you."

"And a dog named Sue," Charlie sang and chinked his glass against hers.

Kate rolled her eyes.

"She's a lovely dog," Charlie said. "Part Chihuahua part Doberman. The mother was the Chihuahua. Not an easy relationship."

"So what are you?" Kate asked. "An unfunny comedian?"

He bristled. "I used to sing, now I act."

"God." She rolled her eyes.

He laughed. "Do you really not recognize me?"

Kate stared straight at him and Charlie saw the moment of recognition strike.

"Oh shit," she said.

Chapter Five

Kate didn't blink. How could she not have realized? Flustered, she reached for a pair of glasses she rarely wore and put them on before she turned to him. Impossible, incredible, inconceivable—as much like a teenage fantasy as it seemed, standing in front of her, in her apartment, was the bad boy of pop, Charlie Storm, with his long spiky eyelashes and mouthwatering good looks, if somewhat currently blotchy face. His records had sold millions. His life was lived publicly in the tabloids. He was a guy whose sudden departure from the music world had left his record company reeling and his fans screaming.

In my apartment!

Kate dipped into a deep curtsey. "Your Royal Highness. I'm so honored to have you in my humble home. How's Camilla?"

Charlie grinned. "Very funny." Then his face fell. He reached toward her glasses and pulled his hand back. "Jesus, no wonder you were all over the road in the car. You couldn't fucking see where you were going!"

"I thought you were asleep."

"I was too scared to open my eyes. Why didn't you let me drive?"

"It's only insured for me."

"We could have been killed," Charlie wailed and Kate grinned.

"My eyes aren't that bad." She tossed the glasses back on the counter and reset the microwave. Charlie sniffed and his stomach rumbled. The slightly sweet smell had made her hungry too.

"So how does it feel to have a celebrity round for dinner?" he asked.

"You mean you actually are famous?" She gaped at him.

"Ha ha."

What would Lucy, Rachel and Dan say? Kate thought about it. No one would ever believe this.

"Why did you want to kill yourself?" he asked.

Kate sighed. "You think if you keep slipping it in, I won't notice and just answer?"

He gave her a sheepish grin. "Yes."

She bit back her smile. "How about you going first?"

"I was out for a swim," he said.

"Then so was I."

"You know you weren't."

Kate wondered how long they could play this game, tennis without balls.

"Who was that at the door?"

"Lucy. She lives downstairs."

"And what happened yesterday to make them sorry and you devastated?"

Kate sighed. "You've got big ears, Charlie." She took two plates from the cupboard and put them on the work surface.

"How come you didn't recognize me? You're not a fan, then?"

Kate's mouth twitched. "You've never made me scream." The moment that left her lips, she wished she hadn't said it. Charlie looked as though he was going to speak and thought better of it. Kate struggled to find something to say.

"Do you know any of my songs?" he asked. "Seen any of my films?"

"Er…I've seen you in the paper," Kate said.

"The one place I don't want to be seen," he snapped.

Kate bristled. What an arrogant shit. "I'm surprised they haven't run out of words to describe you. Unspeakably good-looking, drop-dead gorgeous, heartbreakingly handsome. So many superlatives, it's meaningless."

Charlie gave a short laugh. "You're completely right. They print crap."

Maybe not such an arrogant shit. Kate spooned the food onto blue plates.

"God, this smells great. What is it?"

"Chihuahua and Doberman Hotpot."

He gave a loud laugh. "So I should avoid the chewy bits."

"Aztec beef and sweet potato mash. No chewy bits. Is there any more to drink?"

Charlie looked guilty. "There might be a drop left." He poured the last dribbles into her glass. "Sorry."

Kate couldn't believe he'd drunk nearly all of it.

"Do you have anything else?" he asked.

"Water."

"Right."

Kate sat next to him on the floor with her back against the couch and balanced the plate on her knees.

"Did you make this?" he mumbled, his mouth full.

"Yes."

"It's delicious. What's that taste in it?"

"That will be the Chihuahua. Small, but very spicy."

His fork paused on the way to his mouth and she laughed.

"Chocolate. Only a few squares, but that's what you can taste."

He wolfed it down. Kate had barely touched hers before Charlie finished.

"There's more if you want," she said and he jumped to his feet.

Kate watched him as he walked away. He was so gorgeous. His broad back tapered to a narrow waist and below sat his cute backside. A shiver of lust made her drop her fork.

Charlie scooped the last of the beef onto his plate and chased the remaining olives around the container with a spoon. The chasing took longer than it should have because he was staring at the crunched up ball of paper next to the microwave. He hesitated long enough to convince himself it was the right thing to do, then picked it up and smoothed it out.

"Richard, this was for us, now just for you. Drink it and choke."

Charlie screwed the paper up again, coughing to disguise the sound and put it back where he'd found it.

"Any left?" Kate asked when he sat down again.

"Oh God. No, did you want some? Sorry. Have some of this." He offered her a heaped forkful.

"No, I don't want more. I just wondered how you could eat so much and stay so thin. Hollow leg?"

"Drugs," he said without missing a beat. "You ever tried coke?"

"Yes, with plenty of ice and I don't like it."

He chuckled. "You know, I don't remember tasting anything this good before." He thought about licking the plate and reluctantly decided not to.

"Thanks, but I doubt that's true."

"Kate, it was seriously delicious. I've eaten at some of the most expensive restaurants in London and New York but this tasted perfect. Sort of savory, yet slightly sweet. My tongue's in blissful shock. Maybe part of me has begun to live again. Maybe it's a sign."

Kate smothered a giggle. "You sound like some weird psycho...I mean psychic."

He huffed. "Talking of signs, have you thought about the chances of us colliding in the sea like that?"

"Unlucky," Kate said, at the same time as Charlie said, "Luck."

His heart lurched and Charlie knew, in that instant, she would try again. He swallowed hard, choked by the mere thought of it. Several moments passed before he could speak. "What made you choose that stretch of beach?"

"I went there once. I remembered..."

"What?"

"Having a good time. Burying my father in the sand."

"Please tell me it wasn't a few months ago and you didn't leave him there."

He didn't get the laugh he expected.

"No, we dug him up again. Why did you pick it?"

"I went there as a child, too. I wonder if we were ever on the beach together? My brother and I were always trying to create the ultimate network of sand castles."

"Remember the girl who jumped on them? That would be me."

He smiled. "So why did you want to kill yourself?"

"Charlie, give over. I'd heard that your CDs were a bit repetitive."

"You've obviously never listened to any of them," he blurted and then was cross with himself for reacting to the jibe.

"No. Do you want ice cream?"

He nodded. Had she really never listened to any of his stuff? He was annoyed and then even more annoyed that it bothered him. He got up from the floor and flopped on the couch. How could she look sexy wearing sleep pants and a t-shirt? He sighed. Kate wasn't going to fall in bed with him.

She came back with two blue ramekins, handed him one and sat on the floor facing him, with her back pressed against the wall.

"This isn't ice cream," Charlie said after the first mouthful.

"Frozen zabaglione. Cream, eggs and Marsala."

"It's angel food." He sat up. "God, I'm dead, aren't I? I drowned and this is heaven."

"Do you think you're going to heaven?"

He slumped back, sprawling loose limbed across the cushions. "That hurt."

She looked so edible, sitting there spooning nectar into her mouth. Charlie wanted to kiss her. He wondered how she'd taste. At that precise moment, cold and sweet. God, he *really* wanted to kiss her. Instead, he inhaled his dessert and stared at what was left of Kate's. "Don't you want that?"

She shook her head. He slid from the couch to her side, licked his lips and opened his mouth like a little bird. She spooned in the frozen cream. His lips closed over the spoon and sucked so hard, she had to drag it free. He kept his eyes on hers as he rolled the dessert around his mouth before swallowing.

"Did you make that for Richard?"

Alarm flared in her eyes like sparks from a match.

"You read the note," she said.

She wasn't his type at all, Charlie thought. What did he want with a depressed, miserable woman? He was depressed and miserable enough himself without taking on someone else's problems. But he was intrigued and he owed her because if it hadn't have been for Kate, he wouldn't have made it back to the beach.

"Let me guess," Charlie said. "This is over a guy, right? You're pregnant, but he doesn't want it?" He hoped not. "You found Richard fucking another woman?" He looked for a clue on Kate's face. "Maybe another man? Or he's given you the, 'it's not you, it's me' speech. You still love him, but he doesn't love you? He's married with kids and you just found out? No, wait, I've got it. He's a werewolf."

Charlie was sure he had something right in there.

Kate looked straight at him. "He couldn't cope with the fact that I've been diagnosed with a terminal illness."

He gasped. "Christ, Kate, oh fuck, I'm sorry." When he caught her trying to stifle a smile, he growled. "That wasn't funny."

"Yes, it was."

"So is this illness called 'the rest of your miserable life'?" He cocked his head on one side.

"I hadn't thought of that, but you're right."

"What happened?" Charlie didn't want her to joke.

"I was dumped."

"Yeah, I know that story."

"Who'd be crazy enough to dump you?"

64

"They're standing in line." Charlie thought of Ethan and let her misunderstand.

They sat in silence for a few moments before he spoke. "Have you talked to anyone about it?"

"No."

He reached for her hand, thrilled when she didn't pull away. "How about we talk to each other? Maybe it will help."

Kate liked him holding her hand but knew talking couldn't help. A parade of teachers, social workers and psychologists had assured her it could but she realized at a young age that not talking was far more effective.

"What do you think?" Charlie pressed.

Kate didn't want to talk, but she wanted Charlie to keep holding her hand and if another sleepless night lay ahead, another last night, she could think of worse ways to spend it.

"Getting drunk might help, too. You sure you don't have any more alcohol?" he asked.

"No."

"Cigarettes?"

She shook her head.

"Coke?"

Kate stared at him. "Are you an addict?"

"No, I'm fucking not." He pulled his hand away. "I just enjoy smoking, drinking and doing a few lines of coke every now and again."

"But you wish you were dead."

He fell silent and Kate wondered if she'd gone too far, but his fingers slipped back and he wrapped his hand around hers. Warmth trickled through her body.

"We should talk. I need to talk, but I don't want to go first," he whispered. "If I start, I'll never stop."

"I don't mind. I like your voice."

"I'm not falling for that. You go first. Please."

Kate sighed. "Apart from the obvious, what do you want to know?"

Charlie chewed his lip and didn't speak for a moment. "What's the worst thing that's ever happened to you."

She gave a short laugh. "I need to work up to that. You might faint."

Charlie grinned. "Intriguing."

"Ask me something easy."

"How long have you lived here?"

"Six months."

He waited. Kate loved her apartment and Greenwich, but she didn't deserve to live in a decent, respectable area. She couldn't afford it on the money she made, but then she had no mortgage. She'd bought the place outright. Even so, she struggled to pay the bills on her salary. The apartment had only been affordable because of money she considered tainted, money she'd refused twice but then accepted. Kate thought if she had her own property, she'd be safe. It wouldn't change her attitude, but she hoped it could change her life.

"What's your job?" Charlie tried again.

"Waitress."

She didn't say anything else and Charlie sighed.

"You're supposed to be talking not thinking. Tell me about your neighbor, Lucy, or your job or something."

Kate knew plenty about her neighbors, but they didn't know much about her. After she'd moved into her apartment with a broken arm and a black eye, she'd let them think she was clumsy. She had broken ribs too, but Kate never revealed what couldn't be seen. Rachel, Lucy and Dan talked about their lives because Kate maneuvered them into it, mainly so she didn't have to talk about herself.

Charlie took hold of her chin and turned her face so she looked at him. "Kate, talk to me."

"Lucy's gorgeous, flirty and irrepressible. She fizzes with fun like a huge bath bomb." Kate thought Charlie would love Lucy.

"What does she do?"

"Newsreader for Metro Radio."

"Does she have a boyfriend?"

Kate thought about Nick. Did a married bastard count as a boyfriend? "Yes, her boss, but he's married."

Lucy had gone after Nick in the same way she'd gone after her job. She'd shown him how much she wanted him and reeled him straight in. No letting the line run, Lucy yanked him straight out of his wife's arms. Kate didn't know how much longer their affair could stay a secret. Lucy wasn't good at keeping her mouth shut.

"Is Lucy a good friend?" Charlie asked.

Kate hesitated.

"She came round to see if you were okay after whatever happened yesterday," he pointed out.

"I don't have any close friends."

"Why not?"

"Easier not to."

He sighed. "Who else lives here?"

"Dan's next door. He found me my job at Crispies. It's a café in Greenwich close to the market. His sister's a co-owner. He works there himself sometimes if Mel is short staffed."

"He sounds like a friend," Charlie said.

"He's a talented artist. That's what he does for a living. He walked into an art gallery in Holland Park, saw Rachel and fell in love. Rachel persuaded the gallery owner to take three of his paintings and then Dan found out the owner was Rachel's father. Except her dad doesn't like painters, even if they make him money, only sculptors. Dan discovered Rachel was buying an apartment here and put in an offer on another without even seeing it. Lucy thought he was an idiot." Kate breathed out.

"That was the most you've ever said to me and none of it was about you."

He sat waiting and when Kate didn't speak, he sighed. "Okay, so what did *you* think about Dan buying the apartment?"

"That he must really love her."

"So they're a pair?" Charlie asked.

"No, Dan's shy and Rachel's oblivious. He made me and Lucy swear not to say anything or even hint to Rachel that he fancied her, because he wants to tell her himself. Only I have a feeling they'll be collecting their pensions before that happens."

Charlie rubbed his thumb against Kate's palm.

"You believe in seizing the moment?"

She knew what he was asking and stayed silent.

"Tell me about Rachel," Charlie said in a resigned voice.

"Rachel's the only child of rich, posh parents who sent her to finishing school in Switzerland where she was polished to a high sheen. She's never anything less than immaculately dressed and made-up. She speaks like the Queen, and knows how to cook and eat artichokes. Plus she can fold napkins into a million different shapes."

"See, having a conversation is not that difficult," Charlie said. "Now tell me what happened the last time you saw this Richard guy."

And memories flooded Kate's brain, swamping every other thought, stopping the breath in her throat like a cork.

Richard kissed her on Wednesday night, said the next time he saw her, she'd be in her wedding dress. Kate felt as though she was melting, everything falling away to nothing.

"What happened?" Charlie asked again.

And in a low, flat voice, she told him. "We fucked on that couch, then in bed and he told me he loved me."

Kate tried to pull her hand free of Charlie's, but he didn't let her go.

"And?" he asked.

Tell him. Just tell him. What does it matter? He doesn't know me. If he thinks I'm a fool, so what? Tell him. It was like poison inside her. Hard to spit it out.

"Richard left at eleven on Wednesday night. That was the last time I saw him."

There was a long pause before Charlie spoke. "And?"

"He said he'd see me in twelve hours at Woolwich registry office."

"Oh shit." Charlie groaned.

Kate wondered why it still hurt now she knew what Richard had done, that he hadn't jilted her because he didn't love her, but because it was a game, a bet.

"Richard wanted it to be private, just the two of us. He booked everything—limo, photographer, flowers, honeymoon." She paused. "Well, he told me he'd booked everything. All I had to do was turn up in a…" Beautiful dress, but she couldn't say it. The words stuck in her throat like an oversized gobstopper, too big to even suck. The biting pain of humiliation flared up inside her and the ache in her heart gained strength. It surprised Kate that she wanted to keep talking.

"I made my dress. That was my surprise for him. The limo turned up, but when I got to the registry office, Richard wasn't there. No flowers waiting either and I still didn't get it. They said he hadn't made a booking. I'd left my phone at home and had to ask someone for money to call him. Richard didn't answer. So I sat waiting while brides turned up in their lovely dresses, family and friends all smiling and happy. I waited thinking there had been a mistake but he'd come."

Charlie sat motionless, clinging onto her hand.

"Then I thought he must have had an accident. He was dead. The only thing that would stop him being there was if he were dead. Some freak accident had wrecked my life." Kate couldn't stop the words pouring out now. "*He* was the freak accident. He'd asked me to marry him. He said he wanted to be with me forever, to take care of me forever and I'd believed him." Her head dropped. "I shouldn't have believed him."

Kate took a shaky breath.

"Just before the office closed, a woman came to tell me they'd managed to get in touch with Richard. He said he didn't know why I was there. I gave in then. Stopped hoping. Of course, there was no limo outside. I didn't even have my purse with my travel card. Just my key in my shoe. I asked someone for my bus fare. And all I could think was what had *I* done wrong? What had *I* done that made him not want me anymore?"

Charlie squeezed her fingers. "Jesus, Kate. Look, maybe he realizes he's made a mistake. Have you phoned him, tried to talk to him? He might have had last minute nerves."

She gave him a little smile. "He never intended to marry me, Charlie. Everything was a lie. I found out last night he asked me to marry him to win a bet. I should have been more careful."

"What? That's a bloody horrible thing to do." He grabbed hold of Kate's other hand too. "You'll find someone else to love, someone who deserves you. Just because some fuckwit treated you like shit, doesn't mean you have to kill yourself."

Kate laughed and Charlie stared at her in shock.

"It wasn't so much that Richard let me down, more that I'd let myself down. It served me right."

She saw the confusion in Charlie's face, not sure if she could make him understand.

"Richard was handsome, charming and fun. He brought me flowers, drooled over my cooking. We never argued. He never sulked or got angry. He didn't drink too much or care about football. Apart from the football, Dan thought Richard was great. Lucy and Rachel liked him. The more they told me how lucky I was, the more I began to believe it.

"He *was* a nice guy. He never made me feel stupid, he didn't overwhelm me by wanting to see me all the time. He respected the fact that I'm busy on Sunday and Wednesday nights doing a computer course."

That was a lie but he never asked about the course, never asked about her past. With Richard it was all now, today, the present.

"He liked my friends. He liked my apartment. He liked me. I didn't find much he didn't like. He particularly liked taking me to bed."

He'd bought matching silver rings because the gold one from The Wedding Party sent her finger green and even though Kate didn't like rings, she wore it to please him. He told her she was the best thing that had ever happened to him. Richard didn't try to understand her or uncover her secrets and she'd been grateful when she should have been curious.

"I thought I loved him, but I see now that I don't understand what love is. I liked him a lot. I liked the fact that he'd chosen me. I wanted to marry him because he made me feel safe. He said he'd protect me and wouldn't let anyone hurt me. Funny because I wasn't safe with Richard at all.

"After the woman told me he wasn't coming, my heart emptied. It was like a water pipe had burst and there was nothing I could do to stop everything draining out. I'd wanted my life to change and thought Richard could make that happen. That's all I've ever wanted, a new life, but I don't deserve it. I should have seen through him and I didn't. That's why I was in the sea, Charlie, I'd made a mistake and let myself be hurt. If I'm dead, I can't be hurt anymore."

She wondered what he'd say, if he understood.

"You've tried to kill yourself before," Charlie whispered.

Kate exhaled slowly. "Once. When I was a teenager. A cry for help. I think the fact that no one cared shocked me out of that particular depression." She gave a wry grin. "You know, we didn't really try today. Look how easily we decided against it. I changed my mind when you started to piss me off and you left your clothes in the dunes in case you still needed them."

"I didn't...yeah, I did," Charlie said.

"So what dragged you into the water?" Kate asked.

Now he tried to pull his fingers away and she wouldn't let him.

"You have to promise not to tell anyone."

"I was kind of hoping you weren't going to tell anyone about my wedding that wasn't, either."

"I don't trust anyone."

"You mean you don't trust me."

"I don't trust *anyone*."

"I've trusted you. You can trust me. I can keep secrets. Believe me, I'm an expert in keeping secrets. So tell me, Charlie. I

71

won't be shocked. I won't judge you and I won't tell anyone." She looked into his eyes. "I promise."

Chapter Six

ဆာ

Charlie sighed. "You're not going to like me anymore."

"Who says I like you now?"

He glanced at her. "I've done something very bad."

Kate's heart jumped.

He exhaled a shaky breath. "I've had just about as much as I can take of myself."

Her mind ran off down a disaster-strewn path. "What have you done?"

"Not just one thing. Lots of things. Some worse than others. Christ, I wish I was drunk. It would make this easier." His shoulders slumped.

"Then it's better that you're not."

Charlie laughed, but there was no warmth in it. "Or high," he added.

He gripped her so hard, Kate winced and tried to wiggle her fingers.

"Don't let go of my fucking hand," he snapped.

"I told you I wouldn't let you go." She moved her other hand to his as well, tightening the connection between them.

"I've fucked up everything. Not just my life, others as well." He gulped a mouthful of air. "I fucked a fourteen-year-old schoolgirl at a party and gave her cocaine, and I couldn't even remember her name and she's in a coma. I could get sent to prison. I should be in prison." He kept his eyes down.

Kate had told him he couldn't shock her, but he had.

His voice trailed off to a whispered monotone. "I didn't realize how young she was. She said she was sixteen. I took her word for it. I was pissed off because I thought she'd taken my boxers. I lied to the police about what I'd done. I thought I'd get arrested."

Kate didn't say anything.

"What are you thinking?" he asked in a hoarse voice. "Tell me. Go on. I know what a shit I am."

"Then there's no need for me to tell you."

He groaned.

"Did you make her do anything she didn't want to do?" Kate asked.

He shook his head. "She was downstairs dancing after I left. Brian gave her more coke. The police arrested him."

Kate knew she could have pointed out Charlie wasn't responsible for what happened once he'd left the party, that he didn't know exactly what this guy Brian had done or given her, but none of that excused his behavior.

"Aren't you going to tell me it wasn't my fault?" He raised his dark eyes to hers.

"Is that what your friends told you, what you keep telling yourself?"

"I don't know." Charlie rocked his head against the wall.

"I won't tell you that," Kate said. "You have to take responsibility for what happens in your life, just like me."

Charlie's head spun round. "But what Richard did to you wasn't your fault. Christ, it was no reason to commit suicide, because you got tricked and dumped by some tosser. Find another guy. There are plenty of us out there. We're not all bastards."

"It's not that easy."

"Yeah, it is."

Kate's heart felt squeezed inside her chest, hands trying to force it into a space much too small. "It's easy for you. You're famous, rich and sexy. One smile from you and women line up to sleep with you."

"That's not a good thing."

There was silence for a moment before Kate spoke again.

"Who else's life have you messed up?"

"I'm adopted," he blurted.

"Then you're a lucky guy."

His soft eyes turned rock-hard in an instant. "What the fuck does that mean?"

"Well, I *wasn't* adopted."

Charlie looked at her in bewilderment. "How does that make me lucky?"

Kate knew this was going to make him feel bad, but he needed to stop feeling sorry for himself. "I lost my parents when I was seven. Until I was sixteen, I lived in children's homes and occasionally with foster parents. No one wanted to adopt me. So you were lucky, Charlie. At least someone wanted you."

He sagged back against the wall. "Christ, the one person I choose to confess to and she's got more problems than me." He turned to look at her. "Why didn't anyone want you? You had to be a cute kid."

Kate snorted. "Cute? No, I wasn't. At first, I pretended I didn't need anyone to want me, while I waited for someone to look past all the crap and see the real me. Plus, I wanted to do the picking so I was as bad as I could be. I didn't want friends. My report card said *Kate holds hands with trouble.* Trouble made the best friend ever."

"What did you do?"

"In my first foster home, I dumped every item of food from the kitchen into the garbage. In the next, I flushed a kid's goldfish. I threw all my clothes in the canal and went around naked. I shaved the dog's tail. I scratched my name all over a social worker's new car. I took the hamster out when I wasn't supposed to and the cat caught it." Kate winced. "I tried to get it back. I ended up with half a hamster and had to kill it. It was awful." She shuddered. "After that, no one wanted to foster me, so there was no chance of adoption. It was no more than I deserved."

"Jesus, you were an inventive little shit."

She had her moments, Kate thought.

"And you're right," Charlie said with a sigh. "I was lucky. I was only ten months old when Jill and Paul Storm adopted me. They couldn't have children of their own. Except when I was two, Mum came home from hospital with a baby brother—Michael. I pleaded with them to take him back and swap him for a bike. They bought me one as a present from Michael, so I agreed he could stay for one week. Michael adored me right until the day he died and I treated him like shit."

A tear ran down Charlie's cheek. He dragged one hand free, raised it to his mouth and started to bite his nails. Kate pulled his hand away and pressed his fingers into her thigh.

"How did he die?" Kate asked.

"Car crash. Nine months ago. We were out together. We'd been drinking. Done some lines of coke. He wanted me to fix him up with this girl who'd hung around all evening, trying to get off with me." He glanced at Kate. "Fuck it, they never wanted Michael. They only ever wanted me. I used to call him Ugly Mutt. It was a joke." His voice cracked. "He wasn't an ugly mutt, but maybe I'd made him think he was, because he had his teeth fixed and his eyes and he wanted me to pay for him to have a nose job. He thought if he could make himself look better, his life would be better. He looked perfect to me, only I never told him that. I should have.

"We had a fight over the girl. She'd switched to chatting him up, but still wanted me. I knew she was using Michael but he wouldn't listen. We were drunk. I meant to call us a cab but he'd annoyed the hell out of me and I told them both to fuck off. He nicked my car keys, crashed and was trapped. The car caught fire."

Kate stopped breathing.

Charlie's voice dropped to a mumble. "Mum and Dad wanted to see him after but they couldn't. He had to be identified from dental records."

Charlie exhaled in a rush and jumped to his feet, wiping his palms on his t-shirt. "So what's with the bed?" he demanded. "It's like you're schizoid or something."

Kate didn't think she'd heard the entire story, but accepted the change in direction. She'd not told Charlie everything either. She watched him pacing round the room like a wiry wolf and then he dropped back at her side. "Talk to me," he begged, his eyes wild with pain. "Please."

"About my bed? It's the only new piece of furniture I've ever bought. In all those years spent in care, and afterwards when I lived in squats, I slept on some horrible beds. Blow-up mattresses that deflated through the night, flea-ridden futons a dog wouldn't touch, sofa beds with no padding, beds that reeked of piss and vomit, beds with sheets so stiff they scratched, beds no more than blankets on the floor, beds that *were* the floor with no blankets. All that time, the one thing I always wanted was my own bed, a new bed. I promised myself that one day, I'd have the most beautiful bed in the world. That's what I've got."

"Let's go fuck in it," he said.

Kate recoiled. "No." How could he change so suddenly? From a bird with a broken wing to the boy doing the breaking. But for all his good looks and brash confidence, Kate saw loneliness in his eyes. He was good at hiding it, just like her, but she recognized pain when she saw it.

"We could fuck in here," Charlie said and rubbed her hand with his thumb.

"No." But Kate wondered what she'd do if he pulled her into his arms. She shivered because she already knew. A burning desire to press her naked body against his equally naked body rioted through her.

"I'm not used to women saying no." Charlie laughed and Kate wondered if he thought she didn't mean it. "Is Dickhead better-looking than me?"

She made herself look sad. "Much."

Charlie's brow furrowed.

"Would you take him back?"

"Never."

"What if Dickhead knocked on the door, got down on his knees and pleaded with you? Said he'd made a terrible mistake and he wanted you for ever and ever, amen?"

"No."

"I don't get this, Kate. What this guy has done is horrible. I hope I've never been that calculatingly cruel, but if you don't want Dickhead back, then why can't you move on? All the right is on your side. He's been a shit and everyone will feel sorry for you, unless…unless there's something else. You don't have a deadly disease as well? Nothing contagious anyway?"

He squeezed her hand to show her he was joking.

Kate chose each word with care. "I'm broken, Charlie. When something terrible happens, it makes you question everything else. It shakes the foundations of your life. Richard gave me hope I could have a different future and then snatched it away again. I've spent so many years being rejected that I'd built a strong wall to ensure I never found myself in that position again. But I let Richard through so I know now that I can't be safe. I can't trust myself."

Kate watched Charlie's fingers rubbing hers. "I don't see the point in anything," she said. "I don't feel part of the world. No one needs me or wants me or even likes me very much. I don't like myself. The world will keep turning without me. I'll be no great loss. I'm just a temporary misuse of a minute amount of carbon."

Why was she telling him this? This wasn't like her.

Charlie's grip tightened. "You're going to try again, aren't you?"

"No," Kate lied. But he looked at her with those huge seal pup eyes and she wasn't sure he believed her. "Are you?"

"I should. The world would not only continue to turn without me, it would give a hop, skip and a jump for joy."

He released her hand. Kate stretched her fingers. He'd held them so hard, they'd gone numb.

"What else have you done?" she asked.

"Fucked around and messed up everything."

"Tell me."

He hesitated. "I'm as bad as Dickhead. I've slept with more women than I can count and when I found one I liked, I slept with her sister." He paused. "And her mother."

Kate's mouth dropped open. "At the same time?"

"That might have been worth it." Charlie gave a cheeky grin and Kate couldn't help smiling.

"I hope you didn't get them all pregnant?"

"God, Kate, I'm not that bad." He thought for a moment. "Well, I am, but I'm careful."

"What was the name of the one you liked?"

"Jennifer. Why?"

"Checking you could remember."

"Who are you again?"

"Mermaid."

He raised his hand to her face but let it drop before he touched her.

"Have you lost her forever?" Kate asked.

"Since she and her mother caught me in bed with the sister, I think so, don't you? Anyway, it isn't just the sleeping around. There's other stuff. I'm rarely sober before midday and generally unconscious before midnight. I smoke too much. I drink too much. I use too much coke. I fuck too many women, though still not as many as people think. I've even fucked a few men." He looked at her as he said that, but she didn't let her face change.

"I don't care about stuff I should care about. I'm the biggest fuck up I can be. I've made an art of it."

He was on a roll now. Kate could almost see the words pouring out.

"Everyone wants a piece of me. They all think they own me, just because they know my face. They come up and say 'I know you'. They don't fucking know me at all."

"What about your friends?"

"What friends? I can't trust any of them. How do I know the ones who say they're my friends, really are, that they aren't going to sell me out to the highest bidder? How do I know you're not going to ring the *News of the World* the moment I leave here?"

"How much could I get?"

"A lot. Pay your mortgage on this place," he snapped.

"I don't have a mortgage."

He looked taken aback for a moment.

"Has a friend sold you out, Charlie?"

She watched his cheeks hollow. "Yeah. Not kiss and tell, kiss and lie. The bitch."

"I would never tell the papers anything," she said.

He glanced at her and Kate saw a glimmer of hope in his eyes.

"My agent was the only one who cared, but I'm a client. I made him money. It was in Ethan's interests to keep me happy. Once I started to have problems, he dumped me. My family never wanted me to go into this business in the first place, but they don't understand the pressure. After what happened to Michael they…" Charlie took a few deep breaths before he could continue. Kate rubbed the back of his hand.

"I can't trust anyone. I'm tired of being followed. I'm tired of people waiting for me to fuck up. They know I will and what's worse, they want me to. They're happy knowing I'm no different to them. They think I don't deserve what I have and they're right. But they don't see the other side. I'm tired of my life not being mine, of not being able to do what I want, when I want. So I figured I'd exercise the last piece of control I had and kill myself."

He'd raced through that, almost to the point of not taking a breath and now he opened his eyes wide and looked at her.

He's so beautiful, Kate thought.

"We're both feeling sorry for ourselves. No one wants me and too many people want you," she said.

"Sounds like I could solve part of that. I want you," he whispered.

"But then I'd be adding to your problems by being one of the too many people who want you."

"I don't care," Charlie said. "You're making this more complicated than it needs to be. Listen to me, Kate. I want you."

"More than a cigarette, a drink or a line of coke?"

"At this moment, yes."

"Not good enough," she said.

Charlie smiled. "Okay. So can I ask you something?"

Kate nodded.

"If you're not going to go to bed with me, would you go and buy me some cigarettes?"

"No. It's a nasty habit. They can kill you. It says so on the packet. Give them up."

"How about some booze?"

"No. According to the government, excessive consumption of alcohol can be fatal."

He got to his feet and glared. Kate struggled not to laugh.

"Go yourself, if you're that desperate," she said.

"Dressed like this?"

"Yesterday I got on a bus wearing a wedding dress. I think you could go to the shop in my sleep pants without raising an eyebrow. Anyway your clothes are dry, just not your shoes."

"Please. I'll get recognized."

"No. This is the moment to give up cigarettes, at least. You must have some willpower, although judging by the state of your nails, it's probably a weak little thing confined to a poky corner in your head."

"God, you're a bitch."

But Kate caught the glimmer of a smile on his face as he slumped onto the couch.

"Where's your TV?" He looked around as though it was going to pop out of the floor like some state-of-the-art gizmo.

"Don't have one."

"Music player? CDs?" He swung his feet up and lay back.

"Nope."

"Why not, for fuck's sake?"

"I like the quiet. I was brought up in places that were continuously noisy. There was always someone shouting or fighting or the TV blaring and nowhere to get away from it."

"Don't you like listening to music?"

"I listen on the computer sometimes when I'm sewing."

"You are so weird. What am I going to do to amuse myself? No TV and you won't let me fuck you. How about you model some of your underwear?"

Her head shot up. "Been through my drawers, Charlie?"

"Not the ones I'd like to go through." He gave her a lascivious grin.

"Like what you saw?"

"Even better if you were wearing them, only the removing would be fun."

"Well, maybe there is something we could do together. It involves careful finger work and some manipulation. And there is a huge amount of satisfaction when you finish. Wait there."

Kate left the room and came back carrying a box.

"A jigsaw puzzle?" He gaped at her.

"Two thousand five hundred pieces."

"Is it rude?"

Kate pretended to read the box. "Swinging in the suburbs."

His eyes opened wide.

"Not really. It's a jungle scene," she said.

Kate sat on the floor, opened the box and looked for the edges and corners. After a few minutes spent muttering crossly to himself, Charlie got down by her side. His hand fumbled through the pieces at the other side of the box.

They worked together in silence, but when their fingers touched as they reached for the same straight-edged piece, Kate felt a jolt of desire. Her eyes rose to Charlie's and she watched the bony lump in his throat go up and down.

"What do you do in the evenings if you don't have a TV?" Charlie asked.

"Sew, read, mess around on the computer."

"Do jigsaws?"

"Yes."

"A corner," he said. "Hey, look these bits go together."

"Yeah, if you force them." Kate took them apart again.

"Is being a waitress hard work?" he asked.

"Yes. Is acting?"

"Miss Snippy."

"I'm not just a waitress," she said, feeling defensive.

"What else do you do?"

"Take calls on a phone sex line two evenings a week."

His hand froze in the box and he raised his head to stare straight at her.

"You're kidding, right?"

No, she wasn't kidding. Kate wasn't sure what had made her tell him. Well, not quite true. She wanted to shock him. She picked out a few more pieces.

"So not a computer course?"

"No. I also help write the catalogue for Rachel's art gallery."

Charlie was quiet for a moment. "So, the phone sex…" he began and Kate smiled. "You're kidding, right?" he repeated.

"No."

"Are you doing it tonight by any chance?"

"Sundays and Wednesdays."

"It's only Friday," Charlie whined.

"That's true." Kate spread out several pieces of a similar color.

"I could ring you anyway. What's the number?"

"Where's your phone?"

Charlie swore under his breath. "Why do you do it?"

"Why did you decide to be an actor instead of a singer?"

"I haven't finished talking about the phone sex. We don't have to have a phone. I could go in another room and we could shout."

Kate burst out laughing. "Why did you want to be an actor, Charlie?"

He sighed. "I didn't want to be me anymore. I wanted to be somebody else."

"What sort of roles have you played?"

"Haven't you even seen *any* of the films I've been in?"

Kate shook her head.

"I like making people cry and scream," he said, his tone curt.

"So you usually end up dead after you've smacked a few people around?"

"True."

"You like being hated," Kate said.

He shot her a quick look. "I'm fed up of being loved. Most of my mail comes with photos of naked women offering to sleep with me. Maybe I see playing bad guys as a way of balancing that."

"I doubt it's worked. Didn't anyone ever tell you women like bad guys? Particularly ones on screen that they know aren't bad in real life."

"The thing is, I am."

"You aren't going to stop women wanting you. Isn't it a perk of the job?"

"Not anymore. I wonder had I known what it would be like, if I'd still have taken the path I did. No one told me that once I was famous it was forever, and everyone would be waiting for me to cock up. There's always someone ready to snap me looking hung over or taking a swing at a guy, because seeing me fuck up makes them feel better. Do you think they get some sick sense of satisfaction knowing that deep down, I'm the same as them?" He paused. "All right, worse than them."

"You know, Charlie, I reckon you like acting because you don't know who you are. You think it will help you find yourself and it won't. You're running away from reality, running away from the truth."

"We're not the right people to be talking to each other about this," Charlie muttered.

"There's no one else around."

"I want to *be* someone," he said in a quiet voice.

"But you *are* someone. I don't think it matters what you do for a living, whether you're an actor or waitress. What's important is to be a decent human being and to treat other people as you'd want to be treated yourself. Not to be selfish. I don't like selfish people, those who don't think about others."

"I'm selfish."

"But you have a redeeming quality."

"What's that?"

"You know you're selfish. You have to learn to like yourself, Charlie, otherwise how can anyone else get to know and like you?"

He stared at her for a moment and then the pissed-off expression dropped from his face, and she saw the hint of a smile.

"So did Dickhead listen to you while you were doing it?"

"Doing what?" Kate asked, though she knew what he meant.

"Helping guys jerk off."

"I never told him. He thought I was doing the computer course."

"Why didn't you tell him?"

She'd had the chance to tell Richard on lots of occasions, but something stopped her. A knowledge that he wouldn't approve?

"He wouldn't have understood."

"What? Why the hell did you plan to marry this guy? I'm really interested in your life, particularly the underwear and the phone sex."

Kate smiled. "You have a one-track mind."

"That's the title of one of my songs." He waited a moment before he continued. "You didn't ask me to sing it."

"No." Kate saw the tension seeping from him. "You'll give me a headache."

He roared with laughter. "Why did you tell me about the phone sex?"

"You need honesty. You shared part of yourself with me and I wanted to do the same. Anyway, I'm not doing it this week. I'm supposed to be in Hawaii."

"Hawaii?"

"Don't say it. I know I should have realized it was crazy."

"Were you going to stop once you were married?"

"Are you still on the phone sex?"

He gave her a sheepish grin.

"It depended," Kate said.

"On what?"

"Whether I still needed to do it."

"If you own this place, it can't have been for the money."

But it was.

"What then?" He looked puzzled.

"Whether I still needed the rush of getting men to cry and scream."

He chuckled. Kate looked down into the box as he drew one of his fingers along one of hers, over her knuckle, down the back of her hand to her wrist. *Oh fuck.* Her nipples tingled and she felt a rush of warmth between her legs.

"Look at me, Kate."

She raised her eyes to his.

"What do you see?"

She thought for a moment. "You've got a spot."

Charlie gave a snort of laugher. "You're not supposed to tell the fifth-sexiest man in UK, he's got a spot."

"Who voted? Senior citizens?"

"I really want to fuck you." He growled in his throat.

"I really want to be in Hawaii, but we don't always get what we want."

"Fuck me and I'll take you to Hawaii."

"That's what Richard said."

Charlie sighed in frustration. "I'm nothing like Dickhead."

Kate cast her eyes over his face. "No, he never had spots."

Charlie glared. "I've been under a lot of stress and you're not helping. Go and put on your wedding dress."

"Why?"

"So I can take it off."

"No."

"You could have at least thought about it," he complained.

"I'm going to bed." Kate jumped up. If she stayed any longer, she'd be unable to resist him. "I'll get you some sheets and pillows."

But when she turned away from the cupboard in the hall, he stood right behind her. "Can I sleep with you?"

She brushed past him. "The couch is comfortable."

He leaned in the doorway as Kate made up the bed.

"I won't hurt you," Charlie said.

Kate struggled with a pillowcase. How could he not? He'd sleep with her and dump her. She turned to look at him.

"You're right," he said in a dull voice. "I would hurt you. I hurt everyone I touch. Keep away from me. I'll leave first thing tomorrow."

"Charlie." She wanted to go to him, put her arms around him, but knew what would happen if she did.

He fidgeted, biting his nails, then rubbed his neck.

"Why should I think I've changed because I didn't die when I expected to? I'm still the same fucked-up wanker I've always been."

Kate walked over to the door. "Then prove you can change."

"How?"

"No more cigarettes, alcohol or drugs. No sleeping with someone just because you can."

"I'd rather die."

"Fine. Go ahead and kill yourself. Don't make a mess in my apartment."

Charlie laughed. "You're crazy."

"And you're not?"

"Help me," he muttered. "Please."

"What do you want me to do? Chain you up?"

"I wouldn't mind being handcuffed to your bed."

He'd moved closer. Kate backed away and bumped into the wall.

"What's the matter? Run out of smart comments?" His face stopped inches from hers.

"Just thinking maybe I wouldn't mind handcuffing you to my bed," she said.

She didn't miss the spark in his eyes. Kate ducked under his arm and stepped into the hall. "Then I know I'd be safe on the couch." She shut herself in the bathroom.

Kate's heart hammered as she cleaned her teeth. She might as well juggle with knives as flirt with an expert like Charlie Storm. She was going to bleed. It was only a matter of time.

Chapter Seven

๛

Charlie tossed and turned on the couch. He wanted a cigarette and a drink. No, he *needed* a cigarette and a drink. He wouldn't have turned down a line of coke, and he grew increasingly desperate for Kate. His hand slid toward his mouth and he attacked his nails, chewing the edges. What did he want most? Maybe if he had a cigarette, he'd stop thinking about a drink, only he really needed to stop thinking about fucking Kate. He could help himself to a few quid from her purse, nip out now it was dark and buy some cigs and maybe a bottle of wine, but he couldn't buy Kate. Her, "you've got a spot", had thrilled him more than she could know. Telling him he was blotchy— Charlie smiled. No one had ever dared say that.

But he couldn't figure her out. She'd felt that connection between them, he'd seen it in her eyes. She wanted him, but wouldn't admit it. He'd had women like that before, playing hard to get, thinking it made them more attractive. They didn't continue once they found it didn't work, but Kate wasn't playing a game. Charlie rolled over and groaned, trying to get comfortable and knowing it wasn't going to happen. Not the getting comfortable, but the getting a shag. He wanted to climb into her beautiful bed and into her body. He wanted to feel her hands around his cock, then her wet lips and after that the tight clasp of her pussy. He wanted to hear her moan while she begged him not to stop fucking her, but more than all that he wanted to make her happy and help her forget Richard—which had to be why he hadn't pushed harder to share her bed. His cock didn't agree with that strategy. It was so hard, it hurt.

Charlie wasn't used to people saying no. Not being able to have what he wanted was a novelty, albeit a frustrating one. The more he tried not to think about her lying in the next room, the more she occupied his mind. He could have gone to check on her, asked if he could lie on top of the covers and talk, knowing it would only be a short time before he'd be under them with her, but he didn't move. His balls were rock-hard and aching, but Charlie was determined to do the right thing for once in his miserable life, and leave her alone.

Leaving himself alone was another matter. His hand slid inside his pants and grasped his cock. Shouldn't take long. He managed one caress before the living room door opened. Charlie's hand froze in mid-squeeze and his breath caught in his throat. *Oh God.* She'd put on her wedding dress. He removed his hand from his tackle, because that was definitely one right move, but he wasn't sure what else to do. Pretend to be asleep? Wait for her to come to him? Leap from the couch, peel off that dress and fuck her senseless? None of the above?

Instinct told him she wouldn't move again and he got up. But she stepped over the jigsaw and stood in front of him. Charlie kept his arms at his sides, fingers twitching.

"I lay in the dark, wondering if the door would open and what I'd do if it did," she said. "Pretend to be asleep? Drag you into bed? Everything's been running through my head on a continuous loop—the two of us colliding in the sea, how we have nothing in common and everything in common."

Charlie hoped she couldn't see his erection. If he held her gaze, she might not look down, though how could she miss the huge tent in his sleep pants? And it *was huge.*

"I feel guilty because I want you," Kate whispered.

He stepped from intolerable heat into the cool of air-conditioned comfort as relief swept through him, only to slide straight back into the sun when his cock pulsed in excitement, knowing something better than his hand was possible. Charlie suspected pre-cum was leaving a large, wet spot on his pants. Thank fuck it was dark.

"You made it clear how much you hated the fact that everyone wants you. Why should you think me any different to the women who've fallen for your good looks and sexy smile?"

But she *was* different. "Do you think I've got a sexy smile?" Oh God, was that the best that he could manage?

"Once you've got rid of that spot," Kate said.

Charlie laughed.

"You asked me to help you," she whispered.

"Yes." His voice was thick with emotion but had he asked for her help? He couldn't remember, not with a brain fogged by lust. Only one thing he needed help with at the moment and it was crying for attention.

Kate sighed. "I wondered what the hell I was doing lying alone in there, with the door closed. Why did we both have to be unhappy? After what's happened over the last couple of days, why shouldn't I sleep with you?"

Charlie wasn't about to argue. Kate reached for the side of his face, brushed the back of her fingers over his cheek before her hand fell to his jaw. One finger ran along the line of his lips. The hairs stood up on his arms and the ache in his groin shifted to bloom in his chest.

"Are you real?" she asked.

He licked the pad of her finger with his tongue and put her hand over his heart. It beat hard and fast and he knew she could feel it. Charlie smiled and she sighed.

"What's wrong?" he asked.

"You look so bad and so sexy. I've unleashed a demon I have no hope of controlling."

"I won't do anything you don't want me to do," he said, worried she was talking herself out of this.

"If you're my reward for all the bad things that have happened to me, then what am I for you?" Kate asked.

"My angel."

She snorted and he laughed.

He opened his arms wide. "Have me."

"I've changed my mind. I've gone off you now."

"I'm bloody perfect, apart from the spot, obviously. What's to go off?" He dropped his arms.

"You can't hold a pose for more than ten seconds. You can't sit still for more than twenty. You have the concentration of a flea, the mind of a sewer rat, the mouth of a docker and your nails are bloody awful."

"So, do you fancy me?"

"You may be ridiculously good-looking, but you're also arrogant and whiny."

Charlie bit his lip, trying not to laugh.

"You're a bad guy, Charlie Storm. A total shit."

"You fancy the pants off me, then?"

"Did I mention you were big-headed and greedy?" Kate growled. "You probably think you're a better lover than…"

"Who?" Charlie pressed.

"Richard," she said.

He raised his eyebrows. "I *know* I'm better than Dickhead."

"Now you have something to prove."

"You talked me into that. Smart woman."

"No, I think you talked *me* into that."

"Oh Kate," he whispered. "You're so cute. He must have been mad." And at last, he reached for her.

His hands moved to her hips, pulling her against him. When Charlie buried his face in her neck and felt her soft, warm lips on his shoulder, he was swept away in a flash flood of desire. He slid his hands up the sides of her body, curved them around her neck, tipped up her chin and kissed her.

Charlie's first kisses were always the same, the oft-practiced light brushing of lips, allowing him to taste a woman, letting her taste him.

Not this time.

He was as tormented with desire as if he'd been a schoolboy offered his first chance to snog a girl. He hovered on the verge of implosion, explosion, complete bloody destruction.

Too hungry for slow, too desperate for gentle, he kissed Kate as if it were the last thing he'd ever do. If she'd shown the slightest resistance, he thought he might have cried, but he knew she felt the same. Their tongues invaded each other's mouths, twisting together, surging, discovering. His mind reeled with the scent of her, the taste of her, the feel of her, and Charlie growled deep in his throat like some sort of animal. It bloody scared him, but he couldn't help it. Neither of them breathed.

When their lips slid apart, their eyes wide, they gasped simultaneously and rested their heads side by side, ear to ear, panting in unison.

"Fuck, fuck. Are you okay?" Charlie whispered.

"No."

"Me neither." He was in imminent danger of coming in his pants. His balls had drawn up to the base of his cock and had started their telltale tingle. *Shit, from a kiss?* Women didn't know how lucky they were. If they came fast, everyone was happy. If men came too soon, everyone was disappointed.

He pressed his forehead against hers and they stood for several moments not doing anything other than holding each other while they dragged their breathing back under control. *This* was different. *She* was different.

"What are you thinking?" he asked. Had he ever asked a woman that? Not something he needed to do because he always knew what they were thinking.

Not with Kate.

"That I've never been kissed before," she whispered.

Charlie pulled back and gave her a bemused look. "I'm the first guy to kiss you? What was Dickhead playing at?"

"No, you're the first guy to *kiss* me."

His heart swelled with pleasure and his fingers played with the material of her dress. "You made me lose control."

"Me too. Maybe we're not good for each other."

Charlie swallowed hard. "Maybe we're perfect for each other."

Her hands wrapped around his and squeezed.

"I was cheated of this moment," she said. "I spent so long sewing this, pouring all my love into it. I wanted— Will you undress me?"

If Dickhead had been in the vicinity, Charlie would have beaten him to a pulp, smashed his teeth down his throat and kneed him in the balls. Probably. Most of Charlie's fuck-ups hadn't been deliberately cruel. Then he thought of the fat girl he'd told to piss off and gulped. He glanced at the curtainless window. Kate's gaze followed his.

"I don't care," she said.

He spun her around and lowered the zip. The slinky material fell open to reveal her smooth, bare back with the intriguing white scar. Charlie stroked her shoulders and her skin fluttered under his fingers. As though he'd touched a live wire, white heat flashed through his hands and raced to his groin. What was already hard, grew impossibly harder. There was something to be said for baggy sleep pants, even if they were on the short side. He tugged the wedding dress down so it fell past Kate's hips to puddle on the floor and then he moaned. The only thing she now wore was a pair of not-there panties, the silver beaded band crossing her lower back and dropping down the crease of her butt. It looked so perfect, the breath froze in his throat.

"You have the sweetest backside."

He slid his fingers over her bottom, stroked the soft skin, trailing a fingertip down the beaded cleft before slipping his hands around to the front of her body. He dragged her back against his chest and buried his face in her neck. As he feathered his fingers under her breasts, Kate's breathing turned noisy. Charlie let her go for a moment, just long enough to secretly yank down on his balls to buy a few more minutes, and then wrenched the T-shirt over his head. He tossed it to the floor and moved back against her, trembling at the skin-to-skin contact, nudging her toward the wall so the side of her face rested against the plaster. He couldn't remember ever being this turned on.

"I love the dress but I like you better out of it," he whispered.

Charlie threaded his fingers through her hair and dropped his other hand to trace the line of the beaded band crossing her lower back. Kate's hips jerked into the wall.

"Steady." He breathed the word onto her shoulder and followed the line of her panties to the front of her body. At the same time as he cupped her between her legs, Charlie pushed the hard ridge of his erection into the cleft of her backside and then nipped the side of her neck with his teeth. Kate reacted as powerfully as if she'd been shot. She tensed, cried out and unraveled in his arms.

"Oh God," she gasped. "God, God, God."

Charlie's heart sang. He clung on to her, sensing she'd collapse if he let go. He kissed the place on her neck he'd nipped, covering it with tiny licks, tasting her skin as she came back to earth.

"You are so hot," he murmured. "My little fireball."

Kate took a deep breath. "Right, that's better. Thanks. I think I'm ready to go to sleep now. Night."

Charlie chuckled. "Am I allowed in your bed?"

"Only if you promise to stop biting your nails, you're naked, and get there before I do."

She was already moving as she spoke, but Charlie slipped ahead, dashed through the hall and slammed the bedroom door. He leaned against it while he shucked out of the sleep pants and then leapt for the bed. When Kate walked in, he was under the sheet and pretending to snore. She slipped in next to him and pulled the cover from his face. He looked up to see her dark eyes gazing down at him and felt guilty. He'd seen so many women look at him like that, wanting his body, but also wanting something he couldn't give.

"If you're going to snore, you can go back in the other room," Kate said. "It's not an attractive habit."

Charlie's face lit up. He loved the way she spoke to him.

"I'm not going to be sleeping," he said. "And neither are you."

When Charlie pulled her mouth to his, Kate expected another hard and fast kiss, but this time he surprised her. His lips slid along hers in a tempting caress, lingering for a while before he let them slide to her neck. He seduced her with every part of his face, licking with the tip of his tongue, laving with the whole of it, his cheek brushed hers, his thick eyelashes tickled her skin, his nose gently nuzzled, his teeth nibbled, breath teased until Kate could stand it no longer and pushed her tongue into his mouth, pressing her lips against his, so that Charlie had to respond in kind.

There was a time for soft but this wasn't it. Kate needed him to be forceful and strong, to make her forget. They writhed together, twisting in the sheets, almost fighting. Her on top and then him. Half on the bed, half off as they explored each other's bodies, found places to make the other squirm. His rigid cock was a constant reminder of how much he wanted her. It didn't matter that this was just fucking, at least they both wanted the same thing — no illusion, no pretending.

Finally, he pinned her down and hovered above her, breathing heavily. "You're trying to eat me."

"On toast. With butter."

She bucked him off, then reached for him again. Charlie grabbed her hand and brought it to his mouth, sucking her fingers.

"Butter's bad for you," he said.

"Who says?"

He bit her palm and Kate yelped. As she opened her mouth, he welded his lips to hers and at the same time, pushed the front of her panties aside and slid his middle finger deep inside her. The suddenness of the intrusion made Kate groan into his throat and buck into his hand. Another finger joined the first and she sighed. A moment later she whimpered in frustration when they withdrew.

"Don't be greedy," he whispered. "I haven't finished playing with you yet."

Charlie's head dropped from her neck and he nibbled his way to her breast. Where his mouth touched, Kate burned. Where it didn't, she longed for the fire. His tongue flicked her nipple, his teeth circling and teasing before he sucked hard and strong. At the same time, he pushed his fingers back inside her and Kate felt the desperate draw of desire as fiercely as if he'd reached in and dragged out her heart.

"Christ, Kate. You're soaking wet. You're driving me crazy."

"I'm not feeling anything yet," she gasped and he shook with laughter.

His mouth slid from her breast, over her ribs and stomach, down until it joined his fingers between her legs. When his tongue touched her clit, every muscle in her body clenched, nerves sparked, cells expanded. A few moments of gentle pressure and she hovered again on the brink of falling apart, her fingers entwined in his hair.

Charlie lifted his head. "Will you get me some cigarettes?"

Kate forced her eyes open and saw his smirk.

"Okay." She tried to move away.

His face fell and then he laughed and pulled her back, resting his chin on her belly.

"Well, do you want cigarettes or not?" Kate tried to wiggle free of his grasp.

"Not."

He dipped his head and buried his face between her legs, using the flat of his warm, wet tongue to lick her over and over before he thrust it between her folds. Kate stopped trying to get away and tried to stop pulling at his hair. His soft lips closed gently around the sensitive bud of her clit and sucked hard, then he tapped it with the tip of his tongue until her moans came faster and faster. Kate's legs stiffened, her heels drummed into his back and her hands clutched his shoulders as she fell into the grip of an immense, rippling orgasm that enveloped her body like some super-long effervescent bath bomb.

"Charlie," she gasped. "Oh God. I'm falling apart."

Lights flashed behind her eyes, her limbs shook and she could barely breathe. Kate couldn't remember the last time she'd come like that, if she'd ever come like that. When she forced her eyelids open, she saw the strain on his face, his dark eyes staring at her. She reached for a condom from the drawer and Charlie snatched it from her fingers. He had it on before she'd taken another breath.

"I think you've done that before," she teased.

"I've never been this desperate," he said, settling back between her thighs, nudging at her opening with the blunt head of his cock. He groaned and then hesitated. "Are you sure?"

Kate melted at the question, a gush of cream soaking her sex. After all they'd just done, he thought enough of her to ask that?

"Ask the audience, phone a friend but do it fast," he whispered.

Kate gripped his shoulders. "I know what I want. You, Charlie. I want you now. Fuck me."

In one slick movement, he thrust deep inside her. One long hard drive and she felt every inch of his thickness and length. Kate arched her back, drawing him even further into her body before she clenched around him.

"Oh Christ, Kate!" One gentle cry of her name before he began to move, stroking in and out of her, concentration etched on his face.

She knew he was trying to be careful and she didn't want careful. Kate reached for the back of his neck and pulled his head to hers, brought her hips up to kiss his. Their lips melded as he began to pound into her, his tongue mimicking the action of his body. His cock seemed hotter, bigger, swelling inside her and Kate felt herself coming, the vibration spreading through her body as tension ratcheted to its limits. Charlie dragged his mouth from hers, panting in short bursts, and rearing back, with one final thrust he exploded inside her with a loud groan. Kate tightened around his cock as it pulsed inside her. Her climax rolled into his and they unraveled together, perfectly matched.

Neither moved, frozen in the intensity of the moment. They took a gulp of air at the same time and then laughed. Charlie was still suspended above her body. He lowered his head and slid his lips across hers, so gently Kate wanted to cry, before he sank down and rolled so he didn't crush her. He held her tight, still semi-hard inside her, still kissing her.

Charlie knew he ought to get rid of the condom, but he didn't want to move. His head spun as if he was drunk. He didn't have a problem making women come, but he didn't often come at exactly the same time, nor in such a spectacular way. He'd been shaken by how much he wanted Kate, how much he still wanted her. He'd had mind-blowing sex before, but there had been something about what they'd just done that was different.

Kate was different. She was neither in awe, nor scared of him. She fucking laughed at him and Charlie could hardly believe how much he liked her doing it. No pussy-footing around, she wasn't afraid to tell him what she thought. She hadn't asked him to sing for her and that was a big deal for Charlie. It pissed him off when women did that, partly because it was almost the first thing that came from their mouths, as if that was all they saw, not him but a different Charlie. Kate had just been herself. He'd finally met somebody real.

He held her in his arms and ran his fingers over her skin. He couldn't stop touching her, didn't want to stop, yet couldn't push back that nagging voice that said the feeling would pass. It always had. A vicious worm nibbling at his heart that wouldn't go away.

"I have to get rid of this rubber and wash," he said. "Come with me?"

"Worried you might get lost?"

Yeah, he was. He was good at getting lost.

They both groaned when he withdrew from her. Charlie swung his feet over the side of the bed and pulled off the rubber. When he stood and turned, Kate held out her hand and the worm spoiling his pleasure began to shrivel.

"Come on," Kate said. "I'll stop you falling into the bottomless pit in the hall but look out for the quicksand in the bathroom."

Charlie let her wrap her fingers around his. She tugged him out of one room into another. Charlie was about to drop the condom in the toilet when she stopped him.

"You shouldn't do that. Better for the planet to put it in the waste bin."

Charlie hesitated. He always flushed them. He didn't want anyone siphoning off his little swimmers and making a baby. How could that be better for the planet? More wankers like him? He had no idea if it was even possible but he always played safe.

99

He wrapped the rubber in toilet tissue and tossed it in the bin.

Kate pulled him down to sit on the edge of the tub and reached for a cloth. She soaked it, soaped it and wiped his cock. Charlie's fingers curled around the edge of the bath and he spread his toes on the tiles. No one had ever done this for him before. No one had ever thought to. Kate knelt and rubbed her fingers in his curly pubic hair, twirling it in her soapy fingers. Her other hand stroked up and down his semi-tumescent cock. Charlie almost felt his blood hesitate in its circuit around his veins before diverting to the place in his body that had the most fun.

"Can I shave you down here?" she asked.

The blood flow reversed. Well, it didn't but he shuddered, his cock shivered and his balls quaked. Was she mad?

"Let me?" Kate whispered.

"Okay."

Was he mad? Wouldn't it itch and give him spots? What if her hand slipped? How could he backtrack without looking a wimp?

"Want to shave me too?" she asked.

"Okay."

Kate threw a fluffy towel on the floor. "Lie down."

Charlie lay facedown.

"Want me to do your bum too?" she asked.

"What?" He rolled over. "I don't have a hairy bum." Did he?

She laughed. Charlie leaned up on his elbows and watched as she knelt between his legs with a canister of some sort of shaving foam and a disposable razor. He flinched at the first jet of thick blue liquid but when Kate began to massage it all over his groin he sank back and closed his eyes. The combination of her soft but firm fingers and the cool, slippery foam made his cock swell in her hand. No bloody sense of danger. No bloody sense. With the first long stroke of the razor, Charlie held his breath.

"Don't make any sudden moves," she said.

Maybe he should keep holding his breath. Then his stupid cock jerked. "Shit. How am I supposed to manage not moving when my dick has a mind of its own?"

"I'll be careful."

Charlie wondered what he was doing, letting a woman he'd only just met hold a razor against his best friends. Yet he trusted her.

Kate rinsed the razor in the wash basin and started again. The combination of a hand caressing his cock, another pulling the blade firmly against his taut skin, that mix of acute pleasure and imminent danger made Charlie's stomach quiver like a snare drum. He lay back and went with the flow.

Once he'd stopped thinking what she was doing, he relaxed. Shit, it was the first time he'd felt so relaxed in ages. She soaped, shaved, washed and then massaged him with some sort of oily stuff that smelled nice. His cock was on the way back to full hardness and his balls were building up steam. In a moment, it would be his turn to shave her and he grinned.

"All done," Kate said. "I've wiped off the blood."

"What?"

He sat up so fast he almost nutted her in the head. "Christ." Charlie stared at his tackle. No blood, but he looked bigger. Wow, a lot bigger. His gaze drifted to Kate. "I was hoping for a skull and crossbones."

She laughed. "Too late. Use a new razor on me. Do what you like."

She lay on the towel. Charlie took one look at her pink folds and gulped. He thought he'd done just about everything with a woman but this was something new. Was any landscape more beautiful that this? Little valleys and folds, glistening with arousal. What he was going to do was sexy and not sexy at the same time. He'd never touched a woman here without the aim being to make her wet and make her come. Now, he chewed his lip, rubbed Kate with the soapy gel before carefully drawing the razor over her skin. No way could he leave any sort of shape with her pubes. He'd cock it up so it didn't look like anything. Besides, he wanted her as naked as him.

Charlie wiped her down and tossed the razor in the waste bin.

"This was not a good idea," he said.

Kate raised her head to look at him. "Why not?"

"Because now I'm incandescent with lust. You're irresistible." He licked a wet trail from her navel to her mons and groaned. "I am so good with that razor. Maybe I've missed my calling. I'd work for free."

Kate laughed. "I wonder which of us is smoother?"

Charlie grinned. "Only one way to find out."

One of Dickhead's condoms retrieved from the cupboard, slipped on in a flash and Charlie leaned over Kate. He slowly pressed his cock home until their bodies were tight together, then flexed his hips so they rubbed against each other.

"Why have I never done this before?" he asked. "It feels so good. You feel so good."

"There is a downside."

"Nooooo. Don't tell me."

Charlie pulled out and spun Kate onto her knees. He had a hand on her breast, another on her bare mons as he thrust into her, ground into her. His hips pulled back and drove forward, his hand dragging her into him as he crammed his cock inside her. Kate whimpered as his finger found her clit.

"What…downside?" he gasped.

"Forgotten," Kate mumbled.

He needed her to come because he needed to come. Charlie could barely suck in enough breath to fill his lungs. A warning shot pulsed up his cock and the ache in his belly intensified. Hard cock into soft pussy. Over and over. He licked the shell of her ear as his fingers worked her swollen clit.

"Now, Kate," he gasped.

She tensed beneath him, her breathing choppy and when Charlie felt the telltale tightening clasp around his cock, he let himself go.

They fell asleep on the bathroom floor. Woke, showered and fucked again. When she staggered back to the bedroom, he followed like a shadow. He couldn't bear to be away from her, not for even a second. They fucked in every conceivable position, all over the apartment, including the balcony as dawn broke. Charlie lost count of how many times he'd been inside her, how many times she'd come and he'd come. More than he thought physically possible. They couldn't seem to stop fucking and that scared him. He'd even woken up from a semi-doze to find himself sliding into her from behind with no rubber in place. He only had to look at her to want her and as soon as she saw him looking, she knew what he was thinking. He'd forgotten about wanting a cigarette or a drink. He didn't need the coke. Kate was his drug.

Chapter Eight

ဢ

When they came round the following morning, neither of them had done much sleeping. Charlie thought it was more like slipping into periods of unconscious exhaustion. He was relieved to find they were back in bed and not on the floor but he ached. He had his arm wrapped around Kate, his leg between hers, her back pressed against his chest.

"Oh God," Charlie groaned.

"Are we still alive? I thought we'd killed one another."

"It's the only way I want to die. You—" He paused and then whispered in her ear, "You're not thinking about killing yourself, are you?"

"My capacity—for thought—destroyed—you—have."

"Funny girl."

"I can't feel my legs." Kate let out a long moan.

Charlie's fingers ran along the top of her thigh. "Don't worry. Still there and they feel lovely."

As his hand wandered lower, the door buzzer made them jump. Kate banged her head into Charlie's chin.

"Ignore it." He blinked tears from his eyes.

But whoever was outside didn't give in.

"It's probably Lucy. I'll go and shut her up."

Kate rolled over, swung her feet off the bed and stumbled naked out of the room. Charlie ogled her backside and followed.

"What?" she snapped into the intercom.

"Kate?"

Male voice. Her whole body tensed and Charlie guessed Dickhead stood downstairs.

"I want to talk to you. Can I come up?"

Charlie clenched his fists.

"No," Kate said.

"Please. I'm sorry. I need to explain. I feel terrible."

Charlie pulled Kate to one side.

"Let him come up," he said. "Don't you want to hear what he has to say?"

She stared at him, but didn't reach out to stop him when his finger touched the door release button. He walked into the bathroom and then popped his head out.

"Better put something on. Only, not much. Give him a hint of what he's lost."

Charlie leaned against the washbasin, his heart hammering. What if Dickhead was bigger than him? What if Kate wanted him back?

When Kate opened the door wearing a long t-shirt, Richard held out an enormous bunch of flowers at waist level. Maybe he hoped they'd offer some protection.

"Kate, I'm sorry," he said.

"Right."

She couldn't believe she was standing there talking to him, not racing into the kitchen for a knife, not launching her foot at his groin. Hmm, she should have put shoes on.

"May I come in?"

She moved back and Richard walked in, closing the door behind him.

"These are for you."

Because she wouldn't take the flowers, he laid them on the floor. Kate leaned on the wall and kept her hands behind her back. She didn't want him to notice she was shaking.

"So the whole thing was a bet," she said.

"Yes," Richard said. "I can't tell you how much I regret it. To be honest, I never thought you'd go for it. It sort of snowballed."

Kate gritted her teeth.

"You look…t-terrible," he stuttered.

She guessed she had swollen lips, a stubble-scratched face and messy hair. Loved up, Kate thought and smiled.

The toilet flushed and Richard's eyes moved to the bathroom door and then back to her. As he opened his mouth to speak, Charlie emerged with the lower half his face covered in shaving foam, a razor in his hand, a towel slung low around his hips. He looked like he'd walked straight out of a TV advert. Richard gawped and his eyes opened wide. She knew Charlie had shocked him in a way she'd never have managed.

"Charlie, this is Richard."

"Oh, yeah. Hi, *Dick*." Charlie emphasized his name.

Kate's pulse jumped.

"My name's Richard."

"Dick suits you better," Charlie said.

Richard's eyes flicked between her and Charlie.

"Kate's been ill," Charlie said. "She's just recovered from a severe case of Dick-itis."

It took Richard a moment to get it. Then he glared. Kate listened in growing delight.

"I wanted to be sure she was okay. I can see I needn't have bothered."

"Yes, you should, Dick. You pulled a shitty trick," Charlie snapped.

"Didn't take you long to recover," Richard said to Kate.

"Hey, thanks for the razors and shaving gel. You didn't mind me using them, did you, Dick? I had your Aztec Beef as well and that great ice-cream thing. Big thank-you for the multi-buy on the condoms. Saved us having to waste time shopping."

Richard's face turned thunderous. Kate didn't try to hide her amusement.

"Seems like they weren't the only things you used." Richard stared at Kate.

Charlie put his arm across her shoulders.

"You're the one who hurt her. Fuck off." His voice was quiet but deadly.

"She's a slut."

Charlie was so fast, Kate staggered as he whisked away from her. The two men stood face-to-face, so close a blob of shaving foam transferred to Richard's nose.

"You know, I thought I was a shit, but you are a bubbling cesspit all on your own. You ask Kate to marry you for a bet? You're off the fucking evolutionary ladder altogether. Why are you here? Fancy a shag, did you? Don't bother answering because we know it's the truth and don't you ever call her names again, *Dick*. You don't even deserve to breathe the same air as my Kate."

Charlie pushed Richard out, picked up the flowers, threw them after him and slammed the door. They heard him swear and then stamp down the corridor.

My Kate? Her heart buzzed with excitement.

"You've frightened him off," she said and pouted. "I so hoped we could get back together, but now I don't think he'll want to see me anymore."

Charlie laughed. "You'll just have to manage with me, then."

Kate smiled and wrapped her arms around his waist. "Thank you, Charlie."

He had no idea how much it meant to her, that he'd defended her like that. She'd always had to stand up for herself with no big brother, no family, no friends.

"What for?"

"Playing my hero."

"I wasn't playing." He put a hurt expression on his face. "I *am* your hero."

He pulled the T-shirt over her head, tossed it to one side and guided her toward the bathroom. "We have a tight schedule. Shower first, then bath, then shower again, then bed. Possibly a pause to eat."

Kate chuckled.

"You don't think he recognized me, do you?"

"I doubt it."

She unfastened Charlie's towel, let it fall to the floor and smiled as his cock twitched in anticipation. He had a fabulous body, well-defined pecs and chiseled abs. As she looked at him, his copper nipples hardened and she laughed.

"You know, looking at my body and laughing does nothing for my ego."

"Your ego's big enough. Didn't you have an album called 'The Ego has Landed'?"

"No, that was Robbie—" He broke off when he saw her face. "Ha ha. Very funny. Not."

Kate wiped her hand across his chin and removed the foam, smearing it down his chest and onto his shaft. He was already rigid. Kate loved the way his body responded to her touch. She pushed him into the shower and reached for the controls before dropping to her knees.

The water cascaded over them as Kate washed the foam from his cock. When her mouth closed around him, Charlie reacted like he'd been hit by lightning. He froze with his back pressed against the tiles. She licked the bead of moisture from his tip and ran her tongue down his length. When she took him slow and deep into her mouth, his breath hissed between his lips. As the water poured over her head, Kate sucked rhythmically. His fingers sank into her hair and he released a guttural groan. When she looked up and saw him looking down at her, his face changed.

"Shit, Kate, I'm sorry. I'm sorry," he gasped and spurted into her mouth.

As he sank back against the wall, he pulled her to her feet, and wiped her lips with his fingers. "I should have warned you I was about to explode."

"I already know you're dangerous."

"I usually have more control than that. It's all your fault."

"Want me to show you a trick I know?"

Charlie licked her lips. "Will I like it?"

"Yes. Trust me?"

He nodded.

Kate switched off the shower and tugged him back to the bedroom without bothering to towel dry. Charlie was still hyper and she didn't know how to bring him down. Well, maybe this would work. She piled pillows against the bed head.

"Make yourself comfortable. I've just got to get something."

"Cup of tea and toast?" he asked.

Kate rolled her eyes but came back with breakfast, plus four long pieces of material and a couple of other things. She watched Charlie eye them but he said nothing. They fed toast to each other, Charlie teasing her by almost letting her catch a bite then pulling it away.

"You seem to like tormenting me," Kate said with a growl.

"Yep." He dragged back the last piece of toast from her lips and popped it in his mouth.

Kate pulled the strands of fabric between her fingers. Charlie paused mid-chew, then hurried to empty his mouth.

"No." He shook his head.

"I promise you'll enjoy it."

He sagged. "Oh God. Can't we play phone sex instead?"

"This is better. I promise to stop if you want me to."

Charlie sighed and held his wrists to the metal bed head. "No pictures."

Kate faltered as she tied his wrist. "I don't have a camera."

"Mobile phone?" Charlie asked.

"Not mine. It's a million years old. Charlie, if you don't —"

"Sorry, sorry." He pulled her close with his free hand and brushed his lips against hers.

He'd been hurt. Kate saw it in his face. He couldn't quite let go.

"You can trust me, Charlie. I promise. I'll never let you down. No kiss and tell. Only kiss kiss."

He smiled and Kate tied his other wrist. She used the longer pieces of fabric to secure his ankles with his legs spread wide.

Charlie frowned. "Have you read that book by Stephen King?"

"The one where the writer got tied up by his fan? Or Gerard—Gerald's Game? It was other way around. He'd tied her."

"I'm not sure I could chew off my fingers to get loose."

Kate giggled. "She didn't do that. She was in handcuffs. One tug and you could break free."

"Spoil my fantasy, why don't you?"

Kate pulled the curtain across the side of the bed facing the window. "Just in case. Okay?"

"What are you going to do?" he blurted.

"Stick pins in every inch of your body and stand on you in stilettos until you howl for mercy."

He gulped. "Alternatively?"

"Do everything I can to make you come but not let it happen for an hour."

His shuddery groan lit a fire in her belly. "An hour?"

She sat between his legs and cradled his balls, working her thumb between the delicate eggs in a gentle caress. His cock unfurled like a shooting sprout.

"How about ten minutes?" Charlie asked.

Kate settled her hand around the base of his cock and tightened her fingers, pushing down on his balls at the same time. She heard his breathing quicken and looked into his face. Charlie stared right at her. Kate used her other hand to stroke his swelling cock, fingers trailing up and down, following the line of the veins, sweeping under the bulbous head and into the delicate dip beneath.

"Oh God," Charlie mumbled and his eyes closed.

They sprang open again when he felt the oil. Kate dribbled it over him, letting it run onto his cock head and trickle down over her hand wrapped around the base of his cock and from there onto his balls. She released him and, using one finger, traced an oily path from his glistening crest, down his shaft, over the darker midline of his balls and onto the triangle of flesh beyond. When she rubbed him there Kate heard the change in his breathing, shifting slower and deeper as he attempted to control himself. More fun there later.

She moved a hand back to the base of his dick and watching his face, squeezed almost hard enough to hurt. A slight flinch and his eyes opened to watch her. Kate slid her fist the tiniest bit higher up his shaft and squeezed again, twisting at the same time. She repeated the same thing over and over, moving up as slowly as she could until she reached his cock head and a drop of fluid oozed from the slit.

"Oh fuck," Charlie gasped.

"Watch, Charlie."

The pearl of pre-cum grew until it was too heavy to stay in place and then hung from his cock like a melting icicle. Kate lowered her head and licked it up before it hit his stomach.

"Fuuuccckkk."

Her hand back at the base of his cock, she began again. Squeeze, move up, squeeze, move up. Every movement slow and measured while Charlie quivered like a wet puppy.

"How about...not letting me come...for six minutes," he gulped out.

Kate used her thumb and forefinger to massage the tip of his cock and this time the drop of fluid she milked was larger. Her hand settled around his root and held tight as the ball of pre-cum grew.

"Oh my God." Charlie tugged at his restraints.

Kate kept looking at him as she swept her tongue over the head of his cock, scooping up the salty-sweet treat before dragging the flat of her tongue back and forth over the sensitive head. She knew she was exciting Charlie, but her body clamped and relaxed as cream coated the lips of her pussy.

She wasn't sure how many times she milked pre-cum from him but Charlie's desperate groans warned her to pull back. His balls were pulled up tight and his cock looked almost angry, the crest dark-red with blood. Kate didn't touch him but draped a cold cloth over his groin. Charlie gave a long sigh.

"That has to be at least fifty minutes. Right?" he asked.

"Three."

"Noooo," he wailed.

Kate laughed. "All right. Ten."

"You are such a witch."

She whisked off the cloth and tossed it aside. "Ready for more?"

Charlie found himself nodding. The ache in his balls was intense but he could last longer than ten minutes. Couldn't he? Kate's finger touched his asshole and he jerked almost all his body off the bed.

"Christ, Kate. Some warning?"

"Where would be the fun in that?"

Her hand clenched around the base of his cock and Charlie knew the torture wasn't over. She lowered her head and sucked the tip of his shaft, pulling with short, rhythmic tugs that send his blood pressure rocketing. At the same time, she circled the puckered ring of muscle of his anus with her oily finger.

OhGodohGodohGodohGod.

He wasn't sure what he wanted. Well, yes he was. He didn't particularly want to have sex with a guy again, but the sensation of something in his anus while he jacked off was worth repeating. Hell, he *had* repeated it.

How the fuck could Kate do so much at the same time? While a fingertip pressed insistently against his asshole, another of her fingers had found and was rubbing the pressure point midway between his balls and his anus—something that *made him go fucking insane*. And still her mouth worked its magic on his cock. She had him in her hands and mouth. She could make him come, stop him coming. She had the power to give him a head-spinning orgasm and the power to drag it from his grasp and change its nature to something else entirely. Did she know?

Her finger teased and pressed its way into his body. Of course she fucking knew. Her tiny hands against the desperate need of his body and she'd win. Charlie let out a muffled laugh. In return, Kate changed the way she sucked at him, twisting her mouth as she went down and spearing her finger into his anus, reaching for his prostate. He was helpless. Charlie couldn't speak, could barely think, could only feel.

She massaged him down from the brink time after time and each time left his body racked with dry shudders. He forced his eyes open to watch her, saw the intense concentration on her face, his pre-cum shining on her lips, and thought that was enough to make him come. Yet again, she pulled him back, dragged him from the edge just as he was about to throw himself into oblivion. The pressure on that short strip of flesh behind his balls was intense enough to make his eyes ache.

Charlie could swear he was harder than he'd ever been, his balls tighter than they'd ever been. He'd never been closer to coming and not come. Never been as desperate to come. The muscles of his thighs blazed, pinpricks of fire attacked his spine, he was wet through with perspiration and he could feel his cum rising to the boil. Orgasm loomed, lurked, threatened. Kate crooked her finger, found his prostate again and Charlie whimpered. He opened his mouth to speak and nothing came out. She rubbed him inside and out, flickered her tongue at lightning speed over the tip of his dick, loosened her hold on his root and Charlie's brain exploded.

As the first spurt erupted from his balls, he felt Kate press down on that point behind his balls, halting the jet of cum in its tracks. *Fuckfuckfuckfuck. What the hell?* Charlie thought his whole body was going to come, except it wasn't and didn't. Long, wrenching spasms seized him and he cried out. No pulses of cum, no streaks of jism flooding her mouth, drowning her, just intense ripples of sensation that shook him from head to toe as if he'd been seized in the jaws of a killer whale—in a nice way. He couldn't speak, couldn't breathe, couldn't stop his hips bucking and he threw Kate off. She shoved her finger back inside him and he fucking came again.

Charlie couldn't stand it, but he couldn't stand for it to stop. His back arched as another contraction gripped his groin. Then his legs were free, his arms free too and he lay quivering in Kate's embrace.

"My PIN is 1234. My burglar alarm code 4321. My luggage locks 9999. It was me who set fire to all the German textbooks, me who put red dye in the swimming pool." He sighed.

Kate stroked his face. "Okay?"

"Okay? My God. That was incredible. I'll never be able to walk again, but that's fine so long as you're my nurse. I cannot believe Dickhead let you leave his sight."

"I've never done all that together before."

Charlie managed to turn his head to look at her. Was she lying? It was the sort of thing women said to him all the time— they'd never come so hard, they'd never slept with anyone like him, that he was the best, the biggest, the hottest.

"When I started the phone sex I spent a few days looking up interesting sites on the Internet and made notes so I could sound authentic."

"Did anyone ever manage to get to the end of talking to you without coming?"

She laughed. "No. Unless they were faking it."

Chapter Nine

❧

Rachel looked at Lucy, then at Dan and then back at the coffee table. She was waiting for one of them to speak and the way this conversation was going, she thought it more likely she'd get a response from the coffee table. Kate's flattened-out suicide note lay in front of them.

"I wish I'd never found it," Rachel said. "I wish I'd never told you."

The ball of paper had fallen out of the bin that morning when she'd lifted the lid to drop her trash inside. She'd picked up the paper, and when she'd seen handwriting she'd been too nosy not to open it up. She wished she hadn't. Rachel knew that in telling the others, she'd made the problem worse. Kate didn't want anyone to know about this and now they all knew and every time they looked at her, they'd think about what she'd planned to do.

"Maybe it's not what we think," Dan said.

Lucy rolled her eyes. She picked up the paper by a corner as if it were something that could infect her, and read it again.

To Lucy, Rachel and Dan,

If you're reading this, I guess either you haven't seen me for a while and figured you'd better check on me to see whether I'm okay. Or you already know that I'm not. If it's the former, then sorry, but I won't be back. If it's the latter, then you know I won't be back.

Don't think that you've failed me in any way. You haven't. Not even Richard. There's something in the fridge for him. Please make sure he gets it.

There's no blame to lay at anyone's door. This is my decision.

I've simply had enough of my life.

Thanks for being my friends. Be happy.

Best wishes

Kate

PS My solicitor is Kevin Martineau. Ring him.

"How can that not be a suicide note, Dan?" Lucy asked.

Dan opened his mouth and then shut it again.

"So what should we do?" Rachel glanced at Lucy, who shrugged.

"Do we need to do anything? We know she didn't go through with it," Dan said, as a loud bump came from upstairs. "I mean, she screwed up the note and threw it away. She changed her mind. And she's definitely in her apartment. I've never heard her make so much noise."

"But it sounds so final," Rachel said. "And it doesn't sound like it was just over Richard. She says she's had enough of her life. That's so sad."

There was another bang from upstairs and a peal of laughter.

"I think she's fine," Lucy said. "This new friend seems to have cheered her up. I saw Richard storm out of here this morning, so she's obviously over him."

"It seems awfully fast to jump into another relationship," Rachel said. "You'd think she'd want to mourn for a bit first."

"Over a prick like Richard?" Lucy guffawed.

"Should we do anything?" Rachel asked Dan.

"I don't think we should tell her we know about the note. If she wants to talk to us, she will," he said.

"I'll chuck it away," Lucy said as the sound of a man laughing echoed through the ceiling.

Charlie unplugged the phone and disconnected the buzzer.

"Don't answer the door if anyone knocks," he said. "I want you to myself."

He followed her everywhere, never more than an arm's length away and generally, not even that. He held her hand or pressed his body against hers, desperate to feel her next to him. He didn't want either of them to leave the apartment, and got so stressed when Kate insisted on taking rubbish down to the bin, he was hyperventilating by the time she returned. Charlie couldn't function without her. He'd never felt anything like this before. He didn't get dressed and kept her naked too. But it wasn't just the sex. It was Kate. Without her next to him, he felt lost.

For a while, he didn't want to eat and then he couldn't stop eating. They ate their way though her freezer and cupboards, consuming broccoli and baked beans, prawns and pizza, Thai green curry and cheese-filled pasta.

"Pretty soon, I'll only have ice cubes left," Kate said.

"I can always eat you." Charlie dropped onto the couch and pulled her with him.

"And which bit would you eat first?"

"Toes." He lifted her foot and nibbled.

Kate squirmed as he tickled her. "Not my backside?"

"I'd save the best 'til last."

He wrapped his arms around her and pressed his face into her neck. His body was shaking. "What's wrong with me?" But he knew. He was going through some sort of withdrawal. Detoxing himself.

"You're coming back from somewhere," Kate said. "You're like a plant that hasn't been watered and then there's a deluge. You're coming back to life."

"It hurts."

Kate held him tighter, tracing figures of eight on his skin.

His mind buzzed as if a line of bees went in one ear and zoomed around his head before flying out the other ear. And the noise got louder and louder until he thought he'd go mad.

"Go buy me some cigarettes and get me something decent to drink," he gasped.

"I thought you didn't want me to go out."

"Well, I do now. I'll pay you back."

"I'm not buying you cigarettes or booze."

He glared at her. "You fucking cow." But he clutched her tighter.

"You don't need them," Kate said.

"Yeah, I do," Charlie snapped. "I want a line or two of coke as well, to cheer me up."

"You've got a fucking cow, what more do you need?"

Charlie gawped and then started to laugh and once he'd started, he couldn't stop. He laughed until he cried, great heaving sobs that racked his whole body and through it all, Kate never left him. She held him and stroked him and soothed his face with a cold flannel. When he was too exhausted to move, she ran the cloth over his body, along each finger, every inch of his skin except the one place he wanted her to touch.

"Please, Kate," he pleaded, his hand inching toward his cock.

She lifted his fingers away. "See how long you can stand it."

Even watching her caused his erection to rise like a charmed snake. She resumed her teasing caress and he found himself thinking only of Kate and what she was doing to him. In the end, he was so turned on, he came without her even touching him and spurted over his belly. A wet dream in broad daylight.

But Charlie liked to touch her. He couldn't keep his hands off her and Kate never pulled away. He couldn't sleep, so he kept her awake. He woke her to make love to her. He dragged her away from cleaning her teeth to make love to her. In the middle of cooking, he pulled her down and fucked her and she never said no when sometimes he wished she would. Charlie realized he was substituting her for every one of his vices. Why couldn't she see that?

He was irritable and bad-tempered. Sometimes he was mean to her, downright unpleasant. But he always apologized, always wanted to make things right again. When he was wild, she calmed him. When he cried, she held him. When he wanted to talk, she listened. When he wanted silence, she didn't speak. And Charlie came to realize that he didn't want the cigarettes or booze or coke anymore. He only wanted Kate.

Kate thought she knew what was happening to Charlie. Something bad inside him was worming its way out. She watched his mood swing from affectionate to vicious, from tearful to manic, and handled him the best way she could. He needed her so much, she had no time to think about what had happened to her. Richard didn't matter. Charlie did. Charlie's need for her saved her. When he couldn't stop shaking, she held him. When all he seemed able to do was pace around the apartment, dragging her with him, she thought up ways to distract him.

"Take a seat, sir. The show will begin in two minutes," Kate said. She sat him on the couch, gave him a pad of paper and a pen. "Marks out of ten," she said.

Then she modeled her underwear — cotton, lace and leather and Charlie's boxers — until he forgot to write anything down, forgot why she'd started in the first place.

When they did start to sleep for longer periods, nightmares plagued them both. Sometimes Charlie woke her, his face etched in fear, hers bathed in sweat. Other times, she pulled him away from whatever demon had grabbed him. They had their own torments and they held each other, resorting to humor to defuse their anxiety or sex to forget it. Their conversations were rambling outpourings of hopes, dreams and fears. But even as Kate teetered on the brink of revealing too much, she kept her deepest secrets while Charlie revealed all of his. And when she was tempted to tell him everything, she used sex to distract herself.

They lay exhausted in a tangle of arms and legs and Kate knew this was the closest she'd ever been to any person.

"I'm scared I've exchanged one addiction for another," he murmured, running his hands over her skin.

Kate knew he had, because she was addicted to him, to the sight and sound of him, the touch and smell of him, his soft brown eyes that changed with his moods, his sexy smile and that place behind his ear that sent him wild when she licked it.

As each day went by, she watched the gradual lifting of the dark circles under his eyes. His appetite improved, though he seemed to survive on virtually no sleep. She ached from all the sex, but it stopped her from thinking. Kate knew she'd undergone a detox of her own, not physical, but mental, purging guilt and sorrow from her system. Her thinking became clearer. What happened with Richard wasn't her fault. Charlie made her believe in herself.

And all the time, as they came back to life, the day drew closer when they'd have to face the outside world. They both knew it but in all they talked about, neither of them talked about that.

They lay facedown on the bed, staring at each other.

"What are you thinking?" Charlie asked.

He asked that at least five times a day and Kate never rolled her eyes. She always gave him an answer.

"We're running out of food," she said.

"Then there's no choice. I'll have to eat you. I've decided to start with your backside, sautéed in a knob of butter." His fingers feathered down her spine until his hand rested on her bottom.

"I thought you were going to save the best until last? Anyway, we've run out of butter. I have to go shopping."

Charlie's heart ached with the thought that he might not have her with him forever. He pulled her into his arms and hugged her.

"You're the best friend I've ever had," he whispered.

He looked her straight in the eyes and willed her to understand how important that was to him.

"Thank you, Charlie."

"Am I your best friend too?"

"You're up there with Edward."

He stiffened. "Who the hell is Edward?"

"According to my psychologist, he was a coping mechanism that helped me deal with deep-seated unhappiness. Although I think he wanted to transfer me to the psychiatrist when he realized I'd chosen Edward Scissorhands as my imaginary friend."

Charlie laughed and relaxed again.

"Didn't you have any real friends when you were a kid?" He traced his finger over her cheek.

"Sometimes I thought I did, but the answer is no."

Kate ran her hands up his back and he took a deep breath. Every time she touched him, it was like the magic first time and ripples of pleasure trickled through every limb.

"Didn't you want friends?" he asked.

"One would have been enough. I thought having a friend would be the answer to everything. But the kids I knew always let me down. They lied about me or told my secrets. They were never there when it mattered, so in the end I stopped thinking friends would make my life better. If I didn't have any, then they couldn't hurt me. That was the theory. In practice, everyone thought I was a stuck-up bitch and found other ways to get at me."

Charlie held her a little tighter, kissed her forehead. "I wish I'd been there."

"Don't worry, Charlie. I'm all grown up now. I don't get bent out of shape if Rachel nicks my doll or Lucy flushes my book."

"I wish I'd been a better brother to Michael. I ignored him at school. We boarded and I was supposed to look out for him, but didn't. Much too busy being Mr. Popular to worry about a homesick little boy. I was captain of the football team, played tennis for the county, fenced for the country and even managed to fashion three guitar players and an average drummer into a half-decent band. I didn't have time for my brother."

"What happened to your band when you left school?"

"Dissolved like snow falling in springtime. I started another at university, though. I put an advert on the union notice board and made people audition. God, I was cocky."

Kate coughed and he laughed.

"All right, I'm still cocky. But if they were crap, I told them so. The new band wasn't bad. I wrote all our stuff and one night when we were performing, someone who mattered in the music world was in the audience. Much to my parents' disappointment, all thoughts of doing a proper job flew straight through the window. Michael was the one supposed to make their dreams come true." Charlie heard the catch in his voice so he knew Kate had.

"Who's going shopping?" she asked.

Grateful she changed the subject, he slipped a hand between her legs. "Do we have to?"

"Three cheese biscuits left and I'm not sharing," Kate said. "We could both go. I'll hold your hand so you don't get lost."

"I don't want to go out in case someone recognizes me. You go. And bring a couple of newspapers. Not the decent ones."

When Kate returned, Charlie was asleep, sprawled naked on the floor next to the jigsaw puzzle, his hair mussed and his long lean body stretched over the cushions like an indolent big cat. Kate felt a rush of affection. The jigsaw was half complete. In between bouts of frantic lovemaking, they'd worked on it together, made up silly rewards for the first one to position five pieces. A kiss on the belly button. For ten pieces a kiss somewhere more intimate. Charlie always cheated and Kate sometimes let him.

Feeling sorry for each other had stopped them feeling sorry for themselves. He'd opened his heart to her, and Kate felt bad she hadn't done the same to him, not completely. It still seemed unreal. Every time she looked at him, she couldn't quite believe it. He was the best thing that had ever happened to her, but she knew it couldn't last. He was a star and she was space debris.

Kate crept to his side with a bottle of Stopit, a vile tasting liquid for painting on nails, to stop kids biting them down to the quick. Holding the miniature nylon brush between her thumb and forefinger, she coated each of his stubby fingernails.

By the time she'd put the food away and had cooked them their first normal meal for days, Charlie was waking up. He stretched like a cat too, arms and legs extended, and then turned to look for her.

"India's okay," he said.

Kate smiled.

"I looked on the internet. She's awake and...thank God. What can I smell?" he asked.

"Food."

He scampered to her side, running his fingers through his spiky hair.

"It's not fair," he mumbled.

"What?"

"You've got clothes on and I haven't."

"You know where your clothes are," she said.

"Okay, I'm going to put them on and it will serve you right."

Kate laughed as he stamped out of the room. A moment later, he was shouting her. "Kate! Get in here. Right now!"

When she went into the bedroom, she couldn't see him for a moment and as she registered he'd hidden behind the door, he jumped forward and propelled her onto the bed, spinning her over, pinning her on her back. He sat on her thighs and Kate groaned.

"That hurts," she said.

"So does this."

Charlie stuck his finger in her mouth and ran his nail over her tongue. Kate gagged, grabbed his wrist and pulled his hand away.

"What have you done, you witch?" he hissed. "I was all set to have a comforting nibble since your boobs weren't available and I thought I must have stuck my fingers in poison."

"It's to stop you biting your nails." Kate struggled to get free.

Charlie frowned and reached toward her mouth with his fingers.

"If you do that again, I'll paint my nipples with it," Kate said.

He grinned. "You wouldn't dare. You like me licking those." He pulled a face again. "Take it off."

"It's for your own good," Kate said.

"But my mouth tastes terrible."

"Don't bite your nails then."

"I don't like you anymore."

"So you don't want what I've cooked?"

"Maybe I do like you. What are we having?"

"Tripe and onions."

Charlie held his fingers over her lips. "Try again."

"Enchiladas."

He rolled off her.

"And I bought something to drink," Kate said.

"I thought I wasn't allowed alcohol."

"It's for me."

"We have to share. It's only fair."

"With rhymes like that it's no wonder you gave up writing songs." Kate avoided the hand heading for her backside and went back to the kitchen.

Charlie pulled on the sleep pants. He thought he'd stopped writing songs, but he'd written one in his head about Kate's eyes. The fear in them when she was in the sea, how they lit up when she teased him, their feline quality when she lay beneath him, their wildness when he made her come.

After they'd eaten, Charlie flicked through the newspapers. He didn't see his name mentioned once and the Internet search he'd done while Kate was out hadn't thrown up anything significant about him over the last week. Except India Westerby was okay. Two miracles.

"I need to ring my agent," he said.

"I thought he'd dumped you."

"He might not have meant it."

"Okay."

"I don't want to ring him, but I should."

"You've grown up, then." Kate pulled her legs onto the couch. "Doing things you know you should, rather than what you want."

"What about you? When did you grow up?" He dropped his arm across her shoulders.

"A long time ago, once I'd accepted there wasn't someone out there desperate to give a little girl a home."

Charlie's heart hurt for her. "I bet you were really sweet. Shame what you've grown into. Get your photo album and let's see what you were like when you were younger."

There was a pause before she spoke. "I don't have any photos."

Charlie was taken aback. "What? None? Not even of your mum and dad?"

"No. I don't like photographs."

Kate kept her eyes down and a few days ago, Charlie might have left it, but now he wanted to know everything. "Why not?"

"I just don't."

"Tell me why."

Charlie could almost see the cogs and wheels turning in her head as she wondered whether to lie.

"After I ran away from a foster home for the third time, I got sent to a residential care center in Berkshire—this huge place housing twenty-five kids. I was given a big room in the attic with its own bathroom and that started me off on the wrong foot with the others. I thought I was being kept away from them because the staff had me down as a bad influence. They did, but that wasn't the reason."

Charlie pulled her feet on to his lap and massaged them.

"I meant to be different. I planned to work hard at school, pass exams, try to get on with everyone, but…"

Charlie sensed she'd changed her mind. She wouldn't tell him the truth.

"I fell out with one of the girls. She was telling lies about me at school, so I cut her hair while she was asleep. In revenge, she ripped up all my photographs."

"Remind me not to piss you off," he said. "Christ, with your upbringing, I'm surprised you aren't a misogynistic lesbian."

"I was, but you've fucked me up, Charlie."

"Yeah, I suppose I have." He laughed. "But you can hardly claim it was one-sided."

"No, I think I remember upside down and backward as well."

"Will you put on your leather underwear and sit on my lap while I phone Ethan?" he asked.

"Why?"

"So I know I'll get a reward when I've spoken to him."

"No, I'll distract you. Do it now. You'll have to plug the phone back in."

Charlie had no idea how Ethan would react. He'd said they were finished, but he was the only guy Charlie had ever trusted to handle his interests. Ethan had been his agent, business manager, personal assistant and publicist for a long time and Charlie didn't want to begin again with someone else.

"Ethan?" Charlie said hesitantly.

"You fucking wanker," Ethan yelled.

Charlie winced and held the phone away from his ear.

"Where have you been? I've been trying to contact you all week. Your answer machine has had a bloody apoplectic fit. It won't take any more messages. Your mobile is dead. I've been round to your house. No one's seen you. I thought you'd been abducted by fucking aliens."

"I've been sorting my head out," Charlie said.

"You've been doing my head in," Ethan snapped back.

"What's wrong?"

"You don't fucking deserve it, but you've had two lucky breaks. Malcolm Ward says if you perform in his charity concert in September, he'll forget taking out a contract on you for destroying his family. I think he was planning to string you up by the balls."

Charlie shuddered.

"And for some fucked-up reason you're being given another chance on *The Green*. God, I can only presume the others who auditioned must have farted in the director's face or thrown up in his lap for him to want *you* back, but he does. Kesner's in Scotland and tomorrow's his last day before he flies to Europe. I'll book you a ticket to Edinburgh. You can fly up first thing. Don't fuck this up, Charlie."

"So, are you still my agent?"

"I'll tell you when you get the part."

"I've given up smoking," Charlie blurted and saw the smile on Kate's face.

"Good. Given up fucking as well? I've had Jody Morton ringing daily wanting to know where you are. Did you fuck her too?"

"No, I didn't."

"Well, the smoking is a start," Ethan said.

"Anything more happen over India Westerby?" Charlie couldn't look at Kate now.

Ethan's voice changed. "The police have charged Brian Jackson with supplying. He's out on bail."

"They're not looking for anyone else?"

Silence at the end of the phone.

"Is there something you're not telling me, Charlie?" Ethan's voice was cool.

"No."

"Did you give her coke?"

"No." Charlie couldn't look at Kate.

"Right, I'll send a driver to get you tomorrow. It will be early. I'll ring you when I know the time of the flight."

"Give me chance to get back to my place," Charlie said.

127

"Where are you? Don't fucking tell me abroad."

"Greenwich."

"London?"

"Yes."

"Thank Christ for that. Go home. Now."

Charlie put the phone down.

"Did you know she was only fourteen?" Kate asked.

"No. I swear I didn't. I fucked her once and because she asked me, I dropped a wrap of coke on her stomach before I walked out of the bedroom. If anyone finds out, I'll be arrested and that will be the end."

He and Kate stared at each other.

"Do you think I deserve to be arrested?" he asked. "Don't answer that. I know I do."

"She asked you for the coke?"

"Yes, but I didn't have to give it to her."

"You're not a bad man, Charlie. You're not up there with Nelson Mandela and Gandhi or even the Osmonds, but you're not deep-down bad."

He gave her a little smile.

"You think you don't care, say you don't care, but I know you do," Kate said.

He reached out and pulled her into his arms.

"I care about you," he said.

"But you do tell lies and lying will send you all the way down the slippery sidewinders, when you've spent this week climbing loose-limbed ladders."

"I don't lie to you."

"Good."

"I have to go to Scotland to audition again for that part."

"Another chance?" Kate's face lit up. "That's great, Charlie."

"Only I have to go tomorrow."

"Okay."

128

"I don't know how long it will take. I'll ring you, text you, email, send smoke signals," he said.

"Good."

"You could come with me."

"You don't need me to hold your hand. You're all grown up now. But take care crossing the road. Look both ways. And put on clean underpants, just in case."

"I don't want to go."

"Yeah, you do. This is your opportunity to put things right. Look how much good you've done already. Saving me from dangerous seaweed, rescuing me from the vile clutches of Dickhead Dastardly, introducing me to the delights of whole days of continuous shagging and a lifetime of aching limbs."

"Come with me." *Please.*

"I've got to go to work tomorrow. The honeymoon's over." Kate's voice cracked and the seismic tremor shook Charlie's heart. "I'll lend you the money for a taxi," she said. "You better phone a locksmith and get him to meet you, otherwise you won't be able to get into your place."

Charlie held her tighter, his hip bones pressing hard against hers.

"Kate, don't tell anyone you're seeing me. I'm not saying that because I don't want people to know, I just don't want the press to know and if anyone finds out, anyone at all, the press will too. You don't understand what they're like. I do. Reporters have no respect for your privacy. They'll write lies about you, twist everything you say and do. Every word you utter will be recorded and used against you and against me. It's much better if no one knows about us."

"Okay," she said.

"There is an 'us', Kate. I'm not walking out of your life."

Charlie pressed his face into her hair. "You don't still want to die, do you? I won't leave if I think you're going to do something stupid. Forget the film. You're more important."

"I promise not to be stupid unless you're with me. Now let's go and get your proper clothes on before I have to ravish you again," Kate whispered.

She took hold of his hand and pulled him into the bedroom, pushed down his sleep pants and then dressed him, pulling his boxers up his legs, then his chinos. She zipped him up, stroked his erection and then fastened the button.

It was like being a child again, Charlie thought, but so bloody erotic he was choked with lust. He forced himself not to reach for her because if he had, he didn't think he'd have been able to leave.

Her fingers brushed his chest as she fastened his shirt.

"What are you thinking?" he asked.

"If I'll ever touch you again, taste you again."

"Don't," he gasped.

Kate sat him down on the bed and eased on his socks, then his boots, tied the laces and there was nothing left to do. She sat beside him on the bed.

"Open your hand," Charlie said.

He gave her the little bottle of Stopit.

"Put some more on so I'm not tempted."

Kate painted each of his nails. When she'd finished he grabbed her hand and coated her nails too.

"Just so you're not tempted."

They stood holding each other until the buzzer went. Charlie let her go.

"Bye, Charlie," she whispered. "Be brilliant."

"Hey, I'm a star."

He walked away backward, watching her until the very last moment.

Chapter Ten

ಸಂ

Charlie spent the journey across London torn between excitement and misery. He wished he was back with Kate, but he wanted this role. The locksmith waited outside his house. Ten minutes later, Charlie was inside. He rang Kate.

"Hello, gorgeous," she said.

"How did you know it was me?"

"Oh, it's you."

"You witch. You're not allowed to call anyone else that. It could have been the vicar."

"I call him darling and he only rings on Wednesdays and Sundays."

Charlie laughed and then stopped. "You're not serious, are you?"

"Have you heard from Ethan yet?" Kate asked.

"No." She hadn't answered his question and Charlie felt a twist of jealousy.

"Then you better ring me later, otherwise he'll come round with instruments of torture because he can't get through."

"What do you know about instruments of torture?"

"You didn't open that drawer."

There was a short pause before Charlie answered. "I'm not into pain."

"Liar."

"I'm not."

"So you don't want me to tie you up again?"

Charlie felt a tug at his groin as he remembered. "I could come back after Ethan's called."

Now there was a pause from Kate before she answered. "You need a decent night's sleep. I'll see you in a few days, Charlie. Be good."

"You too."

The moment he put down the phone it rang again. Charlie snatched it up. "Hello, gorgeous," he said.

"You won't get around me like that," Ethan snapped.

"How about I bring back a bottle of whisky?"

"That might work. Right. Find a pen."

Charlie copied down all the instructions. He was not going to mess this up.

With Ethan's final words echoing in his head, "Don't screw up, stay sober, this is your very last chance," Charlie went to pack. His house was spotless. He'd grown so accustomed to a week of living in a mess with Kate he'd forgotten a woman came in twice a week to make his home look unlived in and buy him groceries. It occurred to him that he could have collected a key from his housekeeper and he groaned.

Charlie destroyed every packet of cigarettes he found, breaking them up before tossing them in the bin. He was surprised how little he cared. He took a long look at the beers in the fridge, but left them alone. He didn't have a problem with alcohol. He liked to drink, but had proved to himself over the last few days that he didn't need it. There were no more little packets of coke hidden anywhere. But Charlie spent thirty minutes checking, just in case. He'd had some fantastic sex while he was high, but now he'd had fantastic sex without it.

He grinned when he thought about Kate. Even thinking her name sent shivers of anticipation coursing through his body, but he knew he'd have to be careful. He didn't want the press to find out about her. If they did, it wouldn't take them long to dig up Dickhead and before you could spit, they'd have Charlie as a heartbreaker, Kate as a slut and Dickhead as a victim. Kate's childhood had been rough. Charlie knew he'd only heard part of it. She didn't need to see her past dissected by the papers. If they managed to link her to him, her background would belong to everyone and there would be no hope of any sort of relationship between them. She'd dump him.

Charlie froze as that thought filtered through. She'd dump him because unlike every other woman he'd been out with she wasn't impressed by his celebrity. She valued her own privacy. He ran his fingers through his hair. That sounded good and bad. If the press started poking around, would she run? He knew he had to strengthen their relationship before anyone else got to hear about it. Kate would have to learn to cope with the media attention because sooner or later, it would come.

In the meantime, he'd keep her a secret as long as he could. He sent her a quick text.

Missing u already, Mermaid. Just chewed my nail.

Love Hippo x

The reply came back almost instantly.

Miss u 2, Hippo. Did I tell u Stopit only comes off as yr nails grow? Unless u have my magic removal formula, only 2b revealed under torture.

Love Mermaid xx

As did his message to her.

Look forward 2 it. Got some good ideas 2 make u cooperate.

Love Hippo xxx

* * * * *

Kate knew she had some groveling to do with her friends and neighbors, starting with Lucy. She and Rachel had taken turns yelling at her through the door over the last few days while Kate had snuggled up to Charlie and ignored them.

She rang Lucy's mobile. "Hi, it's me."

"Who?" Lucy retorted.

"Want to come round for a drink?"

"We're on the roof. Come up and join us."

Kate picked up the bottle of wine she and Charlie never got round to drinking and headed for the stairs.

Dan had introduced them to the roof. When he'd been handed the keys for his apartment along with ones for the post box, underground storage and bin room, he'd also accidentally been given one for the door to the roof. All four of them had keys now and the area was decked out with four pale blue plastic Adirondack chairs, a table and parasol, a few sickly looking plants and an occasional disposable BBQ.

When Kate opened the door she saw Lucy and Rachel in their bikinis, lying on towels, faces to the sun. Dan sat under the parasol talking to another guy. Kate realized it was Fax, Richard's friend and wondered if he'd made a move on Lucy.

"I brought a peace offering." Kate held up the chilled bottle.

"What a coincidence. We've got glasses," Dan said with a smile. "Nice to see you again, stranger."

Kate sat next to Fax.

"How are you, Kate?" he asked.

"Fine."

Rachel sat up and put on her sunglasses. "We've been worried about you. For all we knew, you'd done something stupid."

"Rachel!" Lucy snapped.

"I did do something stupid," Kate said. "I didn't see through Richard Winter."

Fax sighed as if he were about to say something and then fell silent. Dan poured out the wine and handed it round. She heard him mutter something to Rachel, who then looked sheepish.

"I'm sorry about what happened with Richard," Fax mumbled.

Kate blinked hard. She knew they'd talk about this.

"I thought he cared for you," Fax said. "He fooled me, too. It was a shitty thing to do."

"How much was the bet?" Kate asked.

"Two thousand quid," Fax said. "I'm sorry. I never thought he'd go through with it. When he suggested it the night of The Wedding Party, after you'd so clearly not wanted to be picked as the bride, I thought he was joking. Then I thought he'd fallen in love with you. I mean, you seemed right together."

Her chest tightened. There had never been a moment when Richard was genuine. He'd walked to that table where she, Lucy and Rachel had sat, looking for a gullible fool and found one.

"What shall we drink to?" Dan asked.

"Kate's new boyfriend," Lucy said before anyone else could speak.

Kate flinched.

"What's his name? What does he do? Where did you meet him?" Rachel asked.

Dan and Fax turned to stare at her.

"What?" she asked.

"The Secret Service should never have turned you down." Dan smiled at her.

"Very funny, Daniel."

Kate knew telling them nothing would make them suspicious.

"His name's Hippo. He's tall with straight dark hair. He's kind and funny and between jobs at the moment. I met him at the seaside."

"What's his real name?" Lucy asked.

Kate thought quickly. "Hippolytus."

"God, no wonder you call him Hippo. Is he Greek? If not, what were his parents thinking?" Lucy said.

"When did you go to the seaside?" Rachel took on the questioning.

"The day I was supposed to be going to Hawaii."

"Hawaii? Why...oh," Rachel paused.

Kate thought it might shut her up, but she was wrong.

"You bumped into him, then?"

"Literally. We were swimming. He was doing the crawl and hit me on the nose."

Kate saw the look that Rachel shot Lucy but Dan tipped up his wine and there was a flurry of activity as they shot back from the table. Grateful for the distraction, Kate hoped she'd told them enough, but Lucy and Rachel couldn't leave it there.

"Where does he live? On the coast?" Lucy asked.

"No, North London." But she didn't know where and Kate's pulse jumped. Why hadn't Charlie said?

"What sort of job is he looking for?" from Rachel.

"It's like twenty questions," Dan said. "Is he animal, vegetable or mineral?"

Definitely animal, Kate thought.

"No wonder women know so much." Fax raised his eyebrows.

"Yeah, but men know the important stuff," Dan said.

Rachel turned to glare at Dan and then looked back at Kate. "What sort of job?"

"She's like a heat-seeking missile." Dan caught the bottle of suntan lotion Rachel lobbed at him.

"I think he can turn his hand to most things," Kate said, smothering a grin.

"Is he married?" from Lucy.

"No."

"When are you seeing him again?" Lucy asked.

"No idea."

"But you do want to see him again?" from Rachel.

Kate nodded, unable to speak the truth, that she didn't think she could live without him.

"You aren't on the rebound, are you?" Lucy said. "We don't want to see you get hurt again."

"I'm over Richard, believe me." Kate wished she could jump in the air and scream it out loud.

A pigeon landed near Lucy's towel. Dan threw a piece of lemon and it flew up to look for another resting place.

"So life's looking great?" Rachel pressed. "Future looking peachy?"

Kate cocked her head on one side. "Yes, life's fine."

"Planning for the future?" Rachel added.

Kate didn't miss the glare that Lucy shot Rachel, but she had no idea what it meant.

"Rachel! Weren't you going to ask Kate a favor?" Dan said.

Kate had the distinct impression he wanted to change the subject.

"Ooh yes, we've had the paintings in for the new exhibition," Rachel said. "I'd be really grateful if you could spare the time to help with the catalogue."

"I could come after work tomorrow."

"Thanks, Kate. That would be great." Rachel beamed at her.

Kate leaned back in the chair and closed her eyes. She'd survived the interrogation without giving anything away. She was a little surprised they hadn't asked her more about what happened with Richard. They didn't seem angry she hadn't told them she was getting married. Maybe they didn't care. She still hovered on the periphery of the group. Were they her friends? Kate wasn't sure, but she was trying. Her skin tingled. The sunshine felt good after being in the apartment for so many days, even though they'd been spent having fun with Charlie. Her mouth twitched, wanting to grin.

"Don't fall asleep," Dan said. "I drifted off for an hour at lunchtime and look what happened."

Kate opened her eyes. Dan lifted his t-shirt to reveal a pale outline of a circle on his chest. Rachel giggled.

"I'm just biding my time, Rachel," he said.

Kate wondered if Rachel had finally seen how much Dan adored her. Life was too short to waste time apart they could spend together.

"Are you two going out yet?" Kate asked.

Judging by the shell-shocked faces, the answer was no.

"Why don't you ask her, Dan? If she says no, at least you'll know where you stand."

Kate closed her eyes. She knew that had been totally out of character, which accounted for the complete silence. Maybe she shouldn't have said anything.

"Want to go to the cinema tonight?" Dan's voice squeaked a little.

"Okay." Rachel spoke almost before Dan had finished.

Kate smiled to herself.

"Lucy, would you like to go to see a film with me?" Fax blurted out.

God, she really had got the matchmaking touch, Kate thought.

"Why not? Nick's busy tonight," Lucy said.

Out of the corner of her eye Kate saw Fax's face fall.

"We'll go together," Rachel announced. "Do you and Hippo want to come too, Kate?"

"I've got something on tonight."

But Kate had a surge of longing to be part of a group of friends going out together. Richard rarely wanted to go out with anyone that Kate knew. He tolerated occasional trips to the pub with Simon and Fax. And it couldn't happen with Charlie, who didn't want to be seen in public with her at all. Kate knew he was worried about the press pestering her and she worried about that too, but for a different reason.

* * * * *

Kate was supposed to be available from eight until twelve on Sunday evening, taking calls from guys who wanted to talk dirty to her or wanted her to talk dirty to them. She was well paid for the number of hours she logged on and she needed the money, but she didn't want to do it anymore. No one would chase her to continue. No one knew what she looked like. In fact, Kate thought it likely that the women who worked on these chat lines and pretended to be sirens in their twenties, were likely to be lonely fifty-year-olds. The men made them whoever they wanted anyway.

Kate deleted her account before she could change her mind. She'd have to cut back on her expenses.

At two minutes to eight the phone rang.

"What are you wearing?" Charlie whispered.

Kate laughed. "Green underwear."

"Lace pants?"

"No, the ones with holes."

He groaned. "I am suffocated with lust."

"I'm giving up the phone sex."

He whined. "What a moment to choose."

Kate tucked the phone between her shoulder and cheek and carried her coffee to the couch. "Why? What are you doing?"

"I've got my hand down my pants. Listen."

She chuckled. "What am I listening for?"

"The sound of an unhappy but rampant steel piston."

Kate burst out laughing. "What have you been reading?"

"I'm trying to hold a telephone sex conversation here."

She smiled at the indignation in his voice. "I told you I'm giving it up. I'm no good at it."

"Well, maybe you need to practice."

Kate didn't say anything.

"That was a hint," he said.

"Do you have anyone there with you?" she asked.

"No."

"Well pretend."

"Consuela, dust my platinum discs again."

"I've got my hand down my pants too, but I wish you were down my pants," Kate murmured in a sultry tone and took a sip of her coffee.

"Mmm," Charlie muttered. "Keep dusting, Consuela."

"I want to eat you," Kate purred. "I want to run my tongue along your long, thick cock and taste every glorious inch of you." The cup wobbled in her hand and she put it down.

"You missed a bit, Consuela. Do it again. Dust up and down, and do it fast."

Kate swallowed the lump in her throat. "Can you feel my teeth on you, Charlie, tracing that thick vein? See it pulsing? Do you trust me? How about if I take your velvety balls into my mouth and suck. Do you like that?" A shiver of desire rippled through her.

"How can you talk at the same time?" he asked in a hoarse voice. "Consuela, take that duster out of there."

"Wrap your fingers around yourself, Charlie. Push down. Now move your hand up. Hold yourself tighter."

"Christ, Kate. That's enough. You're not too far away, you know. I could drive over."

"I'm so tight and wet, Charlie. Thinking of you has made me horny. My nipples ache. My heart's fluttering. If you walked into the room now, I'd come without you even touching me." She meant it.

"Kate," he choked out.

"I've taken off my bra." She slid her hand to her nipple and it hardened in her fingers.

"Don't do this for anyone else."

"That's why I'm not doing it anymore, Charlie. I only want to come for you. I only want to feel your cock inside me, all long and thick and hot. I want you to fuck me harder and harder. I want you to make me scream."

She heard him give a shuddering groan. A long pause followed.

"Consuela's going to have to give me a wash now," he said.

"Tell her to clean behind your ears."

"It didn't go that far."

Kate laughed. "Good night, Hippo."

"'Night, Mermaid. See you when I get back."

A single tear slipped over Kate's eyelashes and trickled down her cheek. It made her skin itch and she wanted to rub it away, but didn't. She needed it to remind her to be strong, because she'd fallen in love with Charlie Storm and knew he would break her heart.

* * * * *

When Kate bounded into the lobby on Monday morning, Dan was leaning against the wall, waiting for her. He only worked sporadically at Crispies, but when he did, he waited for Kate so they could walk there together.

"Morning." Dan pushed open the outer door for Kate to go through.

"Good morning. How was the film?" she asked.

"No idea." Dan grinned.

Kate glanced at him and smiled. "Don't tell me you made 'the move'?"

"I might have."

They went into Greenwich Park, sharing the path with a group of geriatric joggers.

Dan yawned. "I was up all night painting. I could have done without coming in today, but Mel rang at seven this morning and demanded my presence. Sam is sick. Again."

"Who were you painting?" Kate asked.

Dan walked faster and when Kate caught up she saw the remains of a blush on his face.

"You painted Rachel?"

"She fell asleep. She looked so cute. Only I don't think Jack Bellingham will want that painting in the gallery."

Kate laughed.

"Don't tell Rachel. I want to finish before I show her."

"Okay. Er…Dan?"

He glanced at her.

"Don't tell anyone at work about what happened with Richard."

He nodded. "You sure you're all right? I still can't believe he did that."

They stepped aside as a power-walker shot ahead of them, his bottom wobbling like two bags of jelly.

"Were you all mad I hadn't told you about the wedding?" Kate asked.

"Lucy and Rachel huffed a bit. I wish you had, Kate. We'd have been there for you."

She shot him a grateful glance, but was glad they hadn't witnessed her humiliation.

Kate worked at Crispies Monday to Thursday for just above minimum wage, on the basis that the tips were huge. Sometimes they were, but often they weren't. At least her hours weren't bad and she could walk to work. The café opened in the evenings as well, but Kate only worked the daytime shift. Mel, Dan's older sister, didn't like Kate and Kate wasn't fond of Mel, but Tony, the head chef and co-owner, *did* like her. He was a forty-year-old Italian who still lived with his mother and flirted like crazy with everything in a skirt, though never with Mel.

"Had a good holiday?" Tony asked when Kate walked into the kitchen.

"Lovely." Kate smiled, thinking how in all the disgust she felt for Richard, she was at least grateful he'd made her keep the wedding a secret.

"You're not any browner." Tony looked her up and down.

"Terrible weather."

"You should let me take you to Italy. The sun always shines on me. I could show you a really good time." He winked.

Kate rolled her eyes. "Tony, whoever told you that you were an Italian stallion got it wrong, You're more like a piebald pit pony."

"How insulting." He stroked his thinning hair. "I thought I was the love of your life."

"Only when you cook for me. At all other times, no."

"Oh yes, that's Richard," he grumbled.

Kate made herself keep smiling. "Not any longer."

Tony's face lit up. "Seriously? You mean I'm in with a chance again? Come over here and taste my *puttanesca* sauce. I want you eating out of my hand."

"Unbelievable as this may sound, Tony, I'll have to decline. It's eight fifteen in the morning. I'd rather have a coffee."

"You're breaking my heart."

"I thought Lois did that?"

Lois was another of the waitresses who teased Tony.

"You all break my heart. Except Mel," he muttered. "She breaks my spirit."

Kate laughed.

"Stop wasting time chatting and get on with what you're supposed to be doing," Mel snapped from behind them.

Tony started banging pans and Kate retreated to the dining area.

* * * * *

Charlie apologized to James Kesner, the director, for his behavior at the last audition. He didn't grovel, nor offer any excuses. If Ethan knew he'd been drunk and high then Kesner was the one who told him, so Charlie figured he just needed to be perfect today. He shook hands with everyone in the room, toned down his megawatt smile and put everything he had into landing the role of a lifetime. Charlie performed the piece he'd prepared and ran through several pages of the script. When he'd done, Kesner leaned back in his chair and stared at him for several seconds without saying a word. Charlie's heart pounded but he met his gaze and didn't drop his eyes.

"When did you last take any sort of dope, Charlie?"

"Over a week ago."

"Alcohol?"

"The same."

"Tell me why I should have you in my movie?"

"Because I've cleaned up my act and I'm perfect for the part."

"And?"

Charlie wondered what he wanted him to say. "I admired what you did with *The Way Back* and *Rainwalker*." Not too much sucking up. "But I would have been better than Depp. He was too off the wall."

Kesner laughed. "You may be right. Okay, Charlie Storm, you're in."

For a moment, Charlie didn't react. For a few elongated seconds, he didn't grasp he'd been offered the role. Then he smiled. He'd done it. He wanted to jump up and down and scream. He supposed kissing the guy was a bad idea. Polite thanks, on the other hand, should be totally acceptable.

"Thank you. I appreciate you giving me another chance."

"Don't let me regret it. My assistant will send a contract to your agent today and email you later with a shooting schedule. We have a pre-production meeting coming up soon in Ireland. Looking forward to working with you, Charlie."

Charlie shook hands again with everyone, walked out of the airport meeting room and then rushed around looking for the Gents so he could throw up. His stomach eventually moved from rock and roll to a slow waltz.

When he'd pulled himself back together, he took his phone from his pocket. The first person he should have called was Ethan.

"Kate? I got it! Kesner just told me. I made some crap comment about being better than Depp and he laughed and gave me the part. Christ, I can't believe it."

"Well done, Charlie," Kate whispered.

"Why are you whispering?"

"I can't let Mel catch me on the phone. Hang on. I'll hide somewhere."

Charlie tapped his foot, excitement bubbling through every pore.

"Okay, safe now," Kate said.

"Are you going to tell me how great I am?"

"Didn't anyone else show up for the audition?" she asked.

His heart sang. He loved the way she reacted to him. "Of course they did."

"People who were actually trying out for the part?"

When Charlie thought about that, he realized he didn't know.

"Hey, stop thinking," Kate said. "You know it gives you a headache. You got the part because you're going to be great in the role. Let's face it. You're a fantastic, talented, wonderful human being. You're too good for this film. With your unrestrained energy, brutal power and visionary futurism, Kesner should be thanking you. They're lucky to have an actor with your incredible artistic integrity."

"I knew I'd impressed you."

Kate guffawed.

"There are quite a few love scenes," he said in a silky voice.

"Well, that's why you got the part. This last week was one long audition. Kesner and I go way back. He wanted me to be sure you were up to the job."

"And was I?"

"At times."

"Hmm." Charlie wished she was there. He wanted to kiss her, kiss the smile he knew was on her face.

"What are you doing to celebrate?" she asked.

"Taking you to bed tonight around nine?"

"Ah, Bed, that new restaurant in Knightsbridge where they get out the whips if you spill ketchup on the table?"

He laughed.

"Sorry, I'm already going out tonight," Kate said.

And disappointment swamped his happiness. "Where?"

"I'm helping at Rachel's art gallery."

"When will you be back?"

"Eleven, I think."

"Okay." He'd be there at five past eleven.

"Where are you now?" Kate asked.

"In the Gents at Edinburgh airport. Where are you?"

"In the Ladies at Crispies." Kate chuckled.

"I've just thrown up."

"I've just had a wee."

He laughed. "While I've been talking to you?"

"The toilet was too tempting and I don't get many breaks."

"Kate? I phoned to tell you first."

"Don't tell Ethan. He'll be jealous."

"Bye, Mermaid."

"Bye, Hippo."

Charlie didn't ring Ethan until he'd booked a seat on the next flight to London. Ethan had him on a flight at four and Charlie didn't want to wait that long. A few words charming the desk clerk, a couple of autographs, and he was now due to leave in a little over an hour. He settled down in a corner of the executive lounge with a newspaper, coffee and a chicken tikka sandwich and rang Ethan.

"Hi Ethan, I got it."

"Thank God."

"I meant the whisky. I didn't get the part."

"Charlie, don't joke."

"Yeah, I got it," Charlie said, his voice overflowing with happiness.

"I knew you could do it. Well done. When's the contract coming?"

"Kesner's assistant will send it today."

"Don't fuck things up now," Ethan said. "You don't need to get drunk or high to celebrate."

"Nope, not anymore."

There was a slight pause. "So the rumors about you and Jody Morton are true?"

Charlie slammed his cup back on the table and splashed coffee over the newspaper.

"I told you I never slept with her. She wanted to, but I wasn't interested. Not my type."

"I don't believe you."

Charlie sighed.

"You're not taking her to the AIDS dinner?" Ethan asked.

"Is she going?" Charlie asked. "I didn't even know she was in the UK."

"Who are you taking?"

"No one. I *was* taking Jennifer Ward, but I don't think she'll be available."

Charlie heard Ethan mutter under his breath.

"So, who are you currently fucking?" Ethan asked.

Charlie stayed silent.

"Come on, Charlie. I know you too well. If you're off drink and dope, you've found something else to do. Actress or model?"

Charlie pressed his lips together.

"I'm your fucking publicist. I'm supposed to know. Actress or model?"

"Neither."

"Singer?"

"She's a waitress."

"Oh shit."

Charlie's good mood evaporated. "Fuck off, Ethan. I really like her."

"You really like everyone while you're fucking them," Ethan snapped back.

"Kate's different."

"I suppose she's pretending not to be impressed that you're Charlie Storm?"

"Actually, she's not impressed," Charlie said.

"Jesus, Charlie. Get a life. You are who you are. You know what this world is like. You can't trust anyone. This is the wrong time to start a relationship with a nobody. You're supposed to be committed to your job, not to shagging a fucking waitress."

Charlie struggled to find the off switch on his phone, his fingers shook so much.

Chapter Eleven

৪০

By the time Kate reached Bellingham Gallery, it was almost seven. An incident on the underground had left lines closed and everything chaotic. She hoped to get a lift back to Greenwich with Rachel and Dan, but if it didn't look as though they planned to set off by ten, Kate would go back alone. She knew Charlie would come.

The closed sign was up, but the door opened at a push and the bell tinkled.

"Lock up after you," Rachel called.

Kate couldn't see anyone. "How do you know it was me?"

"The latest piece by Gustav Mazov. A hole. Look." Rachel poked her head though a huge red canvas hanging in the center of the gallery and pulled a grotesque face.

Kate gave a mock scream.

Dan emerged from the office, holding a bottle of wine. He looked at Rachel and sighed. "I wish I could say it improves the artist's work, but I can't. Want a drink, Kate?"

"Just a very large glass."

"You've guessed what pleasures lie ahead, then?" He pulled a face similar to Rachel's.

Kate took the glass from his hand. "When are you two next going out?"

"Meal tomorrow," Dan said with a goofy smile.

"Well, you can go to the pub tonight, if we do this quickly." Kate didn't add that she'd like them to pick a pub in Greenwich so they could drive her home.

Bellingham Gallery catered mainly for London tourists, but Rachel used one annex to showcase more innovative work. Her first exhibition had taken place a few weeks after they'd moved

149

into the apartments in Greenwich. Rachel invited Lucy and Kate to help make the gallery look busy and to pretend to buy paintings. Dan was there because one of his pieces hung on the wall. That evening, he'd eavesdropped on a conversation between Kate and Jack Bellingham and afterwards Dan had dragged Kate past every painting, demanding her opinion. Fifteen minutes later, he accused her of being a professional art critic and frequently pestered her to find out how she knew so much. Kate hadn't told him.

"Number one on the list," Rachel said, pen poised, clipboard ready. "Go slow so I can write down every word."

"It's called Wall." Dan read from the label.

Kate ran her eyes over the piece. A medium-sized oil on canvas, showing part of a deep red brick wall with a brilliant blue, cloudless sky as the background. She took a deep breath.

"Okay. The cropped image is offered as a contradiction, a balance between the intimately familiar and the clinically abstract. The backdrop one of static energy with the suggestion of suspended dysfunction in the way the bricks are aligned. The sense of dislocation, arising from the incompleteness of the image, poses questions about the functionality of everyday objects."

Rachel scribbled. Dan gawped.

"I still can't see how you do this," he said. "It's like listening to someone spout Korean. Are you sure you didn't study Modern Art, History of Art, Art of bullshit?"

Kate laughed. "No. I left school at sixteen."

"Then you must be an artist."

"I told you, I can't paint a circle."

"Stop disturbing her," Rachel said. "I don't care how you do it, Kate. Keep going."

"Do you like the painting?" Dan asked.

"No, simplistic crap," Kate said and moved on.

The next one featured a young child pulling off or putting on her clothes. The child's head was covered by the garment.

"Ready for Bed," Dan muttered.

"I like this. It's cute," Rachel said.

Kate swallowed hard. "Is it?"

"Don't you think?" Rachel looked confused.

Kate bit her lip for a few moments before she spoke. "A shocking and unsettling image, where bold, sweeping brushwork is used to match the blurring of the distinction between innocence and sexuality. The sense of catastrophe waiting to happen is echoed in the way color is compartmentalized, so that the painting appears to descend into dysfunctional breakdown."

"Another dysfunctional?" Dan asked.

"Aren't all artists dysfunctional? Anyway, I like the word." Kate grinned.

"But not the painting?" Rachel asked again.

"Not much. Nicely painted though." Kate moved on.

"I don't think I like it anymore," Rachel said.

Kate turned to her. "Don't say that, Rachel. If you see it as cute, that's fine. It's what it means to you that's important. You shouldn't be influenced by what I think."

"So remind me why we're here?" Dan asked. "What's the point in a catalogue?"

"Because what Kate says gives the pieces authenticity," Rachel said.

"You mean it makes them sound better than they are?" Dan raised his eyebrows.

"And you can charge more for them." Kate moved to the next work.

"Careful what you say," Dan said.

Kate stood in front of one of his portraits. "A talented new artist reveals his sparkle and irreverent style in its full, explosive glory. The subject's mischievous state of mind is paralleled in the twisted brush stokes and exquisite detail given to the eyes. How about that?"

"I love you," Dan said.

Kate grinned. "Who is it?"

Dan pretended to thump her. The portrait was of his sister, Mel.

"I haven't finished," Kate said as Rachel started to move on. "But beneath the surface lies a confused individual, whose face both frightens and attracts. The hint of madness is subtly present."

"God, don't write that, Rachel. Mel will kill me."

"Oh, is it Mel?" Rachel asked.

Dan turned in horror, only to see her smiling.

Kate romped through the rest, particularly admiring one artist's work, where in a very dark painting of a kitchen, the single area of light issuing from a fridge had been created using a mass of silken threads. Unless you stood close, it looked painted.

"Is that it?" she asked, looking at a bare patch of wall. "Or is this *very* modern art?"

"The artist promised it would be here by tonight, but it isn't, so tough. Thanks so much for this, Kate. I know I should be doing it, but I can't come up with the right words."

"To be honest, no one ought to write about paintings. That's the whole point of them, isn't it? Images, not words. The only person who can say what they're meant to be is the one who created them. Assuming they know. Maybe you're right about the child getting ready for bed. Maybe that's just what it is, painted by a loving father or mother. But maybe it was painted by a pedophile."

Rachel paled. "Goodness, I hope not."

"The problem is half the time these modern artists have no idea what they're doing. Isn't that true, Dan?" Kate asked.

"I always know."

"That's because you do portraits," Rachel said.

"A painting should be interesting whenever you look at it, not just the first time you see it, otherwise what's the point having it on your wall?" Kate said.

"How do you get your ideas?" Dan asked. "When you were a kid, did your parents drag you round the Tate and the National Gallery?"

"I don't know where I get the ideas. I open my mouth and crap comes out. Are we done?"

It wasn't as simple as that, but Kate had no intention of telling the truth, that her interest in art was a way of keeping an eye on her father.

* * * * *

"Delivery for a Miss Mermaid," Charlie sang into the intercom.

He grinned in anticipation. The door-release buzzed and he went in. It had just gone eleven thirty. Late, but not too late. He'd been caught up in a meeting with a financial advisor, though Charlie handled most of his own business affairs. His economics degree ought to be used for something.

"I didn't think you'd come." Kate leaned over the banister, watching him running up.

"I wasn't going to. You're so mean, going out tonight. I don't like you anymore."

He made a grab for her and Kate ran.

"Fine. Piss off then," she shouted.

She tried to shut her door, but Charlie put his foot in the way and forced it open. He grabbed her, pushed her inside and thrust her back against the door, slamming it shut in the process. He pressed his lips against hers, groaning into her mouth. They kissed so long that when they broke apart, they simultaneously gasped, as though they'd popped to the surface after a deep free-dive. Charlie stroked her cheek.

"Christ, Kate. I've missed you. You didn't really want me to piss off, did you?"

"Not yet."

He stood upright and looked at her. "So how was your day?"

"Perfect now."

He gave a slow smile.

"And apart from landing the role of a lifetime, how was yours?"

"India is out of hospital and I haven't had a drink, a cigarette, a line of coke or a fuck."

"And which of those were you offered?"

"Only the drink."

Charlie took Kate's hand and moved into the apartment. "Done any of our jigsaw?"

"No."

He picked up a square of material from the counter top and raised his gaze to Kate's.

"Have you cut up your wedding dress?"

Kate's eyes sparkled. "Want to see what I've done with it?"

Charlie thought he probably would.

"Help yourself," Kate said and held out her hands as if she were balancing trays of drinks on her palms.

She wore a little gray denim skirt and pink cotton V-necked T-shirt. Nothing on her feet. Charlie's fingers hovered.

Kate laughed. "Make a decision."

He glared and then lifted her top over her head. Charlie felt as though he lay in the dentist's chair with all the moisture being sucked out of his mouth. He was even in discomfort, though in an area somewhat lower than his mouth.

"What do you think?" Kate asked.

Charlie was barely capable of thought. His reaction to Kate was pure reflex. His already perky cock, became perkier. His heart rate doubled and his need for her quadrupled. The strapless bra was a frilly beaded thing that actually didn't seem to hide anything. In fact it seemed to be offering him Kate's luscious nipples. His fingers unzipped her skirt and tugged it down. A deep groan rumbled from somewhere inside him. Her panties were a scrap of heart-shaped fabric with three thin satin strings pulled away either side to curve over her hips. In the center of the fabric was a little hippo.

He opened his mouth and nothing came out. She stood with her hands fidgeting, her hair all messy and a nervous smile on her lips. Charlie sighed.

"Say something nice or else," Kate said.

Charlie whipped his shirt over his head and dropped it. "Something nice or else. You are soooo bad. You've spoiled my surprise." He toed off his shoes and unbuttoned his pants. "Want to unzip me?"

Her fingers slid into the top of his pants, brushed the tip of his cock and she laughed. "What happened to your boxers, Rambo?"

"I was so nice and smooth after that shaving, I thought it would be interesting to go commando."

"And was it?" Kate slid her hand deeper inside his pants and wrapped her fingers around him.

"Not until now."

She led him to the bedroom by his dick.

"I've been thinking about you all day," he said. "I was on my best behavior. Kesner really liked me. I even remembered to say thank you."

Kate pulled his pants the rest of the way down and he stepped out of them.

"I kept imagining you shouting at me if I fucked things up. I wanted to…"

"Wanted to what?"

"Wanted to make you proud of me," he mumbled. "Wanted to show you I've changed."

She cupped her face with his hands. "I didn't know the old you. I only know the Charlie who made my nose bleed, the guy with sad eyes I thought was a shark, the Charlie who saved me. I don't know the Charlie who smoked too much, drank too much and took too many drugs, because you haven't done any of those things with me. And I quite like the Charlie who fucks too much, so long as he only does that with me."

"I want you so much I'm scared," he whispered.

"I'm scared I want you so much," Kate whispered back.

He slid his fingers under the sides of her panties and squeezed her butt, tugging her to him, rocking her onto his cock before edging her to the wall. Charlie pressed his lips against Kate's and dived into her mouth. The heat he found there surged through his body and his toes curled. The smell of her drove him wild, the taste of her was almost more than he could bear. Charlie kissed his way down her neck and licked a path to her nipples while he brushed his thumbs under the half-cups of the bra. He discovered a hidden fastening at the front, flicked it open and the material fell to the floor.

"Oh God, your breasts," he said with a groan.

"Not very big."

"Just completely perfect—the shape, weight, feel and taste of those raspberry-tipped nipples."

"Why do men like breasts so much?"

Charlie looked up at her with his mouth fastened around her nipple. He let her loose with a gentle pop and licked his lips. "You're asking me to think when every cell in my body is working toward achieving those lovely few moments of not thinking?"

She laughed. "Yes."

"Christ. You're so demanding." Charlie nipped his way down her body, punctuating each sentence with a kiss. "I have no fucking idea why men like breasts." Kiss. "Because they don't have them?" Kiss. "Because most women hide them and they want what they can't have?" Kiss. "Because they feel so great?" Kiss. "Because it turns women on when men suck them?" Kiss. He'd reached her navel.

Charlie pulled her panties off as he circled his tongue around her neat bellybutton. When he rubbed his cheek against her, Kate moaned. He dropped down farther to nuzzle against her inner thighs. She was already wet. He could see her folds glistening. Her pussy seemed to shimmer as he watched. Kate groaned as he kissed her between her legs, his tongue slipping through the valleys of her sex until it found the hood of her clit. Charlie's cock pulsed as he sucked.

He settled his knees more comfortably on the floor and pinned her against the wall, his hands on her hips. A few moments of fluttering his tongue over the tight pearl of her clit and she came against his mouth with a quiet cry and a flood of cream. Charlie lapped and sucked and felt her orgasm roll through him, from his mouth all the way to his cock, which released a spurt of pre-cum in response. He kissed her back down, held her until she stopped trembling and then kissed his way back up Kate's body.

"More," Kate whispered against his mouth.

Charlie smiled and turned her to face the wall. He angled his cock so it slid between her legs, along the folds of her sex, wrapped in her wet heat until his hips were shoved tight against her backside. She wriggled and tightened her thighs around him and he hissed.

"Don't move," he said. "Keep still a minute."

Not that Charlie thought Kate keeping still would make any difference. Every part of him ached for her. He ran his hands over her shoulders, loving the satiny feel of her skin. His eyes lingered on the scar, wondering when she'd trust him enough to tell him how she got it. Then he slid his fingers up the front of her body to fondle her breasts. Charlie groaned as the tips of her nipples grew tighter under his touch. Even as he told himself not to, he rocked his hips against her, letting his cock slip and slide in her slickness.

"Oh you feel so good," he whispered.

He wished she was on the Pill, wished he could just thrust inside her without having to put on an overcoat. The broad head of his cock nudged against the entrance to her body and Charlie found himself bending his knees so he could push up and slip inside her. *So easy. Just push.*

While he still had a few functioning brain cells, he yanked himself away. She tempted him beyond reason. Kate wrapped her trembling fingers in his and led him to the bedroom. She lay on one side and watched as he reached into the bedside cupboard for a condom and peeled it over his cock.

"I always think I want to play for hours and then I can't help myself," he said with a groan of frustration. "It's all your fault."

She laughed. Charlie growled and pushed her onto her back. He lifted her legs in the air and levered them toward her chest. When he looked down at her, he groaned.

"Oh God. You need locking up," he whispered.

Keeping hold of her ankles, he spread her legs. Charlie knew his cock was the same, but with no hair to blur the edges, he looked bigger and felt bigger. His eyes closed despite his efforts to keep them open as he slid straight into her. *Down, down, down.* It was like diving into a deep pool, the heady sensation of senses being totally overwhelmed.

Kate began to make little mewling noises, and all hopes Charlie had of taking this slow began to evaporate. Within three long strokes into her, he'd deteriorated to short, frantic bursts, dragging his cock in and out of her tight channel. His fingers gripped her ankles as he thrust. He could feel her pussy tightening around his cock, pulling at him when he withdrew, and Charlie's last fingertip hold on the cliff edge slipped. He powered into her like a super-stud porn star he'd once watched and had decided they'd speeded up.

Maybe not.

"Oh Christ," Charlie groaned, "I can't stop."

"Think…I want…you to?"

The force of his mounting climax left him hovering between bliss and pain, but he was seriously incapable of slowing. He felt Kate come and she bucked into him, her head thrashing from side to side. About the only bit of her she could move.

"Charlieeee," she wailed.

His balls on fire, Charlie fell into the thrall of relentless, hot, slick friction. His muscles grew taut and his heart rate flew off the scale. He had a sudden, momentary fear that what he and Kate had was too good, that to be this perfect wasn't allowed. Something would go wrong. Then everything rushed together, sucking him inside a physical and mental vortex and he jetted into her with loud cries of pleasure.

After the last delectable shudder had slipped from his body, Charlie pulled out of Kate and eased her legs straight. He dealt with the rubber and then pressed his face next to hers. His limbs still trembled and his breathing remained jerky.

"Did I hurt you?" he whispered. "Sorry."

"More," Kate whispered and snuggled closer.

Charlie wrapped his arms and legs around her. Along with the feeling of deep sexual satisfaction, he was afraid. He feared he'd fuck this up because that's what he always did. No matter how much he didn't want to ruin it, that's what would happen.

He continued to hold her in his arms long after she'd fallen asleep.

* * * * *

Kate's eyes flashed open when Charlie shook her.

"What is it?"

"No...I want," he gasped.

"What?" She reached up to stroke his face.

"I had a bad dream," he whispered. "I dreamt I'd lost you. Oh God, don't leave me. Don't leave me."

She tugged him into her arms. "It's okay, Hippo. I've got you."

"You're mine."

"I'm yours," Kate said.

"I don't want to fuck this up. You mean so much to me."

The lump in Kate's throat was hard to swallow. She'd thought she could never trust anyone again after Richard but Charlie was impossible to resist.

His hand slipped between her legs. The moment he began to rub her clit between his finger and thumb, her body responded. He stared at her intently, watching her face as he brought her off. Kate felt like something was expanding inside her, a thundery storm on a summer's day, promising lightning, dark clouds rolling overhead until the weight of the air made it hard to breathe.

"You are so hot and wet and sweet," he said with groan. "I love making you come. Tell me what it feels like."

"Oh God, I don't know if I can."

"Try."

"It starts off warm and soothing but right from the outset, there's that sense of it building toward something." She gulped. "A sort of an intense…tightening in my belly." Words began to run. "If you change what you do, the angle, the pressure, that changes something inside me too, might speed up, might slow down but it keeps coming. Like a mushroom cloud from an explosion or a big wave rushing into the shore. Nothing can stop it and you know it's going to swamp you, engulf you and you want it to but don't want it to, not yet, so you run and run only you can't do anything to make it not happen."

She released a long groan as Charlie's persuasive fingers pulled her into the heart of darkness, only for her to be hurled back into the light, fast as an arrow.

"Oh God, Charlie, Charlie."

Kate stiffened and shuddered as her body tensed and relaxed in the tenacious grip of her orgasm. Then his lips were all over her face, kissing and kissing and Kate knew she was going to die when he left her because she didn't want to live without him.

He threw off the sheet and straddled her, his knees either side her hips, his hand on his erect cock. His eyes looked black in the dim light.

"Kate." He breathed her name in a long sigh.

"Yes."

"Oh God. I want to come all over you. I want to fuck your navel, fuck your breasts, fuck your sweet mouth. I want to shoot my cum all over your belly. I want to rub it into your skin. I want you to taste me. I want to taste you."

Kate reached out and snagged the bottle of oil she'd used before. She trickled some between her breasts, shoved the bottle out of the way and then pressed her breasts together. Charlie groaned. He moved further up the bed and slid the rounded head of his cock into the crease Kate had made. The long, shuddering sigh as she held her breasts tight around him, told her she'd got this right. This was another first for her, another act researched for the phone sex. A lot of men had this fantasy and this time, with Charlie, it turned her on too.

"Oh fucking hell," Charlie gasped.

He was the one shunting his hips back and forth but Kate controlled the movement of his cock. Tight, loose, squeeze, release and she let him surge forward so she could lick his crest.

"Fuck, fuck, fuck."

He pulled back and crouched as silvery ribbons of cream spurted over her. Charlie flung his head back and gasped his release, bathing her belly in warm, thick cum. *He is so beautiful.*

Charlie eased his knees down onto the bed and hovered over her. He swirled a finger in the pearly fluid and trailed it around her nipple. Kate scooped up a smear and licked her finger slowly.

"I wish it was inside you. I wish I could have come inside you." He smeared his hand over her stomach. "Never wash again."

"That won't be very hygienic."

He bent his head and licked the nipple he'd coated. "Is the romance dead already?"

Never, Kate thought. What she and Charlie had would never die.

Chapter Twelve

ಏ

Kate hadn't thought Charlie was awake, but as she closed the door of her wardrobe, he opened his eyes.

"What you doing?" he mumbled.

"I have to get ready for work."

His eyes opened. "This minute?"

Kate smiled. "Well, if I skip breakfast, don't dry my hair and run all the way there, you could cuddle me a bit longer."

"Why do you have to go to work?" He moaned and shifted to try to grab her.

Kate stepped back. "Well, let's see. Because I need to earn money, because they're expecting me and I don't let people down, because I quite like work although one of my bosses is a pain, because if I have any more sex with you, I'll be crippled for life."

"No, don't go. Come back to bed. I want to lick you all over."

"That sounds lovely, but the shower was quicker and I have to go to work."

He leaned up on his elbow and glared at her. "You washed me off."

"Charlie! I can't go to work with your cum all over my chest."

"Why not?"

She sighed and rolled her eyes.

"Oh all right," he grumbled. "Give me a kiss then."

"Promise you'll let me go afterwards."

"Absolutely."

Kate looked at him, sprawled on his front across her bed, the sheet wrapped around his slender hips, and her heart flipped.

"Charlie, I can't *just* kiss you."

"Well, I can *just* kiss you. Promise. Come here."

Kate moved to the edge of the bed and he looked up at her and groaned.

"God, what are you wearing? Little black skirt, white blouse and black rimmed glasses? You look like a schoolgirl. This is not going to take me long."

"You make that sound so enticing." Kate leaned over and licked his lips.

"Toothpaste. Cheating," he whispered.

He ran his hand up her leg, under her skirt, along her thigh and slipped his fingers under the material of her panties, wrenching them down her legs.

"Oh, pink lace. Now you definitely can't go to work yet."

"I'll be back in five seconds." Kate stepped out of her pants and slipped back to the bathroom.

When she returned, Charlie leaned back against a pile of pillows, a twinkle in his eyes, his hand gently stroking his erect cock. Kate briefly debated stripping, decided she didn't have time and knelt at the foot of the bed. She put one hand around the root of his cock to keep it upright, wrapped her lips around his tip and braced herself with her other hand.

"Jesus Mary Mother of Christ," Charlie gasped and almost jerked her off the bed.

Mouthwash works then. Kate giggled and swallowed by accident, though most of the green liquid trickled down his cock and onto the bed.

"Very clever, Kate. I'll get my own back." He shuddered. "Oh fuck. You wait and see. Bloody hell. When you least expect it. Oh Christ, that feels good."

"Want to try – ?"

"Yes," he said.

Kate held back her smirk. "To go without sex for a day."

His face fell and then he smiled. "What were you going to say?" He squirmed around and pinned her on her back.

"Try and go without sex for a week, but that's too cruel." Kate gave a heavy sigh.

Charlie nodded. "I can't expect you to last that long."

She laughed. His fingers flipped open the buttons on her shirt.

"Oh, pink bra. Nice. I'm nearly deflected but not quite. Try what?"

"Deep-throating."

He groaned and yanked down on his balls. "Not in front of the kids."

"I've never done it but I've read about it. The phone—"

"Sex?" he asked.

Kate nodded. She reached to drag the pillows down the bed and then lay on her back so her head hung over them. "Don't be too enthusiastic or I'll bite."

He let out a gurgled whimper. "I won't move."

"Knees here. Cock here," Kate said.

Charlie's eyes were so wide, Kate felt her heart lurch. She thought he'd probably done this loads of times. He slid his hand inside her bra and played with her nipple, while she licked his cock. The wetter it was, the easier this would be.

He started to breathe more heavily and Kate took her hand off his cock and put them both on his hips. He stared straight into her eyes as she slid his cock into her mouth.

"Oh my God, Kate. You have no idea."

She didn't try to take him too far but concentrated on pulling him in and then pushing him out, letting her tongue slide along his underside, letting the curve of his cock match the curve of her throat. When he pulled out, a trail of saliva still linked them together and Kate felt a flood of cream gush from her pussy.

"Sweet, sweet," Charlie gasped as he slid back and forth.

The mouthwash had desensitized her a little but she concentrated on not trying too hard, and the fact that she remained in control and not Charlie allowed her to relax. A moment later Charlie bottomed out on her face. He shifted his knees slightly and snatched back a little control.

The fingers of one hand stroked her neck and he grabbed one of her hands and put it there.

"Feel me...in your throat," he gasped. "Oh fuck. Kate. Angel. No one's ever..."

Kate waggled her tongue as much as she could. Not that there was much room, and swallowed. She knew he was close to coming. His cock felt different.

"N-now," he gasped.

Kate swallowed hard and dragged his hips onto her face. His cum shot straight down her throat and she almost felt cheated. Charlie gabbled incoherently. He was doing his best not to thrust too violently and Kate stroked his backside as he shunted in and out of her mouth, his breathy cries of pleasure sending echoing blasts of heat through her.

When he finally pulled out, he was shaking so hard, he collapsed on his back. "Can't speak," he grunted.

Kate levered herself off the bed and refastened her shirt. She drank half the glass of water by the side of the bed and pulled on the pink panties. He'd been fairly quick, but if she didn't get a move on, she was going to be late.

"Thank you seems a bit inadequate," he said. "And I haven't made you come five times."

Kate frowned. "Only five?"

"I seem to have lost feeling in all four limbs. Jesus, Kate, that was unbelievable."

"All that practice with a banana worked then?"

His eyes widened. "You're kidding."

"Er...yeah. What if it broke? I might choke."

"So, I'm..."

A little grub nibbled at her. "I told you that you were."

She headed for the door.

"Kate? I've got to go somewhere tonight, so I'll give you a call, okay?" he asked.

She put on her shoes. By the time she turned back, her smile was in place.

"Okay. Make sure you pull the door closed when you leave."

Dan wasn't waiting for her downstairs to provide a buffer, so Kate ran most of the way to work. She had to admit a degree of self-interest in the deep-throating of Charlie. For all his protestations of how much he thought about her, Kate still felt like Cinderella. Charlie could have his pick of starlets. Why would he want her? Well, maybe if sex with her was great it might make a difference. Except it hadn't. He was going somewhere tonight. Fine, except why hadn't he told her where he was going? Kate hated to be jealous but she couldn't help it.

Kate had hoped Mel wouldn't be gracing the café with her presence, but her boss stood inside the door, looking at her watch as Kate rushed in.

"Sorry," Kate said, panting, trying to ignore the stitch in her side.

"Something come up?" Mel snapped.

"Yes, sorry." Kate bit the insides of her cheeks to hold back the giggle.

"You can stay twenty minutes at the end of your shift and make up the time."

"Right."

Kate worked hard, trying not to think. She wiped tables, refilled salt and pepper pots, folded napkins, and once customers arrived, served them. Even as she struggled to empty her mind, all she could think about was Charlie. It would end badly. How could it not? They lived in different worlds. She wasn't his type. He was using her. She understood his paranoia over the press, but surely they could go out somewhere together? A proper date. It would be dark in a cinema. No one would recognize him.

Was he ashamed of her? Okay to fuck, but not to be seen with. But the sex was fantastic. The best she'd ever had. Something about them matched, felt right, although Kate knew all relationships were like that in the beginning. Mad, passionate bouts of shagging until things settled down and the guy started to fart in bed, belch in your face, or roll over and go to sleep instead of cuddling. Would she and Charlie even get that far?

Kate couldn't help but keep coming back to the fact that he hadn't told her where he was going that night. A feeling of hurt morphed into an annoyance that she wasn't invited. Why hadn't he told her?

"Is there anyone in there?" Tony knocked on her head with a wooden spoon. "Food's ready for table five."

"Sorry."

Maybe she'd built this whole thing into too big a deal, but she couldn't help it. Had she thought she could sleep with him and not get emotionally involved? She'd hardened her heart long before Richard and still been taken in. Now Charlie had snuck in while her defenses were down. They were having a relationship whether they meant to or not.

The terrible, awful, wonderful thing was that Kate knew exactly what was wrong. She'd fallen in love. That was supposed to be a good thing, but not for Kate. She was frightened. Allowing herself to love meant giving someone the power to hurt her. And Kate had been hurt so many times, because people always let her down. They said they loved her and then they left her. Or hit her. Or threw her out. Or walked out. Or died. So it was better not to fall in love. Better and safer. Only it was too late. Too late for Kate, anyway. People fell in love with Charlie all the time. She was one in a long line. It wouldn't last. But oh how she wanted it to.

* * * * *

Charlie failed to call that night. Kate sat staring at her phone, her mobile by her ear, knowing she was an idiot but unable to do anything about it. She lay in bed wide awake, waiting for the buzzer to sound. It didn't. When there was no call the next morning, Kate got the message.

She'd never chased anyone in her life. She wasn't stupid. Not really. She struggled with enough problems without leaving herself wide open to rejection. Kate unplugged her phone, switched off her mobile and left it in her apartment. The thing was a waste of time anyway. No one rang her. She had no one to ring. If it hadn't been for the fact that it was a pay-as-you-go, Kate wouldn't have bothered with it.

Then, late in the afternoon while she worked, another thought struck her, one that made her stumble and drop a bowl of apple and blackberry crumble, prompting a tirade from Mel. What if he'd gone back to the beach? He'd told her he'd got the job, but he was an actor, what if he'd lied, what if something had gone wrong? Kate's stomach churned. Now she was desperate to phone Charlie and she couldn't. Without her mobile, she didn't have his number.

When Kate returned to the kitchen with the mop, Lois perched on a stool by the window reading the newspaper while Tony stared at her legs.

"*Phwooar*," Lois groaned.

"Thinking of me again?" Tony asked.

"No, Charlie Storm. He's so good-looking he ought to be shot. Then I could stuff him and stick him on my wall."

Tony muttered under his breath and went back to pounding pizza dough. Kate edged over to Lois.

"What do you think, Kate? Fancy him?" she asked.

"Who wouldn't?" Kate stared at a picture of a smiling Charlie, his arm wrapped round a beautiful redhead. "Who's he with?"

"Jody Morton, that American actress. They were at some charity do. It says she's recently split up with her boyfriend. I thought she was supposed to be marrying that guy out of *Lord of the Rings*? Didn't take her long to find somebody else, did it? Don't they look perfect together?"

Kate's swollen, suffering heart lay squashed under her ribs.

"Still, the likes of us would never stand a chance. They keep to their own. Nice to dream though."

Kate knew gossip and rumor sold more papers than the truth. But the photograph hurt. Most likely the picture meant nothing. It still hurt.

At least she knew he hadn't killed himself.

* * * * *

Kate arrived home, exhausted by her attempts to suppress thoughts about Charlie. She saw him everywhere she looked, in everything she touched. His face when she teased him. His face when he came. His lovely smile. Surges of pain spread through her body like a rampaging grass fire. She checked her mobile, but he hadn't called, left a voice mail or texted. She switched it off again. Kate could have called him, but she hung on to the last vestiges of her pride, left the landline disconnected and clicked off her buzzer. Now, she didn't want to speak to him. She'd stamp out the flames while she still could.

A slice of cheese on toast in her hand, she went to sit on her balcony. Even though she'd accepted her future could never be what she wanted, her dreams made life bearable, a way of escaping a grim reality. When she'd been taken into care, Kate made the mistake of revealing her dreams to others, not realizing it gave them ammunition to tease and hurt her. She learned to keep things to herself and live in her own world.

It hadn't been so long ago that she started to believe what she thought would be a miserable future could be changed. Kate accepted money she'd previously refused so she could buy a place of her own. She'd resisted for a long time but realized she was punishing herself as well. What was the point of that?

With her own place and the nearest to friends she'd ever found with Rachel, Lucy and Dan, plus a regular job, even in a little café, life had looked brighter. But she'd allowed Richard to hurt her and now Charlie had swum into her life. One photo of him dancing with a beautiful woman had shown Kate she was still the same damaged, insecure, pathetic individual. A snapshot of a moment in time didn't have to mean anything.

But it did.

Kate was losing her hold on a world with Charlie because it was a creation of smoke, a hollow illusion. No one would ever truly love her.

* * * * *

Charlie felt control of his life slipping through his fingers and he didn't like it. He'd spent an entire day sitting in a sterile hotel room being interviewed by a succession of journalists from all over the world. He'd answered the same questions over and over. No, he was not going out with Jody Morton. No, he and Jody Morton were not having a relationship. No, Jody was not living with him. No, he'd never met her ex-fiancé.

No one believed him. The more he denied it, the smugger their smiles. But Charlie smiled too and played the charming, considerate and thoughtful guy Ethan had told him to be. When the last fawning woman journalist and her limpet gay photographer had left, Charlie slumped on the couch and farted.

"Glad you held that in," Ethan said.

"She'd have told me it was the sweetest thing she'd ever smelt. Bloody hell, I thought she was about to offer to have sex with me then and there, with you and the photographer in the room."

Ethan laughed. "And her piece on you will be the cruelest."

"I know, but I did *not* want to take her out to dinner."

"You couldn't anyway, I've arranged for you to escort Natalie Glass tonight. I've booked a table at Nobu."

Charlie groaned. "No, I'm busy."

"No, you're not, Charlie. Natalie's been told she's got the female lead in *The Green*. You two are going to be working together. I want your pictures in the papers."

"Not tonight, Ethan, please. I want to see Kate."

"I wouldn't worry about your little waitress. I think she'll have realized by now you're out of her league."

Charlie sat up. "What do you mean?"

Ethan threw him the paper.

When Charlie saw the photograph on page five, he swore. He and Jody Morton had their arms around each other and Charlie was laughing. He couldn't remember why. It wouldn't have been at anything she said. She could bore for an oil company. She'd done nothing but talk about people she knew in Hollywood and her enormous house. They'd only danced, but it didn't look as simple as that. The article with the photo didn't imply it was as simple as that either. No wonder he'd been fending off questions all day. He hadn't wanted to go to the damn event, but Ethan had insisted and now he'd managed to get back on the right side of Ethan, he wanted to stay there.

Charlie knew he could have asked Kate to go to the charity event with him. Maybe he should have, but he hadn't because she was his and he didn't want to share her. He wondered if she'd seen the photo. His arms might have been around Jody, but Kate was in his heart. Did she know that?

He wanted to call her but he couldn't find his mobile.

"Table's booked for eight. A car will pick you up and then go for Natalie," Ethan said.

"Must I?"

"You need each other."

"I'd made plans."

Ethan's mouth tightened. "Cancel them. You owe me, Charlie. You're on a knife's edge here. Your life's not yours. It's half mine and half everyone else's. The price of celebrity."

Charlie put his thumbnail between his teeth and then wrenched his finger out of his mouth. *Kate*, he thought and smiled.

Chapter Thirteen

ဆာ

On the way to work the next morning, Kate checked her mailbox. A gas bill and a stiff square card — an invitation from Rachel to the preview at Bellingham Gallery. On the other side of the invite, Rachel had written

Free booze and exquisite nibbles. Bring Hippo! xx Rachel

Dan waited for Kate on the street.

"Where is Rachel getting the exquisite nibbles?" Kate asked, as they set off through the park.

"She's making them."

Kate remembered the last preview. Given a very limited budget by her father, Rachel used cheap caterers who considered slimy mushroom vol-au-vents and overcooked sausages on sticks the height of sophistication. Rachel spent the whole evening apologizing for the food.

"I'm helping," Dan said with a grin.

"Now until you told me that, I thought it would be fine. Why don't you ask Tony to give you a hand?"

"That's a good idea. Do you think he'd have time?"

"If he gets an invite, he'll make time."

Kate dodged out of the way as a child on a bike sped toward her. Despite the early hour, there were several mothers sitting in the playground, watching their offspring torment each other.

"How are you and Rachel doing?" Kate asked.

"Great," Dan said. "I'm amazed how much we have in common. She likes vampire movies. We watched my favorite last night. *Underworld Evolution*."

That didn't sound like Rachel. "Are you sure she likes that sort of film?"

Dan's face fell. "You mean she might have just said she does?"

Kate had to chew the inside of her cheek so she didn't laugh. "Did she cower on the couch and hide her face in your shoulder?"

"Yes, but I did that as well."

Kate let the laugh out. "But I guess that wasn't because you were scared. You know the test. Does she know the five sure ways to kill a vampire?"

"Oh shit." Dan groaned.

"Don't worry. It shows how much she likes being with you. Take home a romantic comedy tonight. And flowers. Give her little surprises like that and she'll think you're wonderful."

"Is that how Hippo won your heart?"

"No, he just splashed his way in."

As Kate and Dan walked through the door, Mel handed her an envelope.

"What's this?" Kate asked. "It's not my birthday."

"Written warning for unpunctuality."

"Are you clairvoyant or something?" Kate looked at the clock. The hand tiptoed past the hour.

"That's for the other day. You'll get another one for this morning. Three and you're out."

"Mel, don't be so bloody mean. Kate waited for me today. It's my fault she's late, though to call this late is stretching it."

"You come in as a favor. It's her job. She's paid to be here on time. She shouldn't have waited for you if you were going to make her late."

Dan rolled his eyes at Kate. She knew there was nothing he could do. If Mel wanted her out, then she'd be out. Kate wondered how much more could fall apart.

She found out at four that afternoon when Charlie walked in.

Kate fled to the kitchen.

A moment later, Lois rushed through, her hands flapping in excitement like a schizoid chicken. "Oh my God. It's Charlie Storm. Sitting at one of my tables. I can't believe it. Do you think he'd mind if I took a picture of him with my mobile?"

Mel shot to the porthole window in the kitchen door and turned back to Lois, her eyes wide with delight. Kate felt sick.

"Charlie Storm in my café! Oh God. Lois, get out there and serve him."

As Lois pushed open the swing door, Mel started punching numbers on her phone. Kate picked up an order from a tight-lipped Tony and took it through. She kept her eyes away from Charlie, but listened.

"Good afternoon," Lois said, biting the nails of one hand and offering a menu with the other. "Our specials today are spinach and nutmeg—"

"Sorry," Charlie said. "Forgive me, but I'd like Kate to take my order."

"But you're sitting at one of my tables."

"Is that one of Kate's?"

Out of the corner of her eye, she saw the direction he was pointing and sighed.

"Yes."

Just for once, Kate wished she had customers at every one of her tables.

"You're a sweetheart," Charlie said.

Kate glanced round to see him beaming at Lois. She turned her back and began to clear a table. Dan sidled over.

"Do you want me to serve him?" he whispered.

"Please."

A moment later, she heard Charlie ask for her again. Dan walked past Kate and shrugged.

"Kate, could I have a word please?" Mel called from the kitchen door. The sweet tone told Kate she was in trouble.

Kate carried through a tray of dirty plates. Mel stood, hands on her ample hips, glaring at her.

"Why are you ignoring him?" Mel snapped. "Bloody well serve him. He's asked for you. He—" Mel stopped. "Why? How does he know you?"

Kate rushed out with a menu and dropped it on Charlie's table.

"Something smells good. What are the specials?" he asked.

Kate bent her head to his ear, but spoke quite clearly. "The boiled testicles served with warmed goat's blood are pretty tasty. Perhaps you'd like heart wrapped in peppered sheep gut? Or there's sliced cock in brandy sauce. Oh no, chef's out of the last one and looking for volunteers."

The old man at the next table dropped his knife on the floor with a clatter.

"Is the goat's blood fresh?" Charlie boomed.

Everything went quiet.

"Clotting nicely," Kate retorted.

"Sounds good, I'll have the balls then, with a toasted teacake and coffee." He lowered his voice. "What have I done?"

"I'll be right back with your order, sir."

Charlie watched her walk away and his heart lurched at the sight of that little black skirt and white apron and her shirt hanging out at the back. He wanted to tuck it in and run his hands over her bottom. Her hair needed combing, her collar straightening, her lips kissing. There was no brittle artificiality in the way she moved and dressed. She wasn't trying to lure him. She was just Kate. And he'd pissed her off. He sighed.

By the time Kate came out of the kitchen, the café was full, mostly with women brandishing mobiles, taking his picture. Charlie had just had his hand shaken by a woman called Mel who told him she owned the café and how delighted she was he'd come in.

Kate banged the plate down so hard in front of him that both he and the teacake jumped.

"Any jam?" Charlie asked.

Kate tossed a little plastic container of raspberry jam onto his lap, evoking a communal intake of breath from the other customers.

"Do you have strawberry?"

Charlie caught it in midair and there was a round of applause.

"Kate," Mel called. "Come. Here. Now."

Kate stomped across.

"What do you think you're doing?" Mel demanded.

"Nothing, I—"

The whole café went silent again. Kate froze and Charlie wondered what she was going to do. His gaze moved to her mouth and got stuck. Even pissed off, she filled him with desire. He wanted to shove her up against a wall with the entire length of his body and kiss her until she couldn't breathe, only he suspected she'd knee him in the balls. Charlie expected her to walk out, but she didn't. She strode over, grabbed the collar of his shirt in both fists and pressed her lips against his. She kissed him so hard, it hurt. Then she walked out.

Charlie smiled. She still wanted him.

All at once, he was mobbed by a crowd of women intent on copying Kate. The café owner elbowed them out of the way to get to his side.

"I'm so sorry. I'll sack her. I don't know what she was thinking," she said with a gasp.

Charlie could see she was thinking the same thing. She licked her lips.

"Don't sack her."

By the time he'd extricated himself from the mass of bodies and made it outside, Charlie felt fortunate all four limbs were still attached. He'd written his signature thirty-two times, seven times on body parts, and kissed the cheeks of thirty-six women, one man and a dog. Charlie wiped his lips again. The dog had been an accident—cradled in a woman's arms and dressed in a little pink outfit, with matching bonnet, he'd thought it was a baby and then it had been too late to go into reverse.

There was no sign of Kate outside, but then he hadn't expected her to hang around. He fled to his car, pursued by a determined posse. He tried to call her, but couldn't get through on her mobile or landline.

Charlie drove to Kate's apartment. He had to park on the road because she wouldn't answer her buzzer to let him in the car park. In desperation, he climbed over the security gate and took up a position below her window.

"Juliet," he shouted. "Get your skinny butt out here."

Kate hid behind the curtains, shaking her head. He was a compete lunatic. She laughed and then was cross with herself. Sliding open the glass doors, she stepped onto her balcony. She looked down and Charlie smiled when he saw her. Her heart did a reverse somersault with several twists and landed right in his hands. When he began to speak, she couldn't move.

"But soft! What light through yonder window breaks?
It is the east, and Kate is the sun.
Arise, fair sun, and kill the envious moon,
Who is already sick and pale with grief
That thou her maid art far more fair than she."

He stared up into Kate's eyes. She wanted to follow her heart and dive into his arms. His voice was so smooth and lyrical, it was like drinking nectar. The words poured out of him into her. When he'd finished Romeo's speech, he waited.

At first, Kate didn't know what to say, then she smiled. "Skinny butt?"

"Maybe I need to check. I could be wrong."

"Come up." She had the willpower of a vampire passing a blood bank.

"What have I done?" he asked as Kate opened the door of her apartment.

But when she pulled him inside and kissed him, he forgot what he'd asked.

They were both naked before they reached the bedroom. Once inside, Charlie pinned her against the wall with his weight, his breathing loud and ragged. He circled his thumb around her clit and then slid his fingers between her damp folds. While her body shook, he held her.

"Ready, steady, go," he whispered, thrilled she'd come so fast.

"You think I'm quick?" Kate asked and dropped to her knees. She wrapped her fingers around him, squeezing gently.

Charlie groaned and put his hand over hers. The pressure milked a drop of pearly moisture from the tip of his cock. Kate's tongue shot out and licked it away. He gasped and sank his fingers into her hair. She sucked him deep into her mouth, just once and then let him go. When she moved her head back, he pushed her away.

"No," Charlie said in a strangled voice. "I want to be inside you."

He pulled her to the bed and pushed her onto her back. Taking her wrists in one hand, Charlie held them above her head as he settled between her thighs, the head of his cock already part way home.

"Charlie," Kate whispered. "A condom."

The second time he'd nearly done that. He fumbled in the bedside drawer and ripped open the packet with his teeth. She made him forget. She drove him so wild he couldn't think. He slipped on the protective sheath and then pushed her wrists back over her head. Charlie drove himself into her, deep, slamming thrusts that sent them farther and farther up the bed until she was pressed against the metal headboard. Still he didn't stop, couldn't stop until the noise she made told him he was hurting her. Charlie dragged her back down the bed, folding up her legs so she could see him taking her and lunged into her again.

He kept his eyes on her face, watched her watching him. He wanted to slow down but he couldn't. He wanted to be slow and gentle. Why couldn't he make love to her like that? She made him so he couldn't think.

"Charlie, Charlie," Kate moaned his name and arched into him.

"Come with me," Charlie gasped.

He tried to hold back, managed for a few moments, but the feeling of her clenching around him was too much to resist. Charlie exploded into her like a dragster bursting off the line, the rushing pleasure fusing them together, so neither knew where one ended and the other began.

He lay shaking on top of her for a moment and then lifted himself up, so Kate could straighten her legs. Charlie flopped down again.

"Are you trying to kill me?" she asked.

He grunted. "I could ask you the same thing. I always mean to go slow, but I never can, not with you. I think I'm scared you're going to disappear."

His fingers slid up her neck, over her cheek to her lips.

"Whatever I've done, I'm sorry," he said.

"Whatever you've done, I forgive you."

He kissed her gently, brushed his lips across hers and sighed.

"I lost my phone yesterday," he said. "I'm always putting it down and forgetting where. I phoned you once I'd found it, but you had yours switched off."

"I was busy."

"What have you been doing?"

"Working."

"Doing what?" he pressed.

"Working, at work," Kate said.

"I did lose my phone, honestly. It was in the fridge."

She laughed. "And was the ice cream on the coffee table?"

"Oh, ha ha."

Kate bit her lip. "You lost your phone and I guess I've just lost my job."

"She won't sack you. I told her I'd provoked you by pinching your bum."

Kate gaped at him. "After which I kissed you?"

"Hey, it happens. They were bloody well queuing up after you stomped out. I'd have been here sooner, only I had to smooth things over for you with Mel."

"First name terms?"

"She gave me her phone number. I bet she'd answer *her* phone if I called."

Kate sighed.

"You could have rung me," he said, stroking her cheek with his fingers. "No messages from Miss Mermaid? No voice mail from my sultry siren? I could think you don't care."

It didn't escape his attention she didn't respond to that.

"I suppose I'd better ring Mel and apologize," Kate said. "I didn't even finish my shift."

"Ring her now. She'll still be in a good mood from having met me." He grinned.

Kate held the phone away from her ear while Mel yelled, slotted in "sorry" as soon as she could and finished the call.

"I've got to go in tomorrow morning to make up the time I missed today."

"She's all heart. So, what did I do?" Charlie asked, feathering her nipples with his fingers.

"Nothing."

He sighed. This was going to take work. "I couldn't remember either of your numbers without my mobile. You're not in the phone book. I checked."

"No."

Charlie waited. He'd thought this was because he hadn't rung, now he wasn't sure.

"What are you doing tomorrow night?" he asked.

"Washing my hair."

"I've been invited to a party at Armageddon. Want to go?" He nibbled her ear and Kate squirmed.

"Is there food?"

Charlie rolled onto his back and laughed. "I can't think of anyone else who would ask that." He turned to face her. "Kate, I don't want you to get hurt. If the press link you with me, they won't leave you alone. I made one film with Jody Morton, had one dance with her and they've got us planning our wedding. I don't want to share you, but I want you to come."

"So, is there food?" Kate asked again, smiling.

"Yep, and you'll be the only woman eating, because the rest of them only allow their bodies five calories a day."

"Good, all the more for me."

"I'll send a car for you, so at least we aren't seen arriving together," Charlie said.

He saw Kate ready to get uppity, so he pulled her into his arms and pressed his mouth against her ear.

"It's for your own good. Believe me, you do not want to come to the attention of the press."

"Okay."

"Good, now I want to ask you to do something else for me," Charlie said.

"I need a rest first."

"Not that...well, not yet. I want you to come with me to see my parents."

Her body tensed. He knew he'd shocked her.

"When?" Kate asked.

"Saturday."

"You need me to hold your hand?" Kate slid her fingers through his.

"Exactly that."

"All right."

"Thank you," he whispered, and kissed her on the end of her nose, sliding his lips down to her mouth.

Kate pulled away. "How do you manage that? One minute you make me so mad I want to kill you, and the next you're so helpless I'd kill anyone who tried to hurt you."

"I have a way with words," he said, keeping a straight face.

"No, I don't think it's that," Kate said.

"Then it must be the other things I can do with my mouth." He bent his head to her breast and licked her nipple.

* * * * *

Dan was waiting for Kate outside the next morning.

"Is Mel dragging you in again?" Kate asked. "How many times this week?"

"Since I'm not in the middle of painting my masterpiece, I can afford to be nice to her and at least I get fed."

"Well, walk fast. I daren't be late."

"You're lucky you still have a job."

Kate faltered and glanced at his face.

"I know you don't work on Fridays, so why have I waited for you?" Dan raised his eyebrows.

"Ah, yesterday."

"So, did you kiss him before or after he pinched your bum?"

"After. If he can take liberties, I don't see why I shouldn't."

Kate realized she and Charlie were still a secret. No one had done the math or if they had, they'd not come up with the right answer.

"Was Mel furious?" Kate asked.

"Only that he pinched your bum and not hers."

Kate made herself laugh.

Crispies was busier than usual, the hope Charlie might reappear, almost tangible. Customers looked for him, talked about him, asked about him. Mel's line—given to staff to feed customers — was that if he'd come in once, he could come in again. Kate refused to cave in to pressure from Mel to explain how she knew Charlie but it was only because they were so busy that Kate won a temporary reprieve. Mel pleaded with her to work the afternoon too and although Kate had intended to look for a new outfit to wear to Armageddon, she needed to keep Mel happy, so she stayed. Anyway, now she'd lost the cash for premium line sex chats, she really couldn't afford to buy stuff she'd only end up wearing a couple of times. Something old would have to do.

* * * * *

Ethan pressed Kate's buzzer and waited for her to answer.

"Kate? I'm Ethan Silver, Charlie's agent. Can I come up?"

"Sure."

She was waiting at her door and Ethan saw at once what Charlie liked about her. She was tall and slim, with short, cropped hair. Her large gray eyes shone in her face. She looked like a female version of Charlie — apart from the red dress. Ethan shook her outstretched hand.

"Hello," Kate said. "Come in."

"Good to meet you. You're very pretty."

Kate laughed. "Right. When did you last have your eyes tested?"

For a moment, Ethan thought her reaction genuine, but then dismissed the notion. She was out for what she could get.

"You're not what I expected," Kate said as Ethan walked into her apartment.

"Explain."

"I thought you'd be a bald, red-faced man who spoke like a lightning bolt and moved even faster, but you're taller than Charlie and you look a bit like Kevin Costner."

Ethan laughed. "I take it that's a compliment."

"Assuming I like Kevin Costner."

"Do you?"

"I might," Kate said. "So, have you come to tell me I'm un-invited to Armageddon?"

Ethan shook his head. "Not at all. My driver's on double yellow lines downstairs waiting for us. Charlie asked me to arrange a car and I thought I'd come myself and see who's done such a good job of taming him. What's your secret?"

"Say no and mean it. He's too used to having his own way."

Ethan smiled. "Clever girl. Right, go and get changed and we'll be off."

Kate's mouth tightened.

"Ah," he said. "You had changed. Sorry." He gave a wry smile. "Kate, the dress looks…lovely, but there's going to be a lot of people tonight who'll notice you're wearing something from a chain store. Show me what else you've got."

Kate led him to her bedroom and opened her wardrobe. Ethan flicked through her clothes. Not much to choose from, but the cheap cotton thing she wore was too obvious. He pulled out a green dress, a pair of jeans and a sleeveless pink top.

"Try the dress first. I'll wait in the other room."

While Kate changed, Ethan looked around the apartment. Her bedroom was fabulous, but the rest of the place was weird. How could she live with no furniture? He was surprised Charlie hadn't bought some for her. Ethan gave a short laugh. It was probably on order. He ran his hand over the sewing machine. She didn't look like a woman who sewed. Picking through the material in the boxes, he realized Kate made underwear. He found two half-finished underwire bras, one with tiny beads attached in curving swirls from the nipples, the other made of soft cream leather. They were exquisite and a flicker of lust licked Ethan's groin.

"Is this better?" Kate said behind him.

He slipped the underwear back where he'd found it and turned to look at her.

"No, try the pink top and the jeans."

"They're very old."

"That's not a problem."

Kate emerged a few moments later, but Ethan still wasn't satisfied. Nowhere near tarty enough.

"What are you wearing under that top?"

"Strapless green bra."

"Let's have a look."

Kate hesitated.

"You haven't got anything I haven't seen before," he said, though he wasn't sure that was true.

Kate peeled the top over her head.

Ethan sighed. "It looks like a bra." A fabulous lacy thing, but still a bra.

"It *is* a bra," Kate snapped.

"Did you make it?"

"Been snooping?"

"Let's see what else you have."

He pushed past into her bedroom and pulled open the top drawer. Ethan got the beginnings of an erection the moment he put his fingers on the contents. "Did you make this?" He held up a pink satin bustier smothered in tiny bows.

"Yes."

"Wear that." It wasn't what he'd intended but he had to see her wearing it. When Kate came back in, Ethan swallowed hard and tried not to look at her pert breasts. "That's better. Take a look."

Kate stood in front of the full length mirror fastened to the door of her wardrobe and blinked at her reflection.

"You look sensational," Ethan said at her shoulder. "Ragged denims and a fabulous piece of tight lingerie. A mix of casual and sophisticated. They'll all wonder who you are."

"Who am I?" Kate whispered.

"Really, you look great." He registered the confusion in her eyes and her flushed cheeks. "Doesn't Charlie say nice things to you?"

"Yes, but he expects to sleep with me."

Ethan roared with laughter. "Well, I don't, but you look great." His eyes fell to her flat, black slip-ons. "Do you have any different shoes?"

"Flip-flops?"

Ethan thought about the Jimmy Choos and Manolo Blahniks that would be on display and smiled. "Why not?"

Kate kicked off her flats and slipped her feet into red plastic thongs. Ethan looked her up and down and smiled. This hadn't been what he'd planned at all. He'd turned the look from cheap to sexy, but intriguing. He'd been aiming for slut, but maybe it didn't matter. Charlie would throw a fit when he saw her like this.

Kate thought Ethan would talk about Charlie in the car, but he was more interested in talking about her.

"So, how long have you been making lingerie?"

"Years."

"Where do you sell it?"

"I don't. It's just for me."

"Well, that bustier would sell in Harrods. Five hundred pounds at least."

"Yeah, right," Kate said and smiled.

"I have a friend who might be interested in buying some of your stuff. Why don't you make me a few samples? All sorts of material, but large sizes. Just because women are big doesn't mean they shouldn't wear sexy lingerie."

"You mean it?" Kate asked, wondering whether he was winding her up.

"Of course I mean it." He gave her his card. "Put that in your pocket and send them to me when they're done."

He leaned back against the seat and Kate waited for the interrogation to start.

"Charlie tells me you're a waitress."

"Yes, at a café in Greenwich."

"But you want to be an actress?"

"No."

"Do you sing?"

"No."

"Want to model?"

"No."

"You don't *want* to be a waitress?"

Kate rather enjoyed the surprise on his face. "Why not? It pays the bills."

"What secrets do you have in your closet, Kate Snow?"

Kate was instantly alert, prey facing predator. "I'm pure as the driven."

"So if and when the papers start sniffing, they're not going to come up with a husband and three kids or some other juicy bone?"

"No juicier than anything of Charlie's."

"What secrets does he have that I don't know about?"

Ethan might be smiling, but Kate didn't trust him. She knew his type and flattery didn't work on her. She leaned toward him. "Don't tell him I told you, but he can shoot this strange sticky stuff out of his er…fingers and fly from building to building. Oh no, hang on, that might be Spiderman. I get so confused."

Ethan chuckled. "Anything else?"

"You'd have to ask him."

"How did you meet?"

Kate wondered what Charlie had said.

"Swimming."

"Swimming? Bet you couldn't believe your eyes. What did you do? Pretend to drown?" Ethan chortled and Kate bristled.

"I wasn't pretending."

That made him sit up, but she wished she hadn't risen to the bait.

"Are you serious? Drowning? Christ, that's great."

Kate saw his mind running through ways of enhancing Charlie's reputation.

"What happened?" he asked.

Kate didn't feel she could back out now.

"We were caught in a rip tide. The weather turned nasty. Charlie kept me going."

"I want every detail."

"You'll have to ask Charlie."

"I'd rather you told me."

Kate shook her head.

Ethan sighed, but changed the subject. "What do your parents do?"

"Dead."

"Take drugs?"

"Paracetamol."

"Bad habits?"

"I eat peanut butter by the spoonful and I sometimes forget to flush," she said.

Ethan laughed.

"And I don't like to share," Kate added.

"Neither does Charlie."

"Maybe it's him that forgets to flush."

"He's a mixed-up guy," Ethan said.

Kate didn't respond.

"So, do you see Charlie as your meal ticket, Kate? Fancy life with a rich pop star-turned-actor? Are visions of Hollywood and houses with swimming pools dancing in your head? What do you want out this?"

He sat there so smug and self-righteous, Kate wanted to shock him. She waited a moment before answering. "Someone who won't hit me."

His eyes shot to hers and she gave a little shrug.

"Don't fall in love with him, Kate. He might not hit you, but he'll hurt you."

Chapter Fourteen

⁸⁰

Kate knew of Armageddon, but had never been there. Clubs were too expensive and Armageddon was reputedly harder to get into than anywhere else. Apart from the red neon sign and two men the size of small elephants standing by the entrance, the club looked nothing more than a large double-fronted, triple-pillared residential house.

Almost before the car stopped moving, Ethan's driver shot around to open the rear door and let them out. Once inside, Ethan waved a gold-edged invitation at a stone-faced, wafer-thin guy and ushered Kate toward the source of the thumping music. Kate pulled up short of a pair of grotesquely beautiful double doors covered with carved, snarling animals. She had a moment of unease before Ethan ushered her into the room.

A wave of faces rolled in their direction. Kate guessed what they were thinking. Who is she? Do I know her? Should I know her? Ethan caught her elbow, maneuvering her to the bar. He lifted two glasses from a serried line of champagne flutes and handed one to her.

"Not bad," he said after the first mouthful.

Kate didn't want a drink. She wanted to run. Why had she let Ethan persuade her to wear jeans? Every woman wore a cocktail dress. Standing next to men in black dinner jackets, they sparkled like bright jewels scattered around the room. Kate felt out of place, as if she'd turned up in school uniform on an "own clothes" day. Her eyes hunted Charlie.

She found him with one of the brightest gems. The woman wore the sexiest dress Kate had ever seen—pieces of red fabric wound diagonally around her body, as if she'd been wrapped in a huge satin ribbon. On anyone else it would have seemed as though she were bursting out of her clothes, like a female Hulk, but on this woman it looked stunning. Kate emptied her glass and found a full one placed in her hand.

Charlie spotted Ethan, registered the woman at his side, and then turned back to the woman at his own, before his gaze shot to Kate again. What the hell had she got on? Jeans, for fuck's sake? He was gripped by a pang of guilt. He should have bought her a dress. He hadn't thought. The women around him wore designer labels, probably dresses the designers had begged them to wear. They even approached Charlie to endorse their suits, shirts, ties. Christ, why had Ethan let her come dressed like that? But her top…her breasts… Charlie stared. Fuck it, Kate looked so sexy and stunning his cock hardened against his zipper. Thank God it was dark.

He shouldn't have let her come. How could he keep away from her? He'd thought they could have a few dances and no one would notice but that wasn't going to happen. Charlie made himself put his arm over Natalie Glass' shoulder and watched Kate looking for him, until their gazes collided. Kate smiled. He didn't. He watched her face fall and he turned back to Natalie. *Shit*. What the fuck had he done that for?

Kate saw Charlie's arm move around the woman in red and a flash of pain seared her heart like a piece of meat tossed onto a barbeque. When he deliberately looked away, Kate decided to go home. Why ask her to come, then ignore her? Ethan's arm moved across her shoulder and when she tried to slide away, he kept her in place.

"Gerald, how's it going?" Ethan gripped Kate tighter and shook the hand of the man in front of them.

"Great, Ethan. This gorgeous young lady one of yours?"

"I'm afraid not. Kate, meet Gerald Sweetman, co-owner of Zeron Films."

Kate shook his hand. The two men chatted for a while before Ethan moved her on.

"Ethan, darling. It's been too long."

Ethan released Kate to triple air kiss a woman in a dress cut low enough to expose a ploughed field of furrowed cleavage.

"You're looking lovely tonight, Foxie," Ethan said. "This is Kate. Kate, meet Foxie Merton. Foxie writes for *Hello*."

Kate received the same kiss that wasn't a kiss. The woman handed her a pink business card and answered a few vacuous questions of Ethan's, before he pulled Kate on.

"I didn't know Ethan Silver represented Kate Beckinsale?" someone muttered as they passed.

"Wasn't it Kate Hartley?" another voice asked.

Ethan chuckled. He slid his arm around Kate's waist. His fingers touched her bare skin and she flinched.

"They're intrigued. Keep them that way," he said at her ear.

He picked up another couple of glasses of champagne from a passing waiter and handed one to Kate. She knew she shouldn't drink any more until she'd eaten, otherwise she'd fall asleep or fall over. She tried not to look for Charlie, but he always seemed to be in the periphery of her vision, always with the woman in red. He hadn't even come over to say hello. Disappointment gnawed at her heart.

As Ethan turned to speak to someone else, there was a tap on her bare shoulder. A dark-haired, pale-faced guy stood smiling at her.

"Hi, what's your name?" he asked.

"Kate."

There was a pause and Kate realized he wasn't wondering who she was, but expected her to know him. She didn't.

"And you are?" she asked.

"Morgan Price. You've probably seen me on Arrow. On BBC2."

"I don't have a TV."

Judging by the dropped jaw, Morgan was dumbfounded by the idea of a household deprived of his brilliance.

Kate took pity on him. "What's it about?"

His face relaxed again. "It's a sci-fi drama. A specialist team of detectives travel around the country, hunting serial killers and kidnappers. I'm Paul Arrow, the main character." He looked at her quizzically. "Do you do stage work then?"

"No."

"Singer?"

"No."

"Model?"

"No."

"She's a talented fashion designer," Ethan said as he passed. "She makes her own underwear."

Kate gritted her teeth as Morgan's eyes lit up like candles. "Wow. Did you make this?" He touched the bottom of Kate's bustier.

"Yes." She twisted away from his fingers.

"Now you've switched from no to yes, want to go someplace and show me what's underneath?"

"No, she fucking wouldn't." Charlie appeared between them, a ball of belligerence.

Morgan hesitated, then slid away.

Charlie edged Kate to the side of the room. "What the fuck are you wearing?"

Kate looked down at her jeans and then at the dresses of the other women and knew no matter what she'd worn, she would never look that good.

"Ethan told me to change out of the dress I intended to wear and he was right. I would have looked cheap. Now, I look different. If you don't like what I have on, too bad."

"You look fucking delicious, but everyone is going to notice you. This lot are trained piranhas."

"Charlie, come and dance," someone whined by Kate's shoulder. The woman in the red dress shoved herself between them and draped her arms around Charlie's neck. "Aren't you going to introduce me?"

"Kate, this is Natalie Glass. Natalie—Kate. Natalie's going to be in *The Green* with me."

"What have I seen you in?" Natalie asked Kate. "Weren't you an extra in *The Conservatory*?"

"Yes, the Venus fly-trap," Kate said.

Charlie laughed. Kate watched Natalie edging Charlie away. She tussled for a moment with the slimy green monster intent on consuming her internal organs, but aware that looking any longer at Miss Slashed Dress only encouraged the monster's rapid growth, Kate backed away. Natalie shot her a triumphant smirk and Kate smiled as brightly as she could, before turning her back on the pair of them.

Kate realized now that Charlie had invited her in an attempt to make up for his neglect. He'd known she was upset about the other night and the fact that he hadn't called her but Kate couldn't see why he'd bothered asking her to come here. He didn't even want to stand and talk to her, so she'd rather not be here. She'd leave—after she'd eaten.

The food had been laid out in a side room and when she saw it, Kate took a step back. This had to be the most magnificent spread she'd ever seen. She stood for a moment, devouring it with her eyes. It looked too beautiful to eat. Everything lay on silver plates and everything was miniature. Tiny circles of bread topped with cream cheese, pate or smoked salmon. Grapes so miniscule Kate didn't think they *were* grapes, until she tried one. There were star-shaped pastry cases topped by one curly pink prawn. Petite rolls the size of plums and a display of exotic fruits she'd seen in the supermarket but never bought because they cost a couple of quid each. There were dishes of caviar, oysters on beds of ice and a load of stuff she didn't even recognize. There were also no women anywhere near the food. Only old men.

Kate picked up a plate and reached for the smoked salmon. By the time she'd worked her way along the length of the table, her plate was piled high and her stomach growled in anticipation.

"I do like a woman with a healthy appetite," said a voice near her ear. "Can I get you a drink to go with that?"

Kate turned to see a small man in tiny wire glasses, holding a plate with four neatly placed items. His eyes were level with her chest. Kate had a sudden horror that guests were rationed. She wondered if she should try and put a few things back.

"No, thanks."

Kate wanted to be left to eat in peace, but sensed that wouldn't happen. She found a free corner and leaned on the wall. Moments later, the small guy stood next to her, his gaze still fixed on her chest.

"Quite a novelty," he said.

Kate hoped he was referring to the food.

"You're not going to throw it all up again?"

"No." Only if he tried to kiss her.

"You only eat once a week, is that it?"

"Something like that."

"I'm Matt Reisen. You are?"

"Kate Snow."

"What might I have seen you in?" he asked.

"Crispies?"

He licked his lips and winked. "Sounds saucy. I might well have. Take my card. Give me a ring. I'm sure I can find you something."

Kate balanced her plate on one hand and pushed the card into her pocket with the others she was collecting. She selected a flaky cheese pinwheel from her plate and bit into it. She knew he was watching. His eyes had moved from her chest to her mouth. He edged a little closer.

"Actually, I've got an interesting project on at the moment. The big studios are going to be fighting over it. A sort of *Lock Stock*, *Full Monty* with a twist. It's about a guy who works at a dog grooming parlor in Swansea and he's convinced one of the dogs he's looking after is the reincarnation of his dead wife, Bitsy. He killed her while they honeymooned in Chihuahua."

Kate laughed and then realized not only was he not joking, but this film was not a comedy.

"Sounds fascinating," she said, and ate a little faster. She breathed a sigh of relief when someone came to take the guy away, surprised they weren't carrying a white jacket with very long sleeves.

"Hello, sweet thing."

Kate twisted her mouth in annoyance as a strange hand helped itself to one of her coconut king prawns. When the fingers reached out again, Kate stabbed them with her fork. They belonged to a tall, blond American.

"*Oww.*"

"Get your own," she said.

"There aren't any left. I think you took them all."

Kate's face went hot.

"Won't you share?" he asked.

"No, you should have been quicker."

"Words no woman has ever said to me before." He smiled. A mouth full of perfect even teeth. "I'm Jake Hartness. What's your name? What might I have seen you in?"

Kate sighed again. These people were dull.

"Crispies?" she said.

"Yeah, I remember now. You were great."

She burst out laughing.

Charlie tensed when he saw Kate laughing, and when he realized who she was with he set off in her direction. Jake Hartness was as slick as spit. Ethan caught Charlie's arm as he passed.

"I want a word with you."

"What?" Charlie didn't take his eyes off Jake, who stood far too close to Kate.

"Kate told me you saved her life."

"What?" Charlie spun around to stare at Ethan.

"We could use that, Charlie, and undo your recent negative publicity in one fell swoop. Transform you overnight from dirty devil to appealing angel."

"No."

"What do you mean, no? This is a great opportunity. You're a real-life hero. You didn't manage to rescue your brother, but you did save Kate. Plucked her from the jaws of death." Ethan laughed at his own joke. "Jaws? Get it?"

Charlie's hands balled into fists at his sides. Sometimes Ethan was a prick. "She saved me."

Ethan faltered. "But she said —"

"I'm sure she did," Charlie said in a cold voice. "But she saved me. So forget it."

Charlie's gaze slid back to Kate and he groaned. Bloody Hartness had her backed up against a table. Kate looked as though she'd been confronted by a king cobra. If she leaned any further back, she'd topple over.

"Ethan, rescue Kate," Charlie pleaded.

"Why? She looks like she's having a good time."

Charlie knew from Ethan's tone that he'd pissed him off.

"Maybe that's why I want you to rescue her," Charlie said.

"You're the one she thinks is Spiderman. You rescue her."

"What? Ethan, please. If they think we're together, they won't leave her alone."

"Is that why you're avoiding her?"

"You know what will happen if they find out she's with me."

A woman pulled at Charlie's arm. "Hi, Ethan. Charlie, you must come and meet Cyn." Charlie shot a pleading look in Ethan's direction and let himself be led away.

Kate was exhausted by having to pretend interest in boring, repetitive conversations. She had no idea what anyone was talking about, who they were talking about or why they were talking to her, but that didn't stop them. Everyone who spoke to her was a very important director, producer, promoter, actor. If they weren't already the big thing, they intended to be the next big thing. As far as Kate could tell, the whole industry was made up of pretentious idiots. Yet she could sense desperation in all of them, the knowledge that they couldn't afford not to be seen because if they didn't speak to the right person — and who the fuck knew who that was — they'd miss some opportunity that would never come again.

In a way, she understood. They had a dream and pursued it. If they didn't make it, it wouldn't be for want of trying and those who'd already made it clung to what they had in case someone snatched it away. Like a soap bubble blown from a wand, their beautiful life could disappear in an instant. Charlie had nearly lost his but he'd had a second chance. So had Kate, but this wasn't the life for her.

Kate's gaze returned to Charlie, blazing round the room like a comet, leaving a trail of light behind him, illuminating others for a moment because they stood near him. He felt as alien to her as something from deep space — untouchable, inexplicable and unattainable. This had been a terrible mistake. The only thing they had in common was the sea. Now they lived in different worlds.

Kate breathed a sigh of relief when Ethan caught her elbow and politely drew her away from yet another producer.

"Enjoying yourself?" he asked.

"I can't think when I had so much fun. Oh yes, it would be when I walked out of the loo at school with my skirt tucked into my knickers and no one told me until it was time to go home."

"You're arousing a lot of interest."

"No, I don't think so. They want to talk, not listen. Do I have a sign on me that says, 'I listen to idiots'? And why are the only people who want to talk to me male?"

"Apart from the obvious reason?"

"What obvious reason?"

Ethan looked at her chest. Kate sighed.

"Ethan, the guys I've spoken to would talk to a door if they thought it would listen and make appropriate noises. I've been offered a part in a very classy art film that has a few scenes of essential nudity — a tasteful threesome. I've listened to synopses of films that make *Silence of the Lambs* look like a fairy tale, the worst of which involved vampire chickens and a woman who had a child with an alligator. What do I think about the name *Gatorbaby*?"

Ethan laughed. "The women here are only interested in people who can further their career. All other women are deadly rivals to be avoided or put down because they might be after the same role, modeling contract or man. Every woman in this room wants to be thinner, taller, prettier and brighter. There's already been one major upset because two budding starlets turned up in the same pair of shoes that could hardly be seen under their dresses."

"Is someone else wearing my flip-flops?" Kate tried to sound alarmed.

Ethan chuckled. "You've also not helped things by mentioning Crispies, because no one knows it's a restaurant in Greenwich. They all think it's some hardcore porno movie."

"I know." Kate sighed. "I'm beginning to believe it myself. I've even been offered a part in Crispies Two."

She scanned the room until she found Charlie. He stood still now, not a comet, but a bonfire night sparkler, spreading light and life in a circle around him. Just like a bloody sparkler, she thought, because you want it to stay lit forever but eventually it goes out. It always does. Then it burns your fingers. She watched as he happily chattered to everyone, his hand on the arm of the woman next to him, kissing another who came up to him. He was so beautiful he made her heart ache.

But this wasn't Kate's life. She was a fool ever to think it could be.

"Why doesn't Charlie talk to me? He asked me to come, but he wouldn't bring me. Now, he doesn't even want to stand near me or dance with me."

"He knows a lot of these people. They're good friends."

"I can't further his career. I don't know the right people. I'm just a novelty, aren't I? And we know what happens when the novelty wears off."

Kate's confidence sputtered like a damp squib. She felt cheap. Maybe she'd not judged this right. Maybe Ethan wanted her to see she didn't fit in.

"He's interested in you because you're different, but Charlie possesses the attention span of a goldfish," Ethan said.

Kate shivered. She was fun to fuck, but it wouldn't last. The truth ran through her veins like fast-acting poison.

"Do you want to go home? I'll get my driver to take you."

"No." Kate inhaled a fortifying breath and forced a smile.

She'd changed her mind. She'd never get the chance to come here again. She turned her back on Ethan and made straight for the deserted dance floor. Despite the fact that it was a club, no one was dancing. Probably because the women worried they'd fall out of their dresses. It took only moments before Jake joined her. Then a few others danced around them.

As the American's hands moved toward her, Charlie was suddenly there, pulling her away.

"I was dancing with someone," she snapped.

"You're dancing with me," Charlie said.

Kate knew he'd be a good dancer, but it wouldn't have mattered if he'd moved like a string puppet because her organs reacted as though they were magnetically attracted to his. Her hips longed to kiss his, but each time he reached out for her, she never allowed herself to slide into his grasp. When the song ended and he leaned forward to speak to her, Kate thanked him and walked away.

She made straight for the bathroom. She didn't want to speak to him. He'd asked her to the club and spent most of the evening ignoring her, pretending they weren't together, but he didn't even want her to dance with anyone else. He'd hurt her. She understood he didn't want the press to know they were together, but most of the people she'd met were actors like him or people in the film industry. He was ashamed of her.

Kate was also reconsidering Ethan's motivation, wondering again if he had a hidden agenda. Maybe he wanted her to look stupid, wanted Charlie to see a cheap waitress in old jeans and be embarrassed into dumping her. Would she have looked so bad in the cotton dress? No one else would have been wearing it. Kate needed a few moments to pull herself together. Then she'd go home.

She thought the toilets were empty, but the unmistakable grunts of a couple engaged in a session of mutual satisfaction emanated from the end cubicle.

"Yeah, like that, yeah, oh..."

The woman was vaguely articulate, the guy a groaner.

Kate had never been able to see the attraction of shagging in a toilet. Lucy had done it on more than one occasion and had been full of Nick's athletic ability, but Kate didn't fancy it at all. The less you touched in there the better.

She lingered by the wash basin, not because she was keen to listen to the duet, but because she didn't want to go anywhere near Charlie until she had her emotions under control. But she should have hurried because when the cubicle door swung open and she saw the flushed faces of the pair through the mirror, Kate let out a gasp of her own and fled.

"Kate, stop."

She hadn't got far down the corridor. No point running, they'd recognized each other. She turned and Nick hurried to her side.

"Don't tell Lucy."

Kate put her hands on her hips. "Why not?"

Nick hesitated.

"Why shouldn't I tell her?" Kate asked. "I take it that wasn't your wife?"

The set of his jaw told her it wasn't.

"I don't want to hurt her." Nick's wheedling tone grated on Kate.

"I think you've already done that."

"Look, Sylvie was just—available. We fancied a fuck. It didn't mean anything."

The woman emerged and walked up the corridor behind Nick. Kate wondered if Sylvie thought it didn't mean anything.

"We're both married. We know the score," Nick said. "Please don't say anything."

Sylvie slid her arm through Nick's. Kate stalked off.

"What's wrong, Nick?" Sylvie asked.

"She threatened to tell my wife."

"The bitch. She won't, will she?"

"I hope not."

Kate overheard them and was tempted to tell Sylvie the truth.

Kate found another loo and lingered for a while before going back to the main room. She wondered if Ethan's driver would give her a lift back. As she peered into the crowd, looking for a way to slip out without bumping into Charlie, a glass of wine hit her face. Kate cried out in shock. The glass didn't break but it had hurt her cheek. Kate screwed up her eyes as red wine dripped down her face and neck. A young girl, wearing a black slash-necked dress, stood smirking. She had long blonde hair and a baby face. Kate had never seen her before. She looked too young to be in a nightclub.

"What the hell did you do that for?" Kate asked.

"Keep your hands off my dad."

"What?"

As people began to gather around them, Charlie appeared at Kate's side. He took her elbow and pulled her out of the room. Ethan caught hold of the blonde girl by the wrist and the four of them ended up in the corridor Kate had just left.

"He told me what you tried to do," the girl shouted, struggling to get away from Ethan to reach Kate.

"Hey, calm down," Ethan snapped. "What are you talking about?"

"Bitch," the teenager snarled. "She's a slut."

Kate's face and chest were streaked with wine. Her top was ruined. The front of her jeans felt wet and sticky and when the girl next opened her mouth, Kate's heart developed the hiccups.

"She tried to get my dad to have sex with her in the toilet."

Everything became clear. This was Nick's daughter.

"That's not true," Kate said.

"Are you calling my dad a liar?" The girl was crying now, dirty streams of mascara running down her face.

"Where's your dad? Let's go and find him," Ethan said.

"Make her promise to leave him alone."

"What's happening? Gemma, what's going on?" Nick strode down the corridor.

How convenient to appear now, Kate thought, realizing he'd probably orchestrated the whole thing.

"Daddy, she's the one, isn't she, who tried to get you to have sex with her?"

"This is ridiculous," Kate said.

"What's all this about, Kate?" Nick glared at her.

Nick had ambushed her. He knew Kate wouldn't want to say what she'd seen in front of his daughter. She felt as though she'd been hit by a train that was now shunting her along the tracks at high speed.

"Do you know him?" Charlie asked.

He stood in a loose-limbed slouch, but Kate heard the chill in his voice.

"Yes."

"Were you in the loo with him?" Charlie sounded different. Detached.

"He was in there when I went in, but there's been a misunderstanding," Kate said.

"You're the one who's made the mistake," Nick snapped. "Come on, Gem. Let's get you home."

"I'm going to tell everyone about you," Gemma cried.

"Nick?" Kate called as they walked away. "So will I."

Nick glared, but steered his daughter toward the exit.

"Thank God no one else saw that," Ethan said. "Kate, you should leave. Here's the money for a cab." He pushed two twenty-pound notes toward her.

Kate ignored the money and turned to Charlie.

"That was Lucy's lover. Lucy knows Nick's married, but I think she thought their relationship was a triangle, with his wife at the other corner. She has no idea she's part of a square or, knowing what's Nick's like, a hexagon. I walked into the ladies and heard Nick and a woman fucking. I wouldn't promise not to tell Lucy. I guess Nick just got his own back."

Kate saw Charlie relax, the relief on his face as he accepted what she said. She glanced at Ethan and wasn't sure what she saw on his. He looked at Charlie and then put the money back in his wallet and walked off.

"More like getting the retaliation in first," Charlie said, fingering the wet ribbons on Kate's top.

Kate was disgusted. "I've had enough."

Charlie put his arm over her shoulder. "Me, too. Come home with me."

"You sure you want me to?"

"Yes."

"Better find me a blanket or a brown paper bag."

He looked bewildered. "What for?"

"You don't want to be seen with me, do you?"

Charlie winced. "Well, it might be a good idea if you go first and wait round the corner."

Kate tried to shrug off his arm, but he pulled her closer.

"Please, don't. I'm trying to protect you. The press are out there waiting, slathering like dogs hoping to get tossed a bone. You want them to tell everyone your life story? If they see us together, they'll dig up every boyfriend you ever had, every mistake you ever made. Your enemies will be queuing up to stab you. And all the friends you thought you had will turn out not to be friends at all, because they'd sell you out for a flat screen TV or a holiday. The people outside don't care whether they print lies or the truth. They just want to sell a photo or a story."

"They weren't in here, though. You didn't need to ignore me in here."

His shoulders slumped. "I'm sorry. Sweetheart, you just don't know how bad this can get. It's you I'm thinking of. They're fucking vultures." He twisted a lock of her hair. "Come on. Let's go home."

Chapter Fifteen

ಐ

As Kate stepped outside, a flash went off in her face. She scurried down the street on her own.

"Go or stay?" asked Mike Fry, Simon Baxter's photographer.

"Stay," Simon said. "Let's have a look at that one, though."

Mike changed the setting, checked the image and gave the camera to Simon.

"I don't recognize her," Mike said.

"Fuck-a-duck. It's Kate."

"Moss?"

Simon gawped at the image. "No, Kate Snow."

"Who's she?"

"No one we're interested in. She used to go out with a mate of mine, Richard Winter. I didn't expect to see her coming out of Armageddon. What's that on her top? She had an accident?"

"Looks like she spilled something. Sure you don't want her?"

"No. I told you, she's no one."

Not quite no one. Simon glared as she disappeared round the corner. The stupid bitch had cost him two thousand quid. He couldn't believe she'd said yes to Richard. Who'd want to marry that wanker? What the hell was she doing in Armageddon? Maybe the photo wasn't entirely useless.

"I've changed my mind. Keep it," Simon said.

"Too late. Hey, eyes left. Isn't that Charlie Storm?" Mike lifted his camera and snapped him. "Worth following?"

"Yeah, there's fuck-all happening."

"He's alone though," Mike said.

Simon snorted. "Not for long, I shouldn't think. Get the car."

When the black cab pulled up next to Kate, the door swung open and Charlie grinned at her from the backseat.

"Need a lift?" he asked.

"I need your jacket."

"I'll warm you up."

The moment she got into the cab, he pulled her into his arms and kissed her. It was hopeless, Kate thought. She was incapable of resisting. It made her realize what it was like to be addicted, to feel yourself unable to survive without a fix of whatever you've grown to love. Charlie's soft and gentle lips nibbled at hers as though she were a divine delicacy to be slowly savored.

"You smell fabulous. Soap and wine," he whispered. "What a combination. Tastes interesting too."

"You've been smoking."

He groaned. "One cigarette."

"I don't want you to smoke." Kate stared straight at him. "That's killing yourself in a very stupid way."

"I'll never do it again."

She smiled and pressed her lips against his, diving into his mouth. Charlie's arms slid round her, pulling her closer. This time, the kiss was long and hard. By the time they broke apart, she was gasping.

"I've wanted to do that all night," Charlie said. "Every time someone talked to you, I wanted to hit them." He buried his face in her neck and licked her skin. "I'm sorry if you thought I was ignoring you. I didn't want to. Oh God, I'm paranoid the press will wreck this. I'm sorry. Do you forgive me?"

He clutched her hand so tight, it hurt.

"Yes. I forgive you."

"Good, so can we watch that film you're in when we get back? What was it called? Crispies?"

Kate thumped him.

* * * * *

206

"I'm not fucking climbing up there," Mike snapped, staring at the wooden framework that covered the parked cars.

"Yes, you are," Simon said. "We've climbed over the gate. How much more difficult is this? You'll be able to see straight into her apartment."

"How do you know it's the right apartment?"

"It is, trust me."

"We're on private property, Simon."

"Don't worry. It will be worth it."

Mike sighed and put down his camera. "Give me a leg up."

* * * * *

Charlie almost dragged Kate's arm out of its socket as he tugged her to her bedroom.

"Slow down," Kate said.

"Can't. How is it you make me unable to think?" Charlie whispered as he slid his hand inside the front of her jeans. "Oh God, you're all wet."

"Red wine."

"No, it isn't. It's you, you little minx."

He moved his hand lower and Kate's head tipped back. She gasped and clutched at his shirt. His fingers shifted inside her thong, touched her clit, rubbed it fast and she almost passed out from the explosion of pleasure that swept through her.

"I love how I can do that to you," he groaned.

Click

Charlie unfastened the little buttons on her top and pulled it apart to expose her breasts. He lowered his head and fixed his mouth around her nipple, teasing it with his teeth. Kate drew in a swift breath. The top fell to the floor. Her jeans and pants followed.

Click

Her fingers slid down to unfasten his trousers. It wasn't easy because his erection made them tight. She dropped to her knees and eased trousers and boxers down together. Charlie groaned when she tucked her head under the bottom of his shirt and kissed the inside of his thighs. As she took his balls in her mouth, he sank his fingers into her hair.

Click

"Oh fuckfuckfuckfuckfuck," he moaned. "Kate, you're playing with fire."

Clickclickclickclickclick

* * * * *

Nick launched an attempt at damage control as he drove his daughter home, though Gemma was so drunk he wasn't sure how much was getting through.

"You know, Gem, I think I might have made a mistake," he said. "Kate's a friend of one of my colleagues. I think it was a wind-up. Kev paying me back for a prank I pulled. Better not tell your mum, she'll just get upset."

"Mum'll fink it's funny," Gemma slurred.

"The same sort of funny as throwing a drink over someone? And the glass? You could have cut her face."

Silence.

"Tell you what," Nick said, hoping this would work. "How about I don't tell Mum about what you did? It was a miracle she let you come with me tonight. If we keep quiet, you're not going to get barred from any more nights out for the foreseeable future. What do you think? Do we have a deal?"

Gemma didn't respond. Her head was up against the window, her mouth hanging open. She'd fallen asleep or maybe passed out. Nick sighed.

Nick received an earful of hell from his wife Debra anyway, because the moment Gemma walked in the front door, she threw up on the Persian rug.

"How could you let her get drunk?" Debra screeched.

"She must have been sneaking drinks. I couldn't watch her all the time."

"In a minute you're going to tell me it's my fault for letting you take her," Debra yelled.

Yes, it fucking was, Nick thought.

After Gemma went to bed and Debra made it clear sex was off the menu, Nick pretended to discover he'd lost his wallet. He made an imaginary phone call to the club, and set off in the wrong direction to get it back. He needed to speak to Lucy before Kate did.

Nick thought he noticed a bright flash as he rang Lucy's buzzer, but when he looked around, he couldn't see where the light had come from and it didn't happen again. Then Lucy opened the door in her tiny see-through nightie and his brain turned to mush.

"I thought you were taking Gemma out?"

"I did, but I missed you." Nick pulled her into his arms and kissed her.

"Mmm. You look so sexy in your tux," Lucy whispered.

"Not as sexy as you." Nick kicked the door closed behind him.

He slid his hands underneath the slinky material, up her thighs and onto her bare bottom. "Lucy, I had a bit of a problem tonight. I was buying a wrap of coke from some bird in the ladies at Armageddon and Gemma got hold of the wrong end of the stick and thought I was after something else."

Lucy stiffened in his arms and he kept her tight against him.

"Hey, babe, course I wasn't, but Gemma ended up throwing a glass of red wine at Kate."

"Kate?" Lucy's eyes opened wide. "What was Kate doing in Armageddon?"

"I've no idea, but I let Gemma think Kate was coming on to me to distract her from what I was really doing. Only, I had no idea she'd chuck wine in her face. So if you get a vitriolic neighbor banging on your door, telling you I'm a complete wanker, I'm sorry. Things got out of hand."

Nick thought that sounded reasonable. He slid his hand over Lucy's nipple, but the unoccupied one percent of his brain started to wonder what Kate *was* doing in the club. How the hell did she know Ethan Silver and Charlie Storm? What had he missed?

"We need to do something about Kate, because when I bring Gemma over here, she might bump into her," Nick said. It had seemed such a good idea for him to commission Dan to paint his daughter. While Gemma was posing for Dan, Nick would get to spend an hour in bed exploring positions with Lucy. "I told Gemma I'd made a mistake, but I know I upset Kate."

Lucy moaned as Nick rubbed her breasts. "Can you stay the night?"

"Oh baby, I'd love to, but I have half an hour, tops."

Lucy slipped her arms out of the slinky red nightdress, letting it slide over her hips and drop to the floor. "Better not waste any of it." She took hold of Nick's hand and pulled him into the bedroom. "Have you brought the coke?"

Oops. Nick thought fast. "I chucked it. I was so worried about Gemma finding it."

"We shouldn't anyway." Lucy unfastened his shirt.

"Will you tell Kate I'm sorry? I had to come up with something quick and I wasn't very fair to her."

"Did you really upset her?" Lucy asked, her fingers in his pants.

Nick thought about Kate's face. He wasn't sure he was going to get away with this. "Yeah, I did. I didn't mean to. She was pissed off with me. If I were her, I'd be planning my revenge."

He didn't dare go further than that.

"How upset was she?" Lucy asked, her hands moving away from the place he most wanted her to touch. He suppressed a whimper of disappointment. "Did you make her cry?" she asked, clear disapproval in her voice.

Nick sensed he'd missed something else. "What's the problem?"

Lucy slumped on the bed. "We're all worried about Kate. Richard was such a sod, pretending he'd marry her for a bet. We thought they were perfect together and then he pulled that shitty trick. What a wanker."

Nick thought Kate was the idiot. She'd only known the guy a few minutes. And honeymoon in Hawaii for a week? Crazy.

"You're still feeling sorry for her about that?" Nick asked, sitting at her side.

"She's just…well, unstable. She'd hardly got over Richard before she jumped into another relationship with some guy called Hippo. After Rachel found the note—" Lucy stopped mid-sentence.

"What note?"

"I'm not supposed to say anything."

No words Nick loved more, other than "can I suck your dick"? He adored secrets, wheedling them out by whatever means he could, some means more pleasurable than others.

"What note, Lucy?" Nick pulled her onto his lap and dropped his mouth to her neck.

And over the next thirty minutes, between groans and moans, Lucy told him everything.

* * * * *

When Kate opened her eyes, the morning sun shone straight through the window and hit her in the face. She groaned and rolled onto Charlie, who lay beside her on his stomach, his face pressed into a pillow. He turned his head and his eyes flickered open. Kate watched who, what and where sink in before he gave a little grin. He slithered down the bed, taking the duvet with him, and kissed Kate's bare buttock. Resting his chin in the hollow of her back, he slid his hands underneath her, until her breasts lay on his palms.

"I want to stay in bed all day," Charlie muttered into her kidney.

"I thought we were going to see your parents?"

He withdrew his hands and rolled onto his back. "That's why I want to stay in bed."

Kate twisted around to face him. "And I thought it was because you wanted to see what I could do with my nipples."

He gave her a smile soaked in lust and Kate shivered.

"What can you do?"

"Later." She sat up.

"No, not later, now." He pulled her down. "You know better than to tease me."

It was another hour before they were dressed. Kate was wrinkled from the length of time she'd spent in the shower with Charlie's mouth doing what her nipples had just done. She wasn't complaining.

Kate put on the green dress Ethan had rejected.

"You look so cute in that," Charlie said.

"Really?"

"Well, you look cuter when you're not wearing anything, but that might freak out my parents. The color suits you, brings out the green tinge in your skin." He slid his hands up her thighs, under the material. "And it has the added advantage of being easy to whisk off."

He tried to pull it up but Kate stopped him.

"You're trying to put this off, Charlie."

"And you'll see why."

He tried again to lift her dress, but Kate squirmed away.

"There's a taxi waiting downstairs," she reminded him.

"I don't care."

It was like dealing with a child, Kate thought. She finally cajoled him into leaving with a promise of a treat later. Now she'd have to think of something. Not very difficult. Charlie was up for everything they did in bed and out of it, and if Kate hadn't felt the same, that might have made her uneasy. So long as it was just the two of them, life was perfect. Charlie was all she needed.

Now Kate knew what addiction meant.

* * * * *

"Not worried about someone seeing me now?" Kate asked, as the taxi stopped outside a dazzling white mews house.

"They're vampires. They only come out at night." He unlocked the door. "Take a look around. I'm going to change." Charlie headed for the stairs.

"Make it into someone good-looking and charming," Kate called after him.

"Very old joke and not funny."

She sat on the bottom step and lay back. Kate's eyes settled on the ceiling and as she let out a gasp of alarm, she slammed her hand against her mouth. Overhead, angels and devils frolicked in a landscape of clouds and if she hadn't already been on her back, she'd have fallen.

Kate had worked hard to keep her life as solid as she could, but she'd always known her existence was a delicate balance, a fragile layer sitting between difficult memories and unrealistic hopes. Sometimes, fragments from the past she thought were gone, bubbled through into her mind—her mother's face, her father's hands, the knife, blood on the floor, blood on her mother. Kate kept those memories buried under tons of rock, but occasionally they found a way out.

Charlie had turned her world upside down in a good way and now his house had sent it spinning off its axis. Kate stared at the ceiling, examining the scene. Now she knew why she hadn't seen her father's work in any gallery. He was painting frescoes.

She heard Charlie bounding down the stairs. He stopped short when he saw her lying on the bottom step.

"What's the matter?"

"I'm contemplating your fresco."

Charlie looked up. "Yeah, it's kind of cool."

"You have it done?"

"It was there when I bought the house."

Thank God for that. "How long have you lived here?" she asked.

"Eighteen months. Why didn't you look round?"

213

"Didn't want to." *Too distracted.*

There was a long silence before he spoke again.

"No one has *ever* resisted the temptation to look around my house."

Kate didn't move. "I just got stuck on the ceiling."

"Why?"

She couldn't think of a convincing lie.

"You know, you are sometimes so fucking deep, it's like peering into the Grand Canyon," he snapped.

Kate moved her gaze from the ceiling to him. "Have you been to the Grand Canyon?"

"Yes, I have. It's a bloody strange experience because the more you look at it, the more you have no idea what you're looking at. Rather like you. I have no idea what goes on in your head or what you want out of life. Why won't you let me in?"

"You don't want to be in my head. It's not a good place."

Charlie pulled her to her feet. "Let me in," he said gently.

She wanted to tell him to keep knocking, but the words lodged in her throat. Finally, he shrugged and squeezed her hand.

"Car's in the garage," he said and led her there.

He opened the passenger door of a silver Lexus SC430.

"Nice car," Kate said.

"Bit useless in London. You're lucky if you can do more than ten miles an hour."

The moment they'd driven away from the house, Kate felt better, but Charlie's mood deteriorated.

"Jesus, look at that idiot," he said, as a car pulled out in front of him from a side road more than a hundred yards away.

Kate didn't think the other driver had done anything wrong, but Charlie continued to find fault with every vehicle that came anywhere near him. He maneuvered the Lexus as gingerly as if it were a clapped-out old banger in its death throes. Kate guessed his actions stemmed from a reluctance to make the journey, more than an indication of how he usually drove.

"Can it go over twenty miles per hour?" she asked.

Charlie shot her a pained look. "I'm trying to be a good driver."

"Want me to take over?"

"No."

"I'll be careful."

"Still, no."

"I've only written off two cars."

His mouth twitched and he speeded up.

"So, how long since you saw your parents?" she asked.

"A while."

"Why now?"

"Because."

Kate reached out and put her hand on his knee. "Why do you want me with you?"

"Dilution," he murmured.

"Well, if you're trying to deflect their attention from you to me, you ought to give me a few hints about what to expect."

There was no answer. Kate thought squeezing O-Positive out of a stone seemed simpler.

"How about we start easy and build up. What are their names?"

"Jill and Paul."

"What's your mother like?"

Charlie stayed silent for so long that Kate wondered if he'd forgotten what she'd asked.

"Strict? Cuddly? Two heads? A beak?" she asked.

"Don't put your teaspoon in the sugar bowl. There's no telling what will happen." His tone was so bleak, Kate felt a shiver of unease.

"Your dad?"

"Not an alpha male."

Kate could see and feel Charlie winding up. His hands gripped the wheel as if he expected it to be yanked away, his knuckles forming lines of well-defined white bony lumps.

"Want me to hold the wheel so you can bite your nails?" Kate asked.

He didn't even smile.

"How did your parents die?" Charlie asked suddenly.

"Eaten by piranhas."

He sniggered and Kate saw the tension in his shoulders ease.

"Amazon expedition," she said. "Boat overturned. Lots of thrashing around. People watching thought they couldn't swim, but in fact they were fighting off razor-sharp teeth. It was all over in minutes."

Charlie laughed again. She'd broken the spell.

"What really happened?" he asked.

"Ebola virus. Not pleasant."

"You don't want to tell me." He glanced at her.

"This is your day, Charlie, and I'm not ready," Kate said.

When they stopped for petrol, she got out to stretch her legs and wandered across the forecourt of the fuel station. Kate saw his back stiffen as he lifted the nozzle from the bracket. Two teenage girls had scrambled out of an SUV, paper and pens clutched in their hands. They stood fidgeting until he'd finished at the pump, then one pushed the other forward. Kate felt an unexpected surge of pride that she was with him. The next moment, the girls shot off in tears as Charlie stalked toward the shop to pay.

Their father reached Charlie before Kate did.

"You mean bastard. Would it have killed you to write your name on a scrap of paper?"

Charlie ignored him and walked up to the desk. Kate lingered by the door.

"Don't walk away from me when I'm talking to you," the man bellowed.

Kate heard Charlie's "fuck off", so she was certain the man had too. She winced.

"You people think you're better than the rest of us. My girls nearly exploded with excitement when they saw you get out of that car. They have your picture all over their walls. They play your music all the time. You only have what you have because of them and others like them. You're a selfish, thoughtless bastard."

Charlie stepped away from the desk and walked past the man without a word. He caught Kate by the elbow, but she spun out of his grasp, wanting to apologize for him if he wouldn't do it himself. As Charlie strode away, Kate walked forward. The Asian woman behind the counter held out a sheet of paper and two Mars bars to the angry father.

"He left these for your daughters."

The man picked up the paper.

"What did he say?" the woman asked.

"'*Sorry, girls. Got out of bed the wrong side this morning, but shouldn't have taken it out on you. Thank you for your beautiful smiles. Please forgive me.*' He signed it Charlie Storm and put two kisses."

"Oh, that's sweet," the woman said.

The man harrumphed.

Charlie had driven up to the doors so Kate got straight into the car. She fastened her seat belt and Charlie pulled back onto the road.

"Aren't you going to tell me I'm a bastard?" he asked.

"I don't know, Charlie. Are you?"

"I feel like every time someone asks me to sign my name, they take a piece of me."

"They were kids and their dad was right. You only have what you have because of them and others like them."

"Maybe I don't want what I have," he snapped.

"Then that's your fault. Not theirs."

"You don't know what it's like. They act like I'm some sort of hero."

"Don't whine." She saw his mouth harden. "Is it so hard to be someone's hero?"

"I don't want them to think of me like that. I'm not worth it."

"Then you're in the wrong job," Kate said. "You can't escape it, Charlie. You can't undo the fact that you're famous."

"Would you like me if I wasn't?"

"I've already told you I don't like you."

He gave a short laugh and fell silent again. A moment later, he said, "I left them a note and a couple of Mars Bars."

"I know and they'll love you forever."

"Oh God."

"If you'd bought me one, so would I," Kate said.

"I'll stop at the next service station."

"It's too late, now. I've changed my mind. You'll have to guess what I want. Twenty questions."

"Does it involve licking?" he asked.

"No, that's one."

"Sucking?"

"Two."

"Fucking?"

"Damn."

Chapter Sixteen

ଽଠ

Charlie switched off the engine, but didn't move. Kate looked out at the smart, double-fronted, pebble-dashed house. Two Doric pillars supporting a flat canopy stood either side of a glossy, dark blue front door. Twisted, tapered box trees grew in terracotta pots on each side.

"Are they expecting you?" she asked.

"No."

Kate stepped out of the car onto the gravel drive. As she moved toward the front door, she heard Charlie come up behind her.

"Shall I ring the bell or do you have a key?"

He pressed the bell.

Kate wasn't sure what to expect. She had no idea why Charlie had brought her. As he crushed her fingers in his grip, it was all Kate could do not to pull away. The door opened and she found herself facing a woman she presumed was Charlie's mother.

Jill Storm was small, thin and pale. She wore a shapeless cream sweater and a calf-length navy skirt. Gray roots showed in her hair and she seemed shrunken, as though something had sucked the life from her. Kate watched her eyes as she looked at Charlie. They came alive for a moment before the light disappeared again.

"Hello, Mum." Charlie released Kate's hand and stepped forward.

He slowly moved his arms up and around his mother, hugging her to his chest. The embrace was short-lived. His mother ended it, pulling away and turning to Kate.

"And who's this?"

219

"Mum, this is Kate Snow. Kate, this is my mum, Jill," Charlie said.

Kate reached out to shake her hand. It felt thin and frail like a bird's wing.

"You'd better come in," his mother said.

Charlie's father stood in the hall, a tall version of Charlie's mother, thin and white-faced with salt-and-pepper hair. He stared at Kate so intently, she found herself taking a step backward.

"Hello, Dad."

"Charlie."

Kate watched them embrace. His father's arms wrapped around Charlie, hugged him tight. This time Charlie let go first.

"This is Kate. She's my friend and she knows about everything."

"More than we do then, Charlie," his mother said.

An awkward silence descended. Kate could feel all three of them struggling for the right thing to say.

"What do you want?" Jill asked.

"To talk," Charlie mumbled.

"You better come into the conservatory."

It was a smart house, Kate thought, a tightly controlled house. Everything neat and tidy, no sign of dust, the carpet recently vacuumed and his mother hadn't even known they'd be coming. Kate imagined her always prepared. Everything ordered in her life, but it hadn't been enough to save her youngest son.

Charlie kept hold of Kate's hand as they walked into a glass-roofed conservatory full of large leafy plants and spiky cacti. He pulled her onto a two-seater brown wicker sofa, while his parents sat facing them in matching chairs. No one spoke.

Paul cleared his throat. "Five months and three days, Charlie."

"Sorry. I've been busy," Charlie said.

"Do you see much of your mother and father, Kate?" Paul asked.

"Kate's parents died when she was seven," Charlie said. "She spent her childhood in the care of the local authority. No one wanted her. She thinks I'm lucky because I was adopted."

Kate watched in discomfort as his parents cast stricken glances at each other.

"I *was* lucky," Charlie said.

Kate squeezed his fingers.

"I…er…I…" He shook his head. "How can this be so hard, when I'm supposed to be a master with words?"

Kate knew why. He was looking for his *own* words, not ones given to him.

"I don't want to hurt you, Mum," he said, "but I want to know who I am."

His mother's lower lip quivered.

"I want to know why I'm me." Charlie pressed on. "Who made me? Whose hair do I have? Whose eyes? Is my birth father tall? Is my birth mother tall? Are they crap at math too? Why is music in my heart? Why don't I like milk? Why did they give me up?"

His mother was so pale and still, she looked as though she'd died.

"We made you, Charlie," his father said. "We love music. Your mother plays the violin. I play the saxophone. I'm crap at math. It doesn't matter that your birth parents gave you up, because we wanted you. We made you."

Charlie started to bite his nail and dragged his hand from his mouth.

"I know you wanted me. I'm grateful for all you've done. You're my mum and dad and you always will be. I love you, but this is something I have to do. I've been in touch with the placement agency. They've traced my birth mother. I wanted you to know in case the press find out and make a meal of it."

"*When* the press find out," Paul said.

"Have you been in touch with her?" Jill asked in a quiet voice.

221

"No."

"She didn't want you, Charlie. She never tried to get in touch with you or find out how you were doing." Her fingers dug into the cushion at her side. "She's not the one who cuddled you when you had nightmares. Where was she when you broke your leg?" Her voice grew more shrill. "She didn't hear you sing in Westminster Cathedral. She—"

"I know," Charlie said.

"She left you in a supermarket trolley outside Woolworth's." Jill's voice snapped like a dry twig. "She didn't even leave you somewhere safe and warm. That's how much she cared about you."

Charlie was trembling.

"We wanted you and gave you a home. We protected you and trusted you. Michael trusted you." His mother let out a single sob from somewhere deep inside her.

Kate clung to Charlie's hand as he lurched. The air in the conservatory, already thick and heavy, became difficult to breathe. Kate watched the drama unfold with increasing anxiety, wanting to drag Charlie out of there and run away.

"You've not been back since Michael died and now you come to tell us you're going to look for your real parents because we're not good enough anymore." His mother shuddered. "I'm sorry I'm not the mother you wanted, but do you think your real mother will love you better?"

"You *are* my real mother," Charlie said. "It's not—"

"You know what day it is, Charlie? You pick today of all days to do this?" Jill began to cry.

Charlie paled. He let go of Kate to reach toward his mother and then pulled back.

"God, I'm sorry. I'm sorry for everything. I'm sorry I haven't been back. Sorry I let you hurt on your own."

Paul took his wife's hand and patted it. Kate's fingers crept back to Charlie's and he clung to her as if he were about to go over a waterfall.

"Michael never took drugs. Why did he take them that night?" Jill asked. "What happened? We need the truth now, Charlie."

The two faces staring at him looked like shadows, frail gray wraiths, barely alive because when their son died, part of them died too.

"I told you what happened. I told the police. I've spent the last five months trying to forget. The papers made me look like a hero and I wasn't. A hero would have saved Michael."

"We know you tried, son," his father said. He glanced at his wife. "We need to hear again what happened."

Charlie deflated as though the air had been sucked out of him.

"Michael started the night in a good mood, buying everyone drinks, larking about. He wanted people to like him and the silly bugger thought they didn't. He preferred to go out with me because there was always a crowd of hangers-on. He thought it was because they liked me but they were moths around a light. They couldn't help themselves. They thought I was something I wasn't."

Charlie glanced at Kate and then turned back to face his parents.

"Michael fancied one of the girls at our table and they flirted a bit. The truth is she probably thought she could use him to get at me."

"You gave him drugs to share with her," Jill said.

Charlie's voice was firm. "No, I didn't."

"Michael didn't take drugs," Jill said in a whisper, shaking her head. "It's you that takes drugs. Michael wouldn't. Not my Michael."

Jill wrapped her arms around herself and rocked. Kate felt the change in Charlie and knew what he was going to do.

"You're right. I gave him some coke to share with her."

His mother went so white, Kate thought she would pass out. Charlie squeezed Kate's fingers but didn't look at her.

"I told him he could take my car and pretend he owned it. He'd only had a pint. After that he'd stuck to Red Bull. He wasn't drunk." Charlie's head dropped. "He drove off with the girl and we heard the crash from inside the pub."

His voice broke. Kate saw a tear roll down his cheek.

"Was he conscious when you got there?" his father asked.

"No."

"But you pulled the girl out." Jill's chest heaved as she took gasping breaths.

"Michael's door was caved in. I did everything I could to get him out, but…his feet…his feet were trapped. I stayed with him as long as I could and then the fire…" Charlie's voice faltered, tapered to a soft whisper. "There was nothing I could do. I wanted to get him out. I'm sorry. I'm so sorry."

Tears rolled down Jill's face. Her head swayed from side to side, strange whimpering noises coming from her mouth.

"You told the police the drugs were Michael's," Paul said.

That was what Charlie had told Kate, too. He was lying now to try to help his mother, but Kate thought it was a mistake.

"Mine." Charlie stared at his father.

"You also told them Michael took the car without your permission," Paul said.

"I gave him the keys."

Kate shook her head. This was wrong.

"You blackened the name of your brother to keep your own name clean," his mother said. "I suppose you thought if Michael was dead, it didn't matter."

"I'm sorry," Charlie whispered.

Kate didn't believe this. Charlie was lying, trying to protect his parents from the truth about the son they'd lost. Almost as though he knew what she was thinking, he glanced at her and squeezed her fingers, his eyes saying "keep quiet".

"So why are you here telling us this today? Trying to impress your latest air-head floozy with your honesty and bravery?" Jill asked.

"Kate's not—"

"Is that it?" Jill asked, brushing the tears from her cheeks. "That's what you've come here for, to tell us you lied about Michael and you want to find your real parents? And you weren't even brave enough to do it on your own. Well, thank you very much, Charlie. You can go now. There's nothing more to be said."

For a moment no one spoke. Kate looked between the three of them and something snapped.

"What *is* this?" she asked. "What's going on here?"

"This has nothing to do with you," Jill said.

"I'm here with Charlie, so it does. You lost a son and that's terrible. I can't even begin to imagine what that must be like, the pain you're going through, but you have another son and he's sitting here in front of you. He's hurting and you're acting like he's a stranger."

Paul and Jill looked at one another.

"I care more for Charlie than you do." Kate swallowed hard. "How can that be? You're his parents. He's told you he's sorry. He wasn't driving the car. Michael was. Michael didn't have to take the drugs, he didn't have to take the car. Charlie didn't force them on him. He tried to save him and couldn't. Don't you understand what that's like for him? Charlie blames himself enough without having you blame him too."

When Kate finished speaking, there was silence. His father looked down at the tiled floor. Charlie was sniffing. His mother stood up.

"It should have been you," Jill said.

"No!" Kate gasped.

"Jill, don't." Paul tried to pull her down, but she shrugged him away.

"You should have been the one to die, not Michael. You were the reckless one, not him. He didn't deserve what happened. He had so much to live for, so much left to achieve. He could have done anything, been anyone. He worked hard and you waltzed through life, not caring about anyone but yourself." She spat the words out and Charlie flinched at every one.

"You lounged around, playing your guitar, pretending to be a pop star while Michael spent hours practicing, trying to keep up with you. You passed every piano exam with distinction yet made no effort. Michael wanted one distinction, just one, but he never got it." Jill dropped back, gulping in air.

"That's enough, Jill," her husband said.

Charlie sat frozen. He wasn't even holding Kate's hand anymore. Her fingers were wrapped around his but they were limp and unresponsive.

"Michael's never going to have any more birthdays. He's never going to come here and introduce us to his girlfriend, tell us he's engaged or getting married or going to be a father." Jill was almost shouting. "There are never going to be any of those moments for us. We'll never hold his grandchildren in our arms. And it's your fault, Charlie. Why did you give him drugs? Why did you let him take your car?"

Kate sprang to her feet but Charlie stepped in front of her.

"I didn't," he snapped. "I lied. I sat here looking at two people who've given me a comfortable home, a good education and the best love they could and I felt how much I owed you and knew it was time to repay a little of that debt. And I am grateful, I am. I'm sorry. I thought I could make you happy if you thought Michael wasn't to blame, but I can't, can I? No matter what I say, you'll always blame me, because I couldn't get him out of the fucking car."

They were all on their feet now, Paul holding Jill, Kate behind Charlie.

"The cocaine *was* Michael's. He bought it because he was trying to entice a girl away from me. He took the car without me knowing. He lifted the keys from my pocket. He was never satisfied with what he had. He was a kind, funny guy, but he always felt second best because he wasn't like me."

Kate tugged his arm, but knew she couldn't stop this.

"You could have made him feel special, but you didn't. When he complained about his ears sticking out, you agreed with him and fixed them. You fixed his teeth and there was nothing wrong with them."

Jill tried to interrupt but Charlie raced on.

"You made him practice the piano when he'd rather have been playing football. You *made* him compete with me. You didn't let him be Michael. He was always Charlie's little brother. He was great as he was. He didn't deserve to die, you're right, but he did deserve better from all of us."

Charlie grabbed Kate's hand and pulled her out of the house with his mother in pursuit, screaming at him.

"I'm going to write a book, Charlie. I'm going to tell everyone what you're really like. See what happens to your precious career then, if women still want you."

Charlie tried to yank Kate across the drive to the car, but she dragged her hand free.

"Charlie, calm down. Please."

His eyes blazed with fury. "Don't tell me to fucking calm down. Get in the car."

Kate grabbed the keys from his hand and darted backward.

"Don't move," she said, twisting away as he reached for her. She ran to the house.

The door was still open. Kate took a deep breath and walked inside. She could hear Charlie's mother sobbing and followed the noise. Paul and Jill stood in a Quaker-style kitchen, their arms around each other. Paul motioned for Kate to go back. A moment later he joined her in the hall. He looked like someone had run over his soul. Kate realized what she'd seen in his eyes before and not liked was deep exhaustion.

"I'm sorry you had to witness that," he said.

"Whatever happened that night, Charlie will never forgive himself. You have to believe he did everything he could to get Michael out of the car, even if he can't believe it himself. Whether he gave Michael the drugs or the car keys is irrelevant. He'll always feel responsible for his brother's death. He has to live with that. Isn't it enough?"

Paul looked at her. "I don't care who gave what to whom. We lost two sons that night, not one."

"Charlie is so unhappy. He's desperate to know that you love him."

"We do love him, it's just…he's difficult. The fact that he's looking for his birth mother on top of what's happened is too much for us now, particularly for Jill."

"Charlie tried to kill himself," Kate blurted out.

Even as she spoke the words, she wasn't sure if she'd done the right thing. The remaining color drained from Paul's face.

"Oh Christ." He staggered and clutched his chest.

Kate was afraid he was going to have a heart attack.

"I'm sorry. I…" She wanted the words back.

"Don't tell Jill," he whispered.

Kate shook her head. "No one knows. Only me. I told you because I want you to understand how much pain he's in, how much he needs you to love him. He lost part of himself when his brother died."

"What did he do?" Paul asked. "Tablets?"

"He swam out to sea."

Paul took a deep, shaky breath. "What happened? He changed his mind?"

Kate hesitated before she answered. "We both did."

Paul leaned against the wall. "Oh my God. Was it some pact? What—?"

"We were two strangers. We met by chance. I was unhappy too. So, I do understand how desperate Charlie felt, how lonely, how unloved. Please don't turn your back on him. He has to…to find himself and he wants your support."

"Do you think he'll try again?" Paul asked.

"He needs reasons not to."

"Like you?"

Kate gave a little smile. "Maybe I'm only a fleeting fix for Charlie, a weak glue holding things together." She felt a flare of pain as she said that. "He has to sort himself out, learn to like himself again before he can move on. Part of that is understanding where he comes from."

"His birth mother." Paul sighed. "We told him too late, when he was in his teens. We should have said something when he was little, but Jill didn't want to. She wanted to pretend he wasn't adopted and I went along with it. It was after we told him that things started to go wrong."

Paul ran his fingers through his hair and pressed his lips together. Kate saw Charlie in the mannerisms.

"Tell him I'd like to meet his birth mother, too. Not sure Jill could cope, but I'd like to thank the woman for giving us Charlie. I do love him, you know. So does Jill. Charlie has been very good to us."

Kate looked at a photograph on the radiator shelf. "Is that Michael?" A smiling guy, with curly brown hair and dimples, stood holding a surfboard.

"Yes."

"Could I borrow it?"

"You can keep it. We have another." Paul opened the frame and gave it her.

Kate slipped the photo into her purse.

"It would have been Michael's birthday today, that's why Charlie's timing is poor. Jill's had better days. Bring Charlie back again. I miss him."

Chapter Seventeen

ℬ

Kate came out of the house to find Charlie pacing up and down next to the car. When he saw her, he stopped and held out his hand. "Give me the fucking keys."

"I'm driving," Kate said.

He leaned against the door to stop her opening it. "You're not insured."

"Well, I promise not to kill you on the way back."

His face remained stony.

"You need to calm down, Charlie. I'll drive for a while and then you can take over. Okay?"

He sighed, but went around the other side and waited for Kate to unlock the door.

"What did you go back in for?"

"I forgot my bag."

Kate hoped he didn't notice the lie.

"See, families aren't all sweetness and light," he muttered, as Kate pulled off.

"I like your dad."

"But not my mum?"

"Not right now." Kate chose her words with care. "She shouldn't have said that, but she's blinded by pain."

"And I'm not?" he snapped.

"Charlie, don't. This isn't just about you."

Neither of them spoke again until Charlie said, "This is the wrong way. We missed the road. Find somewhere to turn."

Kate did as he said and followed instructions to get back to the main road.

They continued in silence for a while and then Charlie said, "I'd forgotten it was his birthday."

"I don't think that was the problem."

He twisted his hands on his lap. "I miss him."

"I know you do."

"Like you miss your mum and dad?"

Kate kept her eyes on the road. This was her chance to tell Charlie the truth, but after the scene in the house, she didn't want to.

"Course you do," he muttered.

"I don't remember them," Kate said. "I don't even remember what my mum looked like. I don't remember what it was like to have someone who cared for me because they wanted to, not because they were paid to do it."

"I...that's sad."

"That's life."

"You must have formed attachments to some of the people who looked after you."

No, she hadn't, because nothing ever lasted. People moved on or she did, so there was no point.

"I told you I wasn't an easy kid," Kate said. "I think I misbehaved because I was testing people, seeing if they could love me even when I was bad. And while I pushed them away, I still hoped someone would tell me I was beautiful and clever, that I could be whatever I wanted. You had that."

"And threw it away."

"No, you fed on it, flourished on it. Jill and Paul made you, Charlie, and they love you. They'd love you no matter what you did. That's something special. So when you look for the woman who gave birth to you, remember that's all she did, let you grow inside her. Your real mum and dad are back there."

Kate heard him sniffing.

Charlie let out a shaky breath. "I guess your parents didn't get eaten by piranhas?"

"No."

"Or die of the Ebola virus?"

"No."

Charlie waited and Kate knew he expected her to say more, but she couldn't. Her mouth felt like she'd been eating dry crackers. She didn't want to remember. Even thinking about remembering turned her stomach into a seething mass of worms.

"I've just opened my fucking heart and you still can't talk to me." His voice grew harsher. "Maybe they're not even dead. Are they living happily in a semi in Milton Keynes? Maybe they chucked you out. Maybe you left them. Have you made up your history to make me feel sorry for you?"

Kate chewed her lip.

"Did you sleep around, Kate? Get pregnant? Have an abortion? What secrets are you hiding?"

A red rage rose inside her. How could he turn this back on her? She couldn't stop herself snapping. "Whose drugs, Charlie? Car keys stolen or given?"

"What do you think? You know what I'm like. Stop here."

Kate slammed on the brakes, switched off the engine and turned to face him. "Tell me the truth."

"Michael's drugs. He stole the keys." Charlie fixed his eyes on some distant point. "I was trying to make it easier for them. I thought if they could blame me, then they could forgive me. But it was Michael's coke. He brought it, he lifted the keys from my pocket." He paused. "But I did lie to them." He turned to Kate, his dark eyes full of pain. "He was conscious when I got to the car. I dragged the girl out. She was breathing but unconscious. Michael pleaded with me to get him out, yelled at me that I wasn't pulling hard enough, not trying hard enough. I'd have cut his bloody legs off if I could, but there was no way to move him and the fire got hotter and I knew he was going to die. He knew it too. He begged me not to leave him."

Kate reached out to take his hand, his fingers shaking in hers.

"But I had to. I couldn't breathe. I had to leave him. Oh, God. He screamed. Then, he stopped. He wasn't conscious then, but I…"

He burst into tears, wrenched his hand from hers and jumped out of the car. When he stalked off down the road, Kate went after him. He bounded up to the nearest lamppost and kicked it. Kate took hold of his arm and tried to pull him away.

"Charlie, don't."

"The council sent them a bill for the lamppost. How could they do that? Send a bill for a fucking lamppost to a bereaved family?"

He kicked out again and then hit the post with his fist. Blood sprayed from his knuckles and Kate clung to his arm.

"Please, Charlie."

She held on to him as he struggled to get free, smearing them both with blood, but she wouldn't let go and in the end Charlie stopped fighting. For a moment, he let her hold him. Kate wrapped her arms around his waist and pressed her head into his shoulder. Then he yanked the keys from her pocket and ran.

"I want to drive. It's my fucking car," he shouted.

Charlie got in the driver's side, intending to drive off without her, afraid for her safety if she got back in with him, but afraid for his safety if she didn't. Kate pulled open the passenger door and sat down. He stared at her for a moment, waited until she'd fastened her seat belt and then roared off into the gloom.

He drove fast. Lights flashed past. He overtook every vehicle he came up behind. Other drivers blared their horns, the noise remaining in his head long after he'd left the vehicle in his wake. He was hyper and reckless, teetering on the edge of disaster.

"Do you trust me, Kate?"

"Yes."

"You don't, but you shouldn't anyway."

Charlie shot past a slower vehicle and stayed on the wrong side of the road, only swerving back when approaching headlights flashed him, accompanied by another clashing symphony of car horns. He glanced at Kate, expecting to see her gripping the sides of her seat, but her hands lay folded on her lap. He wanted her to scream at him to slow down, to stop, to let her drive.

"Do you trust me, Kate?" he asked again.

"I'm trusting you with my life."

She let out a gasp as Charlie overtook a line of three vehicles and only just managed to pull back in before a sharp bend.

"When are you going to tell me to slow down?"

"I'm not."

"Aren't you scared?"

"Yes."

"So why aren't you yelling at me?"

"Do you want me to?" Kate asked.

"Yes. You're my leveler. You're the one who stops me spilling over the top of the glass, stops me biting my nails, stops me being a dickhead, stops me killing myself."

"You have to take charge of your future."

"Which shrink told you that? This is your future, too. If I die, you die with me."

The road opened out into a dual carriage way and the car surged forward.

"Tell me to slow down," he demanded.

"Slow down, Charlie."

"I will if you unzip me and wrap your mouth round my cock." He glanced away from the road to her face. Her eyes were fixed on his.

"No," she said. "If we're going to die, it's not going to be my fault."

Charlie was boiling. Fury and guilt surged around his bloodstream, writhing together like battling snakes until every part of him was wound to breaking point. He slammed his foot on the brake and pulled off the road into a picnic spot. Driving deep into an empty car park, he screeched to a halt in a sideways skid before switching off the engine. He turned to face her. Kate's face looked pale in the darkness, her eyes wide. He was breathing in short, fast gasps. He'd wanted her to stop him. Why hadn't she?

"What happened to your parents? The truth," he said.

Kate hesitated.

"I open my heart to you and you can't fucking give me one simple thing." He grabbed her head and mashed his lips hard against hers. Pressing her back in her seat, Charlie pinned her in place. One hand moved to her breast, kneading it through her dress, pinching her nipple between his fingers. She squirmed in pain and tried to kiss him back, but he wouldn't let her. He didn't want her to be kind.

Charlie yanked her back across his seat and out of the car, slamming her up against the door.

"Talk to me," he yelled.

His hands were all over her, surging under her dress, tearing it over her head. Charlie stopped thinking. He ripped her bra away, dropped his head to her breast and bit her.

Kate howled in pain. "Fuck it, Charlie. That hurt."

She tried to push him away, but he knocked her arms aside, caught hold of her wrists and held them with one hand.

"Tell me to stop," he begged.

His fingers plunged inside her underwear and moments later her panties lay in shreds on the ground and his fingers were in her. Charlie pulled her to the front of the car and twisted her around so she lay facedown over the bonnet, sprawled out naked in front of him. When he let her wrists go, she tried to lever herself up, but he kept her where she was.

"Tell me to stop," he pleaded. "Kate, I want you to tell me to stop. Tell me to fuck off, go away, leave you alone. Please."

He fumbled with his zip and freed his erection. She was the only thing important to him, but he didn't deserve her. He wanted her to see what he was really like. Charlie didn't even pull down his trousers, just pushed his dick between her legs and fucked her. Kate gave a loud sob and then fell silent.

She couldn't move. The bonnet of the car was hot, hard and hurting her. Charlie shuddered against her as his cum dribbled down her thighs. Kate knew exactly why he'd done this. He wanted to drive her away. He had no idea how familiar it was, being abused, being loved, then abused again. She felt something wet, high on her back and his body quivered. He was crying. When he pulled away from her, she took a deep breath and eased herself off the front of the car.

"I'm sorry," he sobbed. "I'm sorry."

Kate turned. He stood with tears rolling down his cheeks, his eyes closed, his cock hanging out. She picked up her tattered panties and wiped herself before pulling her dress over her head. Charlie still hadn't moved. He didn't even look as though he was breathing. His eyes were squeezed shut, his fists clenched as if he'd been frozen by the horror of what he'd done.

Kate stepped to him and let her fingers brush over his.

"Open your eyes, Charlie. I'm still here."

"Sorry," he said, his voice barely audible. "I'm so sorry. I can't believe I did that. I forced you, I raped —"

Kate took hold of his hand, wouldn't let him pull away. "Open your eyes and look at me." She held his gaze. "You didn't rape me."

"I hurt you," he whispered. "I didn't want to hurt you. Why did I do that to you? Why did you let me? Why didn't you say stop?" He began to shake. "Oh God, it wasn't your fault. Sorry."

She slid her arms around his waist. "I'll be all right, Charlie. It's okay."

His arms remained at his sides. He stood like a dejected statue.

"It's not okay," he said. "Tell me to leave you alone. Tell me to fuck off."

"No."

He breathed in noisy gasps. "I don't want you to love me. I'm not worth it."

Kate held him tight.

"My mum doesn't love me anymore," Charlie whispered, sounding so much like a little boy that Kate's heart twisted.

"Yes, she does. She's grieving for what she's lost. She hurts just like you do. My God, Charlie, think how you'd feel if you lost your son, someone you'd loved all those years, everything you wanted for him, gone in an instant. Their lives changed forever that night. It killed something inside them. I know you're hurting too. I know you went through something unspeakably awful, but he was their child. They'd watched him grow, fed him, laughed with him and been proud of him. They had dreams for him and they're all gone."

Kate stroked his back, kissed him. He didn't respond.

"They know you're in pain and they're angry with Michael for that. They're angry because if he'd been more careful, it wouldn't have happened. And they feel guilty that they're angry. You're all awash with emotions. Your mum does love you, but she needs time and more than anything else, she needs for you to keep on loving her."

Finally, Charlie put his arms around her. Kate held him close, kissed the salty tears from his cheeks.

"Your dad told me he'd like to meet your birth mother. He wants to thank her for giving you up. He says they were the lucky ones, because they got you. They're frightened of losing you, Charlie."

"I'm so fucked up. I'm sorry," he whispered. "I shouldn't have done that to you. I'll never do it again."

She kissed his nose. "I've had worse done."

"Oh Christ."

She reached down, tucked him back into his pants, gently zipped him up, and fastened the button.

"You wanted me to tell you no? Well, no more driving like a teenager," she said as she got back into the car.

"God, I'm sorry."

"And no more saying you're sorry."

As Charlie pulled back onto the road, Kate pretended to sleep. She was more hurt than he knew. She'd thought he was different, but when he'd taken his anger out on her, Kate wondered if she'd made another mistake. She wished he wasn't hurting, but letting him hurt her had been all she could think of, making him confront whatever it was eating him up. What did she know about any of this? Perhaps she'd made things worse. What if it didn't stop here? What if the abuse continued, as it had with Dex. Was there something about her that drove her to damaged guys? Kate wanted to believe Charlie would keep his promise to never hurt her again. She had to believe it because she couldn't leave him.

Chapter Eighteen

ഔ

"Hey, wake up."

Kate stirred to find Charlie nuzzling her ear. She opened her eyes and blinked. Everything was pitch black. "Where the hell are we?"

"In my garage."

"Isn't there a light?"

"An automatic one, but it's gone off. We've been here a while."

He got out of the car. A moment later the lights went on and he came round to open the door on Kate's side. He took hold of her hand but wouldn't look at her. He led her up a flight of steep steps and unlocked the door that took them into the house. As they moved into the hall, Kate's eyes rose to the painted ceiling and she shuddered.

"Hungry?" Charlie asked, still looking away from her.

Neither of them had eaten since breakfast, but Kate felt sick.

"I'll order a takeaway later, if you like," Charlie said.

Kate knew he felt guilty about hurting her, and so he should, but he had to find a way through this himself. She'd mothered him enough.

"Do you want to go home?" he whispered.

She raised his scraped knuckles to her lips and kissed them. "No. I want you to show me your house." Kate made sure her voice sounded bright.

They were quiet as they walked around and he clung to her hand like a small child. The main room was beautiful, nothing old or tatty. Exotic rugs in shades of blue and brown lay scattered over a pale wood floor. A massive LCD TV dominated one wall and the others displayed a range of paintings Kate might have

239

chosen herself. Three large light-brown leather couches strewn with shaggy blue cushions were arranged around a multi-layered, glass coffee table. Books and magazines sat in neat piles. Nothing out of place.

"Ooh, furniture," she said. "Did you choose it yourself?"

He shrugged, his face etched with distress, dark shadows back under his eyes.

"This is like being at the cinema." Kate stood next to the huge TV. "How do you turn it on?"

Charlie picked up a remote, pressed it and the TV went on then off. Another button brought music. A third closed the curtains.

"Which is the button for the bat cave?" she asked.

Not even the hint of a smile. Kate wondered if she'd cried and sobbed, it would have made a difference. Was her ability to get past it stopping him doing the same?

The kitchen, with its glossy granite work surfaces and brushed steel appliances, looked as though it had come out of a showroom. She ran her fingers over a butcher's block.

"It's a fabulous kitchen," Kate said and meant it.

The music room was dominated by a grand piano, the floor covered in a sea of paper. Charlie snapped out of his lethargy and scooped up the sheets of manuscript in such a rush, Kate knew he was hiding something.

"Do you have a garden?" she asked.

"A small one."

He switched on lights and opened French doors. Kate looked out onto a yard that seemed all plants and trees. A herringbone patterned brick patio curled toward a small lawn, and tucked away in the corner was a blue and white mosaic-topped table and four metal chairs.

"We could eat breakfast out here," she said.

No response.

Kate wondered if she should leave, but he still clung to her hand. The only time he'd let her go was to pick up the music. She wandered back into the dining room and admired the glass table laid with hand-painted plates and blue stone-handled cutlery. Six curvy stemmed, wide-mouthed glasses that looked impossible to use, sat on silver star-shaped coasters. Kate felt certain no one had ever sat there to eat. Charlie's home wasn't a home.

She touched the edge of the dining table. "Is this from IKEA?"

"No, it bloody — Right, very funny, Kate."

But she saw him give a little smile and felt glad.

The final room downstairs was a cross between an electronic store and a music shop. It was full of equipment — wires and speakers everywhere, three guitars on stands, several amps, a selection box of pedals, another flat-screen TV and a keyboard. Chaotic order, *this* was Charlie's heart.

"I thought you'd given up the music?" she said.

"I'm sometimes inspired to write."

"Written a song about me?"

His eyes opened wide.

Kate smiled and put her arms around him. "Charlie, sometimes you are as transparent as glass. What were you racing to pick up by that piano?"

"That was just a piece about this witch of woman who drove every man she slept with completely mad."

"It *is* about me." Kate laughed.

He raised her hand to his lips and kissed her fingers.

"You drive me mad with lust," he said, staring into her eyes. "Sometimes…too mad. I'm sorry."

"I know."

The last place Charlie showed her was his bedroom. The clothes he'd taken off that morning lay in a little nest on the carpet. Socks inside pants, inside trousers, just as he'd stepped out of them.

"If you positioned your feet right, you could put those back on again," she said.

"I sometimes do."

241

Kate rolled her eyes and went into the bathroom, walls and floor covered by pale travertine tiles, a scattering of halogen lights over the ceiling. The silver taps gleamed, as did a huge sail-shaped towel rail holding a set of fluffy bath sheets in decreasing shades of blue. The walk-in shower had a spotless curved glass wall and a large whirlpool tub sat in the corner. As far as Kate was concerned, this was a bathroom made in heaven.

"Does the tub take long to fill?"

Charlie started the water running. "I'll get us something to drink."

And finally, Kate hoped it would be all right because she knew a way to make him laugh again.

When Charlie got back, the bathroom door was closed. Above the hum of the Jacuzzi, he could hear Kate swearing.

"Shit, shit, shit."

"Kate? Are you okay?"

"No, I'm bloody not. Don't come in."

It was like waving a bar of chocolate in front of a child and expecting to hear the words "no thank you". Charlie opened the door.

"Fuck," he said, then laughed.

Kate stood in a sea of foam looking panic-stricken. The froth covered the bathroom floor and was creeping up the walls like an alien fungus. Charlie closed the door to save his bedroom carpet and waded across. He put down the bottle of champagne and the two glasses, lost them in the foam and turned off the jets.

"How much did you squirt in?" he asked.

"The whole bottle. The top came off. When I came back in, I couldn't find a way to switch it off. Will it damage the tiles?"

"I don't care about the tiles."

Kate lifted her dress over her head and let it drop into the foam.

"Oh God," he whispered. "Look what I've done to your beautiful body."

242

His fingers touched a mark on her breast, a bloody graze at her shoulder. There were smudges of blood all over her, fortunately his. But the bruises were his fault. He traced every mark with his fingers, memorizing every one and wishing it all back.

"I should take you to a hospital, I should—"

"I'm all right, Charlie. I'm not broken."

He ran his fingers over her cheek and when she turned into the caress like a kitten being stroked, something shattered inside him. "Please forgive me. I swear to you that I'll never lose control like that again. No matter how furious I get, I'll never, ever hurt you again."

"Not even if I scratch your car?"

"Don't joke, Kate."

Tears gathered in the bottom of his eyes. He blinked and they spilled over, rolling down his cheeks.

"Don't forgive me too quickly. I want to make it up to you. I'll—" He flailed around. "I'll buy you a new dress. A...a new sewing machine. I could get—"

"Charlie! All I want is a bath."

"Let me wash you."

"That would be nice."

Kate stepped into the bubbles. When she sat down, she almost disappeared. Charlie blew away the foam until he found the glasses and then poured the champagne. Crouching in the white froth at the side of the bath, he clinked his glass against hers. "I promise never to hurt you again."

"I promise not to let you. Now get in here and wash me."

Charlie stripped off and slid behind Kate. He saw more marks on her back and bit the inside of his cheek so hard, the coppery tang of blood seeped into his mouth. Kate leaned back against him and slid her hands under the foam, piling mounds of white fluff on her breasts.

"Do you like women with huge boobs?" she asked.

"I like yours. I like the way they exactly fill my hands, the way they cradled my cock."

He caressed her nipples with his fingertips, thrilled they turned pebble-hard at his touch.

Kate leaned forward to put down her glass and Charlie homed in on the mark he hadn't made. "Where did that scar on your back come from?"

"I was stabbed."

She might have been matter of fact but fear and fury flashed through Charlie's body. For a moment, he couldn't speak and then said, "I thought it was a bit high for your appendix."

Kate gave a snort of laughter. He pulled her back against his chest and spat out the mouthful of foam that splattered his face.

"I don't suppose it was an accident?"

"No."

He waited, but she didn't say more. He wished she'd open up and let him in. Smoothing the foam away from her chest, his fingers lingered on the bite mark he'd made on her breast.

"I'm sorry, Kate." Charlie kissed her neck. "You want to hit me or something? I'm no better than the bastard that gave you that scar."

"You are different. You haven't broken my arm or my ribs, split my lip or given me a black eye."

Another surge of adrenaline and Charlie stiffened. "Oh God. Dickhead? I'll fucking kill him."

"Not Richard. Before him."

There was a long pause. "Want to tell me about it?"

"You're not the only one with a self-destruct button, Charlie."

"You can't excuse some asshole's behavior by saying you were asking for it."

"I should have left the first time Dex hit me."

He held her tight and pressed his lips into her hair. She smelled of lemons. She always smelled of something fresh and new. And someone had hurt her. He'd like to fucking—except he'd hurt her as well.

"Why didn't you leave?" he whispered.

"Because he said he was sorry and promised he wouldn't do it again. And...and I thought I deserved it because I'd pissed him off."

Apologies and promises from abusers, Charlie thought. He'd done the same. How could he show her he was different, particularly when his erection was poking her in the butt? "Did you tell anyone?"

"No. I don't like to talk about myself, and I don't talk about other people, either. I learned early on in life, it's best to zip your lip. Secrets are secrets for good reasons. If I complained and whined, it made matters worse. Anyway, even if I'd wanted to tell someone about Dex, I didn't have anyone *to* tell. The only people I hung out with were his friends."

Charlie let out a shuddering breath on her shoulder, blowing the foam into a little shower of snow. *Oh God, I could have lost her before I'd even met her.*

"What happened to him?"

Kate hesitated again.

"Talk to me, Kate. Please."

"One night, Dex really lost it. He shouted, I said something stupid and he hit me. He broke my arm and a couple of ribs, knocked me out and when I came to, he'd gone."

Charlie wrapped his arms around her, held her tight.

"I found out later, he went to the pub and picked a fight. At closing time, a guy he'd bad-mouthed was waiting outside. He only hit Dex once, a fist in the stomach, but it ruptured something and he was taken to hospital. He nearly died."

"Oh shit." Charlie pressed his face into Kate's hair.

"The next day, his parents moved me out of the apartment. They were angry because I didn't raise the alarm when Dex failed to come home. I'd discharged myself from the same bloody hospital at midnight because I was scared what he might do if he didn't find me at the apartment when he got back. I lay in bed with my arm in plaster, grateful to be on my own, thinking he'd probably picked up some woman to teach me a lesson and instead he was worse off than me."

She shivered in his arms.

"I know it sounds bad but whoever hit him did me a favor. I was determined never to trust anyone again. I did okay for a while. Then I met Richard Winter."

"I think that's the most you've said to me about your past."

"Oh God, we're doomed. The moment I open up, people go off me."

Charlie rolled her over, so that they lay curled up facing each other.

"Did you tell Dickhead about Dex?"

"No. I told you I don't like to talk about personal things. I'm a very private person. My business is mine and no one else's."

"But you're talking to me." He lifted her chin with his finger.

"I trust you."

Charlie's heart swelled and he exhaled, blowing foam off her face. "After what—"

"Leave it, Charlie."

"Was Dex the one who stabbed you?"

"No."

He gave a loud groan. "Jesus, Kate. The press would eat you."

"Then I'd better not tell you the real reason I don't like having my photo taken."

"I think you should. You've had such a fucked-up life, you're making me feel a lot less sorry for myself. This is much better than staring at a psychiatrist." He paused. "Oh God, that sounded terrible. You don't have to tell me anything."

"I want to," Kate said and emptied her glass. She snuggled against his chest. "Remember I had the attic room in the children's home? It was so my care worker had some privacy while he fucked me and took photographs."

Charlie jerked and spilt his drink. "Shit, Kate. How old were you?"

"Fourteen."

"Oh my God. India was…" Grief and guilt smothered his voice.

"It was different, Charlie. You were at a party, having fun and you thought she was sixteen. India wanted sex. I didn't. This guy was supposed to be looking after me."

Disgust that he'd been another of the people who'd hurt Kate made Charlie's stomach churn and his heart ache. He'd treated her like… He gulped back a sob.

Kate pressed her head into his shoulder. "I told Linda, my social worker, but someone gave the fat bastard an alibi so she decided I'd lied. When Ray came to my room, he brought another man. He said if I told again, next time there would be three."

Charlie held her as tight as he could. He wanted to protect her and look after her forever and never let her get hurt again, only how could he tell her that after what he'd done? Why should she believe him?

"I have this feeling there are pictures of a fourteen-year-old me floating about on the Internet. That's why I don't like my photo being taken."

"How do you deal with all this?" he whispered.

"By accepting it. I don't drag it behind me like an oversized suitcase. I don't moan and wail about what I can't put right. I have to live in the world that follows."

"But you tried to kill yourself."

"I'd let my defenses down."

"Have I slipped past your guard?" he asked.

"I think you *are* my guard."

She could still say that after what he'd done? Charlie kissed her hair. He could be a better man. Kate would make him one. He trembled as she ran her hands down his body, sweeping away the bubbles.

"Let me wash your back," she said.

"I'm supposed to be washing you."

"But you have such silky, soft skin."

"You sound like a snake and I think you nicked my line."

Kate trailed her fingers under the foam and down his stomach to wrap them around his cock.

"That's not my back," he said.

"I was hopeless at biology." A lick of his nipple dragged a groan from his throat.

"In that case, it *is* my back. Keep rubbing."

Charlie caught her laugh with a kiss. She tasted so sweet his head was swimming. Kate pulled away and slid down his body, landing tiny nips and bites along the ridges of his ribs. Before her mouth settled round his cock, Charlie dragged her back to cup her face with his hands. When her soft satin lips opened at once for his tongue, Charlie understood how close he'd come to screwing this up, how lucky he was she still lay in his arms and hadn't told him to fuck off or even reported him to the police. He wanted her forever and the thought made his heart ache.

"I'm sorry," he muttered.

"You don't need to keep apologizing." She licked her way back down his chest.

"Yes, I do." He lifted her head to look her in the eyes. "You're special to me and I know I nearly wrecked everything. I'm ashamed of myself."

"I could have stopped you."

"Could you?" Charlie asked. "What if you'd tried and I'd carried on?"

Kate slid up and put her hands around his neck. "Charlie, you've had a terrible day. Someone you love, someone who loves you, said an awful thing and you lashed out. It doesn't matter that you lashed out at me. That's what I've been trying to explain. There's something about me that makes — "

He sat up so fast, a wave of water sloshed over the side of the tub. "Don't talk crap. It *does* matter. There's nothing about you that would make me want to hurt you, that should make anyone want to hurt you. Don't you dare blame yourself. I fucked up

248

today. I don't deserve you, but I'll show you I can be a better man. I don't want to let you go. Ever. I've never felt like this before." He took a deep breath, his heart surging into his throat as he looked into her eyes.

"Kate, I...I think I love you."

Oh God, had he managed to say that out loud? Yeah, he had. His heart rate had doubled and his mouth had dried up. He'd held those words safe for so long that Charlie could hardly believe he'd let them go. Except Kate hadn't said anything. She was staring at him but why didn't she say something? Charlie took hold of her jaw and waggled it up and down as if trying to get her to speak.

"Good to know you care about me too," he said in a gruff voice.

"Hippo, I was yours from the thump on the nose."

His heart leapt against hers, as if the two organs had reached out to kiss. Then their lips met and Charlie's head went fuzzy. *Be gentle,* he told himself and at least this time, he managed not to crush her. His hands plastered over her back, Charlie took it slow. He wanted to kiss her back to happiness, back into belief in him. Today had been terrible but something sort of good had come out of it. Kate was talking to him about her past. He didn't like most of what she had to say, but she'd begun to trust him.

He slid his tongue over her upper lip and sucked it into his mouth. Her hands held his head, her thumbs stroking just below his eyes. She was rocking against him, their bodies sliding against one another. So easy to just slip his cock inside— Charlie turned to stone.

Oh fuck, what have I done? What the hell have I done?

Kate tipped her head back to look at him.

"I didn't use protection." He groaned. "Oh God, I'm sorry."

"Charlie, it's okay."

"No, it's not. I've ruined everything. I'm such a fucking cunt. I've never done that before. Never lost my head so I didn't remember. Fuck, fuck. I mean, what if—"

"I'm on the Pill."

He closed his eyes, his head full to bursting with a thousand thoughts. He'd had this vision of Kate, pregnant, and the pair of them struggling with the assembly instructions for a cradle. Then he thought of all the times he'd used a condom with her when he hadn't needed to and he opened his eyes and glared.

"Think," Kate said.

Charlie did as he was told. *Ah.* One chance for a first time and he'd fucked it up, spoiled what should have been special. She did the right thing not telling him. Only now she had. He made himself not smile.

"Were you ever going to tell me?" he whispered.

"When the moment was right."

"I am such a dick."

"Yes you are."

He let out a choked laugh.

"Pretend tonight is our first time."

"But I already —"

"No. You weren't thinking of me then. This time you will be. Make it good."

Kate squealed as Charlie stood and scooped her into his arms. He sat her on the edge of the tub, grabbed a towel and wrapped it around her. Foam flew everywhere.

"We need to eat," he said. "Italian, Thai, Indian? I could try for Argentinian. We might have to wait a while." He'd send a bloody plane to fly a meal back.

"Don't you have anything in your fridge?"

"The fridge?" He blinked. "I have no idea."

"Can I go see?"

He nodded. Kate rubbed her hair and Charlie wrapped a towel around his waist.

"Do you have an old shirt I can put on?" she asked.

Charlie padded into the bedroom and into his closet. He had about a hundred shirts. None of them were old. He picked a thin white one and slipped into a pair of boxers before he came back out.

The moment Kate had fastened the buttons on the shirt, she laughed. "You can see straight through this."

Charlie raised his eyebrows. "Really."

"Come on." Kate took his hand and tugged him down to the kitchen.

Charlie doubted there was anything edible in there but Kate checked out the fridge, opened a few cupboards and smiled.

"Thirty minutes. Is it warm enough to eat in the garden?"

He'd find a way to make it warm if that was what Kate wanted.

Cooking soothed Kate. Charlie had put music on, some soulful jazz thing, poured her a glass of champagne, given her a kiss and disappeared. He'd had a terrible day and she hadn't meant to unload her past on him, but if they were to have any chance together, there could be no secrets. Charlie was so open and straightforward and Kate still hid something huge. One day she'd tell him, but not this day.

The kitchen was like something out of a magazine. Kate kept running her fingers over the beautiful granite countertop. There were specks of iridescent turquoise spattered throughout and depending on where she stood, they shone bright or dim under the light. Kate cleaned up as she went along. Charlie appeared to collect cutlery, glasses and plates and then disappeared again after he'd returned twice to kiss her.

When Kate walked outside carrying the slowly sinking cheese soufflé and the bowl of salad, it was like stepping into a fairy cave. Charlie had put tea lights everywhere—among the plants, along the fence and all over the herringbone bricks apart from a bare strip between where he sat at the table and the kitchen door. He wore a white shirt that matched hers and a black bow tie. When he stood up, Kate laughed. No pants, only boxers. In the center of the table stood a vase of yellow flowers. A lump erupted in her throat.

She put the bowls on the table and threw her arms around him. "Oh Charlie, everything looks gorgeous. Even you."

He grinned and Kate felt his hands slide onto her bare butt. "I hear the food's crap at this place but we can make do."

He pulled out a chair for Kate to sit and poured more champagne as she served up the food.

One mouthful and he was moaning. "Oh God, this is delicious."

"Several eggs past their sell-by date, a hunk of moldy cheese—I cut off those bits, butter, flour—well, once I'd sieved out the weevils, and milk, only slightly smelly."

Charlie stopped chewing.

She smiled. "Only kidding."

"If we buy the ingredients, will you cook that Chihuahua thing again?"

"Okay."

"And the ice-cream dessert?"

"Ah, well if you eat all your dinner, maybe there'll be a treat afterward. Not quite zabaglione but nearly."

Charlie wrapped one of her feet inside his under the table. One hand rested on her arm. Kate lifted her other foot, and as he took a sip of champagne, she ran her toes along his thigh and under his boxers.

He groaned. "And I thought we might get through dinner without me having to ravish you."

He grabbed her ankle and stopped her toes probing any farther.

"Spoilsport." Kate pouted.

"I can't eat if you do that and I need to eat so that I can do that to you."

He watched her as he ate every mouthful and Kate felt as though she was a child on Christmas Eve, desperate to go to bed, excited about what was to come.

She cleared away the plates and dishes, and came back with the concoction she'd thrown together. Ice-cream from Charlie's freezer, sherry and a couple of crushed amaretti biscuits. Charlie pushed his chair back from the table.

"On my knee," he said.

Kate straddled him and spooned the mess into his mouth.

He licked his lips and smiled. "Almost as sweet as you." His fingers fumbled with the buttons on her shirt and pulled it open. "More," he said and opened his mouth.

Another spoonful and then Kate yelped when his lips settled around her nipple. She shivered as the ice-cream melted and Charlie swallowed around her. Then warmth returned and she groaned. Kate groaned even louder when she felt his hands slip under her shirt and stroke her butt.

"More." Charlie stared straight into her eyes. "Except, would you unfasten this bowtie first. It's strangling me."

Kate took a mouthful of the dessert herself before she slid the bowl and spoon onto the table behind her. She didn't stop after unfastening the black silk tie but undid the buttons on his shirt. He looked so sexy Kate couldn't swallow for a moment. His dark eyes, scruffy hair, the slight stubble on his cheeks. No wonder everyone loved him. He could have his pick of beautiful women. Why would he—

"Stop thinking. It'll give you wrinkles." He opened his mouth. "Feed me, Kate."

She put a spoonful of ice-cream just above her nipple. Charlie was on it before she had chance to register how cold it felt. His hands on her waist, he held her angled back as he licked and slurped before lifting his head to give her a broad grin.

"More," he said.

The next spoonful landed on his nipple and Kate leaned forward to catch the dripping dessert, then sucked. She slid her hand into the waistband of his boxers and fondled his cock. Charlie hissed.

"Don't even think about putting a spoonful there. We have to go inside before I find somewhere else to feed off you," he whispered. "I don't want to freak out the neighbors. I'm trying to persuade them that despite the occasional paparazzo parked outside, I'm just an ordinary guy."

Kate climbed off his knee and began to clear the table.

"Leave it. The housekeeper will sort it out."

"An ordinary guy would do it himself," Kate said.

Charlie rolled his eyes but he stacked the plates.

Chapter Nineteen

ဢ

Charlie was a saint. Well, he wasn't, but at that moment, he thought he was. He cleared away all the dirty plates and glasses and stacked the dishwasher while Kate put the kitchen back to rights. She even took his hand and made him go outside and blow out all the little candle lights. And while that should have lessened his ardor, it hadn't. It made him want her more.

"Hide and seek," Kate said. "You stay here, eyes closed and count to fifty."

She shrugged off her shirt.

Charlie's gaze slipped to her pert nipples. "Not fifty. Twenty-five." Charlie tossed his bowtie aside and let his shirt fall, then dragged his hand up his cock and closed his eyes.

On twenty-five he opened his eyes. His heart pounded as he searched the whole of the ground floor. No sign of her. Charlie turned off the lights before he went upstairs, straight to his bedroom. He'd been sure he'd find her in his bed but she wasn't there. Puzzled, he went to check everywhere else, including the next floor. There was nowhere else to hide except—*oh fuck*.

Charlie ran back to his bedroom and flung open the door of his closet. Kate sat on the blue box in the corner. She hadn't opened it. Then Charlie narrowed his eyes. What was she wearing?

Kate stood, hands behind her back, and smiled. His neckties. Wrapped around her breasts, up her arms, around her neck, her legs, her head. Between her legs. He blinked. Then she brought her hands forward to show what she held. *Fuck*. Charlie went up in flames. A lightning strike couldn't have been more effective. His balls tingled and his cock vibrated like a drill bit.

No one touched his box, not his cleaner, no one. He piled stuff on top... He never had anyone around to stay... *Damn*. He opened his mouth to say he could explain, then wondered—how? Props for a movie? Gifts from a fan? Presents for—er—his agent?

"Got any batteries?" Kate asked.

Air whooshed out of him. His knees shook and his asshole quivered.

"Already in," he whispered.

"Kneel on the bed," she said.

Somehow Charlie's legs carried him across the room. He threw off the cover and knelt on all fours on the dark sheet. The blue dildo Kate held was long and slender, made of a soft and smooth jelly material with spirals down the entire length. Purchased after his experiments with guys because while Charlie had liked the sensations, he liked women better. He'd been relieved to see lube in her hand too.

The moment he felt her hand on his back, lust pooled in his groin. This wasn't wrong, neither perverted nor dirty, but it wasn't something he wanted the press to get hold of. Charlie felt as though he'd bared his soul to Kate. Her hand pressed on his spine and he let his head fall forward onto the bed so his butt stuck up in the air. Charlie closed his eyes.

The bed dipped as she climbed on behind him. He felt her arms brush his thighs, a combination of her soft skin and his neckties and he trembled. With every sense on high alert, Charlie offered himself to her. She had all the power. The wet rasp of her tongue at the top of his buttock and he groaned into the bed. A fingertip stroke of his balls and he clenched his teeth around the sheet. She breathed on him and Charlie felt the wetness bloom at his cock head.

When she spread his butt cheeks, Charlie readied himself for the coldness of the lube but it was her tongue he felt, trailing down the cleft of his backside, circling his asshole and fluttering over that triangle of skin beyond before moving on to lap at his balls. Now, she'd use the lube, but she didn't. Charlie groaned when he felt the hot wetness of her tongue back on his anus. He groaned again when she blew gently, warm turning cold in an instant.

What was she thinking? Was she doing this because she thought he wanted it? He flinched at the drip of lube that slid down his cleft. Then Kate's finger was massaging it in, pressing against the entrance to his body until he felt himself relaxing. Two seconds of bliss until the head of the dildo replaced her finger.

Charlie tried to swallow. Couldn't. Gave up and just made sure he kept breathing. Kate leaned over him and rubbed her breasts against his back as she twisted the tip of the shaft around his anus. He could hear her breathing — fast and choppy. He felt her heart beating in time with his. The knowledge that this was turning her on too gave Charlie all he needed. He opened his body and the dildo slid in.

He gave a muffled groan as the swirled jelly shaft speared his asshole and touched his prostate.

"Oh fuck," Charlie gasped.

"Okay?" she whispered.

"Yes. No. Everything in between."

For a moment, everything settled. Slight burn had shifted to pleasurable fullness. Charlie could breathe. Then Kate took hold of the thing and began to move it. Heat exploded in his gut, flashes of fire raced through his bloodstream and his cock swelled.

No, Charlie screamed at his balls. *Not fucking yet.*

He wanted to fuck Kate while she did this, have his cock thrusting into her while she thrust into him but the thought of moving, even an inch, was beyond him. Every little shunt she made, she pegged his prostate. Then the dildo began to quiver in deep, thumping vibrations he felt all over his body. And still Kate pushed and rocked and twisted the thing inside him.

Charlie's knees quaked and he did his best to lock them in place. He wanted her to do this all night.

Another thirty seconds would be lovely.

He wasn't entirely sure he was still breathing. Nor that his heart was still beating.

What a time to have an epiphany.

Charlie mustered every molecule of his willpower and spoke. "Stop."

"What's the matter?" Kate asked. "Did I hurt you? Oh God–"

She pulled the dildo out and Charlie sighed. "No. Not hurt. Good. Too good." He swallowed hard to try to get some moisture back into his mouth. "Want to be in you."

"Let me just do the dance of the thirty-seven ties."

He leaned back against the pillows and watched as she unraveled herself. It shouldn't have been erotic or exotic but it was. Plain ties, striped and checked, ones with elephants, footballs, lips, horrible ties that flashed and one that played "We Wish You a Merry Christmas" in a high-pitched voice that got lower and slower before it finally fizzled out. He had no idea why he'd kept that.

Yes, he did.

Kate was by his side in an instant. "What is it?"

"Michael gave me that."

She pulled him into her arms as he began to cry.

"Fuck it, fuck it," Charlie sobbed. "Why did he take my keys? Why didn't I stop him?"

Kate stroked his hair.

"Why did she say that?" he whispered.

Kate slid down so she lay beside him.

"Don't leave me." He kissed her all over her face. "Don't leave me."

"I won't."

"Oh God," he panted. "I don't deserve you."

Kate nibbled his ear, ran her tongue around it and Charlie moaned. Nothing mattered then except the two of them. Kate was his. She lay there next to him and he had the chance to make love to her with no barrier between them. He'd got so caught up in what she'd been doing to him, he'd forgotten this was supposed to be for her. If it hadn't have been for that tie, Charlie thought he'd have come before he'd got all the way inside her. Christ, was Michael watching over him?

If you're there, thanks. But fuck off now, mate.

He lay over Kate, holding himself up on his elbows and kissed her. Her sweet lips opened and Charlie fell inside. Their tongues behaved like kids allowed outside in the sunshine after being cooped up all day because of rain. Playing kiss-chase, hide and seek, tag until they had to break apart to breathe.

The moment Charlie positioned his cock against the entrance to her body, they both started as though the knowledge of what they were doing had suddenly hit home. Forget what happened earlier, this was a gift from Kate and he knew it wasn't given lightly. Charlie swirled his crest against her silky folds. His pre-cum, her cream, mingled together and he could smell their musk rising around them. Hot, wet, perfect.

His tip parted her folds and slipped just inside her. Heat into heat. Charlie slid into her a fraction at a time, wanting to remember every second of every moment He felt her muscles clasp him, her fingers dig into his arms, her breath hit his face, saw her lovely eyes smile at him.

He ignored his balls, clamoring for permission to fire. He ignored his cock, aching for the chance to thrust.

"Oh you feel good, Charlie," she whispered.

He kept pushing, breeching her with the mushroom-shaped crest of his cock, his thick shaft following. Little by little filling her up, pushing his velvet cock into her satin glove. Charlie would not rush this perfect moment.

"Kate," he whispered as their hips finally kissed.

Kate pulled him down so he lay on her chest and they kissed again with him not moving inside her. She knew Charlie balanced on a knife edge of control because she did too. If she let herself come, Charlie would fall with her and Kate wanted this moment to last as long as they could make it.

She stroked his back, traced patterns with her fingers, wrote words she couldn't quite say. His cock filled her, and though Kate willed them not to, the muscles of her pussy gently squeezed him.

Charlie groaned. "Pack it in."

His hips rocked and his cock surged inside her.

"You pack it in first," Kate said.

He let out a choked laugh and she felt the sound ripple through her body. She could feel the texture of his cock, the heat of it, little quivers running through it when it jerked. His hands settled over her hips and held her down. One hard thrust and Kate began to ache with the need to come. The tendons in Charlie's neck stood out and he clenched his jaw as he began to move.

The force of his thrusts knocked her knees farther apart. Kate wanted to buck into him but Charlie held her firm. They both cried out, breathy moans and groans growing louder as orgasm rose within them.

"Let me move," Kate begged.

She was so close to coming, a greedy fist of need opening and closing between her legs, each side of the equation leaving an exquisite sensation. The moment his hands slid from her hips, Kate rocked up and Charlie drove down. Long, deep thrusts into her body and slow withdrawals. The sweet pleasure of his cock filling her sent her heart tripping in her chest.

A vein pulsed at Charlie's temple. "Kate," he gasped.

Their bodies slapped together, moved in harmony, the friction winding her, teasing her until she lost the capacity to think, only to feel. All that mattered was here, now, her and Charlie, together, and Kate felt the starburst inside her. Fire blazed along her veins and she unraveled in an instant, her whole body caught in the traction of explosive pleasure followed by instant intoxication, spasm after spasm.

But Charlie hadn't come. The tension clear on his face yet his mouth twisted in a smile.

"Again," he whispered.

Was he crazy? But even as Kate opened her mouth, he changed the angle of his thrust, drove into her body in double-quick time and the protest died on her lips. In the death throes of one climax, rose the phoenix of another, ecstasy rippling down her spine.

Kate thought she hardly had the strength to move, but she did. Rising into Charlie's thrusting cock, but letting him take the wheel. Kate moved without thought, caught in his rhythm until every cell in her body ached again for release.

"Please," she begged. "Oh Charlie."

She felt him jolt, felt the first spurt of his cum and then they were coming together, crying, sobbing, shaking.

Kate opened her eyes unsure whether she'd fallen asleep or passed out. Charlie still lay on top of her, though slightly to one side. His cock was still inside her. She sighed and he opened his eyes.

"You are perfect," he whispered.

Kate smiled.

"Do you think we could kill ourselves like this? Let's make a pact. If we want to go, this is the way we do it. Fucking ourselves to death."

"When we're ninety-nine."

"Goes without saying."

Chapter Twenty

Charlie lay in bed next to Kate, watching her sleep. He trusted her and she trusted him and it was a strange feeling, a warm feeling as though she'd wrapped him in something safe and snug. Charlie couldn't remember the last time he'd trusted a woman. Kate was more than his lover. She was his friend, his dreams — his life. He'd done something awful to her, but she'd given him another chance. Kate knew more about him than anyone and hadn't run. She'd tried to help. There was a lot about her he still didn't know, who'd stabbed her for a start, and the issue of what happened to her parents, but he could wait.

He snuggled closer and traced the outline of her lips with his finger. He'd managed to tell her he loved her, but hadn't meant to blurt it out while they lay naked in an ocean of foam. He hadn't even wanted to say it when they were in bed, although when he'd fucked her without a condom, the words had hovered on his lips. Charlie wanted it to be special. He thought about taking her to Paris or Rome, finding the most romantic place with the moon overhead and…he sighed. Lying with her resting on his chest in all those bubbles, when he was still racked with guilt over what he'd done, had not been the right moment at all. But the words had surged up from somewhere and he couldn't push them back.

Charlie wished Kate had told him she loved him. Others had said it, but they didn't know him. Charlie wanted Kate to say it, wanted her to wake up, look into his eyes and say the three words he wanted to hear.

He blew gently on her lips.

Kate twitched. "Pack it in."

Charlie grinned and then the grin slid away because when he thought about it, "I think I love you" wasn't the same thing as telling her he loved her. Did he think it or know it? Knew it. He loved her. So why hadn't he said that? Charlie frowned. For

262

someone who was supposed to be good with words, he'd cocked this up. But she'd said she was his and she was still here, in his bed, lying next to him. She was sexy and funny and the moment he'd finished making love to her, he was desperate to do it again. But he liked to talk to her, argue with her — annoy her. Kate was different. Kate was the one he wanted.

As he lay contemplating a suitable way to wake her up, his mobile phone vibrated on the bedside table. Charlie would have ignored it, but it was Ethan.

"I'm outside. Let me in."

"I'm busy."

Charlie slid his free hand between Kate's breasts and up to her throat. She opened her eyes.

"You need to see the papers," Ethan said. "It's bad."

Once Charlie had gone, Kate rolled into the warm spot he'd vacated. She snuggled into the indentation in his pillow, breathed him in and smiled. Last night, he'd said he loved her. Well, nearly. He thought he loved her. She liked that it was something he'd thought about. She wondered how many times he'd said, "I love you" and if he'd ever meant it. Thinking he loved her was okay. It wasn't something to be rushed into.

Kate turned onto her back and stared at the ceiling. Was she crazy? It wasn't okay at all. What kind of life could she have with Charlie? His world was a million miles from hers. He was clever and talented. She'd left school at sixteen, but in reality long before that considering the amount of time she bunked off. Plus, he was seriously fucked up. Maybe worse than her. She didn't need someone else who one moment almost raped her and the next said they thought they loved her. But he wasn't like Dex. Charlie had done everything he could to push her away and she hadn't gone. Because whether he thought he loved her or not, Kate knew she loved him.

Ten minutes later Kate went down wearing Charlie's fluffy white bathrobe. He and Ethan were in deep discussion. When she saw Charlie's worried face, her heart cramped. Now what?

Ethan handed her the newspaper. "Page two. Take a deep breath."

The deep breath didn't help. Kate gave a moan of horror. The heading was *TAKEN BY STORM*, the photograph a little blurred, but clear enough of her and Charlie in her bedroom, hips and lips together, stark naked. Kate scanned the writing next to the picture. It gave her name and that she worked in a Greenwich cafe. Charlie squeezed her fingers.

"Is it legal to do that?" she asked. "Take pictures through a window?"

"No, it's not. We can sue but the damage is done," Ethan said.

"At least there's only one photo," she murmured.

Ethan grimaced and turned the page. "Sorry."

Kate felt like she'd been punched in the gut. There was a shot of her in her wedding dress, a "before" shot where she still smiled and a couple more of her and Charlie in the apartment, this time with her breasts on display. The article described Kate as a runaway bride who'd jilted her fiancé to get into bed with Charlie Storm. Kate read it twice to make sure she'd not made the whole thing up. She hadn't. They had.

"I don't understand. How did they get those pictures? Who took photographs of me in my wedding dress?" Although she thought she knew the answer to that. Richard or someone he knew. Fax.

Charlie slid his arm over her shoulder. "If Dickhead was doing it for a bet, he probably wanted proof you'd turned up at the registry office."

Kate crumpled inside, her eyes fixed on that shot of her in her dress, the smile on her face, the joy in her eyes. Fax had watched her go into the building, waited until she came out, then told Lucy. Bile rose in Kate's throat.

"I had to fight my way through a pack of African hunting dogs to get in here," Ethan said. "This is just the start of it. They're not going to leave you alone now, Kate. Everything you do, everywhere you go, they'll be watching. Remember what Princess Diana went through? Every mistake you've made will come back to haunt you. Everything you wear will be criticized. Everything you say will be twisted. They'll try to destroy you."

Charlie pulled her into his arms. "Shut the fuck up, Ethan. You're not helping."

"I'm only warning her what she'll have to put up with if she sticks with you."

Charlie gripped her tighter. "Not if."

"Hey, be realistic. Kate's not in the business. She doesn't know what it's like. If she has any secrets, those walking x-ray machines out there will uncover them. Do you have any secrets, Kate? Is there anything I should know about you?"

If Charlie hadn't been holding her, Kate knew she'd have collapsed.

"Guess you do," Ethan said.

The coolness in his voice was unmistakable. Kate wondered what he knew.

"No, she doesn't," Charlie snapped. "Kate didn't jilt anyone. Dickhead set her up for a bet and he set her up for this. I want to sue for invasion of privacy."

"And make matters worse? You stir things up now and they'll really go for you. Let it die down on its own. You've got to leave the country anyway, so that will help."

"What? Where've I got to go?"

"You're needed in Dublin tomorrow. A preproduction meeting for *The Green*. I have you booked on a flight this afternoon."

"Kate's coming with me. Book her a seat too."

"I don't have a passport." Another spasm of pain gripped her heart. She'd filled in an application and Richard had told her he'd sort it out.

Charlie stared at her in disbelief. "You've never been abroad?"

"No."

He pressed his face into her hair. "You can get her one, can't you, Ethan?"

"Not on a Sunday and not that quickly. Let me take Kate home. It will throw them off."

"Why would I want them thrown off? They know we're together now. We *are* together," Charlie said.

"So while you're away, you want them sitting on her doorstep, pestering her, taking photos of her buying toilet rolls and blowing her nose? This is the way we're going to handle it. We'll pretend it was a fling. A couple of dates. That way they'll probably leave her alone. Just be more careful when you get back."

"No way. I'm not going," Charlie said. "I'm not leaving her."

"You fucking well are going," Ethan snapped. "You've no choice. This is your career. No more chances. I'll see to Kate."

Charlie took her hand. "What do you think? I don't want you to have to handle this on your own."

"I don't like people telling me what to do." Kate stared at Ethan, knowing he wanted to get rid of her, wondering how Charlie couldn't see it.

"I'm not going," Charlie repeated, lifting his fingers to her cheek.

Kate put her hand over his and stared into his eyes. "I'll be fine, Charlie. You have to go."

He sighed. "Fill out a passport application while I'm gone. Let Ethan handle it."

Over her dead body.

"When will you be back?" Kate asked.

Charlie looked at Ethan.

"Wednesday."

"That's the night of the exhibition at Rachel's gallery," Kate said.

"I'll come and we'll go out for a meal afterwards."

Kate smiled.

Ethan and Kate left through the back of the house, while Charlie went to distract the group of journalists at the front. Kate had to wear Charlie's clothes — a pair of his drawstring pants and a white t-shirt, her dress, still wet, lay on the bathroom floor.

"What's with the clothes?" Ethan asked as they sat in the car.

"Charlie tried my dress on and ripped it."

"Really?" Ethan turned to glance at her.

"No," Kate said with a forced laugh.

"I was surprised to find you there this morning after what happened at Armageddon."

Kate turned in her seat to look at him. "Nothing happened at Armageddon."

Ethan didn't like her and Kate wasn't sure what to do about it.

When he turned into Elm Gardens, a group of photographers waited outside the entrance to Kate's block.

"I told you. Is this the life you want, Kate? Being pestered by the press?"

"I want Charlie. I'll take whatever comes with him." Her voice was firm and clear.

Ethan stared at her for a moment before he spoke. "I'll distract them while you go inside. Don't talk to anyone. Don't even say no comment."

Kate fled into the building. She ran up the stairs, straight past a guy who sat on the top step, too slow to catch her, and breathed a sigh of relief once she was safe in her apartment. The moment she closed the door, the phone rang. Then the guy banged on her door. The *Mirror* was on the phone. Kate broke the connection, but as she started to call Charlie, it rang again. This time a reporter from the *Star*. Kate unplugged the connection and called Charlie on her mobile.

"I just got in," Kate said.

"Come back," Charlie pleaded.

"Aren't you about to leave for the airport?"

He groaned. "How come you don't have a passport?"

"I've never needed one."

"I want to take you all over the world and I can't even take you for a meal without someone bothering us. And what the fuck's that banging?"

"A reporter at the door."

"Don't open it."

Kate looked through the spy hole.

"Oh, it's okay. It's Dan. Be good, Charlie. I'll see you Wednesday. You want to meet me at the gallery? You remember where it is?"

"Yep. Bellingham. Holland Park. See you then." He paused. "Kate?"

"Yes?"

"Thanks for yesterday with Mum and Dad, for...well, you know."

"You're welcome. Bye, Charlie."

She opened the door and let Dan in.

He offered Kate a handful of paper. "Messages. They've been stuffing them in everyone's mailbox trying to get in touch with you. I've got rid of the guy outside your door. Threatened him with the police. We've escaped to the roof."

"Oh God, sorry."

"You better come up. I should warn you, Rachel and Lucy are a bit pissed off. Well, a lot pissed off. They're beside themselves that you didn't tell them you were going out with Charlie Storm and furious with me because they think I should have known after that incident at Crispies."

"Ah." Kate's shoulders slumped.

"Nice bum, though." Dan grinned.

"Whose?"

"Yours of course, but don't tell Rachel. Not that there's anything wrong with hers," he added.

"Right." Kate laughed at his mortified expression. "Dan, can I ask you a favor?"

"You can ask."

Kate took the photograph of Michael Storm out of her bag. "This is Charlie's brother."

"He died, didn't he? It was in the papers."

"If you're not too busy, do you think you could paint him and Charlie sort of tussling together? I don't have a photo of Charlie, but I expect there's one in the paper you can use. Only put clothes on him."

Dan laughed.

"I'll have to pay you in installments."

"You don't need to pay me at all, Kate. I'll do it as a gift. If you hadn't said something last week, I'd still be staring hopelessly at Rachel."

"I take it things have moved on?"

Dan grinned.

Kate sent Dan back to the roof. She changed into her bikini, relieved to see it covered the bite mark on her breast, and slipped on a long t-shirt. Charlie was more upset about what happened than her. She knew he'd never do it again. Kate sighed. That sounded a little too familiar.

When she walked onto the flat roof she came to an abrupt halt. Lucy, Dan and Rachel stood leaning against the parapet wall looking down at the street. Next to Lucy stood a bare-chested Nick, in low-slung jeans, his hand squeezing Lucy's backside.

Kate stared into the distance. To the right she could just see the golden supports of the Millennium Dome, to the left, the building block skyscrapers of Canary Wharf rose into a hazy sky. Kate walked across and slipped in next to Dan.

"Hey, are you mad? Don't let them see you," he said and ushered her back. "Here, have a glass of wine."

He picked up the bottle from the table and poured her a glass. Lucy and Rachel stepped in front of her. Lucy wore the tiniest bikini Kate had ever seen. Three silver triangles the size of cheese crackers.

"Charlie Storm," Rachel said. "You're going out with a celebrity and you don't tell us? I thought we were your friends?"

"You are," Kate said and glanced at Nick. Three of them were. "The reason I didn't tell you is down there on the street."

Nick sat on a chair and pulled Lucy onto his lap. "Nice photos. Want to give me an exclusive on what it's like to go out with bad-boy Storm?"

"No."

"Do you know what you're doing, Kate?" Lucy asked. "I mean — Charlie Storm? He's going to chew you up and spit you out. He has to be using you."

An iron band tightened around Kate's heart. She sat down on a concrete ledge with her wine.

"How did you meet him?" Rachel asked. "Was it really at the seaside?"

Kate nodded.

"He's going to dump you," Lucy said. "He has a terrible reputation."

Kate's fingers tightened around the stem of the glass.

"You could make some money out of this," Nick said. "Why don't you give me your side of the story? I could get you on tomorrow's show."

Kate regretted having come up to the roof. She swallowed a mouthful of warm white wine.

"We'll pay good money, Kate," Nick said. "After all, you're a friend." His hand cupped Lucy's breast.

Kate opened her mouth and then shut it again.

"Has he taken you anywhere nice?" Rachel asked. "What's he like? Have you been to his house? Have you met anyone famous? And most important, will he come to the opening on Wednesday?"

"Hey." Dan put his hand on her arm. "Kate came up here to escape the questions."

"Just one, then," Rachel pleaded. "Will he come to the opening?"

Kate tossed the answer around in her head before she spoke. "I asked him, but I don't know if he'll come." She wondered what she was going to do about Nick. He sat watching her and underneath his serpent smile, Kate knew he was wondering if she'd say anything to Lucy.

"Could he get some other celebs to come too?" Rachel asked. "Who does he know?"

"I've no idea." Kate turned her face to the sun, wishing the questions would stop. Maybe she should warn Charlie not to come.

"Nick told me what happened at Armageddon," Lucy said.

Kate opened her eyes and turned in her direction. "Did he?"

Nick draped his arms over Lucy's shoulders, his fingers teasing the triangles covering her nipples.

"Sorry, Kate," he apologized. "I know I landed you in it with Charlie. I was panicking because of Gemma. I didn't want her to know I'd been buying a couple of wraps of coke for me and Lucy, so I made up a lie about a woman in a pink top coming on to me. I hadn't even seen, let alone known you were wearing a pink top. Next thing I know, Gemma's chucked her drink in your face. Of course, now she's read the papers about you and Charlie Storm, she knows you wouldn't be interested in a sad tosser like me. She's desperate to come and apologize, particularly if Charlie's around."

"You're not a sad tosser." Lucy turned to kiss him on the lips.

Yes, you are, Kate thought, *you're married and stringing Lucy along and fucking women in toilets when you get the chance.*

"I'll send Gemma round. Dan's going to be painting her portrait, so I'll be bringing her over for sittings." Nick nibbled Lucy's collarbone. "And the longer he takes, the better."

* * * * *

Charlie had just settled into seat 1A and stretched out his long legs, when Natalie Glass appeared. She bent her head and kissed him on the cheek. The musky scent she wore was so overpowering, Charlie only just suppressed the urge to sneeze. He wondered about buying perfume for Kate and realized she never wore any. But was that because she didn't like it or couldn't afford it? Something else he didn't know about her.

"Charlie! You're looking well."

"Hi, Natalie. Want to sit next to the window?"

"No, I'm okay on the aisle. I'm a bit of a nervous flyer."

It hadn't crossed his mind that Natalie would come to the meeting. It made sense, though he did wonder why Ethan hadn't told him.

"I'm really looking forward to working with you." Natalie beamed. "We're going to have such fun." She raised trim little eyebrows one after the other and winked.

The wink made it clear to Charlie the sort of fun she had in mind and he wasn't interested. She was gorgeous. Huge, dark eyes with thick black lashes. A smile that dazzled. Perfect teeth. Long, sleek dark hair. Pneumatic breasts. And he didn't want her.

He smiled.

He didn't even want a one-night stand with her. His smile broadened. If he hadn't realized it was because of Kate, he might have thought he was ill. Charlie leaned back in his seat and thought about the slight twist on one of Kate's bottom teeth, her spiky, tousled hair with the just-out-of-bed look, her breasts that fit snugly in his palms. And her eyes. Oh God, he loved her eyes, the way they changed with her moods. He even loved them when she was cross with him.

The plane taxied to the runway and Natalie squirmed.

"Will you hold my hand?" she whispered.

Charlie took hold of her fingers and Natalie smiled her thanks.

"Saw you in the papers today," she said. "Nice butt."

"Yeah, she has, hasn't she?" Charlie was pleased to see the smile drop from Natalie's face, but didn't manage to deflect her.

"I have a feeling I'm going to be a headline next week. Some prick from 24/7 persuaded my ex to reveal intimate details about our sex life." She pouted. "It wasn't me that wanted to go to the bloody club in the first place."

Charlie wanted to sit next to Kate the first time she went up in a plane, wanted to see the look on her face when she saw the clouds.

Natalie bent her mouth to Charlie's ear. "Rascal's. Have you been? Anything goes and I mean, anything. Ethan's trying to stop them publishing, but he's not hopeful."

"I thought the latest edition of *Hello!* was full of photos of your house and garden." Charlie extracted his hand now they were airborne.

"Did you read it? They were so nice. They kept asking for my opinion on the best place to take the photographs. They supplied flowers and clothes and they let me have copies of every picture after I'd agreed which ones they could use. And they paid. That's the sort of press I like."

"I'm not sure you can have it both ways. We choose to put ourselves in the public eye and have to take what comes with it. We're happy enough with the good publicity and the money. We only get upset when we think they're being unfair. We can't dictate the attention we want."

That was very philosophical for him. Charlie wondered if he sounded as though he meant it. He *did* mean it.

"Not just us that gets hurt though, is it?" Natalie said.

"No. Sometimes they go too far. Today being a case in point and the apology they'll no doubt end up issuing doesn't make up for the damage they've caused, but the press will never change."

* * * * *

By the time the plane landed in Dublin, Charlie was certain of two things—Natalie Glass desperately wanted to get into his pants and he desperately wanted to keep her out of them. It wasn't that he didn't fancy her. Any guy would. Well, any normal guy. Nothing wrong in fancying, but he wouldn't go further. Charlie was determined to prove he could be faithful. Kate trusted him and he wouldn't let her down. But as Natalie pressed her body against his in the taxi on the way to their hotel, Charlie recognized it was going to be a difficult couple of days.

Sure enough, a request to meet up in her room at seven so they could go down together for dinner, had led to him finding her still wet from the shower. The skimpy towel that stood between him and her naked body accidentally dropped to the carpet as she walked back to the bathroom. Of course, she bent to pick it up, giving him a spectacular view of her backside. She left the bathroom door open. Charlie clenched his jaw.

"Pour me a drink, Charlie," she called.

He opened the mini bar, noting the seal was already broken. "What would you like?"

"Vodka and orange."

He found two little bottles in the bin. He had the feeling that after a couple more vodkas, Natalie's bra would mysteriously unhook itself. Then again, she probably wasn't going to wear a bra.

"Hook my dress up, sweetie."

Yep, he was right. The dress was open all the way down the back. He pulled up the zip and Natalie turned and launched herself toward him. Charlie intercepted with his cheek. He bit his lip so he didn't laugh. Her blue silk dress was cut low at the front, with two shadows in the silk where her nipples pointed toward him like gun barrels. He stepped back, reaching for the glass and pushed it into her hand.

"Don't you want one?" she purred and licked her lips.

"Detoxing," he said.

He needed all his wits about him to keep his newly acquired integrity intact.

By the time they got to the last course, Natalie was drunk and Charlie very sober. He'd tried to regulate the amount of alcohol she consumed, but she ate so little, it must have raced through her bloodstream faster than a striking snake. The other thing she did was eat slowly, chewing every mouthful forever. Just for something to do, Charlie began to count. Sixty-five seconds for each morsel she put between her lips. The meal had to be stone-cold by the time she'd finished. He'd never been so bored in his life.

Natalie tried to force him into having dessert, but he knew damned well he'd be the only one eating it. He refused coffee. Charlie wanted to go to bed and ring Kate. When Natalie stood up, she wobbled.

"Oops," she giggled and caught hold of Charlie's arm.

Charlie didn't like the knowing looks they trawled as they left the restaurant and made their way to the lift. Natalie hung on him like an octopus.

"It's your fault I'm drunk. I had to have your share of the wine as well."

"Sorry." Charlie wasn't sorry at all. In fact, he hoped she passed out the moment he got her back into her room.

"Where's your key?" he asked.

After a struggle, Natalie managed to produce it from her purse.

"I don't feel well," she muttered.

He wasn't surprised. Charlie manhandled her through the door and Natalie lurched toward the bathroom. The fall looked genuine and he went to help.

"I'm going to be sick," she gasped.

She was. All over the bathroom floor and all over Charlie. In a way, he was grateful because now there was no temptation at all.

His mobile rang while he was trying to clean up the mess.

"Hey, what you doing?" Kate asked.

"You don't want to know." Charlie looked at the towels he'd thrown into the bath.

"Yes, I do," she said.

"Cleaning up puke. And before you ask, it's not mine. I wish you were here."

"Why? So I could help?"

"Yes." Charlie laughed.

275

Natalie moaned from the bed and bolted back to the bathroom.

"Who's throwing up?" Kate asked.

"Natalie."

"Campbell?"

"Natalie Glass. She's got a part in *The Green*."

"The one in the red slashed dress at Armageddon?"

He heard the change in tone. And lied. "I don't remember."

"Charlie, you're telling fibs. Are you in her room?"

"Yes, but I'm not doing anything." Charlie turned away as Natalie threw up again.

"Just cleaning up puke," Kate corrected.

"This is not in my job description."

"Get someone else to do it then."

"I don't think this is in anyone's job description. Nice shot, Natalie. At least you mostly hit the bowl that time."

"When you're on your own, call me," Kate said. "And we'll play a little game of doctor and patient."

"I need a shower first."

"Is the phone waterproof?" Kate asked.

Charlie perked up. He'd find a plastic bag and make it waterproof.

Chapter Twenty-One

 න

On Monday morning, Kate strolled into Crispies through the door that Dan held open for her. She glanced at the clock. On time. But Mel's toothy grin caused Kate's smile to dissolve like ice cream on a hot pavement. Something was wrong.

"How are you feeling, Kate?" asked the Mel look-alike.

Dan put his palm on his sister's forehead. "You don't have a temperature." He slid his hand to her nose and squeezed it. "Ah, it's warm. Not a good sign." He winked at Kate. "Oh no, I'm wrong. It's a dog's nose that should be cool. Guess you're healthy, Mel."

"Piss off, Dan," Mel snapped.

He laughed. "That's more like it. I thought you really were ill."

Kate took off her jacket and hung it in the staff restroom. Lois walked past, her mouth and eyes wide open as she stared at Kate with something approaching awe. Two of the other waitresses huddled in a corner, whispering.

It was going to be a long day.

Kate made her way to the kitchen, hoping Tony would cheer her up, but instead of the flirting she'd grown to enjoy, he carried on chopping carrots at breakneck speed. Kate was annoyed, self-conscious and worried, all at the same time. She returned to the dining area to find Mel still talking to Dan.

"We're going to be very busy today," Mel said. "I had to serve yesterday because *some* people wouldn't come in and help." She glared at her brother.

"I told you I was busy. I do have work of my own."

Mel rolled her eyes and turned to Kate. "Had a good weekend?"

Kate's mouth dropped open. She clamped her lips together. Mel was never interested in what any of the staff did outside work.

"What did you get up to with Charlie?" Mel asked.

At the mention of his name, a crackling charge filled the air as every person in the vicinity tuned into the conversation. Lois sidled over and dusted the chairs behind them.

"He took me to meet his parents." Kate's hand slammed to her mouth. Shit, was she a complete idiot?

"Oh. My. God. He must be serious. Is he coming in today? Please, can he come in today?" Mel hands danced with excitement.

"He's in Ireland. Don't tell anyone we went to see his parents," Kate pleaded.

Mel frowned and then her face brightened as if she'd seen Father Christmas coming down her chimney with presents for her and not Dan. "Okay, but keep the fact that he's in Ireland a secret, too. If a customer asks, say you're expecting him anytime."

"But—" Kate stopped when she saw the way that Mel looked at her. An order, not a request. "Only—" Kate made one more attempt.

"People will flock here if they think there's a chance of Charlie Storm popping in," Mel snapped.

"But the newspaper didn't say precisely where I work. There are loads of cafes in Greenwich."

"I'm sure it won't take long for people to find out." Mel avoided Kate's eyes. "After all, he was in here last week. They'll think he's a regular. We'll attract a different crowd."

"The only stars will be in your eyes," Dan said and laughed.

Mel turned on the face Kate knew so well. Pissed off and harassed.

"Did you ring and tell them?" Dan asked.

Mel's gaze shifted to the glass ceiling.

Damn, Kate thought.

"Mel, tell me you didn't do that," Dan said. "Please tell me you haven't thrown out Charlie's name in order to fill this place up."

But Kate knew she had, because spreading the word that Charlie might walk in at any moment would be great for business.

"Of course not."

Dan sighed.

"Would you be a kind brother instead of a mean one and sort out the wine delivery?" Mel asked.

Kate knew why she'd got rid of Dan. The moment he was out of sight, she followed Kate like a puppy, eager for any scraps.

"So what's he like?" Mel asked.

Kate ran her cloth over a table top and pressed her lips together.

"How did you meet him?"

Kate moved to the next table.

"You can tell me. We're friends."

Kate turned round and crossed her arms. "Who are you and what have you done with my boss?"

"Oh, very funny. Come on, Kate. Dish the dirt."

"I can't talk about him." Kate tried to explain. "The press will twist everything."

"We're not the press." Mel made another attempt to deliver a sincere beam and failed.

Kate jerked as a brush hit her foot. Lois swept the floor behind her, hunched over with her antennae twitching.

"How did you meet him?" Mel asked. "Is his dick really —"

"Mel," Tony bellowed from the kitchen. "Get in here."

Kate breathed a sigh of relief. Mel always jumped for Tony.

"Has he sung *Just One Look* for you? I love that one," Lois mumbled in a dreamy voice at Kate's shoulder. "I've got all his albums. Do you think you could get him to sign them for me?"

"I don't know," Kate said, almost wishing Mel had sacked her.

Kate heard a tap at the front window. Her eyes shot up. She couldn't believe it. Ten minutes before they opened and a line of people stood on the pavement.

Dan flew past. "I've got to go to the wholesaler. See you later."

Mel emerged from the kitchen, cast a guilty glance at Kate and began to polish the mirrors. Another first — Mel working.

The Charlie fiasco hit the moment the door opened. The curious stares and impertinent questions left Kate with a throbbing headache. The open-mouthed envy she could cope with, but the ill-disguised hatred made her desperate to flee.

Break time couldn't come soon enough.

She hid in the store cupboard, sat on a drum of cooking oil and switched on her mobile. Charlie had sent a text.

Thought of U and now I've got a huge prob 2 deal with B4 I go 2 breakfast. Wish U were here
xx Hippo

U've given me huge prob 2. Millions of people @ Crispies cos they think U might B here
xxx Mermaid

Just after the "message sent" screen appeared, the phone rang.

"How am I supposed to call you if you keep your phone switched off?" Charlie demanded.

Kate smiled. "Good morning to you, too."

"I want you," Charlie whispered. "I want to continue our discussion of last night."

Kate felt a familiar tightening between her legs from just the sound of his voice.

"Haven't you sorted out your little problem?" she asked.

"It wasn't little and yes, I have. I'm eating breakfast. Hey, hands off my toast."

280

Kate heard a woman laugh and felt a pang of disquiet.

"Natalie?" Kate wished she hadn't asked.

"Yes."

There were sounds of a tussle and then a woman spoke into the phone.

"He's such a tease, Kate. I don't know how you put up with him."

Then the phone was back in Charlie's hands.

"I'll phone you tonight," he said. "I'm going to be tied up all day."

Kate heard Natalie giggle.

"In meetings," he added.

"Okay, I've got to go now," Kate said in a quiet voice.

"Bye, Mermaid."

Kate heard more laughter and then the phone went dead. She snapped it shut and pushed it in her pocket, her foot kicking at the drum. The sound of Natalie's giggling echoed inside her head. Kate wanted to go home and bury her head under her pillow but instead she forced herself through the door.

She slunk past Tony, busy cooking extra of everything, and peered through the circular glass window of the swing door. The place heaved with chattering people. Great, Kate thought, Charlie's eating breakfast with a beautiful woman, who even though she puked on him is still gorgeous, while she had to serve breakfast to a few grumpy regulars and a hoard of nosey parkers and look happy about it. She wasn't jealous. She wasn't. She never let herself get attached enough to anyone to feel that way.

Despite her rocky life, Kate didn't feel insecure. She had no hang-ups about her looks or her body. She'd learned never to show that sort of weakness. It was an invitation to bullies. She'd settled into an acceptance of what she had, though that didn't mean she wasn't sometimes envious of other people. Not for their money or cars or houses, but for their loving families, their friends, the fact that they had people who cared about them. Kate had never been jealous about a guy before.

She wished she had a passport.

* * * * *

The one thing about being busy—it stopped her thinking. Everyone was rushed off their feet.

"Yes, we're expecting him later."

"No, you haven't missed him. Should be any time now."

"Oh yes, he's a regular here."

Mel answered the questions that Kate ignored. Customers who wanted to linger were forced to keep ordering and if they tried to stick to tea or coffee, Mel pointed out the minimum order threat she'd stuck on the bottom of every menu that morning.

Kate carried out a plate of lasagna to table twelve and smiled at the young man sitting there, a round-faced, blond-haired guy with a cute smile. The type who usually gave her a big tip.

"Is it always this busy?" he asked.

"Crispies is very popular."

"Worked here long?"

"No. Is there anything else I can get you?" Kate smiled at him.

"I'll have a glass of red wine. I'll treat you to one, too."

"Bit early for me, thanks. So, which paper do you work for?"

He laughed. "The *Star*. Andy Swift. Want to give me an exclusive, Kate? How you met? What he's like in bed? That sort of thing. Five thousand pounds?"

"No."

"Ten."

She gulped. "No."

"Twenty," Andy offered.

Kate walked away, her heart pounding.

Every time she went near his table, he put the price up another thousand.

"Give me some idea if I'm getting warmer," he complained.

"Max told me not to talk to anyone."

The reporter's face dropped. Kate knew he'd think she meant the PR guru, Max Clifford. She turned away from the table, grinning, to find herself facing a tall blonde about her age. Before Kate could step to one side, a hand shot out and slapped her hard across the cheek. Kate gasped and her own hand flew up in a belated attempt to protect her face.

"Bitch," she screeched at Kate.

Kate stepped backward, rubbing her tingling cheek. The whole place had gone quiet.

"Leave him alone. He's mine."

"Right." Kate turned away.

This was becoming a pain. She could see what Charlie had to put up with. Stupid, crazy people. Before Kate had taken two steps, she felt a blow high up on her shoulder and staggered forward.

"For crying out loud," Kate snapped and clenched her fists.

There was a piercing scream from somewhere, not from Kate, and then the place was in uproar. She turned and saw the reporter from the *Star* holding the blonde woman's wrist. He shook a knife from her fingers. Kate watched it drop to the floor and spin away under a table. Bloody hell, she thought, good job he'd been here after all. When the realization hit that he'd have his story, just not the one he'd hoped for, Kate gave a heavy sigh.

"Kate." Tony appeared in front of her and took her arm, pulling her out of the mayhem of the dining area and into the kitchen. Only after he put his fingers on her back and showed her the blood, did Kate realize she'd been stabbed.

"Oh Christ," she gasped and wobbled.

Tony dragged over his stool with his foot, sat Kate down and unfastened her blouse.

Mel came blustering into the kitchen from her office. "What the hell is that racket? What— Tony what are you doing?"

Kate glanced up, saw the distress on Mel's face and knew it wasn't for her.

"How long has this been going on?" Mel's mouth was a hard line.

"For fuck's sake, Mel. Can't you see the blood? Some lunatic's stabbed Kate."

"What?"

"She stabbed me?" Kate still couldn't believe it.

"I'll call the police. What about an ambulance?" Mel asked.

"No," Kate said. "Neither."

"But she stabbed you," Mel shrieked.

"Please. I'll be fine. I don't want you to call anyone. It's not that bad, is it?"

"Don't worry," Tony reassured her. "She hit your shoulder blade."

"Fuck." Kate moaned as he held a paper towel over the wound.

"Get out there and see what's happening," Tony told Mel. "Some guy's grabbed the woman that did it and got her to drop the knife, but be careful. Don't go anywhere near her."

Kate's back hurt now. Throbbed. Tears sprang to her eyes and she blinked. Was this what she got for dating Charlie?

"I knew that health and safety course would come in handy. Never thought I'd have to remove a woman's top though." Tony winked. "This only needs some butterfly strips. Keep your hand here." He pulled Kate's arm across her chest and onto her shoulder, and then lifted the first-aid box off the wall. "Are you up to date on your tetanus?"

"Yes."

"Not keen on hospitals, are you?"

Kate shook her head. She'd refused to go on the course when Mel asked for volunteers. Kate arched her shoulder blades as he ran an antiseptic wipe across her back.

"Not the first time someone's had a go at you by the look of it." Tony's finger brushed her scar.

"Childhood accident," Kate said.

"This isn't too bad. I'm just going to line up the edges of the wound."

"And why are you telling me that?"

"We're supposed to reassure the patient. You're my first one. I don't count that splinter of Lois'."

"I got that out."

"Oh yeah. Well, to make sure the strips stay in place, I'll stick another two parallel to the cut to keep it dry. No vigorous sex, unless it's with me."

Kate groaned.

"Honestly, it's not too bad."

In trying to reassure her, he was worrying her.

"What's not too bad — the sex with you?" she asked, trying to ease the moment.

"No, that's brilliant," he said, laughing. "You better go home. I'll pay for a cab."

"I'm fine, Tony. I was just shocked."

The door swung open and both turned to see the woman who'd stabbed her standing next to the reporter. Tony stepped in front of a shirtless Kate.

"Out of my kitchen," he said.

"Are you okay?" Andy asked.

"Get out."

"This is Tiffany Samuels," Andy said. "She wants to apologize and explain."

"All right," Kate said. The apology was pointless but she'd like an explanation.

"You sure, Kate?" Tony asked.

Kate nodded.

"Go on, Tiffany," Andy urged.

"Until a month ago, I was engaged to Charlie. It was a secret. We didn't want the press to find out. Only…he broke it off and broke my heart."

Tears started to roll down her cheeks. Kate wasn't impressed.

"I'm sorry I hurt you. Please don't call the police. Something snapped inside me when I saw the paper yesterday. I thought

Charlie had finished with me because I was ordinary. I mean, I'm not a film star or a singer, but there's nothing special about you. You're only a waitress, so it couldn't be that."

Gee thanks, Kate thought. "I—" She started to say she hadn't known Charlie very long and then spotted the reptilian eyes of the reporter and shut her mouth.

"I still love him," Tiffany sobbed. "I thought if I could make you go away, he'd come back to me. I wish I'd kept the baby. Then I'd still have a little part of him."

Oh Christ, the woman is crazy.

"But he didn't want it," she whispered. "He said it would ruin his career. He asked me to have an abortion."

"How long were you going out with him?" Andy asked.

Kate wondered if he was recording all this.

"Three months."

"What's your reaction to that, Kate?" Andy turned to her.

Kate walked out of the room. What was she supposed to say? The man's eyes had been gleaming. He didn't care whether it was true or not. He had his story. Kate went down to the staff toilets and locked herself in a cubicle. She sent a text to Charlie.

Do U know Tiffany Samuels?

xx Mermaid.

Kate was determined not to move until she heard from him. She didn't believe the woman. She suspected there were all sorts of weird people out there, waiting for opportunities to surge out of the cracks. But Kate hoped Charlie had never heard of this one. Her phone beeped with a message.

No. Hinting 4 jewelry?

xxx Hippo

"Kate, are you in there?"

It was Mel. Kate flushed the unused toilet and came out.

"Are you all right?" Mel asked.

"Yes."

"You look a bit pale."

"I'm okay."

"I brought this for you to put on. Nice bra by the way. Where did you get it? Did Charlie buy it for you?"

"No."

Mel offered Kate one of her tops, a horrible red and yellow flowered thing. Kate bit her lip to stop it from curling in horror.

"Thank you."

"You can go home if you want."

"I think I'd rather work." Kate slipped on the top and leaned against the wash basin to look at her pale face. An escapee from an old folk's home stared back.

Mel opened the door. "It wouldn't have lasted anyway. They end up with their own sort. People like us are cheap thrills."

That barb hurt more than the stab in the back. Was that what she was to Charlie? A cheap thrill? Maybe this was a test. What would he do when he heard what had happened?

Taking a deep breath, Kate walked into the dining area. There were more customers than ever. Every chair was taken and people still lined up outside. She wondered how long it would be before Mel decided the extra income was not worth the hassle. Crispies would lose its regulars and these gawpers would leave once they realized they weren't going to be treated to a spectacular fly-past by the British acting contingent.

Kate got on with her work, smiled and said as little as possible. Her back felt sore, but wasn't a major problem. The continual, "are you all right?" bothered her far more. She didn't like it when people made a fuss. On the plus side, the tips were great.

When she saw the two policemen walk in, Kate gave a mental groan. Tiffany had long gone, no doubt to reveal all, including her breasts, to the reporter from the *Star*. Kate wondered if she should ring Charlie and warn him, or maybe she should ring Ethan.

"Kate Snow?" one of the policemen asked Lois.

He didn't need to ask. All eyes were on Kate. Every ear strained to listen.

"Is there somewhere we can talk?" the cop said.

Mel let them use her office. Kate had no intention of pressing charges, but she knew it wasn't up to her. By the time she'd finished talking, she hoped she'd convinced them the whole thing wasn't worth bothering with, but she doubted it. They wanted her to go to hospital, but Kate refused. The moment the police left, another load of reporters and photographers arrived.

She didn't know how Charlie could stand it. Why were people so obsessed with celebrities? Why did they feel entitled to know minute details of their lives? They wanted to tour their homes, inspect their toilets, peek in their fridges. It was as if they felt they had a right to know.

Kate knew she'd made herself unpopular by refusing to talk to anyone.

"How long have you been going out with Charlie?"

"Is this a setup? Publicity for his next film?"

"Are you pregnant?"

Jesus Christ!

"Talk to us, Kate. We're going to write about you whether you talk to us or not. Don't you want to make sure we get it right?"

She knew the papers would print their truth, not hers and decided enough was enough.

"Tony, can I go home?"

"Course you can. You should have gone home earlier. Hell, you should have gone to hospital and I'm having a hard time convincing myself that I did the right thing not making you. Have as much time off as you need. In fact, take off the rest of this week. Nip out the back way. I'll square it with Her Highness."

Once Kate reached the safety of Greenwich Park and knew no one had followed, she relaxed though she had a horrible suspicion there would be more press outside the apartment. She wandered along the path until she found an empty bench, then sat down and took out her phone. Charlie's number was out of service. Kate put the phone back in her bag. She didn't have anyone else to ring.

This was what it must be like for Charlie, relentless pursuit, never being allowed to be on his own except in his home. Even then he wasn't safe. The possibility of another Tiffany in the shadows worried her. Charlie would always be photographed; on holiday, at the cinema, in restaurants, even at the supermarket. As he grew old, if he was ill, if he lost his pants, there would be someone ready to capture the moment. If she stayed with Charlie, that would be her life, too.

Kate closed her eyes and tipped her face to the sun. She could walk away from all this but Charlie couldn't. Could the two of them deal with it better than one? Her mobile rang and made her jump. It wasn't Charlie.

"Where are you?" Ethan demanded.

"Walking home through Greenwich Park."

"Don't talk to anyone. Go straight back to your apartment and wait for me."

Kate was about to ask why, but he rang off.

She was right about the press. When she turned the final corner, she saw several photographers waiting outside the entrance. They stood chatting until they saw her and then mobbed her like vultures. Kate closed her ears and pushed straight through. It was no use worrying about photographs now. Her face had been in the paper. If she was going to be found, she would be.

* * * * *

Ethan wasn't sure if this was his opportunity to sweep Kate away from Charlie. It hadn't been what he'd planned, so maybe he'd keep that in reserve and see how this flew. Kate was pleasant enough, but of no value to Charlie and therefore no value to Ethan. He'd asked Charlie again about the life-saving episode, but he refused to talk about it. In fact, he more or less threatened that if Ethan mentioned it again, Charlie would be looking for another agent. Ethan couldn't afford to lose him, not now he'd landed the role in *The Green* and especially not after Ethan's recent conversation with Jody Morton.

When his secretary put the call through, Ethan hadn't believed it was Jody. By the time they finished talking, a whole new life opened up in front of Ethan. He already ran a successful agency, but having Jody Morton on his list would move him into the big-time. The mega time. Jody wanted Charlie and if Ethan could deliver him, she'd leave her agent and sign with Ethan. Straightforward and simple. One favor for another. Except as far as Charlie was concerned, nothing could ever be straightforward and simple. Still, Ethan thought, all Charlie needed to do was stay with Jody long enough for her to be drawn into a watertight contract and then they could break up.

Ethan was a bit surprised to see all the press outside Kate's block. He thought he'd been given a head's up on the Veronica Ward story, but he could see word had spread. He'd been a bit pissed off with Malcolm Ward because Ethan thought he'd smoothed things over after Charlie agreed to do the charity concert in September. Considering Charlie had fucked Malcolm's wife and both his daughters, Ethan thought the guy let Charlie off lightly, but he hadn't expected Veronica Ward to make fucking a tsunami of her own. What was the saying about a woman scorned? Veronica was a walking time-bomb.

Ethan got Kate to open the electric gates so he could drive in and then went back to the railings. The carrion stayed outside. They knew their place. Ethan had made a few phone calls about the invasion of Charlie's privacy and scored a few points for not pursuing the matter but had made it clear any more trespassing on private property would mean serious trouble. It was a balancing act. Ethan needed the press as much as they needed him.

"Hey, Ethan, how about an exclusive?" someone called.

"On what?" Ethan asked, hoping some idiot would give him a clue. He hoped to fuck it had nothing to do with Veronica Ward, otherwise he could be kissing goodbye to Jody Morton's contract.

"Is she really having Charlie's kid?" one of the reporters shouted.

Something curled up inside his chest, but Ethan's face showed nothing.

"He's still a kid himself," Ethan said with a forced laugh at his weak attempt at a joke as he hurried into the building. "Shit," he muttered through clenched teeth as he leapt up the stairs. "Shit, shit, shit."

Kate opened the door.

"Is it true?" he demanded.

"What?"

He strode in and slammed the door behind him.

"About the baby?" Ethan fixed his eyes on hers.

Kate paled and backed up. "He said he didn't know her."

Now Ethan was the puzzled one. "Who?"

"Tiffany Samuels."

Ethan put two and two together and got the right answer, though he wasn't too sure about the question. He knew Tiffany. She was one of Charlie's most devoted fans. Too devoted. And fan wasn't the right word. More like obsessed stalker. Tiffany had to be the most persistent, aggravating and hysterical fuckwit he'd ever come across and he'd come across more than his fair share. She tried everything to find out where Charlie planned to be on any given day in order that she could turn up too. Once they'd realized what she was like, Ethan's employees knew better than to tell her anything. She'd never gotten anywhere near Charlie. Ethan guessed she'd seen the papers on Sunday, read Kate worked at a Greenwich restaurant and it had been a simple process of elimination to track her down.

"What did she want?" Ethan asked.

He listened to Kate's story.

"Did you speak to anyone? Say anything to anyone at all?"

"I've told you what happened. I haven't said anything. Does Charlie know her, then?" Kate asked.

Ethan didn't miss the fact that Kate's level of anxiety had gone up a notch or two.

"Yeah, she's one of his most ardent fans, a truly lovely girl."

"Did he go out with her?"

Ethan made sure Kate saw his shoulders slump. "Kate, I know you don't want to hear this, but your relationship with Charlie is going to end in disaster. All his relationships end in disaster and you're the one who's going to get hurt. Charlie sleeps with a different woman every week. I've just had one of them on the phone telling me how he slept with her and both her daughters."

"Charlie told me about that."

Ethan was surprised. "What he doesn't know yet is that she's threatening to go to the papers unless he admits he's an addict."

"He's given up coke and cigarettes. And he doesn't have a problem with alcohol. He hardly drinks," Kate said.

Ethan laughed. "She means he's a sex addict."

"Oh."

"He can't help himself, Kate. He's not going to change."

"He can. He has."

Ethan put on his best understanding smile. "This is just another of his brief and passionate affairs, Kate, nothing more. You've been a good influence on him but it won't last."

He saw her mouth tighten. "Hey, look on the bright side. Being with Charlie has made you very sought after. You could have a date every night of the week."

Ethan winced. The scowl told him that was not the right thing to say. *Change the subject fast.*

"Have you made that selection of underwear for me to show my friend?"

Kate brought it out of the spare bedroom and wrapped it in a couple of supermarket carriers.

"Great, I'll be in touch," Ethan said.

He laughed as he walked down the stairs. This couldn't have worked out better. There was a flurry of interest when he pushed open the outer door.

"Shouldn't Kate be in hospital?"

"Is Charlie coming to see her?"

"Hey, Ethan. How's she feeling?"

It was only then that Ethan realized he hadn't even asked her.

Chapter Twenty-Two

ജ

"Kate? It's me. Open up."

Kate opened the door to find Lucy clutching an opened bottle of white wine.

"Are you all right?" Lucy asked.

"Yes."

"Thank God. What the hell happened?" Lucy bowled into the apartment.

Kate sighed and closed the door. "How did you find out?"

"If you owned a TV, you'd know. It's been on the six o'clock news."

Kate felt as if a fist had slammed into her head. Instant headache in more ways than one. "Did they give my name?"

"Yes."

Kate's knees wobbled and she sat before she fell.

"I have to ask you this, Kate," Lucy said, "Nick insisted. I don't want to lie to him and say I asked when I didn't."

"No, I won't do an interview."

"That's what I told him. Right, now let's have a drink and you can tell me everything."

Lucy stalked into Kate's kitchen, opened a cupboard, took out two glasses and poured the wine. Kate's mind raced as she went through the implications of this making the news. None of them were good. Lucy handed her a glass.

"Did it hurt?"

"Only when I realized what she'd done."

"Can I look?"

Kate put down her glass and pulled up her top.

"Whoa, nasty. What did Charlie say?"

294

"Haven't spoken to him yet." Kate was beginning to think she'd never speak to him again. What was he doing that was so important he didn't have time to check how she was? Kate remembered Natalie's seductive giggle and tensed.

Lucy slumped on the couch. "Why on earth would this Tiffany woman think stabbing you would make Charlie go back to her?"

"She didn't think, just lashed out."

Kate hesitated. Now they were alone, this was a chance to say something about Nick and Armageddon, but she was torn.

"If you knew something bad about Charlie, would you tell me?"

"After not realizing what a prick Richard was, yes," Lucy said. "But God, Kate, you only have to read the papers. Charlie's always in trouble."

"Would you want me to tell you something bad about Nick?"

There was a long pause before Lucy answered. "Go on, then."

Lucy's mobile rang and they jumped.

"Hi, what's up?" Lucy said.

Kate waited.

"It's Fax. He's downstairs and wants to talk to you. Can I buzz him up?"

Kate nodded.

A few moments later, Fax stood in her apartment, his camera bag over his shoulder. He was white-faced and shaking.

"Kate, I'm sorry. This is all my fault."

"I thought you'd destroyed those photos," Lucy said to Fax.

"I did, on my computer. I'm sorry, Kate. I'm sorry I took them, even more sorry I gave them to Richard. I thought it would make him see what he'd done. The bastard probably sold them to Simon and some woman almost killed you because of them."

Fax pulled his fingers through his hair.

"I wasn't almost killed," Kate said.

"Here, you look worse than Kate." Lucy pushed her wine into his hand.

"I feel terrible. I wish I'd never met Richard Winter, or sodding Simon Baxter." He took a slurp of wine and coughed.

"You know, I don't think you're cut out to be a press photographer," Lucy said.

"I know." Fax sighed.

"Except you are a photographer and you're in my apartment and all the other press photographers are outside on the pavement." Kate smiled.

"I wouldn't take your picture," Fax blurted.

Lucy sighed. "You see? Too nice."

"You think I'm nice?" Fax's mouth twitched.

Kate's eyes jumped between the pair.

"You're kind of cute," Lucy said. "In an occasionally annoying way."

"And not married," said Kate.

As they turned to look at her, Kate shrugged. "If you take Lucy out for a drink, I'll let you take a photo of my back. Sell it and use the money to go somewhere nice."

Fax blushed. "I couldn't do that, but…would you like to go for a drink sometime, Lucy?" His fingers twisted the stem of the glass back and forth, sloshing the liquid.

"I can't tonight," Lucy said.

"Tomorrow?"

"Working."

Kate heard Fax's confidence gurgling down the drain.

"Wednesday?" he asked, slumping deeper into the couch like a tired dog.

"We're going to Rachel's gallery in Holland Park," Kate said. "You could come too."

"You know I'm seeing someone? Sort of." Lucy's eyes met Kate's.

Fax straightened up and took a deep breath. "Yes, but maybe you'd rather see me."

"Maybe I would." Lucy smiled and drew a wide beam from Fax.

Kate thought he had a lovely smile, but not as nice as Charlie's. The thought cramped her heart.

"What time at the gallery?" Fax asked.

"Around seven," Lucy said.

"Great." He jumped up. "Well, I better go."

He looked desperate to leave before Lucy changed her mind.

"Take a picture of my back, Fax."

He hesitated. "Are you sure? I didn't bring my bag up with me because I thought I'd get a picture. I don't leave it on my bike in case—"

"Just take the picture." Kate tossed her top onto a chair and turned to face the wall. "They've already got my face. It's only my back. Maybe they'll leave me alone then."

And maybe Charlie would see it, she thought.

"Does it hurt?" Fax asked.

"It aches a bit."

"Thanks, Kate."

Lucy went with him to the door and came back grinning. Kate wondered if she'd forgotten what they'd been talking about before Fax arrived. Lucy dropped on the couch, dropped her smile and said one word, "Nick." Ah, that would be a no.

"He was in the ladies washroom at Armageddon with a woman called Sylvie. They were in a cubicle. Fucking. Nick asked me not to tell you." When Kate had told her everything, Lucy had her head in her hands.

"I'm sorry," Kate said.

"I know her. Sylvie Dacre. She works for the BBC, the lying two-faced bastard. Both of them." Lucy sat up and took a deep breath. "Nick was supposed... He's coming round tonight. I have to go."

Kate hoped she'd done the right thing. Was it was better to know the truth, even if it hurt?

She kept the phone unplugged, the door buzzer disconnected, but the mobile nearby. Kate wouldn't chase Charlie, but she sent one message.

I'm OK, but miss u

xx Mermaid

Charlie didn't call or text. Kate tried to convince herself he didn't know what had happened, but her disappointment grew to the point that she sank into a physical and emotional slow-down.

She spent the next day in the apartment, kept away from the windows and ignored all knocks at the door. She concentrated on her sewing and the jigsaw. She heard nothing from Charlie. How could he not know what had happened? Or had he lied about Tiffany and wasn't calling because he'd been busted. But Charlie had no reason to lie. Kate had a suspicion Ethan was behind this, that he'd made sure Charlie didn't know she'd been stabbed. Or was she just making excuses? When she thought too much it was like a maelstrom whirled in her head.

Kate had settled down in bed when she heard a loud banging on the door. More reporters or Charlie? She pulled a t-shirt over her naked body and went to check the spy hole. Kate's pulse jumped. Charlie looked furious. The dark eyes and scowl told her everything. He'd only just found out.

She whipped off the t-shirt and opened the door. As his mouth fell open at the sight of her naked body, she reached out, grabbed him by the collar and pulled him inside. His bag fell from his hand as he reached for her.

"Are you all right?" he asked.

"I am now."

He spun her around and gave a deep sigh. Kate turned to face him.

"You turned me into a gibbering wreck," Charlie moaned.

"And how would that be different to normal?"

His body shook as he laughed.

"I wanted to be cross with you," he said in between planting kisses all over her face.

"Have you changed your mind?"

"What mind?"

His hands ran up the sides of her ribs and then down over her backside so he could pull her against him.

"I could kill you," Charlie muttered into her hair.

"Why?"

"Guess."

"I rang but you didn't answer. I sent a text."

He groaned. "I lost my bloody phone, again. But you could have rung Ethan. He'd have found a way of getting in touch with me."

Kate was sidetracked by the first comment. "If you lost your phone, how could I have rung you?"

"It turned up again this morning. I think Natalie nicked it. I've got you on speed dial and I couldn't remember your number, but I've solved that problem. I'll show you how later."

He lifted his hands to her face and smoothed his thumbs over her cheeks. "I can't believe some lunatic stabbed you."

"It's not serious, Charlie."

He knocked his forehead against hers. "Of course it is. She stuck a knife in your back. Christ, Kate, she could have killed you."

"Why did you tell me you hadn't heard of her?"

"Because I hadn't. Tiffany Samuels? I thought you were joking, making a name out of two jewelers."

"I don't like jewelry."

Charlie sighed. "Ah, then I've wasted my money at Dublin airport on a fabulous present."

He blew her hair out of her eyes and slid his thumbs up her ribs to her breasts, circling her nipples. When they hardened in response he gave a happy sigh.

"Is it more fabulous than you?" Her hand cupped the bulge at his groin.

"There's a dilemma. Open my trousers or open my bag."

Kate laughed and Charlie gently set her back against the wall. She caught his head in her hands as he bent to kiss her neck.

"Why would Ethan make me think you knew Tiffany Samuels?" Kate couldn't let this go.

"I don't know. When did you speak to Ethan?"

"He came here yesterday."

Charlie's head shot up, fire blazing in his eyes. "Yesterday? Why the fuck didn't he tell me what had happened? He could have got a message to me, even rung bloody Natalie. I knew nothing about this until this morning. It was a hack who told me while I was eating breakfast. God, I was so scared. I went straight to the airport, but I've had to wait all fucking day for a flight because of fog. The bitch could have killed you. Jesus, Kate." His hands trembled as he clutched her. "I don't understand why Ethan didn't tell me?"

"Maybe he didn't want you distracted."

"He should have told me," Charlie said. "I want to hire someone to protect you."

"No." Kate tried to pull away, but he held her tight.

"I mean it. You won't know they're there, but I need to know you're safe and you're not safe in this apartment."

"You're overreacting. I'm fine."

"No, you're not. You've disconnected your buzzer. I had to get Rachel to let me in."

"Charlie, calm down. There's no need to worry. It was an isolated incident. I don't think she tried to kill me. She wanted to warn me off. She's crazy. She told me she'd been pregnant with your baby."

Charlie tensed. "I don't know her, I swear."

"Hey, I believe you. How could anyone be that obsessed with you? I mean, you snore, you fart, you stick your hand down your pants and scratch your balls and you spread Marmite as thick as jam."

"I've stopped biting my nails." He held up his hand.

"With my help."

He raised his fingers to her mouth and Kate clamped her lips shut. Charlie dropped his hand and smiled. "Take me to bed and I'll show you what I've got going for me."

"Um, well there's a little problem with that."

"What?" Charlie kissed along her collarbone.

"I wondered how you might feel about not having sex?"

"Why? Are you…er, you know?"

Kate smiled when he blushed. "No."

"Then what's the problem?" Charlie looked bewildered.

"Just to prove that you can," Kate said.

He opened his mouth, shut it again and then said, "Okay."

Charlie followed her into the bedroom, wondering what she was up to. Opening the door with no clothes had an instant effect on his whole body, especially his cock although he'd been semi-erect most of the way from the airport just thinking about her. Now she was telling him she didn't want to have sex? Maybe Kate didn't believe him about this Tiffany person, but he hadn't heard of her. At least, he didn't think he had.

He'd bought Kate a silver necklace holding a little star because she was his star, but this wasn't the time to give it to her. He didn't want it to look as though he was trying to buy her. She meant a lot more to him than that, it was just that when he got anywhere near her, every cell in his body wanted to make love to her.

Charlie stripped and let his clothes fall on the floor. He climbed onto the bed and pulled her back against his chest, being careful not to hurt her. He gave a deep sigh. It felt so right to be here, holding her safe in his arms. His cock throbbed but his anxiety began to dissipate.

"So what have I done now?" he asked, breathing into her neck.

"Ethan told me you were a sex addict."

"What the fuck?" So much for relaxing, his whole body tensed to match his dick. "What the hell's a sex addict?" His fingers hovered above Kate's hip, wary now of touching her.

"Someone who thinks about sex to the exclusion of everything else."

Charlie considered that. He liked sex. He wasn't going to deny it. Okay, loved it. A new woman in his bed had always brought a surge of euphoria, but he'd grown tired of having to tell women they were the best fuck he'd ever had, that their emaciated bodies were beautiful, that he'd definitely ring them, when he knew damn well he wouldn't. Charlie wanted something more and he'd found it with Kate. Friends as well as lovers, he adored making love to her, giving her pleasure, letting her please him. Charlie liked being with her. He didn't need to have sex with her to be happy.

Charlie's erection pressed against her back and Kate wondered what he was thinking.

"Do you think I'm a sex addict?" he asked.

"What do you think?"

"I can't think of anything I want more than to make love to you but I didn't jump your bones the moment I saw you," he said.

"True."

"Do you always answer the door stark naked?"

"Only when it's a friend."

"Only when it's a friend you want to torment out of his skull to prove a point."

Kate laughed and turned round. She ran her fingers along his ribs.

"Stop it," he said. "To prove it's not true, we'll sleep together and only cuddle."

"I've changed my mind."

Kate slid her hand down his chest, wrapped her fingers around his cock and squeezed gently. When her thumb swept over the head, Charlie groaned.

"That's not fair. How can you expect me not to want sex when you do that?"

Kate kissed his nose. "You're not a sex addict, Charlie, but I'm a bit worried that Ethan is prepared to believe Veronica Ward."

He tensed again. "What the hell has Ethan been saying? What's Veronica got to do with anything?"

"She was the one who told Ethan about your problem."

"I don't have a fucking problem," he yelled, then dropped his voice. "Do I?"

"No, I don't think you do, Charlie. Our relationship isn't unhealthy and it isn't just sex."

The moment those words came out of her mouth, the air froze in her throat. She waited for Charlie to say something, but he didn't speak.

"I know we're lying here naked, but you didn't rush over to drag me into bed. You came because I'd been hurt," she said, more hesitant now.

"Kate, you're going to have to stop doing that with your hand, otherwise pretty soon I'm going to prove Ethan right."

She laughed. "Maybe it's not you at all. Maybe it's me that's addicted to sex."

"God, I hope so," Charlie said. "I'd be the luckiest guy in the world."

"In that case, make love to me, lucky guy. I insist. I want you inside me now because otherwise I'm—"

His lips landed on hers and he eased her on to her back so he could nestle between her legs. Charlie didn't even stop kissing her as he slid into her in one slow lunge and then didn't move.

He broke away from her lips. "Oh God, you feel perfect. But every time we do this, I struggle to go slow."

Kate's hands grasped his hips as he bucked against her, pulling him closer as he thrust into her. Her head spun from how much she wanted him. Every part of her reacted to Charlie — her skin tingled, her pulse raced and the breath caught in her throat. Every nerve ending sizzled with delight. He wound her up with a persistent rhythm that had her gasping for him to hurry. But Charlie knew her so well, he teased and played until Kate didn't think she could take any more. Her orgasm burst within her at the moment he spurted inside her in a blaze of sunshine that melted them together.

Kate loved him. Loved. Loved. Loved him.

* * * * *

Charlie woke the next morning to the sound of banging on the door.

"What time is it?" he groaned.

"Ten thirty."

"Why is there always someone banging on your door?"

Kate threw off the covers to get up and Charlie caught hold of her arm.

"Where are you going? You don't know who's out there."

"It's probably Lucy or Rachel." Kate stared at his groin. "What the hell is that?"

"Your phone number. I did it in indelible ink, though I did think you could try and lick it off." He gave her a sheepish grin.

Kate laughed. "And how did you intend to access that in public?"

"Very carefully."

"You're crazy." She leaned over and kissed him.

Charlie's arms wrapped around her waist and pulled her down. The banging at the door started again and Kate peeled herself away. She tugged a long t-shirt over her head.

"Don't answer it until I'm there." Charlie pulled on his blue knit boxers and followed her.

Kate turned away from the spy hole. "It's Nick."

"Who's Nick?"

"From Armageddon. Remember?"

"Kate, open this door!" Nick shouted.

She twisted the handle and pulled it open.

"You fucking cunt," Nick yelled. "Why did you have to say anything?"

Charlie moved between them. "Don't speak to her like that."

"You lied. Lucy deserves better," Kate said.

"I love her."

"Well, you have a strange way of showing it, fucking Sylvie Dacre in a toilet," Kate snapped.

"I'm not the only one who fucks things just because they're there." He looked at Charlie and sneered. "Hope you're using condoms. No telling what you'll catch. Either of you."

Charlie coiled like a snake about to strike, but Kate slammed the door in Nick's face.

"He's not worth it." Kate leaned against the door as Charlie reached to open it.

She put her hand to his cheek. "I like your teeth. I'd prefer they stayed in your mouth."

"Are you suggesting I'd lose in a fight?"

"I think Nick fights dirty."

Charlie's eyes narrowed. "So do I."

"Come back to bed." Kate slid her hand over his groin. He let her lead him back to the bedroom.

"Oh, you're too easy to distract," she said with a laugh.

Charlie pulled a face. "I'm just trying to make the most of the time before you have to go to work."

"No work today."

Charlie's face brightened and he yanked off his boxers. "Good, you can come with me."

"Where are you going?"

"I need to go back to my place because a script's arriving. I've got to do a couple of interviews for an American TV network and after that, one for a magazine and late afternoon, a chat show wants me and Natalie on their settee." He drew the t-shirt over Kate's head.

"Can you still come to Rachel's gallery tonight?" She flopped on the bed.

"I'll bring my credit card."

"You don't have to buy anything."

"I know but I want to."

"I'll meet you there. You don't need me hanging around you all day, Charlie."

He lay at her side and circled her navel with his fingers.

"I need to know that you're safe. It was my fault you were stabbed. I don't think you understand how much you mean to me, Kate."

"It wasn't your fault."

"If you'd never met me, it wouldn't have happened."

Kate grabbed his fingers and held them tight. "Meeting you is the best thing that's ever happened to me."

Choked with emotion, Charlie struggled to tell her what he felt. He made his living playing with words, making people believe what he said and he couldn't utter the three words he held in his heart for Kate. He didn't *think* he loved her, he knew it. Why couldn't he say it?

"Meeting you is the best thing that ever happened to me too," he whispered.

"Apart from landing the starring role in *The Green*."

"Obviously," he said and flicked her nipple with his finger. He looked deep into her dark gray eyes. "I mean it, Kate. Our lives are entwined now and I don't want them untangling."

"I still don't need to follow you around today. I'm not a puppy."

Charlie sighed, then jumped off the bed and came back with a little blue box.

"This was for you. Only now you've said you don't like jewelry, should I throw it away?"

He watched her as she opened it. Was she disappointed it wasn't a ring? But her eyes lit up and she smiled that genuine, gorgeous Kate smile that lit up her face and his heart began to beat again.

"Oh, Charlie. Thank you."

"Because you're my star, Kate."

She kissed his nose.

"I'd like to tell you it has magical powers to defend you from crazy people, but sadly it doesn't. Kate, please come with me today."

"I'll be fine. I'll get a cab tonight with Lucy and meet you at the gallery."

"You're not to go out anywhere before then," Charlie pleaded.

She rolled her eyes. "Don't worry about me."

"Right," he said and touched the wound on her back. "Because clearly nothing happens to you when I'm not around."

Chapter Twenty-Three

ဆ

Kate and Lucy didn't leave the building until the cab pulled up outside. Kate breathed a sigh of relief no reporters or photographers hung around.

"You're yesterday's news," Lucy said.

Kate hoped that was true.

"So, are you okay?" Lucy asked as the cab pulled away. "How's your back?"

"Fine."

"Is Charlie coming?"

Kate nodded.

"Nick is trying to win me back. He says once Gemma goes off to university in September, he'll tell his wife about us and ask for a divorce."

Kate didn't say anything about Nick's early morning visit.

"And when we get to the end of September, I wouldn't be surprised if his wife's father falls ill, so he doesn't want to upset her or he runs over her dog and doesn't want to upset her. And then at Christmas there'll be another excuse not to bloody well upset her. I know it sounds hypocritical, but while it was just me and his wife, I didn't mind, but I'll be damned if I'm sharing him with anyone else."

"What about Fax?"

Lucy grinned. "He's growing on me."

The cab lurched to a halt in the middle of the road outside the gallery. There was no room to pull up at the curb.

"I'll pay," Lucy said. "I'll claim it on expenses."

By the time the driver had written a receipt, traffic had backed up behind and horns blared. The gallery blazed with light, people spilling onto the pavement like sweets falling from a bag, an assortment of the well-dressed and well-heeled, drinks in hands.

"Wow," Lucy said. "Rachel must be pleased with the turnout. Sometimes she only has two people come in the entire day."

"Two's okay so long as they buy something," Kate said.

They spotted Rachel the moment they walked in. She waved and hurried over.

"Do you need us to help with anything?" Kate asked.

"I'd rather you mingled, told everyone how wonderful the paintings are and that they're a brilliant investment. No one's buying anything."

"It's still early," Lucy said. "Oh, there's Fax."

Deserted by her friends, Kate lifted a glass of wine from the tray of a passing waiter and worked her way through to the back of the gallery. A man stood next to the painting "Ready for Bed", making sure people knew it was his work. Painfully thin with a long face and a gray ponytail, he reminded Kate of a horse.

Rachel had been wrong about things not selling. Red stickers were appearing like measles. Dan's "Sister" painting had sold and Kate gawped when Dan pointed out who'd bought it. Tony from Crispies. He stood with his arm round Mel. Kate wondered how she'd got that so wrong.

She edged through the crowds to her favorite painting, the fridge light picture. It hadn't sold, but when she saw the price tag was almost twenty thousand pounds, she wasn't surprised.

"What do you think of this piece?" a voice asked.

Following Rachel's instruction, Kate tried her best. "It's excellent. I like the balance the artist's struck between concealment and revelation."

"And?"

"And the way we're drawn into the light, but at the same time tempted to stay in the dark. I guess it's an invitation to explore the ambiguity of the kitchen, a place on the verge of dysfunctional breakdown. It's clever and very well done."

"What about 'Wall'?"

Kate flinched. Shit, now she'd have to lie. She turned to look at the man who was speaking, but he'd twisted away from her to look at the brick monstrosity and was awkwardly positioned in the press of bodies. He was a middle-aged man, tall and slim with short silver-gray hair and a gold earring.

Kate began again. "Another contradiction. The sense of dislocation from the—"

"Ah, you wrote the catalogue," he said.

"Oops, you caught me." Kate smiled.

Then he turned to face her. "Hello, Kate."

The smile on her face disintegrated. She was freezing from the toes up. Her brain told her feet to move, but nothing happened.

"You look very like your mother."

Kate was desperate to escape, but only her heart was moving, going berserk, flailing at her ribs, ripping itself to shreds in an attempt to flee.

"What do you really think of 'Wall'?"

"It's crap," she choked out.

He smiled. "Still my stroppy little girl."

Kate couldn't breathe. Invisible fingers had wrapped around her throat. She wondered if she was going to pass out.

"I remember taking you to the National Gallery when you were knee-high and you walked round saying 'like that' and 'don't like that' in a loud voice. Do you remember?"

"No," she lied.

"One of my pieces is over there," he said.

Kate's head spun round, and the breath rushed into her throat. "I thought you were painting straight onto plaster?"

"Right, you've seen Charlie Storm's place."

She looked at the picture, called "Tree Down".

"Did you recognize my style?"

She hadn't seen it. The one painting Rachel had been waiting for and if it had been there, none of this would have happened because Kate would have known not to come tonight. Without her realizing, he'd taken her arm and walked her over to his work. She looked at it carefully.

"It's very good." A violent picture of a fallen tree, branches broken, limbs twisted as though it was a living thing writhing in agony. All his work was tormented.

"Don't sound so disappointed," he said. "Look, I want to talk to you, sweetheart. Do you think we could go somewhere and have a chat?"

She wanted to tell him not to call her sweetheart. "No, I don't think that's a good idea."

Now that she could move, she edged backward, but he followed.

"I came tonight because I knew there would be a lot of people around. I didn't want to frighten you. I wanted to see you today because I wanted to wish you happy —"

"No," she said, turned and walked into Charlie's arms.

"I want to go now." She propelled him toward the door.

"Don't you want me to buy anything?" he asked in bewilderment.

"No, just go."

As they weaved their way out of the gallery, he caught hold of her shoulders. "What's the matter? Is it that guy you were talking to? Has he upset you? Want me to thump him?"

"Take me back to your place." Kate was unable to think beyond dragging Charlie as far away from the gallery as she could.

"Tell me what's wrong?" he pleaded.

"I will, but I want to go."

She didn't speak in the cab, but pressed herself into his arms, glancing back repeatedly to see if they were being followed. Charlie stayed quiet and just held her. Once she was in his house, Kate made him go round and make sure the doors and windows were locked. She knew she was being paranoid, but couldn't help

311

it. She stayed on the stairs while Charlie checked. Kate leaned against the wall, trying to sink into it.

After several minutes, he returned to sit next to her and took hold of her hand, pressing her knuckles to his lips.

"Okay, Fort Knox is secure. The only danger is from me and that's not inconsiderable, particularly if you don't tell me what the fuck is wrong."

"I lied. My father's not dead. That's who I was talking to."

Charlie took a deep breath. "Why did you tell me he was dead?"

Kate pressed harder into the wall. "Because when I was seven, he killed my mother and he nearly killed me. I wanted him to be dead too, so I said he was. I made him dead."

"Bloody hell." Charlie rubbed his lips against her hand. "What happened?"

"I was in bed. I heard my parents arguing and went downstairs They were in the kitchen. My father had a knife in his hand, and he was covered in blood. Just covered in it, like someone had thrown a bucket of the stuff all over him." She took a deep, shaky breath.

"My mother was yelling, screaming, waving her hands around. There was blood all over her, too. I ran straight at them, grabbed hold of Dad's arms and Mum tried to pull me back. We were all struggling. I remember slipping and being yanked up by my hair. There was this thump high up on my back and I fell again."

Kate fixed her eyes on a speck on the stairs.

"Your scar."

"I came round in hospital. A policewoman sat by my bed. They didn't tell me straightaway, but when no one came to see me, I knew. A woman in a pink suit turned up and said my mum was dead. My dad lay unconscious in another ward in the hospital, but they were going to arrest him. They'd wanted to find a relative to break the news to me, but there wasn't one. No grandparents, no aunts or uncles so I was taken into care. I testified at my father's trial and he went to prison for life."

312

"Jesus, Kate."

She turned to look at him. "Only life doesn't mean life. He's been out for quite a while."

"Has he tried to contact you before?" Charlie put one of his hands on the back of her neck, hugged her to his chest and kept the other hand holding her fingers.

"Yes, but he knows I won't see him."

"Why not?"

"What could he say to me that would make any difference to what I think of him? He destroyed my life. I was mute for six months and wet the bed for a year. I lost my world. Everything had been taken away from me — my family, home, toys, friends, school. I hated everyone, blamed everyone. I was the child of a murderer. Can you imagine how the other kids treated me? I moved from hurt, to hate, to anger and got stuck there. I destroyed everything I was given. It was no wonder no one wanted me. I wouldn't have wanted me."

Charlie sighed. "Why do you think he came to the gallery? Was it a coincidence?"

Kate glanced up at the ceiling. "No, I think he's known where I was for a long time. He had a picture for sale in there. It came in late otherwise I'd have known to stay away. He wanted to confront me tonight in front of people so I couldn't make a scene. He painted your ceiling."

"My ceiling? How do you know?"

"See the demons' curly tails with the three prongs? He used to put those on drawings he did for me. He's always been a painter. He painted in prison and his work was sold to raise money for charity. He made quite a name for himself."

"I don't know what to say," Charlie whispered.

"His lawyers contacted me and offered me money. That's how I bought my apartment. I thought I could change my life. No more men like Dex. No more shabby bed-sits in dangerous areas. I decided he owed me that." She wriggled under Charlie's arm. "How did it go today on the chat show?" Kate hoped he'd let her change the subject.

"You didn't watch?"

"Everyone was out."

"I'm going to buy you a TV."

"I don't want one. I've got better things to do."

"Such as?"

"Let's go upstairs and I'll show you."

"You're trying to distract me."

"And is it working?"

"What do you think?" Charlie kissed her.

His hand slid up her thigh, under her dress to her pants. He slipped his finger under the edge of the material and ran it around until he reached the damp, soft place between her legs and she trembled.

"I don't want to talk anymore, Charlie."

"Neither do I."

She just wanted to forget.

Charlie made her squeal as he swept her into his arms and carried her upstairs. Kate squealed again when he pretended to stumble on the last step. He put her down on the landing, slumped beside her and groaned. "You weigh a ton."

"Bet I could carry you."

His gaze met hers. "Bet you can't."

Kate sprang to her feet, spread her legs and braced her arms against the wall. "Jump on."

Charlie laughed. "What an offer."

"Come on," Kate urged. "Just don't throw yourself on me."

"You're no fun."

She steadied herself as Charlie slung one leg over her hip, then locked her knees as he put his hands on her shoulders and lifted the other. He was heavy but not too heavy. Kate pushed herself away from the wall, reached back to hook her arms around his legs and took a shaky step.

"Okay. You've proved your point. Let me down before we kiss the floor and get carpet burn in an unsexy way," Charlie said.

Kate gritted her teeth and staggered toward his bedroom. Charlie's hand snaked over her shoulder onto her breast to tweak her nipple and she let out a muffled groan. "Cheating."

The door to his room. Ten steps to his bed. She could do that.

"Take me a couple of times around the room, horsey," Charlie said. "Oh I wish I had a whip, you lazy animal."

Kate collapsed facedown on the bed with Charlie still plastered to her back, humping her butt.

"Oh no, Lucky Lady has fallen at the first hurdle in the bedroom stakes," Charlie shouted. "Her rider is trying to rouse her. Will she have to be put down? Is that plucky guy on her back uninjured? Yippee, the handsome, talented jockey is back on his feet." Charlie stood up. "But he's concerned for his mount. Will she ever be fit to ride again? He'll have to check."

He tickled her legs and Kate tried to squirm across the bed. Charlie pulled her back, unfastened her dress and pulled it off her shoulders. She heard the hitch in his breath and knew he was taking in the white underwear, the multi-stranded, many-beaded back on the bra.

"No broken legs. That's a relief, but further examination is most certainly required." Charlie tugged the dress down and off her legs.

"Aarrggh," he moaned. "White lace thong."

Kate sighed as he removed her shoes and kissed her toes.

"Steward's enquiry on the result of the 10:40 p.m. at the Islington race meeting. Cheating suspected. Doesn't appear to be a horse at all."

A moment later, a naked Charlie lay plastered against her back, the hard length of his cock pressed into her butt, the wet tip tickling her above the band of the thong.

"Not into sex with animals then?" Kate asked.

He laughed in her ear. "I'd gone as far down that path as I thought safe." He shifted to one side and rolled her over with him.

"Oh sweet Christ," Charlie whispered. "What the hell are these?"

Kate didn't think he needed an answer. She'd cut out and sewn the crotchless thong earlier in the evening before she'd left with Lucy.

"Men pants," he said. "You bad, bad girl."

Kate sighed as he trailed his finger around the edge of the lace heart that framed her sex.

Charlie slipped a finger inside her. "How come you're always wet?"

"How come you're always hard?"

"At least no one can see you're wet. The moment I'm near you, I'm scared I'm going to get arrested. It's all your fault."

Kate smiled. Charlie sank his finger in and out of her pink folds, his thumb working her clit at the same time.

"I really like these panties. If you wore these when we were out, we could have some fun."

He slid down the bed and pressed his face to the gap in the material. The moment his tongue touched her, Kate trembled. Tongue, lips, finger, thumb and Kate felt the unraveling begin. Tiny tremors in her core grew larger, spreading until her breathing became shaky and her vision shimmered in sparks of light. The feel of Charlie's head between her legs, his soft hair brushing her thighs, his tongue surging into her, the purposeful intent as his thumb strummed her clit over and over drove Kate faster and faster until she stampeded into oblivion.

"Oh God," she gasped and as Charlie grabbed her hands and squeezed tight, Kate fell into blackness.

When she opened her eyes, his face was inches from hers, his chin and lips glistening with her cream. Kate snuck out her tongue and licked his mouth. A moment later, they were kissing as if they hadn't seen each other for weeks.

Charlie eventually pulled back and pushed up her legs. "You taste delicious and you look divine."

He rocked his hips and teased her sex with the head of his cock. Not pushing in, just pressing against her.

"Sometimes I wish I could just do this all day," he whispered. "Like one of those automatons. Drive us both crazy."

Kate wanted him inside her and tried to rock into him.

"No you don't," Charlie said and changed the angle of his slide so his crest hit her clit.

"Yes I do," Kate tossed back and slung her legs over his shoulder to yank him down.

Charlie's cock popped inside her wet folds and he frowned. "I thought I was in charge."

"You are," Kate lied.

When she crossed her legs around the back of his neck and pulled him down hard, he shot all the way into her with a surprised gasp.

"You little…"

"What?" Kate asked.

Charlie groaned as she flexed her hips up into his.

"Little angel. Except…"

"Except what?"

"I'm not sure I can move."

"Well try."

He brought his knees nearer to her backside and Kate loosened her grip on his neck as he pressed his body closer to hers. When he began to shunt inside her in long, slow thrusts to bury himself in her body, Kate felt the fullness of his cock, the wider head, and sighed in pleasure. The weight of Charlie leaning against her made it difficult to breathe, but intensified the sensation of every movement he made.

Kate could feel everything. The heat of his cock as it pistoned into her wetness, the brush of his ragged breathing, the wet slap of their bodies. She could smell his unique scent, his arousal, his sweat and the lingering aroma of tangy aftershave. Charlie's eyes grew wilder and darker as he moved faster. He turned to caress the inside of her thigh with his cheek and as his tongue lapped her there, his cock echoed the kiss.

She gasped with every thrust into her body, groaned with each withdrawal. His arms spread over hers, Charlie pressed them into the bed above her head and reared over her.

"Christ, Kate."

She'd thought he couldn't get deeper, couldn't thrust harder but he managed both. Kate's muscles spasmed, her body shook and she was washed away in waves of pleasure, pounded into the surf as each contraction bit deeper. Charlie's face contorted and then she felt his cock swell. As he jetted into her, her muscles clenched around his cock, dragging his cum out of him.

As their breathing eased, Charlie's eyes opened. "That was fantastic. I never want to move."

"That shouldn't be a problem. I can't move."

Charlie sighed as he withdrew his cock. Kate sighed louder when her legs were back in a straight line.

"Result of the 11:05 race. Snow the winner with Storm a close second," Charlie said.

"I think it was a dead heat."

He laughed. "I'm dead hot, you could be right."

Chapter Twenty-Four

சு

Kate opened her eyes the next morning to find Charlie looking at her. She gave him a lazy smile.

"I love you," he said.

Kate gulped, wide awake.

"I've been waiting for you to wake up so I could tell you. I should have said it before. Properly. I. Love. You." He punctuated each word with a kiss.

For once, Kate had no smart retort. Her heart was sprinting, racing against her brain toward a finish line and winning. He loved her. He no longer *thought* he loved her. He *did* love her. His dark eyes were like deep pools, so beautiful she longed to submerge herself in them.

"And although I love fucking you, it's far more than that. I love you because I can be honest with you. I trust you. I love you because you've made me see I'm more than I thought. I love you because you've made me real. I'm trying to ignore the fact that my dick gets excited when I even think your name." He kissed the end of her nose and then pulled back. "Do you love me?"

"Yes, I love you." She ran a finger along his lips. "You're my other path, Charlie. Of course I love you."

His face lit up and then his smile slipped a little. "What other path?"

"When I was seven my life divided. I went one way into care and my hopes went on another, different path, one where I hadn't stepped in as my parents fought, one where no one died. On that path, I could pass exams, seize opportunities, get a good job, find someone to love me — someone who thought I was sweet and kind and beautiful. I thought, one day the paths will come together, someone will help me bring them together. That's what kept me sane, helped me to survive. That's why Richard fooled me. I thought it was him I'd been waiting for, but it wasn't. It was you. And in a strange, warped way, I'm glad I met Dickhead, otherwise I'd never have met you."

"Who said anything about you being sweet, kind and beautiful?" Charlie asked.

"This sexy guy I know. I'll introduce you one day."

He leaned forward to plant a gentle kiss on her lips. "I wish I could turn back the clock and make things right."

"They're right now and that's all that matters."

"I want to give you the world."

"I only want you."

"Even with all my bad habits?" he asked.

"Well, no, not with those, obviously."

He leapt on her, taking her wrists in one hand and pinning them above her head. "You're supposed to say you love me even with those." His other hand tickled her ribs and stomach and she squirmed.

"I give in," she yelled.

"You're too easy."

But he pulled her back against him and wrapped his arms and legs around her as if he was trying to make her part of him. Kate didn't think she'd ever felt so safe and happy.

"So why do you think no one would have died if you hadn't stepped in?"

She tensed and Charlie kissed her shoulder. "Tell me," he whispered.

"I made matters worse. I think I stopped Mum saving herself because she tried to protect me."

"But you were only seven. You couldn't have prevented anything from happening."

His legs entwined with hers, toes kissing.

"I'll never know, will I?" Kate said, her voice subdued.

"Is that what your father wants to talk to you about? What happened that night?"

Silence.

"Have I got to tickle you again? Talk to me, Kate. Please." He brushed his cheek against hers.

"I think he wants to ask me to forgive him and I don't think I can."

Charlie pressed his face into her hair. "You forgave me for hurting you. He's your Dad, Kate. You should at least let him talk to you."

"I don't want to."

Charlie let her go and rolled on to his back. "I wanted to ask you to do something with me, only I'm not sure that I should now."

"What?"

"I want to go and see my birth mother."

Something squeezed her heart. "Right. Where does she live?"

"Surrey Quays."

"What's her name?" Kate turned her head on the pillow to face him.

"Janet Doyle."

"Have you spoken to her? How does it work? What do you have to do?"

"They suggest someone act as intermediary, in case she drops dead with shock when she sees me. But I'm the one with the rights, not her. She has no access to me, unless I want it to happen." Charlie took a deep breath. "She registered the fact that she left me outside Woolworths so I guess she thought I might get in touch one day. She could have contacted the adoption agency and asked them to get in touch with me, but she hasn't. So, I have to assume she's not interested in what happened to me. Only when she finds out who I am, I think that will change."

Kate saw Charlie's problem.

"Want a cup of tea?" he asked and rolled out of bed, padding naked across the floor.

Kate got up and followed him.

"Look at it another way, Charlie, she could have told the adoption people she didn't want any contact from you, but she hasn't. Maybe she's always hoped you'd want to find her."

He pulled on a blue toweling robe and tossed a white one to Kate, giving her a wry smile. "We are such a pair. You don't want to speak to your long lost dad and I'm desperate to speak to my long lost mum."

"Are you going to ring her or just turn up on the doorstep?" Kate asked as they went downstairs.

"They don't recommend knocking on the door out of the blue. I mean, she really might drop dead with shock."

"What are you going to do?"

Charlie switched on the kettle and took two tall mugs from the cupboard. "Call her and arrange to see her, if…if she wants to." He looked at Kate. "I'd like you to sit in the car and wait for me, so you can give me a hug when I come out."

Kate put the milk on the work surface. "What are you looking for, Charlie? What do you want her to tell you?"

He ran his finger down her forehead, over her nose to her lips. "I need to know why she didn't want me."

Kate's heart lurched. She couldn't imagine giving her baby up, couldn't imagine giving Charlie up. She put her arms around him.

"Could you do that? Give up your child?" he asked and then rushed on before Kate could answer. "I mean we've never talked about children. I don't want to rush you or anything."

"Why? Were you thinking of starting now?"

His hands slid to her backside, and he tugged her against him. She could feel the hard ridge of his erection pressing against her.

"I think I'm going to call you Ever Ready," Kate said.

"We haven't done it in the kitchen yet."

"We haven't done it on your couch either. Or in the garage."

His eyes twinkled. "So much to look forward to."

The noise of the boiling kettle pulled them apart.

"How much do you know about your birth mother?" she asked.

"Just her name and address, and the fact that she left me outside Woolworths. I was nine months old. I guess the fact that it was Woolworths gives me some idea of what to expect. Not Harrods or Selfridges." He shot her a wry grin.

Kate handed him the tea. "Hey, you don't know why she abandoned you, Charlie. She could have just been a kid. There might be lots of reasons why she couldn't keep you. Maybe she was raped."

He stared at her. "But even if she was raped, she went ahead and had me, kept me for nine months and then dumped me. Would you ever do that? Abandon your baby?"

Kate shook her head. "No, but—"

"No buts. She kept me for nine months. Nine fucking months. The same amount of time she had me inside her. I mean, is that significant?" His voice had risen. "I understand about rape. I could see that. It might have happened. Or if there was no rape and she was a kid, maybe, just maybe, I could accept that. But by nine months I might have been walking. I'd have been smiling at her. Trusting her. Loving her. I was a person. And she didn't want me."

Kate wrapped one of her hands around his clenched fist and pulled him into her arms, holding him tight. Charlie needed steadfast love more than anything, she saw that now. It explained his drive to succeed as a pop star, why he'd turned to acting and why it would never be enough. He might moan and wail about the fans, but he needed the adoration, fed on it because he was trying to wipe out the fact that the one person who should have loved him more than her life, had rejected him.

"Ethan's going to kill me," he muttered.

"Why?"

"Because he wants to control everything about me and I'm not going to tell him about this. He's basically a good guy. He bullied me into getting help, pushed me when others would have given up but he's king of the fairground ride, a master of spin. If I told him what I was doing, he'd have the press there and a TV company recording the whole thing for some Sunday night special. Maybe *Hello* or *OK* magazine set up with a mega-deal. Pages of photos of a big, fucking happy reunion. That's not what I want. I want to do this on my own. Only…I want you there, too. Would you do that? To be honest, I don't want you to wait in the car. Would you come in with me?"

"Are you sure?"

He nodded. "I'm a coward. Holding your hand makes me feel better."

"Ring her then."

"What, now?"

Kate smiled at the look of horror on his face and kissed his cheek. "Yes, now."

"Who should I say I am?"

"Charlie!"

"Okay, okay."

Kate leaned back against the counter top and listened. Charlie already had the number in his phone.

"Hello, is this Janet Doyle?… Oh, Janet Crouch. Sorry. I know this is going to be a bit of a shock, but you're my—"

He didn't get any further. Kate saw the relief sweep his face.

"Charlie," he said. "Yes…Yes…Okay…Right…See you then." He put the phone down.

"She guessed when I said her maiden name," he explained.

"How did she sound?"

"Slightly Scots, I think. She sounded okay, not angry, but not thrilled either. Sort of resigned. We can go and see her this afternoon while her husband's at work. He's not my father."

He gave a deep sigh.

"What's wrong?" Kate asked.

"How will I know whether she's pleased to see me or not? Once she recognizes me, she'll react because I'm Charlie Storm and not because I'm the little boy she gave up."

"Do you want to put a paper bag over your head?"

"Ha bloody ha."

"Have you considered that she might go to the press? Sell her story?" Kate asked.

Charlie started to bite his nails, winced at the taste and glared at Kate. "She's not going to look good if she does go to the press, is she?"

"If a lot of money's involved, I'm not sure people care how the papers make them look."

* * * * *

Charlie's birth mother lived in an apartment a stone's throw from the Thames. When Charlie drove straight to her place, without even using his sat-nav, Kate wondered if he'd been there before, trying to spot her. He parked next to a line of wheelie bins and as they walked to the front of the block, he squeezed Kate's hand. The block was a new build, three stories of London brick with gray multi-angled roofs. Charlie's finger shook when he pressed the buzzer. He gave Kate a nervous smile.

"Come in. It's the top floor." The voice from the intercom sounded raspy.

Charlie's feet got slower and slower. By the time they reached the last flight, Kate was all but dragging him.

Janet Crouch stood at her door waiting. When Charlie came into view, her mouth dropped open.

"Is this a joke?" she muttered and looked behind Kate and Charlie, maybe checking for a film crew.

"Hello, er…Mum," Charlie said.

"Fucking hell," she gasped. "Fucking, fucking, fucking hell."

What a lovely way to greet a child you hadn't seen for thirty years, Kate thought.

The three of them just stood there. Kate could see she'd made an effort to smarten herself up. She wore a neatly ironed blue sun dress, but if Charlie had hoped for a sophisticated, elegant mother, he'd be disappointed. Janet was small and thin with startling bright red hair, courtesy of a box.

"It's a joke," Janet said again.

Charlie seemed to have lost the power of speech, so Kate took over.

"It's not a joke. Can we come in?"

Janet moved aside. By the time they'd walked up another flight of stairs and she'd shown them into the living room, Janet's expression had changed from one of disbelief to one of dreamlike bliss. Kate could almost see wheels turning in her head, cogs clicking, money chinking like a jackpot pay-out on a one-armed bandit. Kate looked around the room. Apart from a very large TV and a DVD player, everything was shabby. The curtains looked tired and faded and the cushions on the couch, lumpy and stained. Janet started to tidy, but moving a few newspapers wasn't going to make much difference. Kate didn't think Charlie had noticed the state of the place, his focus was on his mother, as if he was trying to see inside her, to see himself in her.

"Sit down. Would you like a drink? Tea? Coffee? Something stronger?"

"No, thanks," Kate said and pulled Charlie down onto the red couch when he failed to sit.

Janet slumped into a chair opposite. "Fucking hell," she said again. "You mean I gave birth to Charlie Storm?"

She lit a cigarette with shaking hands and then offered the packet to Charlie and Kate. Charlie looked tempted, but shook his head.

"Charlie Storm," Janet repeated as though it would help her understand what she was seeing.

Kate wondered if she ought to offer to make the woman a drink. She looked as though she was in shock.

"Who are you?" she asked Kate, her eyes narrowed in suspicion. "Press?"

"She's my girlfriend." Charlie managed to find his voice.

"What do you want to know?" Janet asked, blowing out a stream of smoke. "Why I gave you up?"

Charlie nodded.

"I was sixteen when I got pregnant. Seventeen when I had you. I don't know who your father was. Sorry." She shrugged. "I slept around in those days and none of the guys wanted to know me once I was knocked up. Neither did my mum and dad. So I thought, fuck them, and managed on my own."

The ash from her cigarette grew longer and Kate watched, waiting for it to fall on the carpet.

"I remember the day you were born, though. No one with me except this snotty middle-aged midwife. God, you were an ugly little sod, all squashed up."

She winked at Kate and Kate's eyes opened in horror. She wanted her to stop, but Janet had found her flow. The ash grew longer, precariously balanced.

"I was in labor for hours. God, if I'd known, I'd have never…well. Anyway, you came out eventually. All babies do. Everyone else had these pretty things with lovely hair and you were long and thin and bald and…well, fucking ugly."

She laughed and then broke into a coughing fit and the ash fell on the carpet. Janet rubbed it in with her heel.

Surely every baby who'd spent hours forcing its way down a narrow birth canal would come out looking squashed. Kate squeezed Charlie's hand. He wasn't ugly now.

"I named you Charlie," she said and Kate heard the upbeat in her voice then. "I left a piece of paper with your name on it. I didn't know if the people who adopted you would keep it. Who'd have thought?" Janet stared at him. "Maybe I do know who your dad might have been. You remind me of him. He had hair like yours, dark and straight and the same color eyes." She stubbed out that cigarette and lit another.

"What's his name?"

Kate heard the eagerness in Charlie's voice.

"Keith. I met him at a party. He said he was in a band. He'd gone the next morning. I never saw him again. He was good-looking, though. I remember that."

She smiled, her teeth small and crooked, stained from too many cigarettes. But Kate saw a hint of Charlie in Janet's eyes and in her smile.

"Did you ever think about me? Wonder what I was doing?" he asked.

"Sometimes, but you weren't mine, so what was the point? It was easier to forget I'd had you. No point beating myself up about what might have been. I've got other kids now. And a husband. They don't know about you."

She got up and brought over a photograph. It was of her at the seaside, standing next to a beefy-looking guy with tattoos on both arms and close-cropped hair. Three young girls sat on a wall behind them.

"That's my husband, Marvin. The girls are Lizzie, she's twelve, Sarah's fifteen and Claire's sixteen. They'd love to meet you. They've always wanted a brother."

Janet clearly expected Charlie to say something, but he didn't. Three half sisters. Kate knew what would happen when they found out about Charlie.

"Are your parents still alive?" Charlie asked.

"Dad died of lung cancer last year. My mother lives in Luton. I don't know where and I don't care."

"Why did you give Charlie up?" Kate blurted.

Janet bristled. Her eyes shot to Kate as though she resented her asking.

"I met a guy, not Marvin, and he didn't want a kid. I thought without a baby, we'd be able to make a go of it. We did, but it only lasted a couple of years."

"You loved him more than you loved me," Charlie muttered.

Janet ground out her half-smoked cigarette. "He had a good job," she snapped. "He took me places. You were a whiney little thing, always crying for attention, always wanting something, but you wouldn't have a dummy. Kept spitting it out. I loved you, course I did, but I wanted a life too. I was a kid myself."

"So you dumped me outside Woolworths?" Charlie's voice was flat.

"Not dumped," she said. "I wrapped you up well. I knew someone would find you. They'd hear you bellowing for something to eat. Right pair of lungs you had." She gave a little smile. "Still have. Eventually I gave my details to the social services so if in the future, you'd wanted to contact me, you could. I didn't have to do that. But...I'm glad I did." She shot him a nervous glance. "Anyway, you must have had a good life. You're doing all right now, aren't you? Rich and famous. The people that adopted you must have brought you up properly."

"Yes, they did." Charlie got to his feet. "Well, thanks for seeing me."

Janet looked surprised. "Is that it? Is that all you want?"

Kate got up too. She had no idea what Charlie was thinking but he couldn't be happy.

"I suppose you're disappointed," Janet said. "Not what you expected, am I?" She smoothed down her dress with fluttering hands. "Not some rich, educated woman."

"I didn't expect anything," Charlie said.

"You should be grateful I gave you up. You wouldn't have amounted to anything if I'd kept you. But look at you now. You're so good-looking." She took a step toward him. "I wouldn't mind if you wanted to give me a hug."

Charlie tried to back off and Kate stood in his way, elbowed him forward.

Janet flung her arms around him. Charlie hugged her, timidly at first but Kate watched the embrace grow into one of sadness for what had been missed by both of them. He pulled away and Janet patted his arm.

"Well, look after yourself, son. Be careful of people who just want to know you for your money."

Kate bit her lip.

"Give me a ring. Perhaps we could go for a meal. All of us," Janet said as Charlie backed away to the stairs.

"You're welcome to come again. Your sisters would love to meet you," Janet called.

329

"I'll ring you and arrange something. I'd like to meet my...sisters."

Janet looked as though she'd won the lottery.

He turned back at the first step. "When's my birthday?"

She looked flustered. "December. It was the fifth, I think."

Charlie stood up straight, and smiled. "Right." He paused. "When's your birthday?"

"January the seventh."

"I'll make a note. Um, please don't talk to the papers about this. Let's have chance to get to know each other first."

"All right."

He turned to leave again and she called him back. "Charlie?"

"Yes?"

"I'm sorry. Sorry for not keeping you."

Kate looked between the pair of them. Charlie gave a little smile. "It's okay. My adoptive parents did a good job. It's me that messed things up. My dad would like to meet you, one day."

Janet nodded.

Kate glanced back as they went down the stairs. Janet stood watching them as though she still couldn't quite believe what had just happened.

Chapter Twenty-Five

ᔕᓕ

Charlie grabbed Kate's hand and led her out of the apartment. Her fingers curled loosely round the handrail to stop herself stumbling as he pulled her down the stairs at breakneck speed. He didn't say anything until they were sitting in the car.

"I wanted to know and now I do," he said, his voice flat.

"It was a good thing you did, Charlie, telling her it was okay about giving you up." Kate took hold of his hand and stroked his fingers.

He didn't say anything.

"Well, it was a good thing to say it, even if you didn't mean it."

"You know, I researched this. I read that most mothers never stop thinking about children they've given away. They feel as if part of them is missing. She hadn't given me a second thought, only I think she will now."

Kate saw the pain in his eyes.

"Christ, I didn't want much. She didn't even remember what day she gave birth to me. Guess she missed out on the mothering gene. I thought my birthday was December the fourteenth. I may as well stick to that." He paused. "When's yours?"

"August."

"It's August now. When?"

"I don't celebrate birthdays, Charlie."

"Why not?"

She picked at an imaginary spot on her skirt. "I don't like them."

"Why?"

Kate sighed. If she told him, maybe it would distract him from thinking about what just happened. "We didn't have proper parties in the children's homes but we got a cake after dinner if it was someone's birthday and they got to choose what they wanted on TV. Everyone resented the fact that they were stuck in there and not with a family. Not with *their* family."

"Did you never have a party?"

"Not after my mum died and so I never got invited to any. Little girls can be bloody cruel. When I was twelve, I decided I'd organize my own so I'd be invited back. We weren't allowed to bring more than two friends to the house so I arranged it in the park. I wrote when and where on balloons. I saved up pocket money to buy party bags and filled them with sweets, pencils with animal tops and plastic yoyos. I bought crisps, sausage rolls and bottles of Coke and lemonade. I'd even managed music. And a big chocolate cake. I hijacked a supermarket cart to transport everything."

She took a deep breath. She could still see all the food laid out on the picnic tables. It had looked great.

"No one came. At first, I thought maybe I'd got the time wrong or the place and in a different part of the park everyone was standing holding presents and cards, waiting for me."

She raised her eyes to Charlie's. His fingers rubbed hers.

"I had the party on my own. Got told off for feeding crisps to the ducks and then into more trouble because not only did I miss evening curfew but I'd borrowed the music player without asking. They'd eaten the cake they'd bought, but left a slice for me and I wasn't allowed to go to bed until I'd eaten it. Only I was so full, I threw up in the kitchen. I never bothered with birthdays after that."

"Is it too late to adopt you?" Charlie whispered, stroking her cheek with his fingers.

Kate grinned. "But then the sex would have to stop. You'd get arrested."

"Oh yeah." He laughed.

"Hey, I'm over it, Charlie."

"So when's your birthday?" His grip tightened.

"Forget it. It's gone."

"When was it?" he repeated. "Don't make me resort to pain or tickling."

"Yesterday."

He closed his eyes and groaned. "Shit. Why didn't you tell me?" His eyes opened. "That was why your father wanted to see you."

He put the car into gear and drove off.

"Where are we going?" Kate asked.

"Shopping."

"What do you need?"

"Not for me. For you."

"I don't need anything."

"I want to buy you something." Charlie glanced at her. "You don't have to *need* something to go shopping."

Kate did. She'd never had the money to buy things she didn't need.

"I don't want to go shopping," she said.

"What would you like to do?"

"Go for a picnic."

Kate hadn't anticipated that she'd be the one walking round the supermarket buying the food, while Charlie skulked in the car, paranoid about being recognized. When Kate got back, he was talking on his mobile. He flicked the switch for the boot, not even emerging to help unload the cart. By the time Kate sat beside him, he'd finished the call.

"What have you been up to?" she asked as she handed him his change.

With such a wide and innocent smile on his face, he was guilty of something.

"Nothing."

"I'm very sad to have to tell you this, but I fear winning an Oscar is out of your reach. You're a hopeless actor, Charlie. You wear your heart on your face. Though it is a lovely face." Kate kissed him.

"Not as lovely as yours," he whispered. "Happy Birthday for yesterday."

The kiss grew deeper and more passionate by the second. Charlie's tongue teased her mouth, sending a frisson of pleasure pulsing through her whole body.

"We could have the picnic on your bed," Kate gasped as she pulled away.

"No. I'm driving us to Richmond Park."

"Great," Kate said. "I haven't been there in ages."

They'd eaten, and were lying on their backs in the sun before Kate spoke to Charlie about what happened that afternoon. She knew he didn't want to talk about it, but she also knew he had to deal with it.

"Was she so much worse than you expected?" Kate asked.

For a moment he didn't answer. "I didn't know what to expect. I didn't think I'd care whether she was pretty or bright. And I don't. I wanted her to have missed me, thought about me over the years and I don't think she did."

"Do you like to think about your mistakes?"

"I'm a mistake?"

"She had you, Charlie. She didn't abort you. She was a kid."

He rolled onto his side.

"Her eyes are a bit like yours. You have her smile," Kate said.

Charlie looked across at her. "Do I?"

Kate nodded. "But not her teeth."

He laughed.

"You run your fingers through your hair like your dad," she added.

He didn't say anything.

"You bite your nails like your mum."

"I don't anymore. Look."

He showed Kate his hands. The ragged edges had gone.

"Why don't you go and see your mum, and take her some Stopit? Tell her about Janet."

Charlie slumped onto his back.

"And tell her what? That she was right?"

Kate put her chin on his chest. "Life's too short to fall out with your family. They love you, Charlie. They're your parents. Let them show you how much they care."

He pulled her up so that she lay on top of him.

"How about I show you?" he said.

"In the middle of Richmond Park? I don't think so."

"But you've got those special panties on."

"No I haven't."

He gave her a puzzled look and then his eyes widened. "Move closer."

"Why?"

He gave an exasperated sigh and yanked her into his arms. A moment later, his hand was between her legs and he was moaning in her ear. Kate forgot about the fact that they lay in a park, forgot everything but what Charlie was doing. He had one arm over her shoulder, pulling her tight as he kissed her, the other hand sliding in her wet folds, teasing her clit out of its little nest and then circling it with his fingertip.

Kate gasped into his mouth and he swallowed her cry as she melted against him. Charlie kissed her back to earth, nibbling her lips until her breathing eased.

"Now we have a big problem. I was going to take you to see the special area of conservation for the stag beetle, but I'm no longer in a fit state."

"Another day," Kate said.

She jumped up, hauled him to his feet and thrust the bag that had carried the food in front of the ridge in his pants.

* * * * *

335

Kate yawned. It was nine at night. They'd spent the evening entwined naked on the couch and she'd been thinking about bed when Charlie told her they were going out. He drove her back to her apartment for her to change into jeans. He also grabbed one of her woolen sweaters despite the fact that it was still warm outside. When he pulled into a parking space and switched off the engine, Kate had no idea where they were.

"Do you trust me?" he asked.

"You know I do."

"I want to blindfold you."

Kate's heart thumped. He held a dark blue tie. He looked so excited, she couldn't say no. But she didn't like it.

"All right."

She felt the slight pressure from the tie as he wrapped it around her eyes. Once she was out of the car, she clung to his arm and kept her body close to his.

"Up five steps," he said.

Kate knew they'd gone into a building. She heard an echoing sound and shivered in the chill of air-conditioning, but could sense nothing more than that. They moved through several doors and then Charlie stood behind her.

"I'm going to take the blindfold off now," he said.

As it fell from her eyes, Kate blinked. She saw a group of people in front of her, heard them yell "Surprise" and jolted back into Charlie's arms. From there, she took in everything. Rachel, Lucy, Dan, Fax and a whole load of other people she didn't know. And an ice rink.

"Happy Birthday." Lucy rushed up and hugged her.

Kate was overwhelmed. Beautifully wrapped presents were thrust into her arms. Champagne corks popped. Music blared from speakers. She leaned harder into Charlie. If he hadn't been behind her, she'd have fallen.

"Open mine first," Rachel said.

Kate unwrapped gloves. Lucy had bought her a hat. Kate had never had so many gifts to open. She was filled with a rush of love for Charlie.

"This is my mate, Ben, from my first band. This is Jed who can't sing in tune," Charlie said.

"That's you, you wanker," Jed said. He turned to Kate. "That's why we had to play so loud, because he kept losing the key."

"You kept changing the key," Charlie retorted.

Ben slung his arm over Charlie's shoulder. "Do you fancy coming and having a session with us, Charlie? We're looking for a guy to play the tambourine."

"Very funny."

Kate was thrilled with the banter, delighted to see a different Charlie, a normal guy, joking and laughing. He introduced her to everyone. Although mainly musicians, there were also friends from university—a lawyer, an architect, a teacher. And Charlie stayed with her, his arm always around her and Kate knew he was saying—she's with me, we're together, and her heart sang with love for him. He was still a star, still the light everyone buzzed around, but this was a different world and what she saw made Kate believe they could have a future.

Once Charlie knew Kate wouldn't freak out and run away, he moved back and watched. It hadn't been too difficult to organize, though he hadn't had to do much other than ring a few people and tell them what he wanted. He'd contacted Rachel at the gallery, asked her about Kate's friends and realized it wouldn't be much of a party if he only invited people Kate knew. So he called his friends and they'd all brought her presents and she sat there with a silly grin on her face, surrounded by wrapping paper and Charlie didn't think he'd ever felt so happy.

"Can we eat?" someone called.

"Go ahead," he said.

Charlie noticed that it was his mates who descended like vultures. He put his arm over Kate's shoulders and walked her to the table.

"What do you think?" he asked.

On top of a plastic tablecloth emblazoned with flying superheroes, were matching paper plates holding party fare suitable for seven year olds — cocktail sausages, bowls of bright curly grub-shaped chips, Twiglets, red jelly rabbits, green jelly fish, cookies, sandwiches piled up in crooked pyramids, tiny iced cup cakes covered with hundreds and thousands and in the center of it all, an enormous chocolate cake, smothered in swirls of brown icing and topped with twelve candles.

Kate pulled Charlie into her arms, pressed her mouth close to his ear.

"I love you so much," she whispered and the air whooshed out of him.

Charlie's mouth swooped on hers and they were on their own, everything around them a blur. This was it, he thought, this was what he'd been looking for, who he'd been waiting for — Kate at the center of his world.

"Ready for the cake?" someone shouted.

Lucy lit the candles.

"Charlie's going to sing," someone shouted.

No, he fucking wasn't but then he looked at Kate's face and he wanted to. He took hold of her hands and looking straight into her eyes, sang "Happy Birthday to you". The others joined in but Kate smiled just for him. As he finished, he was about to pull her into his arms for another kiss when Rachel cried, "Quick, blow out the candles before the smoke alarm goes off."

Kate stepped up, took a deep breath and Charlie saw the excited child she'd never had chance to be. He pushed back a surge of fury that it had been denied her. She beamed as all the candles puffed out and everyone applauded. How could he be so lucky?

"You didn't spit on it," Charlie complained.

Kate laughed. "I still could."

"Did you make a wish?"

"I've got everything I want."

"Well, I'd like a yacht and a house by the sea," he said.

"Really?"

"No, not really." Charlie hesitated. He thought about telling her that he wanted her and a houseful of kids.

"Thank you for singing, Charlie. I know you don't—"

He put his finger on her lips. "I'd do anything for you. Anything."

* * * * *

"Don't make me do this," Kate pleaded.

"You'll like it once you've tried it," Charlie said.

"If you knew how many times I've heard that." She stood up on the ice skates and wobbled. "Ouch," she whimpered. "Do you think I need a bigger size?"

Charlie looked at her feet and laughed. "No, you just need them on the right feet."

Kate slumped back onto the bench and let Charlie lever them off. Around her everyone chattered and laughed, tottering over the rubber matting before they poured onto the ice. Charlie bent to help Kate with the clip fastenings.

"Thank you, Charlie," she said and cupped his head with her hands. "This is a goodbye kiss."

She pressed her lips against his and he pulled away, looking worried.

"Goodbye?" he asked.

"I'm going to die out there and I didn't want to go without a last kiss."

"You've never been ice skating before?"

Kate shook her head.

"It's not difficult."

She laughed. "There speaks someone who's already an expert."

"You can hold on to me," he said. "I won't let you fall."

Kate wobbled over the matting to get to the opening. Fax stood quivering just ahead of her. He was on the ice but both hands were glued to the wooden barrier that ran round the rink. Lucy skated backward in a circle in front of him.

"You go around and let me get the feel of it," Kate told Charlie and watched as he skated straight to the middle.

Well, of course he could skate. The guy was perfect at everything.

But not everyone was as competent as Lucy and Charlie. Dan and Rachel were slogging their way around, hand in hand. Charlie's friends were messing around, falling over and laughing, arms and legs flailing. Kate put on the hat and gloves she'd been given, stepped onto the ice and at once her feet moved faster than the rest of her. She grabbed the side, wrapped her arms over the top and pulled herself upright.

A few yards away, Fax had progressed to shuffling. He'd let go of the side and his arms and legs shot out and then retracted, making him look like a confused starfish. Kate kept a tight grip on the wood and moved an inch at a time.

She was okay until Charlie ground to a halt in front of her, showering her with ice crystals.

"Bastard," she hissed.

He laughed. "Let go of the side and hold my hand."

"I'll fall."

"I'll catch you."

He held out his hand and Kate sighed.

"They're playing one of my songs," he said. "It's a sign."

"You and your bloody signs." But she took his hand and with great reluctance, let go of the side.

"Don't try to walk. Slide your feet out in a V shape. It's like roller skating," Charlie said. "Lean forward not back."

"I've never roller skated either."

But when she copied what he was doing, she felt a little more confident and they began to move round the rink. As they skated, Charlie sang to her, accompanying his own voice pouring out of the loudspeakers. Oh God, he sounded great.

"Well done. That's one circuit," Charlie said, as Kate slid into the side, embracing the top of the wood like a long lost friend. She almost kissed it.

"And it only took two hours."

He laughed. "Well, if you insist on stopping every couple of feet."

Kate pulled herself upright.

"Thanks, Charlie, for today, for tonight. It's been wonderful."

"It's not over yet. I haven't given you my special present, and you don't get it until you've gone round all on your own."

While Kate made tentative independent forays of a few feet, her friends and Charlie's skated over to say good night and in the end the pair were the only ones left.

"Ten minutes and it melts, Cinderella," Charlie warned.

Kate launched out, her arms flapping. She knew she looked stupid, like a fat bird, too heavy to take off but she was determined to complete a circuit on her own. She was aware of Charlie nearby shouting encouragement and she was doing well, the skates gliding, rather than slipping. Kate sensed the curve coming up, panicked at her excessive speed—almost walking pace—caught an edge and went down like a stone. She never hit the ice. Charlie did, underneath her.

"Told you I'd catch you." He groaned.

"My hero. Are you in pain?"

"A ten-ton mermaid just flattened me. Of course I'm in pain."

Kate rolled off and then leaned over to press her lips against his. Charlie put his arms around her, sliding his tongue into her mouth. Moments later, the music went off, the lights came on and there was the sound of male coughing from the edge. Kate pulled away.

"See, I took your mind off the pain," she said.

"Only because you're a bigger pain."

341

Chapter Twenty-Six

∽

It was almost midnight when they got back to Charlie's house.

"Two more surprises," he said as they walked up from the garage.

"Are they big ones?" Kate grinned, her arms full of presents.

"One should be waiting outside, but we're a little later than I thought. Go and have a look."

Kate thought he looked too pleased with himself and wondered what she was going to find, hopefully not a puppy. She put the presents in the hall and opened the door. Her heart lurched.

"Oh Charlie, what have you done?" she whispered.

"Hello, Kate."

Her father stood on the doorstep holding a bouquet of flowers. Charlie came up behind her.

"Rachel gave me his number. I rang him this afternoon. You need to talk to him, Kate. Listen to what he has to say. I feel better now I've spoken to Janet. You need to sort this out." He reached for her hand and she pulled away.

"You had no right to do this," she said.

Everything blurred. Spots danced in front of her eyes as though the world had turned into a Seurat painting. Before Kate knew it, the three of them stood in the living room. Charlie held her arm, pulling her down onto the couch. Her mind raced through a maze, slamming into dead ends, turning round, looking for another way out, all the time knowing there *was* no way out. Her father sat on the couch opposite.

"Charlie was kind enough to give me the chance to see you tonight, Kate. All I ask is that you hear me out."

Kate retreated inside her shell, a scared hermit crab backing into the tightest curve, knowing she was trapping herself but with nowhere else to go. She managed to wrench her hand free of Charlie's grip and wrapped her arms around her body. When Charlie tried to put his arm around her, she shrugged him off. She knew he'd be hurt, but Kate didn't care. He'd turned the best day of her life into the second worst.

"What you saw that night, it wasn't what you thought," her father said. "Your mum was mentally ill, sweetheart. She heard voices telling her to do things. That was okay when they were good things, like bake cakes but not so good when it was stuff like digging up the lawn in the middle of the night." He leaned forward. "Do you remember?"

A hole had appeared overnight in the backyard. Her mother said she wanted a flower bed.

"She loved you so much, I didn't want to take her away from you. Because I worked at home, I thought I could look after her. If I'd ever had any idea she might become violent, I'd never have let her stay in the house."

Kate wanted to put her fingers in her ears, babble nonsense so she couldn't hear this.

"That night, I was in the kitchen drinking coffee, reading the paper. Gina walked in, took a knife from the drawer and stabbed me. No warning, no argument, nothing. I tried to get the knife away from her. When you came downstairs, that's what I was trying to do, not kill her. But you waded in and everything was chaotic. Somehow everyone got hurt."

Kate rocked, staring at the floor at a point between her father's feet, wishing a wild-eyed demon would surge up through the crack between the boards and drag him back to hell.

"Don't you remember what she was like, Kate? We never knew if she'd get out of bed in the morning, if she'd remember to take you to school or collect you. Sometimes, Gina behaved like the woman I'd married and was a good mother, but it was a lottery what we'd wake up to. Your mum or a complete stranger. Don't you remember?"

She didn't speak.

"If I could turn the clock back, I would. Christ, if I had any idea she might hurt you, I'd have put her in hospital and looked after you myself."

Kate knew he'd never have stopped painting. It was all he did, all day, all night, shut up in his studio once inspiration grabbed him. They weren't allowed to disturb him. Sometimes they had fun, but he thought trips to the Tate or the National Portrait Gallery were amusing for a five-year-old. He had no idea. Her mum was the one who made life fun.

"There was no way I could have known she'd go that far. I love you, Kate. You're my child, my daughter. I've missed too much of your life. Can't we start again? Won't you let me be your father?"

Kate curled up tighter. Charlie tried to put his fingers over hers, and she pulled away, sliding to the far side of the couch. He'd ruined everything.

"There's something I need to tell you about that night," her father said. "But before I do, I want you to know that I don't blame you for what you said at my trial. I know what you think you saw, but you were wrong. That's why I pleaded not guilty, why I had to spend longer in prison. But I didn't stab you. It was your mum."

Kate's fingers beat a tattoo on the side on the couch.

"I'm sorry, darling. I know it's not what you want to hear, but it's the truth. You burst into the kitchen and didn't understand what was happening. You thought I was attacking your mum and tried to save her."

Kate closed her eyes. Saw the blood, smelled it, felt it on her hands. A warm, sticky mess that she wanted gone. It pooled on the tiles, spread like a red tide of tipped up paint.

"In the confusion, your mum lashed out and you grabbed the knife. Somehow, you must have caught the blade in your mum's leg. It severed her femoral artery. By the time the ambulance arrived, she'd bled to death."

Kate heard Charlie gasp beside her. She'd never breathe again.

344

"You didn't tell me that!" Charlie yelled. "You fucking didn't tell me that was why you wanted to speak to her! To tell her *you* didn't kill her mother, *she* did. You fucking cruel bastard."

"I'm sorry, sweetheart," her father said.

"Why did you have to tell her that? She was a kid. I mean, what the fuck is this?"

Her father got up and stepped toward her. "Kate."

Kate leaped to her feet and clamped a hand over her mouth. "Excuse me," she muttered through her fingers. She dashed out of the room, slammed the door and didn't stop. Out of the house, down the street, down another street, Kate didn't stop until she climbed into a cab.

When Kate didn't reappear, Charlie went to look for her. The downstairs bathroom was empty. He ran all over the house, checking every room before slamming back into the lounge.

"She's run away. You stupid fucker. What were you trying to do? Get your own back for her disowning you? I was trying to help you make up with her. How did you expect her to react to that? How do you even know that's what happened?"

"She refused to see me after I got out. She even changed her name."

"Jim, you are a complete and utter wanker. If she does anything stupid, I'll—"

"What sort of stupid?"

Charlie had snapped his mouth shut.

"She's just upset. You know how women are. She'll be back," Jim said.

Charlie gaped at him. "I can't believe you thought you could tell her that she killed her own mother and expect to waltz back into her life. I mean, what the fuck does it matter now who did what? Her mother's dead. Kate's spent almost all her life in care because of what happened. She wasn't to blame. She was a seven-year-old child, for Christ's sake."

"But I didn't kill anyone," Jim said. "I don't want her thinking I killed her mum. I spent fifteen years in prison for something I didn't do."

"And Kate's spent fifteen years in a prison too."

"She took the money I offered."

Charlie stared at him. "You've no fucking idea, have you? You didn't even ask her how she was. You just wanted to push your own guilt onto her shoulders. Did you write to her while you were inside? Ever ask to see her?"

Charlie saw the answer was no. He wanted to slam his fist into the guy's face.

"Can I help you look for her?"

"How? You don't know anything about her — what she likes, what she hates, what scares her. Just fuck off. Get out of my house."

After he'd gone, Charlie found Kate's bag next to the couch. He wrenched it open, saw her keys, purse and phone and knew he was in trouble. He drove to her apartment, but she wasn't there and as far as he could tell, she hadn't been back. Her car was outside. Charlie returned home, hoping Kate would be there. She wasn't. He sat and waited. And waited. The sun came up and there was still no sign of her.

* * * * *

Ethan heard the banging at his door and ignored it. But whoever it was, didn't intend to give up. He got out of bed, and just in case, took off the underwear he'd worn overnight, before pulling on a white robe. Ethan somehow wasn't surprised to see Charlie stamping around outside. He wondered which hat he needed this time — financial expert, personal shopper, real estate agent, ass wiper or ass kicker.

"This had better be good," Ethan snapped.

"Kate's gone."

Ethan gave a mental whoop of joy and moved back to allow a pale-faced Charlie inside. "What happened?"

Charlie let it pour out and the more he poured, the brighter the sun shone for Ethan. So much easier to blend Jody Morton into Charlie's life with Kate out of the way.

"I have to find her," Charlie said. "I need a private detective."

"I know a good one," Ethan said. Finding which stone Kate had crawled under wasn't a bad idea, if only to make sure the stone was heavy enough. "It's too early to call now. I'll make you some breakfast."

"I'm not hungry."

"You look terrible."

"I haven't been to bed," Charlie said.

"Grab a couple of hours upstairs."

"I ought to be at my place in case Kate comes back." Charlie fidgeted from foot to foot.

"I'll send Jake over. He's not busy today. Give me your keys."

Charlie handed them over and started upstairs. Ethan went into his kitchen. He'd make sure Jake knew who not to let into Charlie's place. Kate being top of the list. Ethan got as far as holding the jug under the tap, before he slammed it down, splashing water everywhere. He raced upstairs.

His bedroom door was open. Ethan thought he was safe, that Charlie had gone into the right room. He saw Charlie standing next to the bed, holding one of the bras Kate had made. It was the one Ethan liked best—white satin with little pink roses. Charlie had looked pale before, now his face was ghost-like.

"Where is she?" Charlie threw down the bra and stalked over to Ethan's bathroom. He flung open the door, then surged back, his fists clenched.

"She's not here," Ethan said, holding his hands in front of him. He was frantic to find a scenario that would fit, one he could make fit.

"This is Kate's fucking bra," Charlie shouted, throwing it in Ethan's face.

"She made it, yes," Ethan answered.

"Her pants."

Ethan tried to grab them before Charlie noticed how big they were, that they were warm and maybe a little wet, but Charlie yanked his hand away.

"Kate!" Charlie screamed. "Where the fuck are you?"

"Charlie, she's not here. I asked her to make the underwear for a friend."

Ethan was relieved when Charlie deflated like an old balloon, a look of wrinkled confusion on his face. Then he straightened. "So where's your friend?"

"She's gone home."

"Leaving her underwear?" Charlie's eyes were full of distrust.

"Charlie, my sex life has nothing to do with you."

His shoulders slumped again. "No, sorry."

"The spare room's across the landing," Ethan said. "Get some sleep. By the time you wake up, I'll have sorted things out."

When the door closed, Ethan breathed out. That had been close.

* * * * *

When Charlie emerged a few hours later, he still looked terrible. Ethan wondered if he'd even slept.

"I need to go home in case she's back," Charlie said. "Have you got a detective looking for her?"

"I've two guys working on it. I've used them before. They're good."

Ethan hadn't hired detectives. He'd decided it would be a waste of money and he didn't waste money. He'd wait a few days and tell Charlie that Kate appeared to have vanished without trace. By the time she turned up, if she turned up, Charlie would have moved on to someone else and he had just the someone in mind.

Ethan poured Charlie a coffee and set it in front of him.

"So, what happened?" he asked.

Charlie ran his fingers through his hair. "I fucked up. I thought I was doing the right thing and I wasn't."

"What did you do?"

Ethan listened without speaking, thinking if he'd had to describe the worst case scenario, this would have been in there somewhere. The woman was a walking disaster. A tiny part of him thought it a pity Tiffany Samuels hadn't stuck the knife in a little lower and deeper. "*Lover killed by crazed fan*" had a certain ring.

He could see Charlie cared about Kate. He wasn't blind, but the guy was being led by his dick. He needed to take someone else to bed and forget the waitress. This was an ideal opportunity for Jody Morton to step in.

"Is there anything I can do to help these guys?" Charlie asked.

Ethan had to think for a minute to work out what he was talking about.

"No, they'll get back to us if they need anything."

"A photo? They need a photograph." His head dropped. "I don't have one."

"There were plenty in the paper," Ethan reminded him and Charlie shriveled up like an old man.

"I need to go back." He jumped up. "Can you organize a painter? I need my ceiling done."

Ethan stared at him. Talk about a change in direction. "Jake's over there. He'll sort it out. He can stay and look after you."

Charlie gave a short laugh. "Afraid I'm going to start drinking again? Do a few lines of coke?"

"Are you?"

Charlie raised his eyes to his and Ethan met his stare.

"No."

"Good." So Kate had done him some good. "Jake has a copy of your schedule. He'll take care of you."

"I don't need a fucking nurse. I want Kate."

"You've commitments to honor. There's all sort of shit going on this week. You're on that BBC chat show for a start."

"I don't feel like it."

"You're paid to feel like it. You're a fucking actor, Charlie. Fake it."

* * * * *

Charlie spent the week in a daze. Jake drove him everywhere, cooked for him and moved the booze. Charlie couldn't find it. For the first few days, whatever Charlie was supposed to do, he did. That included a joint interview with Jody Morton for a movie magazine. Ethan had already told her Kate had walked out and why, and Jody was all over Charlie, trying to be kind. She turned out to be more sympathetic than Charlie expected. She listened while he talked and talked.

But as time went on and there was no word from Kate, Charlie fell apart. When he was alone, he cried for what he'd lost. He was glad Jake moved the alcohol. He bought cigarettes but thought about Kate and what she'd say and never lit one. Twice a day Jake drove him to Kate's apartment. While Jake sat in the car, Charlie lay on Kate's bed, breathing in the faint scent of her that remained, pressing his face into her pillow, willing her to come back to him. He wrote messages on Post-It notes, covered the walls in her bedroom with yellow squares.

"I love you."

"Come back."

"I need you."

Then he got angry. What the fuck did she think she was doing? She had to know he hadn't meant to hurt her. She'd not given him a chance to explain, just run off into the night. He'd arranged the party, gone to all that trouble. Didn't she think he'd be worried? Didn't she care? No, she didn't. She didn't care.

But what if she couldn't come back? What if she was dead? The thought stuck in his throat, a malignant lump that stopped him eating. He rang the police, but they thought he was crazy. The cop Charlie spoke to said if it was a quarrel, she'd come back.

Charlie wanted to believe that. Ethan's detectives found nothing, but still looked. Lucy, Dan and Rachel were as worried as Charlie. He gave them his number, asking them to ring if they saw her. Charlie didn't know what else he could do.

Then grief, anger and fear combined, swirling him in a whirlwind of misery. He locked himself away in his music room, writing at a feverish pace, crying until there were no tears left. He convinced himself she was dead, that she'd killed herself. He'd told her that he'd fuck up her life and he had.

* * * * *

Ethan was worried. He knew 24/7 planned to run a story on Charlie and that it would be bad, but he had no idea how bad. His sources weren't giving him any clues. A tiny part of Ethan wondered if Charlie had done something to Kate, maybe killed her, but the sensible part of him realized that if 24/7 knew that, then Charlie would be in police custody. Ethan had told Charlie the detectives had traced Kate to Brighton and she wasn't coming back. He'd thought that would calm him down, but it hadn't. Ethan had to get Jake to physically prevent Charlie driving to the south coast.

He considered warning Charlie that trouble was coming, but in the end decided not to. Ethan worried about his young cash cow. Since Kate vanished, Charlie had deteriorated to the brink of meltdown. Bad press could push him over the edge. Ethan decided on a different strategy, using Jody. She'd been ecstatic when Charlie's latest love interest disappeared, but Ethan had been able to persuade her not to climb straight into Charlie's bed, but be an attentive and sympathetic listener. She could pick up the pieces on Sunday after the newspaper had done its worst. Ethan only hoped there would be pieces to pick up.

Chapter Twenty-Seven

&

Charlie stopped halfway down the stairs when he saw the Sunday paper lying on his hall floor. He didn't have a paper delivered, so he knew someone had pushed it through his letter box, probably a member of the press and probably because there was something about him in it. Or maybe about Kate. His feet felt wedged in wet sand. The effort required to walk the few steps to the door made his knees shake.

The headline was *STORM BREAKS*. A large picture of him dominated the front page. He looked drunk and stoned. He was neither. It was sadness and despair in his eyes.

Charlie sat on the stairs. As he read the double-page spread inside the paper, his already disintegrating world dissolved. Everything around him lost focus and color. Only the printed words remained clear. The article had everything — truth, lies and surprises. How he'd taken advantage of an underage girl, committed statutory rape, given her cocaine and left her unconscious. How he'd given his brother drugs and handed him keys to a powerful car knowing he was drunk. How after the crash, Charlie left his brother to die, although he somehow managed to rescue the attractive female passenger. How Charlie seduced Jennifer Ward, slept with her sister and her mother, and walked out on all of them. Apparently, so had Malcolm Ward. Divorce pending. Jennifer had suffered a nervous breakdown, taken an overdose and was in a psychiatric hospital.

Charlie groaned. He didn't want to read any more, but couldn't stop. The newspaper described how he'd deserted the mother who'd brought him up to seek out the one who'd given birth to him. He'd promised his birth mother the world, promised to be a brother to his half sisters and never contacted them again. The paper crumpled in his grasp. The suicide attempt was in there. How he'd tried to drown himself, but had even fucked that up. The implication being it was a pity he'd failed. Charlie began to think that too. Kate had talked to the press. No one else knew about the suicide. She'd done this.

The pain of her betrayal was so overwhelming, he thought his heart had burst open. Charlie lay on the stairs and howled in anguish.

* * * * *

"Of course Kate did this," Ethan snapped. "Who else could it be?"

Charlie slumped on his couch, his head in his hands.

"I don't know who to be most angry with—her for selling you out or you for not confiding in me. You're supposed to tell me everything. You don't take a shit without letting me know." Ethan paced round the room, his brain flying through the options.

"Why would she do this?" Charlie groaned. "I don't understand."

"It's obvious. Revenge. She's been lying to herself all these years about what happened with her mother. You made her confront the truth and she's doing the same to you, albeit more publicly. Christ, she'll have made a fucking fortune from this. We could have made a fortune from this, well, some of it, if you'd told me."

"Do you think I'm proud of it?" Charlie shouted. "My life's a fucking mess."

"But suicide?" Ethan asked, more gently this time.

Charlie didn't say anything. His gaze dropped to the floor.

"Why didn't you tell me things were that bad?" Ethan sat beside him and patted his knee like he was a puppy. A puppy would be less trouble.

"You'd just dumped me."

"Right," Ethan said, his eyes flicking around. "Well, the suicide thing's not as bad as the rest. At least you'll get the sympathy vote from that."

Charlie turned his bloodshot eyes on Ethan. "That makes me feel a whole lot better."

"Sorry."

"I've got to ring Mum. Christ, what's she going to think when she reads this?"

Charlie looked about to throw up.

"She's your mother. She'll cope."

The phone rang twice and then stopped. Ethan knew Jake had picked it up in the kitchen.

"Has Kate been in touch with you?" Ethan asked.

Charlie threw the newspaper on the floor. "Yeah, I think she has."

There was a knock on the door. Jake popped his head around and caught Ethan's eye.

"Jody Morton's outside."

"I don't want to see anyone," Charlie said.

"I need to speak to her," Ethan lied. "Let her in."

He put his hand on Charlie's shoulder to keep him on the couch. Jody Morton was going to open doors for Ethan. Where she walked, others would follow.

Jody swept in, rushed over and threw her arms around Charlie.

"My God, Charlie, you poor thing."

Tears rolled down her face. Ethan caught her wink as she pressed her head against Charlie's. Ethan bit back his smile. What a fantastic actress.

* * * * *

Kate had fled from Charlie's house to a refuge for battered women with two twenty-pound notes in her pocket, a birthday present from a friend of Charlie's. She'd been given the address a year ago by a nurse after one of her "accidents". Dex had been waiting outside the cubicle, so Kate didn't take the piece of paper, but she'd memorized the address. One night, when Dex had frightened her more than usual, she'd gone to the refuge, but not inside. She'd looked at the door, knowing safety was steps away and then returned to the arms of her abuser. And he'd showered her with love as she knew he would, until the next time he hit her.

This time Kate had walked straight up to the faded red front door and knocked. The state she'd been in when she arrived, wide-eyed and almost catatonic, it was easy to let them think someone had hit her. She knew she wouldn't be turned away. The women who ran the center gave her a bed and offered food, though Kate was incapable of sleeping or eating. They wouldn't let her stay in bed all day, which was what she wanted, but she remained indoors, never leaving the house while she tried to figure out what to do.

Charlie had known she didn't want to speak to her father. He had no right to interfere. But because he had, she'd been forced to confront a terrible possibility—that she'd killed her mother. Kate found it hard to move past that. It lodged in her brain—a massive dam, everything piling behind. At her father's trial, Kate had told the judge what she'd seen and afterwards a lady had said that her daddy wasn't coming to take her home. And Kate's path divided.

In the end, when the jury found him guilty, Kate believed he was guilty too. They said her daddy had been sent to prison for killing her mummy, and she wouldn't be able to see him anymore. And Kate had closed down and retreated to a safe place inside her head. When she came out, she knew she would be alone forever.

Her father never admitted his guilt and because of that, he'd stayed longer in prison. Was it her fault? What if she'd been wrong? Kate spent her days in the hostel curled up in a chair trying to think herself back to that night. But after so many years of trying to forget, she could no longer distinguish between what she wanted to be true and what *was* true.

When she walked into the kitchen at the refuge on Sunday morning and saw a sea of hostile faces, Kate thought they'd somehow found out she was a fraud. One of the women tossed her a newspaper.

"I thought I recognized you when you came in here, but no one believed me. Dumped you did he? Getting your own back?"

Kate looked at the headline. *STORM BREAKS*, and something broke inside her too.

"Going to make a donation with the thousands you've got from that?" a voice called as Kate walked out, still clutching the paper in her hand.

She sat on the bus, reading the articles over and over, her fingers smudged with ink. There was scant mention of her which somehow made it worse. She could have written this. There was little in it she didn't know. Charlie might think she was getting even because of what happened with her father. Kate read it again, her heart beating faster. Ethan didn't like her. He'd be only too happy for her to take the blame.

Kate choked on the words of the two reporters. One of them was Simon Baxter, Richard's friend, which made Kate wonder, for a moment, if Richard could be behind this. One problem with that. Even if she could explain how most of the facts could have been wormed out of people, no one knew Charlie tried to kill himself. No one, except her and Charlie. And Charlie's father. Maybe his mother.

Once he'd read the paper, Charlie would think she'd betrayed him, that she'd sold him out to the press. It was the one thing he'd never be able to forgive and Kate couldn't bear to think of him hating her. But she could never tell him that one of his parents must have betrayed him. Their relationship was too fragile. All Kate could do, was to find Charlie and tell him it wasn't her.

A crowd of photographers stood outside Charlie's house, cameras with huge black lenses slung round their necks like monstrous medallions. As she drew nearer, someone saw her and they turned and rushed at her. Kate made herself keep going, pushing through them.

"Kate."

"Over here."

"Give us a smile."

A smile? Kate had forgotten how. They jostled her, but she remained silent, lips pressed together, intent on speaking only to Charlie. She hadn't considered what she might do if he wasn't there.

A well-dressed stocky guy in his forties with gray hair pulled back in a ponytail opened the door. Kate didn't recognize him. She managed to find her voice from somewhere and gave him her name.

"Wait." He shut the door.

The men behind called to her again.

"Kate?"

"Turn around."

"Kate? Go on, give us a smile."

"What do you want to see him about?"

"Talk to us, Kate."

She pressed herself against the door, wanting to shimmer through the glossy blue wood to the other side. She almost fell as it opened. Kate followed the ponytailed guy through to the lounge, her heart beating so hard in her chest, she expected to see it burst out of her ribs and leap into Charlie's hands. It was where it belonged.

Charlie stood alone in the living room, his creased linen shirt half-tucked into his chinos. When Kate saw him, she felt a pull so strong, she stumbled. She wanted to rush up and wrap her arms around him, but the fierce look in his eyes held her back.

"What do you want?" His voice sounded cold and quiet.

"I wanted to see you, make sure you were all right," Kate said.

"Of course I'm not fucking all right."

"It wasn't me, Charlie," she whispered.

"We were the only two who knew. I sure as fuck didn't say anything, so that leaves you."

Kate could hear her pulse drumming in her head, feel it echoing through her body. Her knees shook under her jeans.

"I didn't tell," she said.

Charlie took a step toward her and then stopped.

"Why don't you just admit it?" he said. "For Christ's sake, Kate, do the decent thing and admit it. It was a shitty way to get your own back, because I fucked up with your father, but at least tell me the truth now."

"It wasn't me," Kate said. "I didn't tell." The room was ablaze. Everything on fire. Her lungs burning. She couldn't breathe. Every part of her said run, but she made herself stay.

"Then who the fuck was it? You must have told someone. Who?" Charlie's eyes were granite, shutting her out. He stood with his arms folded across his chest. A perfect statue.

The only person she'd told was his father and she couldn't tell Charlie that. He'd been hurt too much for him to know his family had done this.

"I didn't betray you," Kate said.

"I know you're fucking lying. You told somebody or went to the press yourself. How much did they pay you?"

Kate didn't think she'd ever felt so ill. She trembled on the point of collapse. Charlie was incapable of seeing the truth. She'd thought he loved her, but he didn't. If he had, he didn't now. All he'd ever wanted from her was loyalty and trust, and he thought she'd let him down like everyone else.

"You use the press when it suits you," he said.

"I've never spoken to the press."

"So how did they get the photo of that scratch on your back?"

Kate felt the flush sweeping across her cheeks like a crimson badge. "Fax took it. I wanted him to ask Lucy out, so I let him take the picture."

"See? You use the press when it suits you."

"But I've never spoken to the press about you." She needed to sit.

"You're a liar," he yelled, spitting the words out like bullets. "Liar. Liar. Liar."

Kate flinched at every one. "I've never lied to you."

"Bollocks. You lied about your father being dead, about why you didn't like having your photo taken. You probably lied about Dickhead, too. No wonder he didn't want to marry you. He had a fucking lucky escape."

Kate shrank under the onslaught, but wouldn't run.

"Charlie, we have something here. Please don't do this."

He laughed. "We have nothing. We started this when neither of us were in our right minds. All that time I thought you were the first real thing I'd come across, only you're a fake like all the rest. Worse than the rest." He glared at her. "You lied to me and you lied to yourself. You lied about your father killing your mother. You stabbed her. You fucking killed her." His voice was icy with contempt.

"Charlie," she pleaded.

"Fuck off, Kate. Run away again, just like you always do."

Kate recoiled, but she couldn't let this go.

"I have no reason to hurt you, Charlie. Why would I do this?"

"Because I made you see the truth. Because I brought your father here. You let him sit in jail. You never visited him. Even when he was out of prison, you wouldn't see him. But you took his fucking money, didn't you? He was good enough for that. You could have talked to me, but instead, you ran. Fucked off to Brighton. You didn't even try and get in touch. I was out of my mind. I thought you were dead."

"I haven't been to Brighton." Kate had no idea what he was talking about.

He gave a short laugh. "Still lying? I employed private detectives because I was so worried. I was going to let you think things over, then come and get you. Instead you got me. Congratulations. Enjoy the money."

Kate shook her head. "Charlie, why would I come here to talk to you if I was the one who gave that information to the press? What would be the point? Help me find out who did speak to them. I swear it wasn't me."

"If it wasn't you, then who did you tell?"

She couldn't tell him. She took a step toward him and he backed off.

"Don't touch me. I don't want you anywhere near me. You're poisonous. Just fuck off. I never want to see you again. I never want to hear your name again. You're dead. Do me a favor. Go finish what you started in the sea."

Nothing could have hurt her more.

A door slammed. "Oh, am I interrupting something?"

Kate and Charlie turned to see Jody Morton standing in the doorway. She wore the white robe Kate had worn, loosely fastened around her hips. Jody padded barefoot to Charlie's side and put her hand on his arm.

"The tub's full," she purred in his ear. "Come and wash my back."

Kate took a deep breath. It felt like the last she'd ever take.

"Do you still have my purse?" she asked in a small voice.

Charlie stalked to the cupboard that held his DVDs, grabbed the black leather bag, turned and threw it toward Kate. It smacked her straight in the face and dropped to the floor.

Kate picked it up and clutched it to her chest, her cheek stinging. "Thank you."

Walking out, knowing he hated her, was one of the hardest things she'd ever had to do. She walked straight through the photographers and carried on walking all the way back to Greenwich. It took her four and a half hours. And every step hurt. Every step destroyed a part of her.

Chapter Twenty-Eight

๛

Kate opened the door of her apartment and the fetid smell of spoiled food hit her like a noxious tidal wave. She opened all the windows and emptied the fridge. When she took the rubbish down to the bin room, she found Dan in there cutting up cardboard.

"Hey, I've not seen you for ages. You okay?" he asked.

"Fine," Kate lied and a jolt of pain flashed through her.

"What happened to your face?"

The bag had left a long red scratch from her eye to her chin. She knew Charlie hadn't meant to hurt her but the fact that he had, hurt worse than the blow.

"A branch caught me."

"Looks nasty. By the way, Mel's been trying to get in touch with you."

Kate had almost forgotten she had a job.

"I'll ring her."

"I've finished that picture of Charlie and his brother," Dan said. "Do you want to come and get it?"

He held the bin open for Kate's black bag. She wondered if Dan had seen the article in the paper.

"So where've you been?" Dan asked, as they walked back upstairs.

"Away for a few days."

"With Charlie?"

"No. That's over." Kate's heart was being squeezed so hard she thought she might curl up and die. How could she have thought she stood a chance with a guy like Charlie? If he'd seen her in a bar or in the street, he wouldn't have looked at her twice.

"Ah, the thing in the paper."

"So you *did* read it? He thought I was the source. I wasn't." Her voice broke.

"Come here." Dan opened his arms.

Kate let him hug her but when she crumbled, she pulled away.

"It'll be okay, you'll see," Dan said.

Kate nodded.

"Do you still want the picture?"

She nodded again, unable to speak.

When Dan walked into the hall holding up his portrait of Charlie and Michael, Kate sighed. It was fabulous. Dan had captured Charlie's smile. An open, artless beam. His tousled hair stuck out at one side. His eyes shone like a baby seal's, huge and trusting. They'd never look at her like that again.

"Don't you like it?" Dan's voice faltered.

Kate wet her dry lips with her tongue. "Sorry. Just mesmerized. It's brilliant. I'm amazed." Amazed she could speak without squeaking. "You have to let me pay you, Dan."

"No, I told you. It's a gift."

He placed it in Kate's arms.

Kate got back inside her apartment, closed the door and collapsed, sliding down as her legs gave way. She leaned the painting against the wall and stared at it, her eyes filling with tears. The images of Charlie and Michael lost all focus and shape. Colors merged until there was no form, no Charlie. He wasn't hers. Her heart felt like it was being wrenched apart in her chest, torn to shreds.

Kate thought about the last time she'd sat there crying, when she'd returned from the registry office. She'd hurt then, but nothing compared to this. Kate curled into a ball and buried her face in her arms. The knowledge that Charlie hurt too made it worse. If there was one thing Kate aimed for in life, it was never to knowingly hurt another person, because she knew what it felt like. She should have stayed alone. None of this would have happened. She'd thought she could change her life and she'd been wrong.

What could she do now? Run? Her usual course of action. But this time, not within London. Another town or city. Start again. Hide. Because if she had to see her father, it would destroy her. He wanted her to believe her mother had been sick, but Kate wasn't sure that was true. It was her father who was the obsessive one—no noise, no TV, just painting, watching her paint, shouting at her when it wasn't right. He wanted nothing to be his fault. No money, but it wasn't his fault. Her mum upset, not his fault. Snatches of memories confused her. Had she really stabbed her mum?

She'd never know the truth so no good beating herself up about it. But Kate never wanted to see her father again. She'd sell the apartment. Give back the money. Maybe she could get a passport and go abroad, work in a bar. Thoughts flashed through her head on a loop. Last time, suicide seemed the only answer. Now, it was no answer at all.

Kate shrank a little, remembering what Charlie had said. Finish what she started. Kill herself. But he'd missed the point. Missed the reason why she walked into the sea the first time. She'd told him, but he hadn't heard. It wasn't because Richard dumped her, but because she'd let herself down. That wasn't the case now. She'd done nothing wrong. She hadn't hurt Charlie.

Even if she managed to prove she hadn't spoken to the papers, Kate knew she'd lost him. No way back. He was already in the arms of another woman. Kate couldn't compete with a star like Jody Morton. Everyone said it wouldn't last between Kate and Charlie and they'd been right. Her fingers slid to her neck and touched the star he'd bought. She rubbed it as though it was capable of performing magic, and then wrenched it off. She tried to throw it away but her hand didn't let it go. The chain was looped around her fingers and Kate wondered if that was a sign she shouldn't give up. One of Charlie's signs. She sighed.

When she walked into her bedroom and saw the wall covered in messages of love, Kate froze. How long had Charlie spent doing that? She'd hidden away in the refuge trying to sort her head out and not thought enough about Charlie's head. As she peeled each one away, and read what he'd put—*I love you. Come back. I need you*—she thought of what she'd lost and how much Charlie hated her and how much worse it was to be hated than not to be loved. She'd brought this on herself. When she'd run, she'd hurt him, made it easier for him to believe the worst. He'd loved her and she'd let him down.

* * * * *

Kate coaxed her car all the way to Charlie's parents', petrified it might conk out and strand her in the middle of nowhere. She hadn't been able to call them. They were ex-directory, so she hoped they were in. If not, she'd sleep in the car and try the next day.

Charlie's mother opened the door. Kate watched her eyes narrow.

"What are you doing here?"

"I'm sorry to come unannounced, Mrs. Storm."

"What do you want?"

"I wondered if I could have a word with your husband."

"Trying to get more dirt on Charlie? Don't you think you've done enough damage?"

"It wasn't me who talked to the papers."

"Who else knew all that about him?"

"I would never hurt Charlie," Kate said.

"Too late. He's already hurt. We're hurt too. The paper's full of our private business. Do you think that's what we needed? You've made your money, now leave us alone."

"Can I speak to Mr. Storm, please?" Kate asked again.

"He's not here."

She took a piece of paper from her bag with her mobile number written down. "Could you ask him to phone me? It's important."

Kate handed over the paper. Jill screwed it up and dropped it. The door slammed in Kate's face. She swallowed hard, picked up the ball of paper and put it in her pocket. Back at the car, Kate lifted the painting from the boot. She left it propped under the portico by the front door and drove back to London.

By the time she reached Greenwich, it was too late to go to an estate agent. It would have to wait until the next day. She ought to eat. Kate couldn't remember the last time she'd had food. She cut green mold off the sides of two slices of bread before she toasted and buttered them, then left them untouched.

Slumping on the couch, Kate's hands reached again for the creased Sunday newspaper, rereading it, looking for a clue, desperate to find something she'd missed that might tell her who'd done this. She wondered if the police had been to see Charlie about India, Michael and the drugs. It could mean the end of his career.

Kate rang Ethan on impulse, twisting his business card in her fingers.

"It's Kate Snow."

"What do you want?"

She winced at the sound of another arctic voice, though she wasn't surprised.

"Ethan, I didn't speak to the papers about Charlie. I wondered if you knew who had?"

"Have you any idea of the damage you've caused, you stupid bitch? Stay out of his life. Don't ring me again."

He cut the connection.

As Kate stared at the headline in the paper, she wondered if the answer was right in front of her. She could ask the guys who'd written the article for the name of their source. Maybe if she explained, they'd tell her. The 24/7 switchboard put her through to Simon Baxter's voice mail system. Kate didn't want to leave a message, she wanted to speak to Simon. So she made another, more difficult call.

"Hello, Richard. It's Kate."

"Kate who?"

Kate bit her tongue. "Kate Snow."

"What do you want?"

She kept her tone even. "Simon's telephone number."

There was a short silence.

"Why?"

"Because you owe me a favor."

She waited while he thought about it.

"I'll ring him and ask him to call you."

She started to thank him and the phone went dead.

That was it. Kate couldn't think what else to do. When the phone rang a few minutes later, she snatched it up, but it was Rachel, asking if she wanted to go for something to eat with her and Dan. Kate told her she'd already eaten.

She curled up on the floor next to the jigsaw and kept the phone under her hand.

* * * * *

Charlie wanted to be on his own. It was his fucking house and he wanted everyone to leave. Then, after Jake had gone and Ethan had taken Jody back to her hotel, he wanted them to come back. He didn't want to think and it was easier to keep his mind blank with other people around.

He'd had to go to the police with his solicitor. He stuck to his story. For some reason India hadn't said that he'd given her drugs but she had said he'd fucked her. Though she'd admitted she'd lied about her age. Charlie had been scared. His solicitor kept answering for him most of the time, which was just as well, because he felt like asking them to stick him in a cell and throw away the key.

He could ride out what the papers had printed, apart from one thing—the attempted suicide. That so fucked him up. He still hadn't called his mum and dad, but he couldn't bring himself to pick up the phone. He'd seen their names four times on his caller ID, but he never picked up. He didn't know what to say.

It was Monday evening before he managed to pluck up enough courage to speak to them.

"Mum."

It was all he said, all he could say and she burst into tears and then Charlie cried too, for all the hurt he'd caused and for what he'd lost. His dad came on the line and Charlie had to fight hard not to break out into a fresh round of sobbing.

"I'm sorry," Charlie said.

"You changed your mind, son. That's all that matters."

Charlie promised to go and see them and felt better when he finished the call. He was so exhausted, he slept well for the first time since Kate disappeared.

* * * * *

When Jake turned up the following morning to take him to the Tate Modern for an interview with the director of the Royal Shakespeare Company, Jody sat in the back of the car.

"You don't mind me sharing your ride, do you?" she asked. "Ethan's fixed for me to see them too."

"No, that's fine," Charlie muttered. Ethan had already rung and told him Jody would be going with him and he had to be nice to her. Or else.

"How are you feeling?" she asked but didn't wait for an answer. "God, sorry. You must be sick of people asking you that. It's awful, isn't it? As if you're suddenly naked on stage and everyone is pointing and laughing."

Charlie hadn't quite thought of it like that.

"I can't watch *Lord of the Rings* without wanting to vomit." Jody put her hand over her mouth for a moment. "Breaking up is so hard."

"I thought you dumped him?" Charlie said.

"We weren't right for each other, but that doesn't mean it didn't hurt."

"Sorry."

"You don't know how nice it is to have you as a friend, Charlie. I hardly know anyone in London. Will you have time to show me round the museum afterwards?"

He hoped not.

"I'm not sure how long this will take. Have you done any Shakespeare before?" he asked.

"Only at school. How about you?"

"Same here."

"It sounds like real fun," Jody said with a smile.

Charlie thought it sounded like a lot of hard work, but Ethan had insisted. The RSC wanted to organize a celebrity fortnight featuring ten different plays and a host of stars. Raising money for some charity or other.

"So what are you trying out for?" Jody asked.

"Hamlet."

"Want to practice?"

Charlie sighed. "Why not?"

It was not the fun-filled day Jody hoped for. Forced to sound enthusiastic about playing Regan in King Lear, she'd plastered a smile on her face that cracked her makeup. She'd hoped to wrangle her way into playing alongside Charlie, but they'd already cast Ophelia and there was no way she'd play his mother, Gertrude. Jody was still seething they dared to ask.

She managed to persuade Charlie to walk round the museum with her afterwards, but it was full of crap. Pieces of garish pink plastic dangling from the ceiling on metal chains, the contents of a bathroom cabinet strewn in a circle, a big black square with a bell in the middle. Plain weird. The only time Charlie's eyes lit up, was when he saw the giant slide. But there was no way she was going on that. She'd wreck her new Donna Karan pants. Jody waited for him at the bottom, but then hadn't actually seen him emerge because three cute guys had asked for her autograph.

Jody decided she'd waited long enough to make a move on Charlie. He was depressed after the exposé in the press and she wanted to cheer him up. He was still furious with the woman he'd been fucking. Charlie needed someone to take his mind off things. A good meal, a bottle of wine and her in his bed. Perfect.

"I need cheering up," Jody said. "I want to buy a dress. Wanna come and help me choose one?"

Charlie shrugged. She'd take that as a yes. She'd never found any man enthusiastic about shopping.

Four hours later, she'd lost patience with him. He'd been uncommunicative while she tried on dresses, sullen over a coffee in Harrods and sulky when she tried to buy him a tie. She'd managed to wangle an invite back to his house but he wanted to stay in.

"I want to go out," she whined.

What the fuck had been the point of buying the dress if he wanted to order a pizza?

"I don't feel like it," Charlie said.

"Let's go to Gordon Ramsey's place in Chelsea." Jody put her hand on Charlie's arm. So far, she'd been careful not to overdo the touching, but she was frustrated. After that handbag throwing scene, she'd thought he'd take her up on the offer of the hot tub but he'd bolted off to his music room and locked himself in. Jody stroked his biceps.

"Please?" She tried her puppy-dog look.

"It's always booked solid."

Jody bit back her annoyance. He could get in anywhere he wanted.

"Let me try." She pressed a few buttons on her phone. Minutes later, she'd secured a table and a cab was on order.

"Now go and put on something nice," she said. "And have a shave. I don't want your chin scratching my face. I've got a photo shoot tomorrow."

"I don't want to go out."

"Well, I do. I want to wear my new dress. I need to show I'm strong and brave and well over that prick. You should do the same. You can't hide in here forever. Let the press see that you're above all this. We'll smile and show them a united front."

Charlie did as he was told. Jody thought about joining him in the shower, but she'd just done her hair so she decided not to bother. His naked body was something to look forward to. As she reached for her magazine at the far side of the coffee table, Charlie's mobile rang. Jody leapt at it.

"Hallo," she chirped.

"Is Charlie there?"

Suspicious of any female she didn't recognize, Jody was on guard. "Who's calling?" She deserved an Olympic Gold for repelling rivals, though she hadn't had to do anything to get rid of the lanky waitress. The stupid cow had managed that all on her own.

"I'm Charlie's mother. Is he there?"

Oops, thank God she'd not said anything nasty. "Oh hello, Mrs. Storm. This is Jody Morton. I'm a very close friend of Charlie's. I'm afraid he's not here at the moment."

"Will you ask him to ring me?"

"Of course. Is it important? Could I give him a message?"

"It's about Kate. Please ask him to call me."

"Certainly." Not, Jody thought. There was no way she was bringing up Kate's name. After tonight, she didn't think Charlie would even think of her again.

Chapter Twenty-Nine

80

Kate had finished the jigsaw puzzle. Well, almost finished it. One piece missing. She stared at the picture for a moment, admiring the shapes of the jungle cats, remembering how Charlie lounged like a leopard, how they'd worked on the puzzle together. Then she scooped the whole thing up and put it in the bin. If she wanted a new life, she had to get rid of the old. She filled black bags with all her sewing materials and took them down to the bin room along with the sewing machine and the computer. The latter had seized up and died while she'd been away and Kate couldn't afford to get it mended. She'd lost heart for the sewing. No point anymore.

Before Kate knew it, she'd tossed out almost everything she owned, except for a small quantity of clothes, her mobile and the Post-It notes Charlie had stuck to her wall. It didn't hurt as much as she thought. They were just things. Even the bed. It could go with the apartment. How could she sleep in it again and feel happy? Kate laid her silver star under the pillow. It was all part of her dreams now.

As she made her fourth trip downstairs, dumping another two bags in the bin room, her mobile rang.

"Kate? It's Simon."

She was so shocked he'd rung, for a moment she didn't speak.

"Kate? Are you there?"

"Yes. Sorry."

"Richard said you wanted to talk to me."

Kate sat out of sight on the gravel at the rear of her car and leaned back against the wall.

"I wanted to ask you about the article you wrote on Charlie," she said.

"And here I thought you were going to ask me on a date." He chuckled.

Kate wasn't in the mood to laugh.

"Charlie thinks I'm the source."

"Well, maybe you should tell your side of the story. Like to explain how you got that mark on your face? I've already got the headline — *Snow-storm*."

Kate's fingers rose to her cheek and trailed down the scratch. Someone must have taken her picture as she left Charlie's house.

"Did he hit you?"

"No. I caught it on a branch. Simon, I need to know who told you he'd tried to kill himself."

There was a deep sigh from the other end of the phone. "You know I can't tell you that. I have to protect my sources. You hadn't got the mark when you went into Charlie's house. You had when you came out. Forest in his lounge, is there? Maybe Jody Morton hit you. She's got a temper."

"Was it his mother who told you?" Kate persisted.

"I can't say."

"His father?"

"Kate, I can't tell you."

"But he thinks it was me."

"Then why don't you let me interview you? You can set the record straight. We'll pay. I could come round now. You can tell me how you got that mark and maybe I could drop a hint about what you want to know."

"No."

She switched off the phone. That wouldn't make things right. Tears fell from Kate's eyes. She'd trained herself not to cry, a defense mechanism borne out of necessity. If you shed tears in a children's home, you were doomed to a life of name calling — cry baby, pissy pants, leaky girl. But now Kate let the tears fall. A silent flood, because no sound came from her lips. She sat and cried until not one tear remained inside her.

* * * * *

"Kate? What are you doing out here?" Lucy demanded.

"Looking at the stars," Kate said. Wanting just one.

Fax stood at Lucy's shoulder, his arm around her waist.

"Come inside," Lucy said. "It's after midnight and it's cold."

Kate got to her feet too fast. Her head swam and she leaned back against the wall.

"We've been worried about you. We wondered where you were. You keep disappearing."

"I've been away for a few days."

"You're not back with Charlie, then?" Lucy asked.

"No. That's over. Charlie thinks I sold him out to the papers. I didn't. I don't understand where they got their information." She looked at Fax. "I talked to your friend, Simon Baxter. He won't tell me his source."

"He's not my friend," Fax said.

"Let's go inside." Lucy tapped in the code and pushed open the door of the building.

Kate had a sudden hope that Fax might be able to help. "Simon thinks I should give him my side of the story."

"Don't," Fax said. "Keep quiet. It'll all blow over."

"But Charlie thinks I betrayed him." The band tightened around Kate's heart and she bit back a whimper.

"It could have been any of the people he's messed up," Lucy said. "Bloody hell, I bet there's a long enough list."

"Why is Charlie so sure it's you?" Fax asked.

"Because one thing the paper printed was only known by the two of us."

"Perhaps you said it by accident to someone?" Fax suggested.

"No. I've never told anyone. I wouldn't." Apart from his father. Kate swallowed hard.

Lucy stood by her door, the key in her hand, but she made no attempt to put it into the lock. "What was the thing that only you and he knew?"

What did it matter now? The whole world knew. "About him trying to commit suicide."

"Oh God. The bastard." Lucy put her hand to her mouth. "I think it was Nick who told them. Your note, Kate, the one you wrote, telling us not to worry about you and to contact your solicitor. Remember?"

"But I didn't give it to you. I threw it away."

"Rachel found it. I told Nick. I'm so sorry."

"What note?" Fax asked.

Kate thought Lucy looked ready to throw up. Fax slid his arm around her and hugged her. Lucy clung to him. Kate felt a moment's bitterness that she wasn't the one getting the sympathy.

"Who saw it?" Kate asked.

"Rachel showed me and Dan. Then I told Nick."

Oh Christ. Kate let out a shaky breath.

"What note?" Fax asked again.

Lucy looked at him and then at Kate.

"I wrote a…a goodbye letter," Kate said. "The day after I was supposed to marry Richard, I swam out to sea. I thought I'd never come back, only I bumped into Charlie who happened to be doing the same thing. Since I said I'd met Charlie in the sea, I guess Nick must have put two and two together. He can't *know* Charlie was trying to kill himself, but he could have guessed."

"Can you find out?" Lucy asked Fax. "You could pull a few strings. If I ask Nick, he'll deny it. We're barely speaking, anyway."

"I'll try."

* * * * *

The following evening, when Lucy rang Kate and asked her to come downstairs, Kate could tell by the tone of her voice something was wrong. Fax was there too.

"Sit down," Lucy said.

"I'd rather stand." Kate wanted to be ready to run.

"Do you want the good news or the bad news?" Fax asked.

She felt relieved it wasn't all bad.

"The good," she replied.

"Nick *was* the one who told Simon that Charlie tried to commit suicide."

Kate sighed.

"I confronted him, once Fax confirmed it," Lucy said. "The bastard tried to tell me he did it for us. It turns out the night Simon and his photographer got those shots of you and Charlie in your place, they took one of Nick coming to see me. Nick said he needed to get that photo back so his wife didn't find out. He offered you."

"He wasn't the only source," Fax said. "They interviewed a whole load of others. Apparently Simon had been working on the story for a while."

"No mention of me or his parents saying anything?" Kate asked.

Fax shook his head. Kate shook with relief. For the last few days she'd felt as though she'd fallen through an iced-over lake and couldn't find the way back to the surface. Now she'd managed her first breath of air.

"What's the bad news?" she asked.

"I really think you should sit now," Lucy said and Kate slid onto the couch.

"There's more to come," Fax said.

"More what?" Kate didn't understand.

"More in next Sunday's paper."

Kate shuddered. "How much more can there be?"

"Not about Charlie. About you," Lucy said.

Her muscles tightened. "What are they going to say?"

"The only thing I found out was that it had something to do with an old murder case," Fax said.

Oh God, blood does run cold. Kate could feel them staring, but didn't look at either of them.

"Did…did you kill someone?" Lucy whispered.

"Lucy!" Fax said.

"What can I do to stop it?" Kate asked.

"I don't think you can do anything other than weather the storm." Fax paused. "Sorry, bad choice of words."

"We're here for you Kate, you know that," Lucy said.

Kate thought Lucy was going to touch her hand and she curled up like a clam.

"Is there anything we can do?" Lucy asked.

"Get a signed statement from Nick, saying he told 24/7 Charlie tried to kill himself and that it only was a guess, anyway." Kate wasn't serious, but Lucy nodded.

"I'll try."

Now Fax looked as worried as Kate.

Lucy kissed him on the nose. "Nick owes me. If he doesn't see it that way, maybe his wife will. I've always fancied being a blackmailer."

* * * * *

Kate couldn't believe what she held in her hand. Until Lucy gave it her, she thought there'd be little chance of proving what Nick had done. Kate was desperate to call Charlie, but guessing he'd shout at her again and not listen, she decided to speak first to Ethan.

"Ethan, it's me, Kate. Please don't put the phone down. I have something important to tell you."

"What?"

Kate wouldn't be deterred by his brusque manner. She was too excited, her heart bouncing like a kangaroo.

"I've got proof it wasn't me who told the papers about Charlie's suicide attempt. I have it in writing."

"So?"

Kate thumped back to earth. "I...I want Charlie to know the truth."

Silence at the other end of the phone.

"He thinks I sold him out, Ethan. I didn't. I want to speak to him."

"Okay. Come to the Dorchester tonight at ten. Charlie has a late interview there with Sky TV. Ask for me at reception."

Kate buzzed with the thought of seeing Charlie again. Even if he didn't want her, she had proof she didn't betray him. She showered and washed her hair, put on her denim skirt and a pale pink linen top. A little bit of her hoped Charlie would apologize and sweep her into his arms, but she'd settle for kindness in his eyes.

* * * * *

Charlie was warming to Jody. Not as a person, but as a distraction. At least when he was with her, the press divided their attention between the two of them. She moaned about the photographers, but Charlie knew she loved them. She never emerged from anywhere without checking her hair and face. He was tempted to tell her she had a spot, just to watch her freak out.

Even though she was wasting her time, Jody had done her best to cheer him up. She'd made it perfectly clear she wanted to go to bed with him and he was beginning to wonder why he wasn't fucking her. She wanted him to. Ethan wanted him to. What did it matter anymore?

But it did matter. He didn't want to sleep with people he didn't care about. All Charlie could think about was Kate. He thought he'd gone through every emotion since he'd seen that bloody newspaper and now he was just sad for what he'd lost, sad for Kate too. He didn't understand why she'd done it. He could only think it was because he'd cocked up over her father but she'd not given him chance to explain, to say he was sorry.

He'd had a phone call from Ethan saying he wanted to see him and Jody that night at nine, in the Penthouse bar at the Dorchester, the hotel where Jody was staying. Charlie took her for a meal in the Pavilion first. She spent the entire meal jabbering on about her house in Malibu and how much he'd like it and had he tried surfing and did he know Keanu and when was he moving to Hollywood and could she help him find a house.

Charlie was going off her again.

"Want a dessert?" he asked, sure she'd say no.

"Cherries."

Charlie didn't want anything. He'd drunk most of the bottle of wine and they'd had champagne beforehand. He had a nice buzz but he wasn't drunk. A bowl of cherries arrived and Jody scooted her chair closer to his.

"We'll share," she said.

When her fingers touched his zip, Charlie froze. He scanned the room, but no one looked their way. Luckily the tables were set far apart. He glanced at his lap. The starched white tablecloth covered the fact that she'd unzipped him.

Charlie stared straight at her. "What the fuck are you doing?"

"Wait and see."

She smiled, lifted a cherry to her lips by the stalk and sucked it into her mouth. Charlie didn't like her lips. They were too full. He suspected she'd— He lost his train of thought as her fingers lifted his cock out of his shorts, out of his pants. He glanced around the restaurant expecting a sea of shocked faces but no one was looking.

His cock hardened under her touch and he gave a little groan. Jody picked up another cherry, ran it along her lips and then along Charlie's. When he opened his mouth to take it, she whipped it away. It disappeared, but not into her mouth. Charlie flinched when the fruit touched the tip of his cock and swirled around the sensitive head. Jody withdrew her hand and popped the cherry into her mouth.

He pushed the bowl toward her. "Have another."

Jody laughed and lifted one from the bowl. This time, she bit off the tip before she transferred it to her other hand. Charlie gave a quiet moan. He didn't move. He didn't even blink. He could feel the fruit coating the tip of his cock. He wasn't sure if the moisture was from the cherry or him. Jody grinned, then put the fruit in her mouth, sucked the cherry off the stalk and chewed.

"Another?" he asked.

"I'd rather have a taste of something else."

Charlie stuffed himself back in his pants, zipped himself up and got to his feet.

He knew he shouldn't be doing this, but his dick overruled his brain.

Ethan walked in as they strolled out. He noticed how Charlie carried his jacket, saw his hand wrapped around Jody's and tried not to smile. Jody grinned so broadly she was in danger of losing the lower half of her jaw.

"Is it important?" Charlie asked.

Ethan hesitated. He could take a risk or he could make sure. Making sure won. Charlie was too unpredictable.

"I need a word with Jody." He drew her on one side. "How's it going?"

"We're going up to my room, how do you think it's going?"

"Kate is on her way over here. I think it would do Charlie good to see that flame is well and truly extinguished. She's looking for a reconciliation. Any ideas how we could persuade her it's finished between them?"

Jody's eyes were steely. "How about I push her over the edge of a cliff?"

Ethan chuckled. "You don't need to go that far. Letting her see you in bed together should be enough."

"How are we going to manage that?"

"Give me one of your keys. When Kate arrives, I'll send her up. I'll call you and let your phone ring out once. Keep Casanova at bay until then."

Jody sighed. "I've just worked him up into the right mood, now you want me to get him to wait?"

Ethan checked his watch. "Twenty minutes. She won't be late."

Jody kept her back to Charlie and handed Ethan one of her keys.

Chapter Thirty

№

Kate went to the reception desk of the Dorchester as instructed and was directed to the lounge. Ethan sat reading a magazine and drinking what looked like champagne. He stood as Kate walked over. She held out the note written by Nick like a shield in front of her. Kate watched his eyes surf the words and then he looked at her.

"So you tried to kill yourself, too?"

"A halfhearted attempt, like Charlie."

"I told Charlie about this." Ethan waved the paper she'd given him. "I explained you weren't to blame for the story and that you'd tell him who was."

Kate held out her hand. "I'll show him."

"Can I keep this for the time being? I need to have a word with a few people — make my displeasure felt."

She hesitated. "Charlie's okay about everything?"

Ethan smiled. "He's in the Harlequin Suite, waiting for you." He offered Kate a key.

"He wants me to go up? Are you sure?"

"Go on up. You'll like the suite. Elizabeth Taylor stayed there when she got the news about the record-breaking deal for her role as Cleopatra."

As Kate went up in the elevator, she wondered if everything would be all right now. If there would be champagne waiting and an apology on Charlie's beautiful lips. She pictured herself in his arms, heard him say sorry, imagined him kissing her, making love to her. Her body zinged with anticipation, tingling from the tips of her fingers to the centre of her heart. It was love. She loved him.

Kate couldn't see why they shouldn't start again. She needed to apologize for running out. It had been a mistake, but she'd been scared and overreacted. She could make him understand. If she hadn't run, maybe none of this would have happened because when Charlie saw the newspaper, she'd have been with him and he'd have believed her.

She knocked on the door. Despite Ethan having given her a key, she didn't want to just walk in. No one answered, so Kate let herself in. Music played loudly. James Blunt. Odd. Charlie didn't like him. Kate drew in her breath as she walked through the mirrored lobby. She couldn't believe this was a hotel room.

"Charlie?" she called.

She passed a dining room and a bathroom. He wasn't in the long sitting room, so she walked to another door.

One that was open. The one with the music. The one with Charlie.

On the far side of the room, Charlie stood in black boxers next to a huge bed. On the bed, reclined a naked Jody Morton. When Charlie saw Kate, his eyes opened wide. He looked as frozen as Kate felt. Only Jody was moving, reaching for Charlie. Kate fled to the elevator. She pounded the button and the doors opened at once, as though they'd known she'd be coming straight back.

Something had ripped inside her. How stupid to think Nick's letter would make a difference. The damage was too severe. Charlie had already moved on.

Down in the lobby she saw Ethan standing near the exit. He smirked as she walked toward him. He'd been waiting for her. Kate's fingers itched to slap his face. Instead, she handed him the key card.

"Why didn't you simply tell me?" she asked.

"Charlie wanted to be sure you got the message."

A spurt of pain flared between her eyes at the thought of Charlie setting this up. But if he had, why had he looked so shocked to see her? Maybe he'd wanted to be in bed with Jodie when Kate walked in.

"I rang the moment you made for the elevator and told him it was time to start the show."

Ethan looked her up and down as though she was a cheap slut. Kate didn't understand any of this.

"You orchestrated the whole thing just to hurt me?"

"To make sure you didn't turn into another Tiffany Samuels. It's over, Kate. Finished. You didn't really think you could play happy families with Charlie, did you?" He smiled. All she saw were rows and rows of teeth. "I warned you what he was like. Did you think you'd get married, have kids and live happily every after? You're one in a long line. Charlie's going to be a mega-star and you...you're nothing."

"I am *not* nothing," Kate said. "I'm a person with feelings. I've just as much right—"

"What sort of mother would you make? Throwing yourself into the sea over a minor disappointment. Staying in an abusive relationship. You don't even know what normal family life is like. Charlie doesn't need someone like you."

Kate flinched. "Why are you being so cruel? What have I done to you?"

"It's what you've done to Charlie."

"But I didn't do anything. I gave you the letter. It proved—"

"What letter?"

Kate gulped. It had all been a waste of time. Ethan wouldn't show Charlie the letter and maybe Charlie wouldn't have believed it anyway. Kate felt as if she'd been poisoned, stabbed, buried in an earthquake and then drowned by the following tidal wave. She started to move past Ethan and then changed her mind. She didn't need to slap him to hit back.

"You know, Mr. Silver, I'm glad I'm not in your world if it's populated with people like you, people who don't give a damn about anyone other than themselves, people who'd lie and cheat to get what they want. Don't you even care whether newspapers print the truth?"

He gave a short laugh. "But they did print the truth."

Kate bristled. "I wonder if they'd be interested in the fact that you like to wear women's underwear?"

She felt a small shard of pleasure in wiping the smile from Ethan's face.

"That's crazy."

"I'm not stupid. Why would you only want samples in large sizes? I saw the way you touched my stuff and the look in your eyes."

He opened his mouth, but she spoke again before he could.

"But I'm not a bad person. I know right from wrong. I know how to keep secrets. I might be nothing in your view of the world but I deserve as much respect as anyone else. In all my life, I've never been as cruel to anyone as you've been to me."

She walked away.

* * * * *

"Get out of the bathroom, Charlie."

Jody kept banging on the door but he wasn't going out there until he had his clothes back on. He dressed quickly, trying to work out what had just happened. Where the hell had Kate come from? He'd hardly been able to believe his eyes. Which was why he'd stood there gawking at her like an idiot.

Kate.

Oh fuck.

God, her eyes when she'd seen him and Jody.

Charlie sat on the edge of the tub, his head in his hands, trying to think.

"Charlie, open the door. I've got something I want to show you."

How had she got into the suite?

"Charlie, come out. Lie facedown on the bed and I'll show you what I can do with a mouthful of bourbon."

Everything started to make sense. He'd been played by an expert. Two experts. All that fucking around with the cherries. He'd been set up perfectly. That was all it had taken to pierce his defenses. Fucking cherries. Ethan must have given Kate a key. How else could she have got in? Charlie gritted his teeth as he thought how Jody and Ethan had maneuvered him into this. That was what they'd been talking about when Ethan pulled her aside, how to set this up. The lying bitch.

He thought about Kate's face as she stood for those few awful moments in the doorway. A couple of seconds stretched to hours. He'd seen the long scratch down her cheek, and realized he'd done that when he'd thrown the bag, but far worse was the pain in her eyes. She'd hurt him, but he shouldn't have hurt her back. He wouldn't have hurt her like this.

"Charlie, have you ever tried a cock ring?"

Worse yet, there was a little niggling worm eating away at him. What if Kate had been telling the truth? What if it wasn't her who spoke to the press? How could she have had the courage to come back and face him after all the horrible things he'd said to her, unless she was innocent? And if she was, what had he just done?

"Charlie? Are you okay?"

He got to his feet and opened the door. Jody stood there, still naked, smiling up at him, with capped teeth, dyed hair, breasts that were too round, too pert, too fucking perfect. Her smile faltered when she saw his face.

"What's wrong?" she asked.

"How did you manage to time that so well?"

"Time what?"

"Fucking me, you manipulative bitch." Charlie went back into the bedroom.

"Don't be mad. Come to bed," Jody said.

"Fuck off."

The bedside lamp just missed his head as he walked out. All he could think about was Kate.

* * * * *

Kate walked to her apartment from Greenwich station, hurrying past happy couples strolling hand in hand. She seethed with anger, the subject of her rage changing with every few yards she stamped. Fury with Jody, because people like her always got what they wanted. Fury with Ethan, because he'd played her for a fool. And fury with Charlie for not having faith in her.

She got back at midnight, her pulse racing. Kate's head whirled, she felt restless, nervous, on the edge of screaming. Lucy had asked her to ring to let her know how she got on with Charlie, no matter what the time. Only how could she? Lucy expected happy news. Kate picked up the pile of Post-It notes Charlie had scribbled on and pushed them in her pockets, along with her mobile. Picking up her car keys, she looked around her little home for the last time and closed the door.

Kate hadn't driven far before she was forced to stop. She turned onto a side street and switched off the engine, gasping as pain came in waves, surging from her heart, swamping her body, leaving her shaken and bewildered. She wanted someone to hold her and tell her everything was going to be all right, but there was no one. Charlie had loved her, Kate knew he had, but not now. Instead, he'd done the worst thing he could to show how much he hated her.

She rested her head on the steering wheel. What was she going to do? She was tired of starting over, of trying to feel excited about moving into a grubby bed-sit, when all she really saw was how much work needed to be done to make her feel safe. Every time Kate had moved to live somewhere else, she tried to grow her own home, as though it was some sickly weed that only needed water and food to change it into a beautiful flower. She'd painted dozens of walls, sewed curtains and cushions, but never made a home. Her apartment in Greenwich was going to be different, but it had turned out the same in the end. When she tried to take the different path she kept getting pushed the other way. Only this time, it wasn't her fault. Kate rocked in her seat.

When she'd pulled herself together, she drove out of London with no destination in her head. She thought the farther away she got, the better she'd feel, but instead a growing sense of the futility of her life flattened her mind. Maybe having a home and all that went with it wasn't supposed to be her other path. She'd never bothered much about possessions because they trapped you or got spoiled. Better not to have anything. Not even love. If you got attached to something, it only got taken away. Child or adult. Toys or people. No difference.

The idea that anyone could have ever loved her or would ever love her, seemed as likely as her taking a trip into space. She'd given Charlie her heart and he'd crushed it. And she was angry with him because it didn't have to be that way. Yet again, the pain in her chest made her unable to drive. She wasn't safe on the road. Kate didn't want to hurt anyone. Pulling into the car park of a Burger King, she curled up on the backseat, her eyes wide open, afraid that if she went to sleep, she might never wake up.

* * * * *

In the morning, Kate bought a bottle of water from the restaurant and took it back to the car. Nothing to eat. Not hungry. She reversed out of the parking spot, and as she put her foot on the accelerator and moved forward, a child dashed in front of her. Kate slammed on the brakes and saw the little girl's eyes register what was about to happen. The car lurched to a halt, throwing Kate forward. The child disappeared. The thought that she'd killed her almost stopped Kate's heart. She'd been distracted, not paying attention. What had she done?

Everything seemed to happen in slow motion. Kate saw a woman in a short red skirt run out of the restaurant, her mouth open in a scream. Kate couldn't hear anything. A dark-haired man followed the woman, his face a gray cloud. But he came to Kate's door. *Don't let me have killed her*, Kate thought. *Kill me. Please kill me.* Then she saw the woman stand up with the child in her arms and the child was crying, but alive and air rushed into Kate's lungs.

The man opened the door and she cringed, thinking he'd hit her.

"Are you all right?" he asked.

The woman and the child came to his side.

"I'm so sorry," the woman said. "I thought Ruthie was with us. We only took our eyes off her for a second. I saw her run in front of your car. I don't know what we'd have done if—"

The little girl turned in her mother's arms and looked at Kate.

"Thank God you braked in time," the man said. "Are you okay?"

"Yes," Kate managed to force out. "I'm glad she's all right."

She watched the three of them walk back to the restaurant. The man's arm across his wife's shoulders, his fingers in the fair hair of his daughter. He bent his head and kissed them both.

Life was precious. Was that the message being sent by someone she didn't believe in? If it was one of Charlie's signs, Kate thought she'd missed it. There was nothing left in her now — no anger, no sadness, no hope. Kate got out of her car and walked away.

Chapter Thirty-One

ဆာ

Dan came to an abrupt halt when he saw a strange man coming out of Kate's apartment.

"Who are you? Where's Kate?" he asked.

"Jon Chadwick. I'm with Locton and Moore."

"You're an estate agent? Kate's selling the apartment? Is she in?"

"The apartment's on the market, yes. The sale's being handled through her solicitors. No, she isn't in. The place is empty. Well, virtually. A few bits of furniture left."

Dan rushed down to Rachel and she called Lucy.

"What are we going to do?" Rachel asked.

Lucy pulled her fingers through her hair. "I thought everything was going to be okay now she had the letter from Nick. She didn't ring, but I thought she'd be with Charlie."

"Well, maybe everything is okay," Dan said. "She could be back with Charlie. If she's moved in, she doesn't need this place anymore."

The three of them stared at one another.

"Do you think that's what this is?" Rachel asked.

Dan wanted to be upbeat but knew his face had given him away.

* * * * *

Charlie read the newspaper while he sat outside on his patio. Jody had flown back to the States. He hoped he never saw her again. He'd certainly never agree to work with her on another job, assuming he ever worked again. His hands shook as he held the paper. The headline was *STORM CHASER*. It wasn't a big spread like they'd done on him, just a single page opposite an article on some dog that could bark the National Anthem. The writer had made Kate look like some crazed celebrity groupie. They'd even suggested the Tiffany incident was staged. He swallowed hard. The more he read, the more ill he felt. Last week they'd crucified him, now they'd crucified her for knowing him.

They'd interviewed her father. There was a little picture of Jim with one of his paintings. The story about the night her mother died was in there in gory detail, together with the crazy suggestion that Kate should have been the one in prison. The fact that she'd been a seven-year-old, irrelevant.

Dickhead was quoted too, and he'd twisted what he'd done, made it look as though Kate had been desperate to get married, that *she'd* booked the registry office, that *she'd* been the one who wanted to do things in a quiet way. Dex's family branded Kate a callous bitch. Kate was a damaged woman whose aim in life was to find a man to look after her. She was greedy, manipulative and selfish. Charlie had been one in a line of suckers, but the biggest catch. The paper said she'd even swum out to sea to snare him. And as Charlie read, he realized that in not trusting Kate, he'd made the biggest mistake of his life.

He tried to call her, but her mobile was off, the house phone not ringing out. He drove to her apartment with his heart pounding and then held his finger on the intercom buzzer. A man's voice answered and razor-sharp claws raked Charlie's heart.

"I was looking for Kate. Is she there?"

"No. She's moved out."

"Moved out? Who are you?"

"The estate agent. I'm just showing a couple of prospective purchasers around."

"Can I come up?"

"Not unless you want to buy the place," the man said.

"I might," Charlie shot back.

The door release buzzed and he shoved open the door.

A young couple were leaving as he arrived at Kate's door. They gawped as he went past. He pushed his way into the apartment and rushed from room to room. He knew she wasn't there, but he needed to see for himself.

"What are you doing?" The young estate agent followed on Charlie's heels.

Charlie ignored him. He opened cupboards, drawers, the wardrobe, but everything had gone.

"Where's the furniture going?" Charlie asked.

"It's being sold with the property."

Charlie looked at him. "The bed?"

"Everything that's left."

"I want the bed."

"Well, er, it goes with the apartment."

"I only want the bed. I'll give whoever buys the apartment ten thousand pounds."

"I don't think I can do that."

"You mean you've sold it already?"

"No, but I'd have to ask Miss Snow if that's acceptable. Only everything is being handled through her lawyers. All the proceeds of the sale go to them. I believe she's repaying a debt."

Charlie faltered. A debt to her father. "Well, I want the bed."

The man looked at him as if he'd gone mad and Charlie thought he probably had.

"Call and ask," Charlie said.

While the guy stood in the kitchen, Charlie went back into the bedroom.

"Oh Kate, where are you?" he whispered.

He knelt on the bed, dropped his face and breathed in. He could still smell her. The coconut soap she used, the lemon shampoo. His hands slid under the pillow, pulling it closer and he felt metal against his wrist. He pulled out his hand and saw the silver star.

"They said they'll... What are you doing?" the estate agent asked.

"Nothing." The pillow dropped from his fingers. When Charlie got up and turned to face him, he had the necklace clutched in his fist.

"If you give me your number, I'll let you know once her solicitor gets back to me."

The guy looked at him as though he were some sort of pervert. Charlie wondered if an article on him pillow sniffing was going to be in the paper next week.

He gave the estate agent his phone number and went to knock on Dan's door. When there was no answer, he ran down to Rachel's.

"Do you know where she is?" Charlie asked, the moment the door opened.

Dan shook his head and Charlie's shoulders slumped.

"Come in," Dan said. "We were just talking about her."

"When did you last see her?" Charlie sat down and then got up again. He was working himself into a panic.

"She went to see you with Nick's letter."

"A letter?" Charlie asked and watched the two exchange looks.

"Nick was the one who told 24/7 you tried to kill yourself," Dan said.

Charlie felt everything falling away around him, as though he stood in the middle of an earthquake while the building disintegrated under his feet.

"I found Kate's suicide note," Rachel explained. "It had fallen out of the wheelie bin. Because Kate told us she met you in the sea, we put two and two together."

"I could have dived in to save her," Charlie snapped.

"But you didn't, did you?" Dan said.

Charlie's head slumped.

"Lucy told Nick and he told the Sunday paper," Rachel said. "Kate was upset because you thought she'd spoken to the press. Lucy persuaded Nick to admit it in writing. Kate took the proof to show you and we haven't seen her since. She was supposed to

392

ring and let us know what happened, but she didn't. We hoped you were together, but looks like we were wrong."

"Shit." Charlie's legs gave way and he dropped onto the couch.

"She isn't answering her phone," Dan said. "I've texted her but she hasn't replied."

Rachel clutched Dan's hand. "We're worried about her, but we have no idea where she'd go. She dumped everything she had. Her computer, sewing machine, even her plates and cutlery. It's all in the bin room. Then we found out the apartment was on the market."

Her sewing machine? Charlie didn't want to hear this, he wanted to put his hands over his ears and make a noise so he couldn't listen.

"Where would she go? Do you know where she went before?" Rachel asked.

Charlie perked up. Ethan's detectives found her in Brighton. She must have friends there. He jumped to his feet.

"Maybe Brighton. I can find out."

"Hey, Charlie," Dan said. "The stuff it said in the paper about Kate? Mate, when she moved in, she was pretty battered. She had a broken arm and a black eye. This guy, this Dex, they reckon is a hero, I think he hit Kate. The papers have twisted it."

"Yeah," Charlie said in a bleak voice. "They have a habit of doing that."

* * * * *

When Ethan opened the door, Charlie elbowed his way inside.

"I was about to ring you. I've had a call from the RSC. You must have impressed them, Charlie. They want you to play Hamlet for a complete run, not just for the charity event. Well done. It's going to be tight to fit it in, but filming—" Ethan broke off.

Charlie glared at him.

"Aren't you pleased?" Ethan asked.

Charlie gave a short laugh. "I wonder why they picked me."

"Because you're a talented actor?"

"Do you know the fucking play, Ethan? It's about a young guy who has everything and throws it away. He fucks up his life. The most famous speech in the world, 'To be or not to be', do you know what it's about? Whether he should fucking kill himself. He couldn't even get that right. Great publicity stunt, picking a weak actor whose life has gone down the pan, to play a weak prince, whose life has gone the same way."

Charlie stalked in circles, unable to keep still.

"What's wrong with you now?" Ethan asked.

"I need the name of the place Kate stayed in Brighton."

"Why?"

"Because I have to find her. I was wrong. She didn't tell the papers about the suicide attempt. She came to the Dorchester to prove it only I didn't give her the chance."

"A piece of paper doesn't prove anything," Ethan said. "Forget her, Charlie. You're on the way up, not down."

Charlie stopped moving. There was a long silence before he spoke. "What piece of paper?"

Ethan didn't say anything, but Charlie saw his jaw tighten.

"You fucking knew! You fucking knew, and you still let her come up and see me about to shag Jody Morton." Charlie shook with fury.

"We—" Ethan began.

"You and Jody set it up. I wondered why she didn't rip my clothes off the moment we got in the room. You're unbelievable, the pair of you." Charlie shook his head in bewilderment. "You let me think Kate betrayed me. Don't you fucking want me to be happy?"

"You were happy with Jody Morton."

"No, *you* were happy I was with Jody. What did you get out of it, Ethan? She going to sign with you if you got her into my bed?"

"You're acting crazy. You need to calm down, Charlie. Maybe all this is for the best. Kate's obviously unstable, she—"

"Where did she stay in Brighton?" Charlie demanded.

"I'm not sure."

"Give me the number of the private detective."

"Look, if she doesn't want to be found, she's not going to go back to the same place."

Charlie stepped forward and Ethan backed away.

"Give me the fucking number."

"I didn't hire anyone."

"What?" Charlie's stomach dropped to his feet.

"There was no point," Ethan explained. "She—"

Charlie clenched his fists. Ethan had no idea how close he was to needing new teeth.

"You lied to me. You fucking charged me for a PI company you never hired? Right. That's it. We're finished." Charlie stalked off and then surged back. "You know what the really crazy thing is? I thought you were my friend. I thought at least I could rely on my agent."

"I've always acted in your best interests," Ethan insisted.

"Come off it. You act in *your* best interests. You always will. You're as much of a monster as I am." Charlie stepped up so his face was inches from Ethan's. "Only I don't get off on wearing women's underwear. I guess your other clients will wonder about that too."

Then he stormed off.

But once Charlie stood outside Ethan's house, he didn't know where to go. He'd been so certain Ethan would give him an address, he hadn't thought beyond that. He got back in his car, sat for a moment and then rang Kate's father.

"Jim? It's Charlie. I don't suppose you've heard from Kate?"

"Not since that night at your house, no."

"Do you have any idea where she might be?"

"What's the point asking me? I haven't been in her life for years and she made it clear that's the way she likes it."

"She's disappeared," Charlie said.

"She'll turn up again."

He heard no concern in Jim's voice.

"Aren't you worried?"

"No. This is what she does. Runs away from life."

"She's selling her apartment and giving you back the money," Charlie said.

There was a short laugh at the other end of the phone. "Is she now? So what's wrong, Charlie? Don't you like being run away from either?"

"I love her," Charlie whispered.

"You probably say that to every woman you sleep with. Seems to me that Kate's incapable of accepting love. You'll never make her believe you mean it."

Charlie couldn't bear talking to the guy any longer. He cut the connection. He lowered his head onto the steering wheel and started to cry. This was his fault. He knew what Kate was like. She ran away from problems. She didn't want to confront them and yet despite all that, she'd tried to speak to him, twice. The first time he'd thrown her bag at her, marked her lovely face and told her to fuck off and finish what she started. She still hadn't given up on him. But the next time, she'd walked into the hotel room and seen him about to fuck Jody.

God, what would he have done if that had been the other way round, if he'd seen Kate with another guy? Charlie couldn't stand to think of anyone but him holding her, loving her. He'd destroyed the one good thing he had. *I love her.* He thought about the times he held her in his arms and tried to relive the moments, but they slipped through his fingers like silken rope. He was pathetic. It should be him finishing what he'd started.

Charlie sat up straight and stared ahead. Is that what Kate would do? Go back to the beach where they'd begun? His mobile rang and he dragged it from his pocket. Not Kate.

"Hello," he muttered.

"How are you, Charlie?" his father asked.

"I've been better."

"I've just had a call from the police."

Charlie's overworked heart lurched.

"About Kate," Paul said.

"What?" Ice water surged through Charlie's veins.

"They found her car, Charlie."

"No." He didn't want to hear this.

"Abandoned outside a Burger King on the Flyton by-pass."

"Kate?" Charlie managed to force out her name.

"They don't know where she is."

Relief and fear surged together. "Why did the police contact you?"

"They found a scrunched up piece of paper in the car; our address and the route to our house scribbled on it. She came here, Charlie."

"When?"

"A few days ago. Your mum has only just told me."

"What did she want?"

Charlie heard the hesitation in his father's voice.

"She wanted to speak to me. She brought us a painting. Left it by the door. It's of you and Michael. It's lovely. Your mum can't stop looking at it. Someone called Dan Stevens painted it."

Charlie wondered if he could feel any worse.

"Charlie? There's something else I need to tell you. When you both came here that day, and you slammed off in a temper, you remember Kate came back into the house? Well, she told me you tried to kill yourself. I think that's what she came here to ask me, if I'd told the papers."

Charlie didn't say anything.

"I didn't tell anyone, son. Not even your mother. I don't think Kate did either."

"Oh God."

"Were things that bad?"

"Yes."

He heard the shake in his father's breathing. "Come home, Charlie."

"I have to find Kate. What do the police think? Are they doing anything?"

"No. She's an adult and abandoned her car, that's all. There was an incident involving a child outside the restaurant. Kate nearly ran her over. The child wasn't hurt but no one's seen Kate since."

"I need to find her."

"Is there anything we can do?" his father asked.

"No, but if she comes back, don't let her go."

Chapter Thirty-Two

Kate sat on the sand, staring at a sludgy green sea. The weather was miserable, the sky a thousand shades of gray. She wished she could sweep the cloud away and find a patch of blue. Was that something her mother used to say? Find enough blue sky to make a pair of sailor's trousers and the weather would clear by evening. Maybe it wasn't her mother. Maybe it was one of her many social workers. Kate wasn't sure. She wasn't sure of anything.

It started to drizzle and the few families on the beach began to pack up and leave. Even the seagulls flew away. Kate pulled her cold fingers inside the sleeves of her blue sweater. Had she tried hard enough to put things right? She thought so. She put her hand in her pocket and pulled out the wedge of Post-It notes Charlie had left. A few deft folds and Kate turned one into a little boat. She threw it toward the sea.

Fifteen minutes later, there was flotilla of yellow boats lying on the sand. The water had reached a couple and swamped them. She watched the waves rolling in and wondered if it was the same water continually throwing itself onto the sand, trying to crawl up the beach before falling away. Soon, it would reach all the little boats and then it would reach her. Maybe she should let the sea swallow her and all that was wrong with her.

There was a strange comfort in having nothing left, no possessions. The bag with the remains of her clothes sat in the boot of the car. She'd lost her purse somewhere. Probably in the cab of the truck in which she'd hitched a lift. She still had her mobile. Kate took it out of her pocket. She hadn't switched it on for days. She pressed the little button on the top and cleared the missed calls and messages without looking at them. She was no longer interested in what anyone had to say.

She tapped one text message into her phone, but didn't send it.

To Hippo

Sorry we lost each other

Mermaid XX

She erased the kisses.

Then put them back.

Kate set the phone upright in the sand between her and the waves. After a moment, the light went off on the screen. A few more paper boats struggled in the waves.

Even with her back to him, Charlie knew it was her. He didn't know what he'd have done if she hadn't been there. The thought of arriving too late almost disabled him. He walked across the top of the beach until he was directly behind her looking down from a dune. She wouldn't have heard him above the noise of the sea. She was surrounded by yellow paper triangles and her mobile stuck up in the sand in front of her. He took his from his pocket and tapped out a message.

Kate jerked when the phone blipped. For a moment, she just sat there, and then Charlie watched her reach out very slowly and pick it up.

Run away with me

He waited to see what she'd do. He hoped she wouldn't rush into the sea. It looked bloody cold, and he really didn't want to get any wetter. He sent another text.

Right now

Kate turned. For a tiny, heart-stopping moment, he thought he saw a smile on her face and then it disappeared. As he walked toward her, she got to her feet. Charlie wanted to run and sweep her into his arms but he was scared she'd push him away. It was what he deserved. He stood in front of her. He had so much inside him he wanted to say, and now he found he couldn't speak.

Kate blinked, and he was still there. He held out his hand and opened his fingers. In the middle of his palm lay the last piece of jigsaw.

"Sorry," he said.

She couldn't tell whether the water on his face came from his eyes or the rain.

"I ransacked the apartment looking for that piece," she said. "When did you take it?"

"The moment you opened the box."

He opened his other hand and there lay the silver star she'd left under her pillow. He took a step closer, and Kate edged away. She saw his shoulders slump a little, and then he straightened and looked right at her.

"I've come to save you," he said. "I'm ready to slay dragons, repel pirates, eviscerate mutants and strangle seaweed."

Kate thought for a moment. "How about fighting off a T-Rex?"

Charlie sucked his teeth. "Er, no, that's not in my job description. If you meet a T-Rex, you're on your own."

He took a step nearer and this time Kate stood her ground.

"So, do you come here often?" he asked.

"Only when I need saving, but if you can't face a T-Rex, maybe you're no use to me."

"I was only joking about the T-Rex. Point him out. I won't ever let anything hurt you."

"You can't promise that, Charlie."

He pulled up his collar and rubbed the rain from his eyes. "Then I promise I'll never hurt you again. I know I let you down and I'm sorry. I should have believed you."

"What about Jody Morton?" Kate stared straight at him. His gaze didn't flicker from hers.

"She's gone back to the States."

"So, did—?"

"I never slept with her, Kate. She and Ethan arranged it so you'd find us. I heard her phone ring and I guess that was her signal to—" Charlie stopped.

"But you were going to."

He looked down. Kate saw the shame on his face. His hands hung limp at his sides.

"Why did Ethan do that? What had I done?" she asked.

"Nothing. You'd done nothing. I think Jody told Ethan he'd be her agent if he got the pair of us together. I don't even like her. I'm sorry. Please tell me you forgive me."

"Why were you going to have sex with her if you didn't like her?"

Charlie raised his head. "Because I was hurting, because I wanted to forget you, because without you I'm weak."

"I don't want someone weak."

"You make me strong." Kate heard the catch in his voice. "I've done one good thing. I've sacked Ethan. He had no right to manipulate me that way, but most of all he had no right to hurt you." Charlie ran a hand through his damp hair. "I also keep thinking about him wearing your underwear and it's freaking me out."

Kate gave a little smile.

"Ethan went too far, Kate. He almost cost me everything I care about." Charlie stared at her, his eyes pools of ink in the poor light. "Maybe he has."

"It was Nick who spoke to the papers."

Charlie scowled. "I heard he lost his job with Metro Radio. They didn't approve of the fact that one of their senior people sold a story he should have let them run."

"So everyone is getting their just desserts?" Kate asked.

"I don't know. Are they?" Charlie looked at her, dark shadows under his eyes, despair all over his face. "Let me take you home, get you warm and dry. I'm not leaving you here, Kate. I…" His chest heaved. "I'm frightened to touch you because if you walk away from me, I can't ever leave this beach."

402

Kate knew she had to make the first move. There was only one move she'd wanted to make since the message appeared on her phone and she'd turned to see him standing in front of her. Kate opened her arms and the light in his eyes burst into a brilliant flame. Charlie fell into her embrace.

"I'm so sorry," he sobbed. "I fucked up, and I thought I'd lost you."

He clutched her so tight, Kate could hardly breathe.

"I almost did, didn't I? If I hadn't got here in time?"

"I came to say goodbye, but I'm not sure I'd have gone in the sea," Kate whispered. "It looks a bit cold for a swim and I spotted some vicious-looking seaweed."

Charlie pressed his face into her hair, then raised his head and nodded toward the water. "What are all those little boats?"

"The Post-Its you stuck on my wall."

"Oh, God. I'll never let you down again, I promise." He held her head in his hands and stared into her eyes. "Say you forgive me."

"Would you really tackle a T-Rex?"

"In an instant."

"Even if one's lolloping down the beach, right now?"

Charlie paused. "There isn't one lolloping down the beach right now, is there?"

Kate checked over his shoulder. "No."

"Then yes, absolutely."

"Okay, then," Kate said. "I forgive you, if you forgive me for running away."

"But I shouldn't have—"

Kate put her finger on his lips. "Forgive me."

Charlie smiled. "I forgive you."

He kissed her then, a tentative brushing of his lips against hers over and over until Kate nipped him with her teeth to make him stop. He groaned as her tongue slipped into his mouth. She groaned as his tongue slipped into hers. Charlie kissed and teased, landing kisses all over her face, licking the rain away until Kate's head was as cloudy as the sky.

"I love you I love you I love you I love you," he whispered, holding her tight against him.

"Only four times?"

"I ran out of breath. When we kiss, you suck all the air from my lungs." He wiped a drop of rain from her nose. "But when I'm with you, I feel at my most alive. I don't think I want to act anymore. I want to be me. I want to do something with you. I want to know everything about you, to know your dreams and fears. I want to help make your life what you want it to be. Above everything else I want to make you happy." He stroked her cheek. "Will you let me try to make you happy?"

"Oh God, Charlie." Kate swallowed her sob.

Charlie smiled. "First thing I'm going to do is make it stop raining."

"And how are—oh." Kate laughed as the rain eased off.

Charlie bowed. "Second thing I'm going to do is provide exciting transport to the car. On my back."

Kate jumped on and he staggered.

"Hey, I didn't throw myself on you. I was really careful," he said with a groan.

"Do I have to use my whip?" she asked.

Charlie held her tight and began to gallop to the parking lot. By the time they reached his car, he'd slowed to a walk and it had stopped raining.

"What's the third thing you're going to do?" Kate slid from his back.

"Make the sky turn blue."

She raised her eyebrows.

"What can I say?" He beamed. "I'm a prodigious talent. In many ways." His gaze dropped to his crotch.

Kate couldn't help looking. The ridge in his pants was unmistakable.

"Open the trunk," she said.

Charlie's eyes widened. "We can't fuck in the trunk."

Kate bit back her laugh. When he flipped it open, she stripped to her underwear and threw her clothes and shoes inside.

"Now you," she said.

Charlie did as he was told and took off everything but his boxers and deck shoes.

"Good idea," he said. "We're not going to make a mess in the car now."

She smiled. "Want a bet?"

Charlie looked at the rear seats in the convertible and groaned. They had to be designed for legless anorexics.

"Sit on the passenger side and put the roof down," Kate said.

"No, I'm driving."

She stared at him.

"What?" Charlie asked.

And kept on staring.

"Think, Charlie."

He finally got his brain in gear and leapt into the car. Roof down, seat retracted as far as it would go, a broad smile on his face and a cock about to break into song. Early evening and such miserable weather, no one would come to the beach now, would they?

Kate sat on his lap facing him and smiled. The sweet contact when their lips met made Charlie forget what he'd been worrying about. He forgot they were wet, forgot they were cold, only remembered they were together and he had Kate safe in his arms. Well, maybe not safe but... He wrapped his arms around her and held her tight.

Their kisses were soft and open-mouthed, slow shifts from one angle to another as their tongues tussled in a gentle duel. He toed off his shoes and pulled her legs down so she lay spread against him. Not much room to move but enough.

Kate dragged her mouth from his to take a breath. Charlie's heart pounded as if he *was* being chased by a T-rex.

"I love you," she whispered.

He clamped his hands over her hips. "And I love you but if you don't stop wriggling I'm going to disappoint us both."

"I'm trying to get my panties off."

"Oh, in that case…"

Charlie tried to remove his boxers at the same time. Arms and legs wedged and tangled together, caught in an impossible game of Twister, they laughed as they struggled to maneuver.

"I'm going to swap this bloody Lexus," he grunted. "We'll go round all the car showrooms and find a vehicle with enough room for us to fuck in every position."

"A camper van?"

He laughed.

Finally naked, Kate held herself up while he yanked his shorts the rest of the way to his feet. *At last.* Then he clasped Kate's waist and brought her creamy folds down to kiss his desperate cock. Their laughter faded, swiftly replaced by ragged breathing.

"That feels sooo good," she said.

"Oh Kate, Kate," he whispered.

His balls were tight, drawn up close to the root of his cock, urging him to yank her down and fuck her hard. But Kate impaled herself without him doing anything but sitting there. Charlie tightened his hold on her hips as she sank down and down. He gave a low groan at the feel of her—so wet and hot, the way her pussy held him, the warmth, the tightness. So long as she didn't move for a while, he'd be fine.

She moved.

Fuck. Fuck. His cock pulsed and swelled. No point pretending he was in control but Charlie grabbed her buttocks and dragged her down harder. Within moments his balls hovered in a frenzy of anticipation, tingling with the need to open the floodgates, shoot down his cock to empty themselves into her. *Nownownow.* He gave up and gave in, surrendering to the moment. Kate took over the rhythm and Charlie slid his hands to her breasts as she drove herself down on him.

To think he'd imagined slow and careful. Charlie tried to recall if he'd ever managed that with her? Then his brain fogged. He had a lifetime of loving Kate ahead of him.

He slipped a hand to her mons and reached for her clit. A flick of his finger as he bucked his hips and Kate let out a cry as she came, clamping around him, exquisite little spasms to drive his cock to oblivion. Charlie had words he wanted to say but left them dammed up in his head, while he flooded her pussy with cum, spurting blasts of fire over and over until his cock ceased doing its own thing and he could move again.

"My beautiful girl," he whispered and held her tight against him, his fingers still playing at the point their bodies joined.

"My gorgeous boy."

"Hey, look up."

Kate tilted her head back on his shoulder.

"A patch of blue sky," Charlie said.

* * * * *

When the garage door slid closed behind them, Kate released a shaky sigh and Charlie clutched her hand.

"Do you want this house to be our home?" he asked. "We could find somewhere else, choose a place together?"

Kate's swollen heart neared breaking point. "Home is wherever you are. This is a lovely house, Charlie and I'd adore to live here. Especially since I don't actually have anywhere to live at the moment. I put the flat on the market because I want to pay my father back. I...I got rid of all my stuff. Even the bed."

"I bought it."

She stared at him.

"Well, I spoke to the estate agent and asked him to talk to the owner. I don't know whether the offer will be accepted. I'm not going above twenty quid."

Kate smiled. "How much did you really offer?"

"Ten thousand pounds."

"I'll take twenty."

Charlie got out of the car. "Sounds a bargain."

"Twenty thousand," Kate said as she got out the other side.

"Done."

"You would be."

Charlie laughed as she followed him into the house. "Bath, bed or birthday present?" he asked.

"Present?"

He huffed. "I'm going to try not to be upset that you'd rather have a present than go to bed with me. It's in the music room."

He took her hand, pulled her down the corridor and pushed open the door. The floor was covered in scribbled-on manuscript paper, all except for one spot next to the piano where a rectangular piece of plywood had been laid. In the middle of the board sat a large box, so badly wrapped, Kate knew Charlie had done it himself. She wondered if it had been there since the night she'd run.

She knelt down and ripped off the paper to reveal an eighteen-thousand-piece jigsaw puzzle—a seascape with green-tailed mermaids, a kaleidoscope of tropical fish and a dark shipwreck.

"Lots of seaweed," Charlie said. "I figure you have to come to terms with your fears. Like it?"

"Eighteen thousand pieces? It's going to take years."

He grinned. "I thought you could lie here naked trying to fit pieces together, while I tried to fit words to music."

Kate ripped open the plastic bag and tipped all the pieces onto the plywood. "Start composing then."

Charlie sat at the piano, ran his fingers over the keys and then started to play. After a few bars, he began to sing and Kate turned to look at him. His voice sent tremors down her spine and wrapped her in its embrace.

"She was a stranger

That girl in the sea

Who came to me

She filled my dreams

And I gave her my heart…"

Charlie stared at her as he sang and Kate had to blink back her tears. It was a song about loss, about her and him, the mistakes he'd made and how he didn't know if he'd ever find her again. When the last echoing notes died away, Kate stood and walked to stand behind him. She slipped her arms over his shoulders and crossed them over his chest.

"I hope you find your lost dog," she whispered and Charlie shuddered. "And you were a bit out of tune in that last part. Set my teeth on edge."

For a moment, Kate thought he was crying and then realized he was laughing.

"You are the cruelest person I know," he said.

"It was lovely, really. What's it called?"

"Strangers. That was supposed to be an incredibly romantic moment." Charlie spun round and buried his face in her chest, curling his hands around her waist. "Even though you are the meanest person I know, I still love you." He kissed her forehead.

"And even though you can't sing in tune, I love you," Kate replied.

Charlie planted a gentle kiss on her nose.

"You can sing some more if you like," Kate said. "You'll get better with practice."

"Does that little piece of advice apply to everything?" Charlie nibbled her ear as he slipped his hands inside her panties. Kate groaned.

"You can only get better," she said and yelped when he bit her.

"No more secrets," Charlie whispered.

"You know everything about me." And it was true, Kate thought.

"And you know everything about me," he said.

"And I still love you. It's amazing."

Charlie kissed her breasts. "I want to take you on holiday. Somewhere out of the rain. Tomorrow, you're going to fill in a passport application. Where would you like to go? Pick anywhere in the world."

"The Gobi desert."

"Pick anywhere else in the world."

Kate hesitated. "Hawaii?"

Charlie lifted his gaze from her chest. "I won't let you down, Kate. I want to give you the world."

"I only want you. You're my world."

She could feel his heart beating fast under her hand.

"Kate?"

She looked into his eyes.

Charlie slithered to the floor and knelt in front of her, holding her hands. "I wanted to find the perfect place to do this, the perfect moment. I fucked up telling you that I loved you and I didn't want to get this wrong too. Only I realized that I don't need to find the perfect moment because you're what makes the moment perfect. So…Kate Snow, the woman I love more than my life, will you do me the very great honor of becoming…the person who'll cook me lovely things to eat, who'll cheer me up when I'm miserable, who'll tell me no and mean it, who'll do that thing to my cock with her tongue every night — well, maybe every other night, who'll love me forever and ever — damn, I've forgotten what I was going to say now."

Kate's shoulders shook as she laughed.

"Oh yeah, that was it. Will you marry me?" He looked up at her with his beautiful dark eyes and Kate gulped.

Oh God. "Yes."

He smiled his lovely Charlie smile and tears welled in her eyes. Charlie got to his feet and kissed her. A sweet, gentle caress of her lips by his. When he straightened, his eyes were shining.

"I love you. We're going to have so much fun. We could stop at Las Vegas on the way to Hawaii and get married," he said in an excited rush. "No press, no interference. Just us."

"What about your mum and dad?"

"They'll like Vegas. They can come with us, only not to Hawaii. I want you to myself, there."

"What about Rachel and Lucy and Dan?"

"I'll fly them out too."

Kate laughed. He tugged her out of the room toward the stairs.

"Okay, we'll get married in London," Charlie said.

Kate looked up at the white ceiling and Charlie followed her gaze.

"I paid a fortune to have it painted. I didn't want it to remind you of my stupidity."

"Mine too," Kate said.

He pulled her up the stairs. "Can we go to Vegas?"

"If you promise not to gamble."

"Hey, I'm on a winning streak. I've got you. There's nothing left to lose."

"You can have a hundred dollars a day," Kate said. "And when it's gone, it's gone. And don't think I don't mean it."

Charlie dragged her onto the bed. "I need you so much," he whispered. "You're the beat of my heart, the air in my lungs. You make me feel safe. I don't want to live without you. I want to spend my life making you happy. I want us to grow old together and when we die, I want us to die in each other's arms, because I can't live in a world without you by my side."

"You've not left me anything to say." She reached out and stroked his cheek.

"I want—"

Kate put her finger on his lips. "That didn't mean I don't want to say something. I love you, Charlie. I never thought I could love anyone as much, and I need you, too. My other path led me to you. I'm finally where I belong."

"In my bed and in my bath and—"

"Don't say kitchen," Kate warned him.

"In my heart." Charlie smiled.

411

Epilogue

$\wp$

"Put that down. Right now. I don't want to have to tell you twice. Don't…oh damn…I mean, bother." Kate watched as the ball flew through the air and landed on a half-built sandcastle. "I don't call that putting something down. Come here… No, I said here, not down to the water."

"Mark, do as you're told. Come here." Charlie gave a heavy sigh. "Leave Lizzie's hair alone. It's no use complaining she's bitten you if you're going to do that."

"Lizzie, stop trying to pull down Mark's trunks."

"Mark!"

"Lizzie!"

Kate turned to Charlie and raised an eyebrow. A moment later they were chasing the twins along the surf. Charlie scooped five-year-old Mark into his arms and up onto his shoulders. Kate did the same with Lizzie. The twins screamed with laughter.

After they'd exhausted their two-legged horses, they settled on the blanket to eat the picnic Kate had prepared.

"Is this why they're called sandwiches?" Lizzie asked, picking at the grains of sand stuck to the one she'd dropped.

Kate took it from her hand and gave her another. "No, a man called the Earl of Sandwich invented them when he was too busy playing cards to stop for a proper meal."

"Mummy, do you know everything?" Mark asked.

Kate laughed. "Yes and I know best."

"If you know everything, what am I thinking?" Charlie asked, running his hand up Kate's leg.

"You're thinking what a lucky guy you are to have such a fantastic wife and two delicious children."

"We're not delicious," Lizzie said. "Chocolate's delicious."

Acting in unison, Kate and Charlie pulled the twins onto their backs and blew raspberries on their squirming bellies. "Delicious," they said.

"Grandma!" shrieked Lizzie.

"Grandpa!" echoed Mark.

Kate looked up to see Paul and Jill holding ice creams.

"Who wants to see a jellyfish?" Paul asked.

Kate shuddered back into Charlie's chest and he put his arms around her. The twins walked off hand-in-hand with their grandparents and Charlie kissed Kate's neck.

"I love you," he whispered.

"I love you."

"I love this beach too. " Charlie tightened his hold on her. "It could have been the end and instead it was the beginning. You don't mind having a vacation here, do you?"

"What? Sandy sandwiches, gray sky, freezing cold sea, biting wind, lurking sharks and apparently—jellyfish—what's not to like?"

"Would you still come every year if I didn't bribe you with a trip to Hawaii as well?"

Kate turned and ran her finger over his lips. "I'd go anywhere with you."

"Have I made you happy?"

"Yes."

"Can you forgive me anything?"

"Er…yes."

Charlie smiled. He brought his hand up from behind her back and dangled a piece of seaweed over her face. Kate screamed and scuttled backward off the blanket.

"You bloody—"

"Not in front of the children."

Kate spun round. The twins were way down the beach, but out of the corner of her eye she saw Charlie leap for her. He pinned her down and kissed her and kissed her.

They were the last to leave the beach. The sea crept closer to the place where they'd sat, closer to the word they'd written in the sand.

H E L L O

Also by Barbara Elsborg

ॐ

eBooks:

Anna in the Middle

Digging Deeper

Doing the Right Thing

Finding the Right One

Lucy in the Sky

Perfect Timing

Power of Love

Saying Yes

Something About Polly

Snow Play

Strangers

Susie's Choice

The Bad Widow

The Small Print

Print Books:

Anna in the Middle

Perfect Timing

Something About Polly

About the Author

കൗ

Barbara Elsborg lives in West Yorkshire in the north of England. She always wanted to be a spy, but having confessed to everyone without them even resorting to torture, she decided it was not for her. Vulcanology scorched her feet. A morbid fear of sharks put paid to marine biology. So instead, she spent several years successfully selling cyanide.

After dragging up two rotten, ungrateful children and frustrating her sexy, devoted, wonderful husband (who can now stop twisting her arm) she finally has time to conduct an affair with an electrifying plugged-in male, her laptop.

Her books feature quirky heroines and bad boys, and she hopes they are as much fun to read as they are to write.

Barbara Elsborg welcomes comments from readers. You can find her website and email address on her author bio page at www.ellorascave.com.

Tell Us What You Think

We appreciate hearing reader opinions about our books. You can email us at Comments@EllorasCave.com.

Why an electronic book?

We live in the Information Age — an exciting time in the history of human civilization, in which technology rules supreme and continues to progress in leaps and bounds every minute of every day. For a multitude of reasons, more and more avid literary fans are opting to purchase e-books instead of paper books. The question from those not yet initiated into the world of electronic reading is simply: *Why?*

1. ***Price.*** An electronic title at Ellora's Cave Publishing and Cerridwen Press runs anywhere from 40% to 75% less than the cover price of the exact same title in paperback format. Why? Basic mathematics and cost. It is less expensive to publish an e-book (no paper and printing, no warehousing and shipping) than it is to publish a paperback, so the savings are passed along to the consumer.

2. ***Space.*** Running out of room in your house for your books? That is one worry you will never have with electronic books. For a low one-time cost, you can purchase a handheld device specifically designed for e-reading. Many e-readers have large, convenient screens for viewing. Better yet, hundreds of titles can be stored within your new library — on a single microchip. There are a variety of e-readers from different manufacturers. You can also read e-books on your PC or laptop computer. (Please note that Ellora's Cave does not endorse any specific brands.

You can check our websites at www.ellorascave.com or www.cerridwenpress.com for information we make available to new consumers.)

3. *Mobility.* Because your new e-library consists of only a microchip within a small, easily transportable e-reader, your entire cache of books can be taken with you wherever you go.

4. *Personal Viewing Preferences.* Are the words you are currently reading too small? Too large? Too... ANNOYING? Paperback books cannot be modified according to personal preferences, but e-books can.

5. *Instant Gratification.* Is it the middle of the night and all the bookstores near you are closed? Are you tired of waiting days, sometimes weeks, for bookstores to ship the novels you bought? Ellora's Cave Publishing sells instantaneous downloads twenty-four hours a day, seven days a week, every day of the year. Our webstore is never closed. Our e-book delivery system is 100% automated, meaning your order is filled as soon as you pay for it.

Those are a few of the top reasons why electronic books are replacing paperbacks for many avid readers.

As always, Ellora's Cave and Cerridwen Press welcome your questions and comments. We invite you to email us at Comments@ellorascave.com or write to us directly at Ellora's Cave Publishing Inc., 1056 Home Avenue, Akron, OH 44310-3502.

MAKE EACH DAY MORE *EXCITING* WITH OUR

ELLORA'S
CAVEMEN
CALENDAR

WWW.ELLORASCAVE.COM

ELLORA'S CAVE
Romanticon

Annual convention
for women who
refuse to behave

Discover for yourself why readers can't get enough
of the multiple award-winning publisher
Ellora's Cave.

Whether you prefer e-books or paperbacks,
be sure to visit EC on the web at
www.ellorascave.com

for an erotic reading experience that will leave you
breathless.

15052961R00224

Made in the USA
Lexington, KY
05 May 2012